THE SERRATED EDGE OF FATE

NIKOLA HARVEY AND KIRAN CHARLES

THE SERRATED EDGE
OF FATE

Contents

Prologue

In the year four thousand and twenty, the world nearly ended. There was no grand explosion, no asteroids, and no zombies. A pandemic swept through the world killing a large amount of the population and left the remaining humans devastated and vulnerable. They rebuilt the best they could, but their numbers were small... and they were still only human.

Through study and experimentation, the humans succeeded in summoning another lifeform. These beings introduced themselves as angels and offered their help - they'd mate with the remaining humans and create a stronger race. A race that could resist sickness, and that would live far past a normal human lifespan. Soon, children were being born with amazing healing, psychic, and flight abilities. They had beautiful wings that they could make appear at will.

What they didn't realize was that when they summoned the angels, other, darker entities came with them. These demons passed themselves off as angels and fooled so many before they were discovered.

Their children brought pain with a touch, held dangerous pyrokinetic abilities, and were just as strong as the angels. Veris, an angel favored amongst all others, helped push back the demons and their descendants - but it was far too late to stop what the demons had begun. One demon in particular, Riskel, felt slighted by his angel brethren, and used some of his... less savory talents to bond the offspring of that angel to their own for eternity. Once every ten generations, Veris' graceline and Riskel's shadowline would be soul-bound to one another - an eternal punishment for the hubris and greed of angels.

As time went on and the children grew, these stories seemed more myth than fact. The world was thriving once again. The human hybrids were stronger, faster, less vulnerable. People began to forget that things weren't always this way. Even the sting of the demon's deception was forgotten, and their descendants were slowly integrated back into society.

But when the bond took hold of an angelic girl and demonic boy ten generations later, they couldn't deny the connection between them. Despite the warnings and threats from those around them, they tried to live happily — to let love be enough — but her family held resources more vast than either of them were truly aware of. They were discovered. The process of breaking their bond was cruel, painful, and impossible for the demonic half to survive.

Word passed from father to son, from mother to daughter, from generation to generation. Myths became tradition, and tradition would not be ignored.

One

Vince

"Yeah, yeah. I hear you," Vince sighed. "I've heard this story a million times. A really long time ago, humans begged the angels to screw them to save their own skins, the demons betrayed everybody - and now, once every ten generations, two poor, innocent descendents get fucked. I get it, and I don't go near the angels, okay? I don't want to die. It would be a tragedy to let someone that looks like me perish for something like that."

"I don't think you're taking this seriously!" Vince's mother argued. "You're the next one! This isn't a joke."

"Yeah, Ma, I know that. Don't worry. I'm not an idiot." He kissed her on the head and grabbed a pancake, stuffing it in his mouth and speaking around it like a savage. "I'm going to be late."

She rattled off a list of things he needed to do after work as he grabbed his Stetson. He had hoped that by moving them all out of their tiny, rundown apartment and into a real house, he'd have less work to do... but he'd been very, very wrong. They were still in a bad neighborhood, and despite the job he'd gotten as a ranch hand, they hadn't been able to afford anything fancy.

He waved her off as he straightened his hat, then took off out the door to get to his truck. Ten minutes later, he was pulling into the gravel lot at Strauss Farms and jumping out of the cab.

"Vincenzo!" Johnny yelled from the barn.

"Stop calling me that," Vince groaned as he walked in and grabbed the shovel. "You clean the stalls?"

"Nah, left that for you. Because you're my best friend," Johnny said with a boyish grin. "Besides, I gotta finish that patch on the east side fence." Vince gave him a nod and began to clean the barn. They worked hard until lunch, when Johnny tossed a bag to Vince.

"Peanut butter?" Vince guessed.

"You got it." Johnny grabbed one for himself and watched Vince with a curious expression on his face. "You coming out to Pattie's tonight? Got a fight going."

"Yeah? Think I can make some money?"

"If they let you fight, yeah. I think Pattie is still mad you beat all his guys last time though," Johnny reminded him.

Vince leaned back on his elbows. "Yeah, that was fucking great." They reminisced about the fight until the bell signaling the end of lunch rang, and the men got back to work. Vince helped Johnny get the fence mended, and together, they brought in all the cattle for milking. By the end of the day, Vince was tired. He raised his hands up above his head in a stretch before climbing into his truck.

Johnny knocked on his window a few moments later. "Pattie's?" Vince agreed and drove home to shower, taking his time getting cleaned up and finding something to wear. If he wasn't allowed to fight, he was at least leaving with someone at the end of the night. He put on his favorite ripped jeans and a button-up black shirt. Topped with his slightly beat up Stetson, he looked like something out of a cheesy cowboy romance, which was always a guarantee for a good lay. He sprayed some cologne and met Johnny twenty minutes later at the abandoned warehouse that was unofficially known as Pattie's.

Vince was met with a beer when he stepped out of his truck. Johnny grinned as he led him inside and they checked out the competition, which Vince was sad to see was thin at best. No one new, no one he hadn't beaten before. Chances were good that he'd leave that night with money in his pocket and someone to warm his bed though, so at least he had that going for him.

He took a second to drink down the cold beverage before striding over to look for Pattie, who he found taking bets for the line of fighters ready to go. "I want in." Vince said simply, not finding it necessary to waste pleasantries.

Two beady eyes stared back at him. "Yeah? Good luck finding any-one to fight you." Pattie flicked his fingers toward the group gathering near them. "Go pick a fight with Kos. If you piss him off enough, he might take you on again."

Kos was a lumbering, gigantic moron, but entirely ungraceful. Irri-tating him would be easy enough, but convincing him to hold off until the bets were placed was another thing entirely.

Vince flashed him a playful smile. "If there's anything I'm good at, it's pissing people off." He spun away from Pattie and approached Kos with Johnny on his heels. "Evening, gentlemen — and please be aware that I use that term very loosely — I was wondering who'd be interested in getting their ass kicked tonight?" Vince asked, his hands spread wide in invitation.

Kos scoffed, ignoring him entirely, and turned back around to his meathead friends. One of those friends noticed Vince wasn't moving and nudged Kos. "He's lookin' at you."

Whirling around with crossed arms, Kos regarded Vince with all the same amount of respect one would give a pile of dog shit. "Move on, Vincenzo." The oaf spat his name like an insult, then shoved Vince's shoulder before completely disregarding him again.

Vince dusted off his shirt and smiled at Kos' back. "Look, it's up to you. You can fight me here and maybe make some money if you beat me... or, you can fight me later when I'm done fucking your girlfriend. At least this way, you keep your girl and have a chance at embarrassing me in front of everyone."

"What did you just say?" Kos hissed, flailing back around and ram-ming into Vince hard enough to draw attention. He snapped his head toward Pattie and roared, "This one's mine!"

Pattie offered a wave and laughed to himself as he started accepting bets, and Kos put a thick, gross finger right in Vince's face. "Smile while you can, before I carve it off your pretty little face."

"Whatever you say, sweetheart." Vince winked and blew him a kiss before closing his hand around Johnny's arm and tugging him away. "That was easier than I expected."

"Isn't hard to get someone like Kos upset. Don't know if it was a good idea getting him that angry, though," Johnny said as they looked over to the group.

Vince was pretty sure if looks could kill, he would be dead. He walked away to hang his hat over by the lockers kept for the contestants, then kicked off his boots and began unbuttoning his shirt. Johnny rolled his eyes while the nearby crowd looked on in appreciation as Vince's muscled form was revealed. His body was a sculpted work of art from years of fighting and hard ranch work. Tattoos covered nearly every inch of his upper body, and the ink stood out in the fading sunlight filtering in through the windows of the warehouse. He hung his shirt next to his hat and tossed his boots into the locker. "It doesn't matter how angry he is. We both know he can't beat me."

"You say that now," Johnny warned. "But you should know he's been fighting angels, I think he's learned a couple of new tricks."

Vince frowned, but quickly changed expressions as he started showing off for the crowd. "Angels? Since when do the angels come to fight in demon territory?" He scanned the first few rows to see if he could find anyone unfamiliar that he might've missed in his initial inspection. Having never fought an angel before, he was curious about what that might be like until his mother's words started repeating in his head. Vince wanted nothing to do with the angels, here... or elsewhere.

"You should come down more often, then maybe you wouldn't miss out on all the interesting shit," Johnny said with a shrug.

Vince scoffed and made his way down toward the cage that served as a ring. The last thing he needed to do was go into a fight while dwelling on angels and death. Suddenly eager to get some of the adrenaline out of his system, Vince bounced on his toes and cracked his neck.

Kos was ready for him. His body language was open and threatening, but he couldn't hide the way he was favoring his right shoulder - like maybe one of those angels did more damage than Kos' abilities could handle in such a short timespan. Good, should make it even easier, then, he thought. Vince flexed his fingers to loosen up as Pattie came forward to set the ground rules - or, rather, remind them all there were no ground rules. Everything up to and including kill shots were fair game, but it was common courtesy to let your opponent walk away. There was honor even amongst demons in an underground fighting ring.

Vince waited for the signal and ignored the deafening roar of the crowd as he ducked one of Kos' meaty fists. He countered with a punch to the kidney, and wasn't disappointed by the grunt from his overgrown opponent. Moving quickly, he stood and hooked Kos' arm, placing his other hand on his back to lift him and drop him hard on the floor. As he landed, Vince hopped back to look down at Kos with a wink.

"Cocksucker," Kos spat as he rolled over to push himself back up. He charged, faking a right hook and hitting him square in the jaw with his left, sending Vince stumbling back a few feet. Thankfully, whatever demon spawned Kos' genetic line had nothing on the one that started Vince's. He grinned almost ferally at him, daring him to come that close again.

"You know," Vince started as he watched Kos across the cage, "That's not an insult. I enjoy the hell out of sucking cock." He braced for impact as Kos came running at him, not giving him the satisfaction of hearing the breath leave his body as he gripped Kos around the waist. With a growl, Vince dug his heels in and lifted Kos feet first into the air. After an awkward moment of struggling, Kos was forced to release his hold and Vince dropped him on his head. "Seems like you'll be spending most of the evening on the floor tonight, Kos. Should've kept my boots on. You could've licked them."

Kos roared, the rage finally spilling over. He spun himself around and kicked Vince's legs out from under him, then scrambled to climb on top of him and pin him to the ground with both hands around his throat. "The only one licking boots tonight... will be you."

Vince gripped Kos' wrists, squeezing as he fought to get out the words: "You're... fucking... heavy." His eyes flashed black, warning Kos a split second too late before he shot waves of pain through his arms. When Kos released him to get away, Vince lifted his leg to kick him in his bad shoulder. Vince took immediate advantage of the situation, grabbing Kos' arm on the same side and planting his foot on the sore spot. "Yield, Kos. Don't make me hurt you worse."

It wasn't until that shoulder popped with a disgusting echo that Kos finally yelled, "Yield! Get the fuck off me, I yield!"

Vince let him go, stepping back with his hands raised. He turned a challenging, inviting face to the crowd. "Any other takers?" There were a few quiet murmurs, but most shook their heads. Vince sighed and turned to leave the ring, catching sight of Pattie waving him over with a sizable stack of cash.

Pattie grinned widely with a smile only a mother could love. "Are you ready to finally fight someone a little more your speed?"

"You got someone like that? Haven't seen anyone promising." He counted the money as he waited for an answer, which was the only thing that distracted him from the predatory look on Pattie's face.

"Got an angel that comes around every other Thursday looking for a fight. You manage to win, the payout will be twice that size, maybe more." He gestured to the bills he was holding. "Could get yourself something mighty fine for that price."

Vince whistled as he put his winnings in his pocket. "Double this? There isn't much I wouldn't do for that kind of money, Pattie. Is this week the one he's coming?" Vince did a quick calculation in his head. It was Tuesday, so a fight on Thursday would give him plenty of time to recover and be in top shape. If it was next Thursday, that would give him time to get some training in with Johnny. Either way, Vince was in.

"Next," Pattie said. "He was just here last week. I'll put you down if you're sure you can handle it."

"I can absolutely handle it. I'll see you and your angel next Thursday. Now, if you'll excuse me, I'm gonna go have sex." He walked away from Pattie and up to the redhead that had been eyeing him since the fight was over. "Hello, darling. Did you like that?" he asked as he motioned to the ring.

She uncrossed her arms with a smirk and took a step forward, reaching up to run her fingertips over the bruises on his neck that would be gone by morning. "You look pretty good on your back... I liked that."

"I'm nothing if not accommodating, ma'am. I'm sure we can work something out." He smiled slow and easy, leaning into her touch. "Wanna get out of here?"

Biting her lip, she regarded him for a moment and then nodded once, curling her fingers over his arm and leading him toward the exit. "Your place or mine, handsome?"

"Depends on who lives closer." He stopped suddenly as he remembered he was barely dressed. "I have to get my hat. I'll be back in five minutes." He wrapped an arm around her waist and kissed her thoroughly, hopefully ensuring that she wouldn't leave without him while he ran back to the lockers.

Johnny caught him right as he was heading back out with his things. "Be careful with her. I don't know anything for sure, but I've heard some... rumors about that one."

"Rumors? What rumors?" Vince asked as he struggled with his shirt.

"She's one of those psycho humans that actually wants demon blood in her line. She's been going after the biggest and best, so it's not surprising she targeted you. I'm sure she'll be a hell of a lay, just don't knock her up." Johnny grinned, pushing him playfully and sliding on his own hat. "We don't need any tiny Vince's running around."

"The world would absolutely benefit from a bunch of me," Vince argued.

She ended up being a damn good lay, and though Vince made sure both of them thoroughly enjoyed it, Johnny's warning stayed in his mind. The last thing he wanted to do was intentionally bring a demon child into his world, or into the world as a whole. Things were hard enough as it was.

Jaskian

"Yeah, yeah. I get it, Ma." Jaskian rolled his eyes at his mother, like he had a hundred times that day already. "Stay away from demons, from the bars, from humans, from... well, just about everything fun. I got it." He leaned down to kiss her head as she clicked her tongue at him. "But for the record, this is why I don't live with you anymore. You spoil all the good things about life."

Astarte swatted him playfully and shoved him off of her. "I'm keeping you alive. If I didn't repeatedly remind you to stay away from all the things that could get you in trouble, you'd spend your days wrestling hurricanes and jumping into volcanoes."

Sounds a hell of a lot more fun than going to work, he thought. "I'll be good, Ma. Always am." He knew she could sense the lie, but she let him grab his jacket and duck out the door all the same. As he let out his wings with a shudder, he couldn't shake the feeling that one day, the mounting half-truths he told his mother would catch up to him. He could only be thankful that today wasn't that day.

Jask soared over the city below him and watched the buildings pass until he neared the right one, then skidded to a stop on the ground outside of his small office. She might've thought he merely did research for a private investigator, but in reality, he was that private investigator. He ran his fingertips over his name on the door and unlocked it with a wave of his hand. A single blink had the lights illuminating the room, and he sat down with a plop in his chair as his computer booted up. Maybe she wasn't wrong about his pension for natural disasters, but lately, chasing criminals had been all the thrill he needed to burn off some of his chaotic energy.

His caseload was unusually light; he couldn't pinpoint the reason, but he also didn't care. There was a stack of cold cases on his desk that he'd been neglecting for weeks, and this seemed like a good time to take another crack at the one that had perplexed him the most. Twenty years ago, a boy just... vanished. No one broke in, no fingerprints were left, none of the suspects he'd interrogated even told as much as a little white lie. No one knew what happened to him, and the actual cops had long since stopped searching for him. "Alright, Pavo. Let's see if you'll tell me your secrets this time around..." He flipped open the folder and stared at the only picture he had of the boy. From his features alone, he knew Pavo had demon blood. That was probably what caused the police to back off in the first place - the whole force was made up of angels, and not the kind Jask wanted to associate himself with. They were stuck up dickbags that never saw the value in demons. But Jask? Jask saw it, and even if he didn't, it wouldn't matter. His job was to solve crimes, it didn't make a lick of difference to him who sired the victims or the culprits. Money was money, and justice was justice.

Every lead he ever managed to dig up had run dry a long time ago, but he knew he had to have missed something. Someone, somewhere, knew what happened to Pavo, and Jask was determined to find him this time around. He stood up and slid his jacket on. The hat he chose looked ridiculous with his king hair, but did a decent job of casting a shadow over his face. Where he was going, the less people that knew he was an angel, the better.

In times like this, he did take his car - a beat up old Cutlass that probably wouldn't make it five feet down the road if Jask didn't have powers. He revved the engine and looped around the block a couple of times before heading toward Pavo's father's house. By all accounts, he was the last to see the boy alive, and demons were notorious for avoiding an angel's ability to detect lies. He knows something, I just have to ask the right questions.

Saros lived on the edge of the demon territory, so Jask kept his car as close to the line as he could when he parked. He scoped out the house, noting a handful of lights on and only one silhouette inside. He tapped his jacket pocket to make sure he had his blade and got out of his car, closed the door quietly, then made his way to the front door and knocked a couple of times.

Saros opened the door with an angry huff. "Whataya want this time?"

"You know the drill, let me in." He ducked under Saros' outstretched arm and stepped inside, keeping away from the windows. "I'm still look-ing for your son, I haven't given up."

Saros closed the door behind them. "It's been twenty years. Do you realize how painful it is that you keep bringing this up to me?" He stomped into the kitchen to grab a beer, not offering Jask anything.

"Yeah, no thanks, I don't drink on the job," Jask said sarcastically. "I know this isn't easy for you, but I'm the only creature on this planet that is still trying to find your kid. One of you knows something, and I'm not going to stop until I figure out what. I think Pavo might still be alive."

"After all this time? Hope is a dangerous thing." Saros shook his head after taking a drink. "No one knows anything, and if they do, they aren't going to tell you."

Jask already knew that. "Perk number one of being me is the fact that they don't have to tell me anything - they just have to lie to me at the right time." He sat on the arm of Saros' couch and studied his body language. "Look at the facts. No one came in, no one saw him leave, there wasn't a speck of evidence left behind... no ransom note, no pack-ages including body parts or demands, and no verifiable crime scene. I've scoured both ends of Ares from the Dreadlands to the Gardens, and haven't so much as come across a hair from Pavo's head. Do you know what that tells me?"

"I'm sure you're just dyin' to tell me," Saros deadpanned.

"It tells me that he either ran away, or he knows the person that took him. No matter which direction that coin lands... there's a better than average chance he's still alive. Can you think of anywhere outside of Ares he would've gone? Anyone he trusted that disappeared around the same time Pavo did?"

"I've already told you everything I know!" Saros frowned, slamming down his bottle.

The lie raced up Jask's spine and set the hairs on the back of his neck on end. "No, you haven't. Damnit, Saros!" Jask stood, taking a danger-ous step closer. "Is there somewhere Pavo might've run to?"

Saros eyed him warily. "Getting pretty close there, buddy. I think it's time you left."

"I'm not leaving until you give me something I can work with. You already learned the hard way I'm a lot stronger than you are, and I'll track you to the ends of the earth if you try to run. Where would he have gone? Who would he have gone with?"

Saros clenched his teeth. "He may have gone to the train yard. West of here. Been talking about it since he was a kid."

It wasn't much, especially since the chances of Pavo still being there two decades later were almost nonexistent, but it was a start. Jask nodded once and tipped his hat to Saros. "See, that wasn't so hard, was it? I'll be in touch." He left the house without another word, keeping his head bowed as he got into his car and drove straight to the train yard.

It took two days to comb the entire thing. Two days, and yet again, not a single piece of evidence turned up. By the time he was done and made his way back to the Dreadlands to find Saros and beat the truth out of him, he was gone. Nothing but ashes remained of the house, which meant any lingering evidence he may have missed was gone, too. Jask swore quietly under his breath and ran a hand through his shoulder-length loose curls as he stared at the rubble. "I don't know where you went, Saros... but I warned you. I'll track you to the ends of the earth."

~

While tracking was a particularly powerful aspect of the Veris graceline, Saros had hidden himself well. Jaskian knew it would take more than skill to find him, and he had a fight coming up in a couple of days that he didn't want to miss. Drazan - Jaskian's friend, occasional crime-fighting partner, and general hooligan - couldn't tell him much about the fight except that he was going up against a pretty foul demon.

"That's not saying much, Draz. All demons are foul, but that's why I love them so much." Jask winked at him and carefully slid his coat over his shoulders. "They're a lot more fun than angels, that's for sure."

Drazan eyed him with all the skepticism their storied friendship called for. "It still baffles me that you're not worried at all. If it were me, and my family had been the ones killing off mates for generations, I'd be steering clear of demons altogether. Better never to meet them at all, if you ask me."

"Well, I didn't ask you," Jask said while swiping his keys off the table. "Doesn't matter anyway, from everything I've been told, she lives clear on the other side of the world. Can't exactly blame her, y'know? If it was me that ran the risk of dying, I'd have moved away, too."

He had his own reasons for seeking out demonic company, and none of them had anything to do with his supposed mate. He was the eldest child in the tenth generation, which meant the mate would be his, but even if he found her, he doubted he'd be interested. Women were fun occasionally, but he vastly preferred the company of men - which wouldn't do the curse a whole lot of good.

"You're just pissy you think they're a girl," Drazan teased.

Jask headed out the door to get in his car, Drazan right on his heels. "This has happened how many times now? And every single time, it's been a woman and a man. Never two women, never two men. Wouldn't really make sense to do it any other way if the goal was to join the bloodlines."

Draz stayed silent as they drove to the bar, but right before they pulled in, he said, "I don't think the point was to just join the bloodlines, Jask. I think it was also a punishment for the angels... to make them watch one of their own give up everything for a demon. To love a demon, not just use them for sex or fights or slavery."

Somewhere deep down, Jask knew that. But believing his mate was a woman made things a lot easier for him. It quelled that deep-rooted urge to seek them out, despite a mountain of evidence proving that would be a horrible idea. Absolutely no good would come of him ever finding his mate, and staying away was the only way to ensure they both stayed alive. Maybe I should write her a thank-you note for moving away, he thought. That little maneuver might've saved both of our lives.

The bar was right on the edge of the Dreadlands, not far from where Saros used to live. It was far enough away from the Gardens that it would be crawling with demons, but not so deep into demon territory that he'd be in danger. Most of the demons that hung out at Barrage already knew Jask, and they either enjoyed his company, or were scared enough of him not to make a move against him. Either way, it meant he was pretty much guaranteed to have a good time.

The barkeep was a sleazy-looking little thing, no taller than one of Tolkien's hobbits, but far greasier. He handed Jask a drink that was not-so-affectionately known as Angel Blood, and Jask took it without complaint. Drazan was already mingling with the crowd — he was descended from one of the weaker angels, and his graceline had diluted enough that he passed for a human in most circles — not that it was ever safe to call him one to his face. Jask watched with an amused expression as Draz was cornered by a particularly predatory demon, and slowly raised the drink to his lips. *Maybe this will be the night he finally understands my predilection for the kinkier class.*

As for himself, Jask spotted at least a couple of demons he wouldn't mind rolling around in the sheets with, and he was in desperate need of some release before his fight. One of the downfalls to being one of the most powerful angels left was the hurricane of chaotic energy constantly swirling inside of him; chaos that only grew when he was let down, disappointed, or angry. Thanks to Saros, he was all of the above, and he knew that going into a fight like that would make him sloppy. Luckily for him, sex was a pretty damn good remedy to that.

He slid off his barstool with cocky, delicious intent, and headed straight for a demon almost twice his size. That feat alone was impressive, as Jask stood over six feet tall with muscles for days. The demon let his eyes drag up and down Jask's body, seemed to accept whatever he saw, and dropped the pool stick he'd been holding. Two steps later, they were broad-chest to narrow-nose, and Jask tipped his head back to look up at him. "Heya, big guy. Ever had an angel inside of you before?"

"No," he grunted, his foul breath reminding Jask that some demons were little more than stunted entities of heat and sickness. "And I don't plan on starting now."

A chase, huh? Alright. Jask pouted, running his hand over the oaf's meaty chest and sending a shiver of grace down that giant body. "You sure? They say 'holy fuck' for a reason, y'know."

Not a moment later, Jask was roughly pushed onto his back on top of the pool table. A rush of adrenaline and lust raced through his veins and he grinned, settling right where he was. Okay, so... not gonna be able to top this one without getting into some weird territories. Got it. "I normally don't care to have an audience, but if you insist..." A quick invasion into the demon's mind told Jask his name was Tazgath, and the things that he wanted to do to Jask would send most angels running for the Gardens with their wings tucked so far inside of them they were barely existent on this plane. But not Jask. No, Jaskian had a penchant for pain, and at the end of the day, he knew Taz wouldn't truly be able to hurt him. Jask could smite him with a wave of his hand if it came to it, but the game was fun to him regardless.

Tazgath leaned over him, pressing him harder into the pool table, and Jask huffed an excited breath. "C'mon, Taz. You want it, I want it. I'll even let you top if you promise to keep throwing me around like this. Let's get out of here, yeah?"

"Foolish little angel," Taz growled. "Do you know what happened to the last feathered fuck who found himself in my bed?"

Another cursory trip around the mudpit Taz called a brain showed Jask exactly what happened to the last angel, and Jask found himself filled with fury instead of the previously good things he'd been experiencing. Demons screwing angels was one thing, and talking down to them during it was expected. But Taz had ripped that angel's wings off slowly after using him, and that wasn't something Jaskian would ever be able to look past.

Letting that rage guide him, Jask reached up and wrapped a hand around Taz's throat, channeling his powers to a single focal point of silver light which wracked through Taz's body and ended his life. The force of his dead weight falling on top of Jask sent the rotted old pool table splintering to the ground, and in an instant, every demon inside of that bar was on him.

He sent another, weaker burst of power out to clear the space around him and then stood, wiping the wood dust from his peacoat. "No one else needs to be hurt here, I came in peace. But let that be a lesson to any demon that takes it upon themselves to rid an angel of their wings... I don't show mercy."

Either they believed him or were too scared to say anything else, because the other patrons returned to what they'd been doing before. One of Taz' friends — an attractive blonde — came over and sat next to Jask as he attempted to finish his drink. "That was rude," she said, but the amusement in her voice took the sting out of her words.

"So was what he did to Rasiel. I was just looking for a good time, but... I can't let that kinda shit go. You understand." It wasn't a question, most demons clearly understood the line between fair play and outright torture, and while their very natures made them partial to the latter, the fear of retribution kept most of them in line.

She nodded, placing a hand on his arm. The warmth he felt even through his coat had him letting out a soft sigh, and he leaned into her touch whether he meant to do it or not. "I know you, I've seen you around. You angels are all so cold and boring, all you're looking for is a little warmth and a good lay. What do you say we go back to my place and I give you what you need?"

Jask nodded in spite of himself and stood up, pulling her close and relishing every inch of heat radiating off of her body onto his own. She was right; he was so, so tired of being cold, and if that meant he had to settle for a woman, well... he'd settle for a woman.

Two

Vince

Vince slammed his hands down into the water of the large creek he'd just fallen into. He watched the clouds for a second before standing and motioning to Johnny. "Again." An audible pop sounded as he stretched and shook off some water. He was covered in mud, blood, and honestly, he didn't want to think about what else might be in the creek on the farm. The fight with the unknown angel was soon, and he had to be sure he was able to hold up against whatever he was hit with - hence this incredibly stupid idea he and Johnny had concocted.

Vince's boss had an old farm truck that he let them use, wisely not asking for what. As Vince looked on, Johnny backed the truck up and waited for the signal. Vince clenched his jaw and nodded once. The truck tires spun and shot dirt and rocks into the air as Johnny floored it toward Vince, who dug his feet into the earth and kept his eyes on the rapidly approaching vehicle. Vince met the grill with his shoulder and listened to the tires squeal in protest. He screamed in victory as he pushed up and lifted the front of the vehicle off the ground, successfully getting the truck chest-height before having to drop it.

Johnny had cut the power as soon as the truck was in the air and before it had finished bouncing, he was jumping on Vince. "You fucking did it!"

"Son of a bitch, that hurt." Vince laughed. "But it didn't knock me on my ass, so that's an improvement!" They checked out the damage to the truck and then packed up and drove back to the main parking area. Vince toweled off and jumped in his own truck, checking his rearview to make sure Johnny was following before heading home. He had two beers open and was waiting on the couch by the time Johnny walked in the front door. "You drive like a grandmother."

"You never met my grandmother, she would've beat us both here," Johnny said as he grabbed his beer and downed half. "How are you feeling about your angel fight now?"

"Your what?" his mother demanded as she walked downstairs.

"Fucking hell, Johnny," Vince sighed while shaking his head. "It's nothing. Absolutely nothing."

"Vincenzo, we *just* talked about this!"

"Evening, Ms. Amaranth," Johnny said pleasantly while making a point to examine the wallpaper and avoid Vince's glare.

"You *cannot* have anything to do with the angels!" she continued.

"Angel. Singular. It's one night, and once I kick his ass, there won't be a problem," Vince tried to reassure her.

"You're *fighting* one?" Somehow, her voice became impossibly higher.

"For a big pay out!"

"No amount of money is worth your life!"

"That is absolutely not true." Vince and Amaranth were so busy arguing that no one noticed Johnny slip out. Vince continued to make his case and fight with his mother until she stormed upstairs and locked herself in her room. He walked outside and punched a hole in a tree, which stung like a bitch, but looking at the hole made him feel better. He could win this fight. He could do whatever it took to keep food on his family's table and a roof over their head. What could meeting one angel hurt?

~

Thursday morning found Vince strangely nervous. His mother had barely spoken to him over the course of the week, and his sister wouldn't even look at him. He'd explained numerous times that the odds of this angel being *his* angel were very low, but they weren't listening. He'd even explained he wasn't in the business of fighting women, so if that's what Pattie had in mind, it wasn't happening anyway. Nothing he said seemed to assuage their fear, and by the time he was brushing his teeth, Vince was seriously considering dropping the entire thing. After dressing for work and hugging his mother goodbye, he forced himself to ignore the look in her eyes and walk out the door. He threw himself into work, and when the time came to leave, he'd almost forgotten what tonight was.

That is, until Johnny came running from the east fields with a grin. "I am so ready to see you kick some angel ass!"

"Your faith in me is heartwarming." Vince shook his head as he locked up the barn.

"Come on, I'll give you a ride. We are definitely going drinking after this." Johnny clapped him on the back and Vince followed him. It was better if he didn't go home to give his mother a chance to stop him, anyway.

He was quiet on the way to Pattie's, watching the world fly by out the window. They pulled up sooner than he would've liked, and he slowly got out of the cab of the truck. The redhead from last week was there again and he struggled to remember her name. After trying for a moment, he decided to just avoid her *and* the slap that particular slip-up would cause. The crowd was much larger than his last fight, and the adrenaline started flowing in his veins. He couldn't believe he'd thought about not coming.

Pattie approached him with a weary look in his eyes like he hadn't been sleeping much. "You sure you wanna do this, Vincenzo? Your opponent seems to be in rare form tonight, and he killed Taz a couple of nights ago."

"I'm sure Taz probably had it coming." Vince shrugged, a little relieved to hear it was a man he'd be fighting. He'd be laughing about this with his mother later. He'd foregone getting dressed up tonight since he'd come from work, and pulled off the old t-shirt he'd been wearing.

He tossed it into Johnny's truck and his boots followed. Soon, he was only wearing a pair of ripped jeans. He took a deep breath. "Alright, Pattie. Where's your guy?"

Smiling a little, Pattie gestured toward the ring. "He likes to make an entrance. Just get in there, he'll show up soon enough. But be careful, you hear me? You're one of my best, and this angel... he's apparently got a thing for killin' demons."

He stepped aside and Johnny placed a hand on Vince's bare chest. "Last chance to tuck and run, Vinnie. There are other ways to make money, but I gotta say... on behalf of demonkind everywhere... kick this son of a bitch's ass for all of us."

Vince winked and walked into the warehouse, making his way down to the door of the cage. "I'm not the tuck and run kind, Johnny. You know that. I'll win or die trying." He meant it as a joke, but a little shiver ran down his spine nonetheless. Vince distracted himself by look-ing over the crowd as they filed into the arena. He sped over the red-head and deliberately ignored the look she gave him. As he looked straight across, he caught sight of someone standing behind the crowd. His breath caught a little in his chest as he shamelessly checked the man out. Beautifully chiseled muscles and long, pullable hair that his fingers itched to dig into.

He reached behind him for his friend, unable to take his eyes off the gorgeous specimen. "Johnny, tell me you know his name. Please tell me you know who that is."

"Sure I do, Vincenzo," Johnny answered, sounding amused. "That's your opponent." Vince could feel his jaw drop as Johnny shoved him into the ring amidst the cheers of the crowd.

Several seconds passed, and all that happened was Vince lost sight of the angel. He whirled, fists raised, trying to pick him out of the sea of people. The floor shook violently enough that Vince was temporarily thrown off balance. He caught himself just in time to spin his body and take in the fifteen-foot wingspan and ice-colored eyes of the creature crouching in front of him. Just him landing created craters in the middle of the damn cage. "I'm Jask," he said, with a voice like thunder and sunshine. "Nice to meet you."

"How polite," Vince muttered, tilting his head and getting a good look. "Name's Vince. You know, in case you want to scream it later." Vince blinked and shook himself out of that. This was *not* the time to be flirting. He straightened up to his full height and waited for the bell to ring. As soon as he heard it, he headed for Jask.

Right before Vince's fist was about to connect with that stupidly gorgeous jaw, Jask disappeared. Vince's legs were kicked out from under him a heartbeat later, and his ass hit the concrete with a thud. Jask paced around him as Vince planned his next attack, and then Vince pushed himself to his feet.

"That's how you win? Cheating?" His eyes went black as he cracked his knuckles and moved faster than possible for the human eye to follow. He had one arm around Jask's waist and lifted him up, preparing to throw him over his back.

Jask let out a low chuckle as he teetered over Vince's shoulder, like the whole damn thing was happening in slow motion. Something Jask did made him unbalanced, and they both hit the ground, hard. "Ah, fuck," Jask groaned. "Who told you I like it rough?"

"A little angel on my shoulder." Vince got back to his feet, ignoring the fact that nothing about Jask was little. He looked up at the timer and the restless crowd around them and held out his hands. "Sorry, handsome, but we're gonna have to speed this up. I got money to make." He stepped forward and put a good bit of strength behind an uppercut. He had hoped it would knock the angel out, because something was feeling increasingly off about this fight.

Jask stumbled back, unfortunately staying on his feet, but rubbed his jaw like that was the first time he'd ever been hit. Feeling empowered, Vince sent a blast of energy his way and knocked him back into the wall of the cage. The angel rolled, tucking his wings around him and springing back up right in front of him, landing a blow to Vince's stomach.

Vince cursed and was forced back a step, but he'd been taking hits from a Chevy for the last week. He recovered quickly enough to grab Jask's hand as he pulled away, and pulled him flush up against him. For a moment, he allowed himself to focus on how nice that felt, but then he flipped him. He'd prepared to slam him into the ground, but hesitated as one of Jask's wings brushed his arm. He didn't use as much force as he could have, and when he landed on top of Jask, the angel looked... horrified? Confused? Like he wanted to fuck Vince's brains out in front of an audience? It was hard to tell, but Vince didn't have time to figure it out.

Right as Jask pulled Vince's hips down and whispered something lost to the sound of the bell, rough hands dragged Vince off of Jask.

Johnny pulled Vince out of the ring and Vince could hear him saying something about the fight being over. They'd run out of time. Vince couldn't take his eyes off of the angel still laying on the ground. He went along with Johnny mindlessly, but something was telling him to go back. As Johnny pushed through the crowd Vince once again lost sight of Jask, and that made him feel things he couldn't quite put his finger on.

Before he realized what was happening, he was outside breathing in lungfuls of clean night air. He put his hands on his knees and laughed. "Johnny. I'm fucked."

"What the fuck happened back there? You *had* him, Vince. You *had* him!" Johnny turned, pacing in front of Vince. "But okay, okay. You're not fucked, you tied. Pattie is shiesty, I bet he still takes the money from everyone that said the angel would outright win, since he didn't."

"No, definitely still fucked." Vince ran a hand down his face and looked up at the stars. "We gotta get out of here. As far away as we can," he said sharply as he started walking toward Johnny's truck.

"Why? What the hell is going on?"

"Fate, apparently. Come on, Johnny, before he comes looking."

His friend didn't ask any more questions until they were a full five miles out of town. "Where are we going, exactly? And why? Vince, tell me what's going on."

"Remember all those stories Mom likes to tell? About true mates or some shit?" Vince dropped his head back against the seat. "That was him."

"*What?*" came Johnny's incredulous reply. "No way, nope. Nuh-uh. No way... wait, *way?*" He looked at Vince, fear evident on his face. "You're sure?"

"Pretty damn. See?" He looked back out the window. "Definitely fucked."

Johnny nodded a little, then reached over to squeeze Vince's arm. "How do you know? What did it... what did it feel like?"

"Like everything I ever wanted was right in front of me and all I had to do was reach out and touch it." He put his shirt over his face and screamed into it before continuing calmly, "What the *fuck* am I going to do? My money is on him running back to the Gardens and telling mommy and daddy about the dirty little demon he found. I'll be dead by morning."

"So we hide you," Johnny said quickly. "No way I'm letting a puffed-up feathered asshole kill you, Vince. But wait a minute, why didn't *he* just kill you? I've seen him fight, he's more than capable of it."

"I don't know, and I sure as shit wasn't hanging around to ask." He shook his head. "And I can't hide. Can't leave Mom and Leota like that." Vince closed his eyes and remembered the look of horror on the angel's face. He didn't want this anymore than Vince, and that made him dangerous. Although, a small part of Vince was starting to wonder if he really didn't want it, or if he was just scared to try it, and *that* was what was really dangerous.

After another argument about hiding, Vince convinced Johnny to drop him off at home. The house was dark, and he made his way up to his room with no interruptions. Vince dropped his boots and clothes on the floor of his room, ignoring the bed despite the ache in his bones.

He climbed out of his window and pulled himself up onto the roof. Placing a hand underneath his head for a cushion, Vince watched the stars as he thought back over the night. He'd been so excited to get to this fight. To *win* this fight. Not only did he not win, he'd practically signed his own death warrant. They'd be coming for him sooner rather than later. Jask's family wasn't known to take chances with the demons they were bound to, and Vince was sure he wasn't the exception.

His first reaction was to fight, to take as many of them down with him as possible. He knew, however, that decision would come back to haunt his family. He should've listened to his mother. Johnny was right, he should hide. Keep his family safe. He thought about what he'd need to pack. *Do I even own a suitcase?* His eyes traced the constellations as he continued to think. What could he sell so he could have money to get out of town? Where would he even go? He could talk to Strauss, see if he could take the Chevy. Leave his truck to his mom so she could use it.

He closed his eyes, and without his permission, his mind wandered to the angel again. *No,* he corrected himself. *Jask. His name was Jask.* He'd been struck dumb the moment he'd laid eyes on Jask. Unbidden, he remembered the way that toned body had felt underneath him, and he started imagining a completely different scenario. Jask, naked and moaning, writhing beneath him as he thrust up into Vince. Vince let his hand trail down his shirtless chest, unbuttoning his jeans and sliding his already interested cock out of his pants. He hissed a little at the cool night air, but slowly started to stroke himself, and soon, the chill was forgotten. He kept his eyes closed as he imagined Jask flipping them, sliding down to get between his legs and taking Vince into his mouth. He could see the way Jask would look up at him, how it would feel when Jask moaned around him.

"Fuck," Vince cursed as he sped up his hand, twisting it a little. He pictured Jask's light blue eyes lust blown as Vince gripped his hair to move him where he wanted him. Or even better, Jask sliding into his mouth so *he* could taste *him*, using Vince's mouth to chase his own pleasure. He bit his lip to keep quiet as he spilled over his own hand to the thought of sucking Jask off. After a moment, he came back to his senses, fixed his jeans and climbed back into the house to shower. He was definitely, irrevocably fucked.

Jaskian

"Well, that was a fucking disaster." Jask sat down in a heap, letting his wings mostly shield his body from Drazan's view.

"What happened? It all looked pretty cut and dry from where I was standing." Draz said as he crossed his arms.

Jask shook his head, covering his face with his hands and replaying the fight in his mind. He'd been so sure he could win, but one look at Vince had him feeling off balance and thrown. "He's my mate, Draz. Y'know, the one my family has sworn to murder if they were ever found. The one that's *supposed* to be a girl, living in China or some shit."

Draz stared at his best friend, arms dropping to his sides. "*Him*? You can't be serious. How do you know?"

"I've never pulled a punch in my life, and I did tonight. It was like I couldn't bring myself to hurt him. Not to mention, look at this." Jask pulled his wing toward the light and pointed out the spot where the white feathers had turned black, right where it had made contact with Vince. He tucked them away after and stood, pacing in his bedroom. "That only happens with a mate. And fuck, when he pinned me? I don't think I've ever wanted anyone that bad. Every touch felt like... ah, hells. I don't know how to explain it. Like it was too much and not nearly enough all at once. Like I'd burn up if he didn't stop, but die if he did."

"Shit." Draz leaned against the wall, watching Jask attempt to wear holes in the floor. "What are you going to do?"

That was the question, and Jask didn't have an answer. "If I tell anyone else about it, he could die. He *will* die. He couldn't even outright beat me, and I could barely bring myself to touch him. If my family finds out..." Jask stopped, turning to face Draz. "Do *I* leave? Find him and tell *him* to leave? Pretend it never happened? He's probably scared to fucking death of me." The thought made his stomach churn.

"He did run pretty quickly. Didn't even stop to see if he'd made any money. I could look for him? Feel him out for you. Did you even get a name?" Draz pulled a pen out of his pocket and prepared to write it down.

Even after knowing Drazan his entire life, Jask was suddenly skeptical as hell. He shook his head a little bit, working out a way to avoid telling the truth. "I'll handle it, I just need a few days to figure out what to do."

Draz waited another moment and then put the pen away when Jask didn't change his mind. "Well, let me know what you decide. I'm happy to help."

Lying to his best friend only made him feel worse, but he couldn't take the chance that Draz would betray him. This wasn't some stupid, meaningless thing... this was the life of his mate. And whether he actually cared about the demon or not, Vince's death would hurt like hell. Jask knew his parents had ways of making sure it didn't kill him, but it would still be the most painful thing he'd ever experience, and on that selfish note... he was pretty keen on keeping Vince alive.

He jerked his chin toward the door, giving Draz some half-cocked excuse about needing sleep after the fight, then closed the door behind his friend. Sleep was the last thing on his mind, but no matter what he chose to do, he should probably be alone.

Jask almost immediately teleported to his office. One way or the other, he needed more information about Vince and his family, and the best way to do that was research.

"Okay," he mumbled to himself as he typed. "Vince... Riskel, tell me your secrets." Not much came up from his original search except for articles talking about Riskel, the demon that spawned Vince's shadowline and gave him his surname. Jask was lucky, he may not have found anything at all if he hadn't known his entire life his mate would be a Riskel.

Digging further, he *was* able to gather a few, probably useless pieces of information. Familial ties, place of employment, things like that. Jask tucked the information away with a disappointed sigh - he wasn't exactly sure what he'd hoped to find out, but he'd absolutely wanted more than that. *Who is he, really? Why was he fighting? What makes him happy? Is he seeing someone? Are **they** happy?*

From there, his mind didn't take him anywhere good. Jealousy burned in his gut at the thought of someone else touching Vince, of bringing him to that edge and tipping him over, of having a place in

Vince's life at all when he, himself never could. He slammed his lap-top shut and got up, determined to do whatever he needed to do to get Vince to leave town so he could put the demon - and the bond - far from his thoughts.

Jask didn't want to waste the time it would take to drive over there, so he extended his wings and kicked off from the ground the moment he was back outside. Vince's home was deeper into the Dreadlands than he'd been in quite some time, but in this case, he wasn't the one that needed to fear for their life. Vince was, and it was dark enough outside that Jask wasn't afraid of being seen. He kept to the clouds, far enough overhead that even those demons with night vision abilities wouldn't be able to spot him, then landed with a soft thud on Vince's back porch.

The state of the house nearly broke his heart. It looked sturdy enough, but it was small, and from what Jaskian discovered, he lived with his mother and sister. It certainly wasn't big enough to be comfortable, and it suddenly made sense to him why Vince would be stupid enough to fight an angel in the first place, knowing what he must about their fates.

He knocked twice, tucking his wings away and lowering his eyes to the floor, hoping whoever answered wouldn't immediately take him for an angel. The chances were still slim, but he made himself as small and non-threatening as possible nonetheless.

Jask could see Amaranth looking through the window by the door after telling her daughter to go upstairs. In this area, opening the door without some caution wasn't a good idea, so he couldn't blame her when she only opened it a crack. "Who are you?"

He considered lying, making up a fake name or using his considerable powers of persuasion to get her to let him in, but if she sensed any of those things happening, Jask knew she wouldn't listen to a word he said. And he *desperately* needed her to listen. "Mrs. Riskel, my name is Jaskian. I'm asking - no, I'm *begging* you - to give me ten minutes of your time. I won't hurt you," he added quickly, knowing the timbre of his voice would give him away if his name alone did not.

Her eyes widened. "You're one of them. That damn fool son of mine didn't listen, and now there's an... *angel* on my doorstep." She said it like it was a dirty word, and indignant pride for all of angelkind swelled in his chest.

Biting back a retort, Jask kept his voice low and his demeanor un-threatening. "I didn't hurt him during the fight, and I'm not here to hurt him now." Jask took a deep breath, folding his hands in front of him so she could see he was unarmed, not that it made much of a difference when *he* was enough of a weapon on his own. "But he's still in danger. He needs to run, the quicker the better."

"Right. I'm so sure you're concerned about his safety. Who is she?" Amaranth asked. "Your sister, I'd suspect. You don't look old enough to be the father."

Jask shook his head minutely, taking a shallow breath. "He's mine. And I know you don't have a reason to believe me, but I *do* care about his safety. I haven't told anyone his name, not even my best friend. I came here to warn you, to tell him he needs to leave before my family finds out. I'm not strong enough to stop all of them."

"He's yours? What in the hell do you mean? This isn't a funny joke. You thought you'd come mess with us before taking him away?"

"I wish it were, ma'am. I really do." Jask finally looked up, making eye contact with her as something a little like pain spread through him. "He's my mate, I don't have any doubts. And I promise you, I have no intentions of letting any harm come to him. I'm telling you, he *needs* to run. My family, I... I can't keep them away forever. You should *all* run - you, Vince, Leota. Get as far away from Ares as you can."

The door opened a little more as she leaned on it. "He isn't here. You're sure? That he's yours, I mean."

"I know it seems... absurd, given the fact that there haven't ever been two bonded males, but I'm telling you, it's true. The moment I laid eyes on him, I knew something was different about him. I didn't quite real-ize what until I actually *did* try to hurt him in that fight, and couldn't bring myself to do it. Hurting him would've been like hurting a part of me, and there's no way I'd have had that reaction to anyone but my mate." Jask bowed his head, his voice growing impossibly quiet as he said, "Please. Save him, don't let history repeat itself again. Save him."

She sighed, obviously looking him over. "It's not absurd. You're exactly what he would've picked for himself. I'm sure it's engineered that way. Make it harder on him to resist." She paused for a moment. "But you listen to me, Jaskian Veris, just by coming here, you've put us all in danger. All you had to do was stay quiet, not tell a soul and keep away from my boy. You did the opposite. You interfered, and now we'll never be safe. Hopefully neither me nor my son will see your face again." She slammed the door closed, and Jask jerked like he'd been slapped.

It hit him all at once. She was right, she was absolutely right. If he'd have stayed away, no one would've ever found out except for Draz, and he could handle keeping Draz quiet. Now, his scent was all over the Dreadlands and led right to Vince's door. Word would spread, people would talk, and eventually, Jask's father would hear of it. No lie in the world would save any of them at that point.

He backed up a step and looked around wildly, his grace sparking through his body like nervous, chaotic electricity. All that would do was make his imprint on the area stronger, so he teleported as far away as he could in one leap.

Landing roughly, Jask curled up on the ground to calm himself and try to think clearly. His brothers, Cidos and Edis, would ultimately be the ones tasked with the job of killing Vince. He could talk to them, try and reason with them, but in the end... he knew he wouldn't win. The twins had been groomed for this from a young age, brought up to believe there was no greater sin than crossing a graceline with a shadowline. Even if Jask pointed out that they couldn't procreate so the line wouldn't continue either way, no one would listen. There were spells, other curses, body swap rituals. A number of things that would make it possible for one of them to bear a child.

At a loss, Jask did the only thing he'd ever been good at. He picked himself up and began tracking Saros, convincing himself that if he couldn't save Vince, the least he could do was save a *different* innocent demon.

With a renewed sense of responsibility, he extended out his grace and ignored his body's warning signs to sleep, ultimately locating the demon several hours away in a mundane little cabin. It took him almost an hour to break through the defenses that Saros placed around the property, but once he was in, the exhaustion tugging at him ebbed away.

This time, he didn't bother knocking. He kicked open the door and strode in, extending out his wings and gripping his blade at his side as Saros whirled around to see what the hell was going on. "Sorry I'm late," Jask quipped. "I didn't want to come."

Saros cursed. "How'd you get through the wards?"

Jask tilted his head and laughed. "My surname is *Veris*, you insufferable cretin. Your wards don't work against me, and I tried to tell you I'd be able to track you anywhere. It's a gift of the graceline." Jask waved a hand behind him, closing and locking the door. Another flick ensured Saros wouldn't be able to teleport out of there - he was stuck.

"Why can't you just leave me alone?" He looked around, presumably for a weapon, so Jask tossed him a regular knife.

"I told you a hundred times, Saros. I'm not giving up until I find Pavo, and that lead you left me was bullshit. Care to try again, or should I carve it out of you this time?" Jask swung his own blade in a circle, hoping Saros would just start talking on his own. Torture wasn't his forte, it went against his very nature, but it was one of the few languages demons seemed to understand.

"You won't find him! There's nothing left to find!"

It was truth, plain and simple. Not a guess, not a lie, not a twisted version of something half-accurate. It thrummed through Jask's veins for exactly what it was. This man *knew* there was nothing left of Pavo. Rage had Jask's wings expanding further, knocking pictures off the walls and making him appear even larger than he really was. "What... *happened?*"

Saros shrunk away, trying to hide. "I was drunk. I didn't stop after the first hit and by the time... when I'd stopped... he wasn't breathing. It was an accident! I dumped him at the train yard, cleaned everything up. The angels, they don't look too close at us."

That little ten-year-old boys' face flashed through his mind, and the memories from all the years he'd spent searching for Pavo followed until Jask was shaking with sickened disgust and anger. "He was a *child!*" Jask screamed, the force of grace coming unbidden off of him strong enough to shatter the glass windows and send Saros slamming back against the cupboards. The sound of the demon's skull cracking echoed over the rest of the reverberating noises, and he slumped to the ground, his eyes wide in fear, but completely lifeless.

Jask picked up his useless, disgusting body and clenched his jaw, another wave of devastating power turning his skin and bones to ashes on the ground. Clenching his jaw, Jask turned on his heel and teleported back to his office.

The walls shook around him from the unbridled chaos he still wasn't able to reign in, and he found himself grateful he'd chosen office space far enough away from anything that mattered.

He couldn't save Pavo, despite an overwhelming belief that the boy had still been alive. He wouldn't be able to save Vince. All he'd managed to do was kill two demons with his own hands and put an entire family in danger, and for what? Out of some self-righteous sense of worth? Who was he, Jaskian Veris, to decide who lived or died? To decide who needed his help, or who should be left alone? He wasn't even a real cop, he was a poser with a hero complex, and death followed him. In the last week alone, his body count was higher than Saros'. What made him any better? Divine retribution?

No, Jask scolded himself. *I'm not any better, and for all I know, Taz had a kid that I left fatherless with my decision to kill him. Vince obviously takes care of his family, and by showing up at that fight, I probably handed him a death sentence. And Pavo...* He dropped his head to his desk, the world around him finally going calm as all the fight was knocked out of him. Jask knew, realistically, that he never had a shot at saving the boy. He, himself, was only twenty years old the day Pavo died, which for an angel, meant he'd technically still been an adolescent.

He needed sleep and sustenance, already having pushed the bounds of his body and his grace too far. But he made a vow to himself that one way or the other, once he got what he needed, he'd scour the world for Pavo's body so he could give him a proper burial. Jask might not be able to do much else, but he could do that. He had to.

Every bone in his body was screaming for his mate as he made his way back home and collapsed in his bed. It was a foreign feeling, one he was already growing to hate, but it was nearly all-consuming. He needed something good, something comforting, and Vince was the only thing he could think of - and the only thing he couldn't have. *I never should have gone to that fight. I had no business being there in the first place, and now that the bond has clicked into place, I'll have a gaping fucking hole in my chest forever.*

He rolled onto his stomach, letting his wings droop over the sides of the bed so he couldn't see the blackened feathers, and made himself one final promise. Jask would do whatever he had to do in order to get the Riskel family to safety, and then he'd take off. Maybe see the world, maybe set up shop somewhere overseas. He'd never be able to face his *own* family again, not with their abilities to sense lies and deceit, nor would he be able to get anywhere near Vince once he got them somewhere safe.

Somehow, Jask had managed to ruin his own life in one fell swoop, and he had no one to blame but himself. Instead of sleeping, Jask forced himself back up and headed out to the Dreadlands, knowing a certain demon owed him a favor after Jask had solved a case for him and he couldn't pay the fee. It was time to call it in, in a big, big way.

Three

Vince

Vince couldn't sleep at all after getting home from the fight, so by the time five AM rolled around the following morning, he was ahead of his alarm clock. He was already dressed and in the kitchen when Amaranth came down to start breakfast. He gave her a small smile and sipped his coffee, avoiding all of her questions about the fight, only answering that he was alive and home. He looked away from the uncertainty in her eyes and hugged her tightly before leaving for the farm. He drove on autopilot, no music playing, and nothing on his mind but the growing ache in his chest. He rubbed it absently as he thought again about his plan from last night. He was at war with himself. He knew he probably didn't have a choice, but just leaving everything behind was sitting uneasy with him.

He pulled up to see a worried-looking Johnny. He assured his friend that everything was fine and they got to work like any other day. Vince tried so hard to throw himself into the physical labor, but his mind kept going back to Jask. More often than not, his hand found its way to his chest before he realized what was happening - but no matter how hard he pressed, that empty feeling wasn't going away.

When the bell for lunch rang, he decided it would be better to go home. He didn't want his bad mood to affect Johnny or the others. He drove back and let himself into the house, opening the fridge to see what he could scrounge up. He didn't realize he'd been staring without actually seeing until his mother pushed the door closed. He smiled at her out of habit, but the smile left his face pretty quickly.

"What's wrong?"

"Had a visitor this morning. Shortly after you left. Introduced himself as Jaskian," she said, watching him.

"Jask." Vince realized he said the name a little too softly and cleared his throat. "What'd he say?"

"That you were his mate, and he wanted you protected. He said you should run, that we all should." She opened the refrigerator back up and started making him a sandwich.

Vince sat at the table, hanging his hat on his knee. "Shit. That doesn't make any sense."

"He was different, that one. Didn't even make a move to come in."

"Why would he? No point if the one he came for isn't inside." He watched her place the food in front of him, but suddenly, his appetite was gone. They knew where he lived. He had no choice but to leave now. They'd never be safe if he stayed here. Without touching the food, Vince stood and headed up to his room. He packed a duffle full of clothes and essentials and left his mother after a tearful goodbye.

On a roll, he drove back to the farm and sat down with Strauss. "First," Vince started, "I don't want to leave. You've done so much for me and my family. I hate this almost as much as saying goodbye to my mother."

"I say let the bastard angel come." Strauss leaned forward, smacking his palm on the desk. It was just like him to want to put up a fight. "I'd like to see him try."

"You and I both know that's a terrible idea. I wouldn't run if I thought I could win," he said, and that stung, because Vince hadn't lost a fight yet.

Strauss reached over and gripped Vince's shoulder, squeezing gently. "I'm sorry, Vincenzo. Ya've been like a son to me, and it's rubbish that someone supposed to love ya is tryna kill ya. What do ya need from me?"

"Can I take that old Chevy? The one Johnny was running me over with."

With no hesitation at all, Strauss nodded. "Of course ya can. It's yers, whatever ya need. I don't have a whole awful lot of money, but I can give ya some to get ya started. Ya've been one helluva worker, son."

"I don't need your money, Strauss. I'll find a way to make it, but can you take my truck back to my mom? Have Johnny drive it or something?"

He nodded once, reaching over to take the keys. "Yer leaving your family here? Is that... smart?"

"They're after me. They don't have a reason to go back if I'm gone. I'll do something to make sure they know I'm leaving. Start a few fires in the Gardens, maybe."

Strauss sighed, leaning back and tossing the key into the air. "Ya don't think those angels will use yer family to draw ya back here?"

"What reason would they have to do that? I'm staying away from their precious heir." Vince ignored the stab of pain to his chest. "That's all they care about."

Nodding a little, Strauss spoke to him quieter. "Ya feel it yet? The effects of the bond? Every single bonded pair has tried and failed to fight it. No way the Veris' just believe ya and let ya live."

"Nah, haven't felt a thing." Vince rubbed his chest again, showing his lie for what it was. He stayed quiet for a moment. "You think if they kill me, think they'll leave Mom and Leota alone?"

"Yes, I do. But that doesn't mean ya should go sacrifice yerself. All I'm sayin' is take them with ya. Protect 'em. Don't leave 'em here defenseless. I'm over a hundred and fifty years old, scout, I can't fight off no angels."

Vince ran a hand through his hair. "Yeah. Yeah, you're right. I'll go get them first." He laughed quietly. "I don't even know where to go, Strauss. Been here my whole life. Thirty three years is a long time to just... drop."

"I'm sorry this is happening to ya. We always knew there was a chance, but..." Strauss whistled. "An angel that willingly comes into the Dreadlands? I ain't ever heard anything like it."

"He was after a kill. Pattie said he took out Taz a few days before. Seems he enjoys it."

His boss eyed him skeptically. "And yet, ya don't appear to have a scratch on ya. How's that possible?"

Vince shrugged. "I'm too good looking. It distracted him long enough for me to get away."

Strauss stood up, walking around to Vince and pulling him into a hug. It was a completely unexpected gesture and spoke to the finality of this goodbye. "Well, ya ever see that angel again... don't give in. Ya think whatever's happenin' inside of ya is bad right now, ya don't want to know what it'll be like if ya give in and let it happen."

Vince hugged him tight, clapping him on the back. "I have no intention of seeing him again or giving in. Don't worry, boss."

"Then alright." Strauss pulled back, sadness lining his face. "Ya be good, and yer keep your family safe. If anyone comes round here askin' after ya, I'll tell 'em yer whole damn house blew up or somethin'."

Vince grinned. "Couldn't ask for a better cover story. I'm gonna get my family, probably swing by to say goodbye to Johnny later. Thanks again for everything." He hugged him one more time before leaving to make the drive home.

Vince turned the key in the ignition and tried not to look in the rearview mirror as he pulled away from the farm - he'd have his chance to say goodbye when he came to talk to Johnny. Right now, he was more worried about getting his family to safety, and that worry was growing. He had a little money saved from the fights, but that wouldn't last long. He could probably get a letter of recommendation from Strauss, but getting an interview as a demon - and a well-known, violent one - would be the hardest part. He didn't want either his mom or sister to work, especially somewhere unknown. Vince tapped his fingers against the steering wheel as he sat at a red light. Everything had gone to shit, and it hadn't even been a full day since he'd met Jask.

All he could do was try and get as far away as possible. A small, traitorous part of his brain suggested what everyone was saying about Jask was true. He was different from the others. Vince could find him and ask for help, for protection. He could ask Jask to join him and they could blow town together. They were strong descendants of the two most powerful bloodlines. Together, they could stop anything that came their way.

Vince blinked as he realized he wasn't driving home. The pull in his chest and his own daydreaming had led him to the edge of the Dreadlands. He was driving toward the Gardens, toward *him*. He slammed on the brakes and turned the car around, flooring it in the opposite direction and pulling into the first abandoned parking lot he could find.

He was breathing hard and fast, everything in him fighting to get him to turn around. To find his safe haven in the arms of the man whose family would have him dead. Because of what? Because of his shadowline? Because he wasn't worthy? Vince gripped tight to the anger those thoughts brought. Let it fuel his determination to get his family and leave. It hurt, more than he'd ever admit, but he turned the truck back onto the highway. This time, he didn't allow his thoughts to drift to what may lay in the other direction.

His mother stood up in surprise when he finally walked back in the door. "Vincenzo! I thought you were gone? Did something happen? Did they find you already?" She hurried to him, patting him down and checking him for injuries, even as he lightly grabbed her arms to steady her.

"I came back to get you and Lee. I'm taking you with me, and we're going now. Grab whatever you can carry. Toss it in the back of the truck. If it can be sold, even better."

She pulled back with fear in her eyes. "Did someone threaten you?"

"Not yet. Strauss just helped me see the light. Come on, gotta get moving," he said, then yelled the same instructions to his sister.

His mom refrained from asking any more questions until they had practically everything they owned thrown in the back of that truck, but once they were all squeezed inside the cab, she turned to face him. "Are you going to explain now?"

He opened his mouth to do just that, but then jumped back out, motioning to the steering wheel. "Gotta blow up the house first. Drive, please. Fast and far. I'll meet you at the end of the property."

Luckily for him, Leota wasn't in the mood to ask questions. She climbed over their mother and hit the gas, barely giving Vince enough time to move out of the way before she was streaking off down the gravel driveway.

Vince laughed a little and ran back into the house. He turned on the gas stove and let it saturate the building, then stood outside, looking at the place he'd called home for the past three years. Three years, and everything worth taking had fit in the bed of a rusty pick-up. He turned his head to make sure said pick-up was far enough away before moving on to the next step of the plan. His eyes flashed black as he lifted his hand and brought a happy little ball of flame to life.

"To new beginnings," he murmured before tossing it like a baseball, then turned and hauled ass toward the truck. He felt the heat as the house erupted behind him. Vince couldn't deny how nice it'd felt to do that, but he stayed focused on getting to the truck.

"So," his sister started, once Vince was back in the driver's seat and they were officially on the road. "We're running from... who, exactly? Mom wouldn't tell me, and your goodbye was shit."

"Don't talk to me like that, you little fucker." Vince frowned at her and then rubbed the back of his head when his mother slapped him there. "And we're running because... I had my heart broken. Remember that the next time you look at an attractive person. They aren't worth it. Fall in love, get your shit blown up." It was as close to the truth as he was willing to joke about, and if it kept Leota from dating, even better.

She scowled, crossing her arms and trying to make more room for herself. "You blew up our *house* because you couldn't hold a boyfriend? Mom, how does he get away with this kind of shit?"

"You watch your mouth too, Leota. I'll smack you harder than I smacked him." She pursed her lips, glancing briefly at Vince before looking back at her daughter. "We're running from Jaskian Veris, and his family. It's not that your brother couldn't hold a relationship, it's that the Veris' would rather see us all dead than let him try."

Leota's eyes widened for a moment, but it did little else to relax her bitchy demeanor. "Dang. He's your mate, huh? That must suck."

"Yeah," Vince agreed quietly. "It does, and you didn't even get to see him, Lee. Ass you could bounce a quarter off of, eyes the color of a clear sky, and arms that could definitely hold me against the wall as we... *ow!* Stop hitting me, Ma!"

"Stop talking like that in front of your sister!"

Lee burst out into a fit of laughter, trying to double over in the tight space to hold her side. "Gross, Vinnie! Gross."

"I'm just trying to tell the truth," he shrugged, merging back onto the highway. "But the Veris clan? Not something to mess with. We'll head east, maybe go to Savannah. Live on the beach. It's a new start, that's all." He deliberately left out that traveling that far and finding a place to stay was going to cost money they didn't really have, but Vince would find a way.

Leota immediately started babbling about the merits of beach-living, and neither Vince or Amaranth stopped her. If getting Leota excited was the only way to make this drive bearable for them, then they'd let her drone on as long as she wanted about sand and stupid waves. *Anything* to make this easier.

The trip to the farm didn't take as long as Vince might've liked. He knew this goodbye wasn't going to be easy. He pulled the truck into the parking lot and left it running, giving both his mother and sister instructions to stay there. Vince jumped out of the truck and gave Strauss a wave, then leaned against the hood as he waited for Strauss to let Johnny know he was there. His friend came out of the barn a few moments later with his arms crossed, checking out the truck and the items strapped down in the back before heading over.

"So, you're going." It wasn't a question.

"Yeah, got a good night's sleep and thought about what you said. Distance seems to be the best option for everyone," Vince said.

"Ain't gonna be the same around here without you messing everything up." Johnny smiled, hitting Vince on the shoulder.

"Me? I had to do most of the work on that fence." He tilted his head up to the sky. "I'd say you could come with us, but there's no room in the cab. Well, we could always tie Lee to the top of the truck, I suppose."

"Fuck you, Vinnie! Ow, mom!" Leota cried out from the truck.

"Nah, I've been here too long. Twenty years almost. Wouldn't know how to act in the real world," Johnny said with a sigh, shaking his head.

"I blew up the house, so I hope you hadn't left anything there of value."

"No shit? Well, I'll be damned. What a way to announce your departure."

"You know me, gotta make everything a big deal," Vince joked, and he could hear Johnny speaking but the words stopped reaching his ears in a coherent manner. Something was happening. The ache in his chest was easing and he felt like he could breathe for the first time all day. Vince pushed himself off the truck and ignored Johnny calling after him, didn't feel the tug at his arm. Jask was here, his *mate* was here. Some supernatural compass inside him had him turning in the direction of the house. There, coming from the main entrance and headed straight for them, was Jaskian Veris. Vince's feet seemed to move on their own and he couldn't take his eyes off the angel. It wasn't until Johnny's fist connected with his jaw that he snapped out of it.

"Vince, go! I'll hold him off, just get the fuck out of here!" Johnny was screaming. With one last look back at Jask, Vince turned and ran back toward the truck. His mother and sister were talking over each other when he threw the truck in gear and swerved out of the lot.

"Fuck!" He hit the steering wheel, mad at himself for almost throwing it all away that easily. Driving faster than was probably safe, he risked one last look in the rearview to see Johnny standing fearlessly in the path of the angel. He could only hope his best friend would live to tell him what happened.

Jaskian

Watching his mate drive away was almost unbearable. He fell to his knees, staring after the truck and completely ignoring the demon standing close enough to kick him. Nothing mattered except for staying still long enough that Vince and his family could actually leave. If Vince could have enough strength to drive away, then Jask could stay on the fucking ground and let him go.

"You're not... You don't want to go after him?" Johnny sounded surprised, frowning down at Jask.

"Of course I want to go after him," Jask snapped, digging his fingers into the dirt like he was trying to hold onto the earth itself. "It's not safe. I only came here to-" He broke off, dropping his head to the ground as he felt Vince cross over the property line and head further away. "Fuck!"

"If you didn't come here for him, then why the hell are you here?" Johnny asked skeptically, crossing his arms again.

Jask huffed a bitter laugh. "I came here for him. But to make him leave, to make sure he was safe. Looks like he's got that handled all on his own." He hated the way his body was shaking, but couldn't bring himself to do anything about it. "His mother listened, then. Good."

"His mother? I told Vince to leave. I don't think Ms. Amaranth had anything to do with it. Hey, man, you look like you could use a drink." Johnny was obviously trying to distract him and Jask was nearly thankful for it.

"I told her to... nevermind." He pushed himself to his feet and turned toward Johnny, but stopped dead in his tracks as recognition rocketed through his system. "You - what? No, you're... how?"

"You okay, buddy? I know Vince leaving couldn't have tickled, but you're white as a ghost." Johnny genuinely looked concerned.

Jask paced around Johnny, trying to age him backward in his mind. The eyes were right, for sure, and the rest... His heartbeat quickened as he circled back around in front of Johnny, noting every angle of his jaw. *There's no fucking way... and yet...* "Pavo?"

This time, Johnny's face was the one to go pale, and he stepped backward quickly. "Who told you that name?"

Tears. Traitorous, stupid tears. They welled in Jask's eyes, and he wished he'd have just stayed on his knees. "You're alive? I - fuck, I looked for you for *years*. I just spent four fucking hours looking for your body."

"My body? What the fuck are you even talking about? Look, if you know my dad please don't tell him where I am," Johnny pleaded.

"Who, Saros?" Jask shook his head, still trying to come to grips with what was happening. "I killed him. Yesterday. Wait, this morning? Yesterday morning? Did I sleep? Fuck." With a jolt, Jask abruptly realized he'd murdered Saros for killing a child. A child that was apparently all grown up and standing right in front of him. His voice got a little softer, and he made eye contact with Johnny again. "You're Pavo? Seriously?"

Johnny leaned against the wooden fence surrounding the employee lot. "He's dead? Shit." He scrubbed his face before looking back at Jask with a nod. "Yeah, or I was, twenty years ago."

It was too much. *Too* much had happened, and this... Jask took a step forward and yanked Johnny into a hug, squeezing him tightly until Johnny started squirming. "Seriously, man. I've been looking for you for a *really* long time. I'm... fuck, I'm glad you're not dead. Saros told me he killed you. How'd you survive that?"

Johnny stepped back again, putting distance between himself and Jask. "I've never told anyone this story. Not even Vince, but if you've been looking that long..." He took a deep breath. "My dad was a mean drunk. My mom had died in childbirth, and maybe he blamed me? I dunno, but without fail, every time he'd get drunk, he'd hit me. Once or twice, and then he'd pass out. I tried to stay out of his way, you know?" Johnny rubbed his face again, probably hiding his own tears. "One night he'd had *a lot* to drink. I think it may have been my mom's birthday. The hits didn't stop. I blacked out at some point, and when I woke up, an old homeless lady at the train yard was patching me up. She did the best she could, but that bastard had left me for dead. I healed quickly thanks to the demon blood and took off. Trespassed here and Strauss took me in. The rest is history."

Memory transference was one of his favorite powers, especially in situations like this. Jask stayed put so he didn't startle him, but pointed to his own temple. "Do you want to see what happened to him?"

"Can you do that?"

Nodding, Jask extended his hand and took a step forward, careful not to make any sudden movements. "Just gotta touch your head."

Johnny watched his hand warily, but nodded slowly. "Yeah. Go ahead."

He touched two fingers to Johnny's head and closed his own eyes, clearly replaying every moment of what happened in that cabin. When it was over, he dropped his hand and took a step back again, knowing damn well how badly most demons hated to be close to violent angels. And that's all he really was, at the end of the day. A violent angel.

"Fuck," Johnny gasped, his eyes wide. He stared at Jask for a moment as the tears fell, and this time, he was the one that hugged Jask. "Thank you."

All he could do was hold on, bracing his arms tightly around the boy he thought was dead. "I know I didn't do a fucking thing to save you, but damn... I'm happy you're alive." He pulled back, huffing a relieved, overwhelmed laugh. "At least I did one thing right lately."

"Were you really coming to warn Vince away?" Johnny asked, watching him.

Jask suddenly found the dirt beneath their feet incredibly interesting. "I might be strong, but not strong enough to fight off my whole family. My brothers alone could take me if they worked together, so... yeah. I did." He fished a key out of his pocket and handed it to Johnny. "It's for a house, I... bought it off one of the Razal brothers. No angel knows it even exists but me, they should be safe there. I was gonna give it to him and tell him to go, but..." He trailed off, knowing damn well that Johnny saw Vince drive away from him just as clearly as Jask had.

"I had to make him leave," Johnny offered. "I'm sure you saw the punch, but... yeah, I'll get this to him. I'll make sure he's safe."

"Honestly?" Jask shook his head, gallic shrugging. "Knowing he's struggling with this doesn't make it any easier. But I'd rather lose my wings than know any part of that family was hurt because of me, so... I'm gonna stay away."

"Then that's something else I have to be thankful for. Let me call

Vince, set up a place to meet him for this and then we can go get that drink. I think we can both use one now." Johnny walked away, pulling a phone out of his pocket.

Part of Jask wanted to say no, to go home and crawl under his blankets until his chest stopped aching. To hide from the world as a whole until his memories of those few, precious encounters with Vince were lost to time itself, but he knew none of that was an option. This was real, and it sucked, but there was only one way through it. Forward.

When Johnny finally came back, Jask had his hands shoved into his pockets and was toeing the ground with his boot. He wasn't sure he was prepared for whatever Johnny was about to say, but he needed to hear it, one way or the other. "Will he take it?"

"Yeah," he answered. "All I had to do was tell him how uncomfortable his mom and sister would be in that tiny ass truck for a long drive. You give me the address and I'll text it to him. I'll meet him there with the key."

Now that it was time, every instinct was screaming at him to go himself. To make *sure* that Vince was safe, to see him one more time. He struggled, longer than he should have, but eventually scribbled down the address and handed it to Johnny. "We're gonna have to reschedule that drink. If you're going now, I need to be far away from here or I'm gonna end up following you."

"Rain check, then?" Johnny asked with a sad look as he tucked the paper in his pocket.

Pity from a demon, that's new, Jask thought. "I'll be around. I go to the Barrage sometimes, but... really, you don't have to. I promise, I'll do everything physically possible to stay away from Vince, you don't need to babysit me. I think I have a more vested interest in his survival than you do."

"It's not completely about Vince. I owe you for Saros. That weight has been on my shoulders for years."

"I didn't do it for a reward, Johnny. I did it because he killed a child - or, at least... he thought he did. Anyway, the point is your kinfolk at the Barrage don't like me a whole lot right now, so it's probably best you aren't seen associating with me. Just... thank you. For fighting back then, for not letting that son of a bitch kill you. Something always told me you were alive, and here you are. That's reward enough for me."

He didn't have much else to say, and Johnny hadn't been wrong - he needed a drink. He let out his wings and took off into the sky, forcing himself to stay on the path away from Vince. One way or another, he was going to keep that damned promise.

~

Drazan was waiting for him at a bar in the Gardens with a drink and a curious expression. Jask sat down, not wanting to talk about anything at all, but knowing he owed his friend an explanation. That didn't mean he wasn't going to try to put off *giving* that explanation, but at least he knew he owed him one.

They polished off a couple of drinks and Jask was forcefully reminded why bars in the Dreadlands were superior. The music was boring, the patrons were boring... the whole place was too... *clean.* Even the alcohol tasted different, muted, like it was hardly alcoholic in nature at all.

"Barely spiked fruit juice, that's all this is." Jask downed his fourth drink and set the glass down with a dull thunk. "I miss the Dreads."

His friend rolled his eyes and gestured for the barkeep to pour them another round. "So why are you here, instead of there? It's not as if that bar *ever* closes down. I'd have even gone with you for once."

The urge to leave and actually go there was strong, but Jask knew it wasn't a good idea. "Nah, I need to steer clear of demons for a little while. Guess I'll just have to deal with the cold, huh?"

Drazan huffed a laugh and shook his head. "You're the only angel I know that looks for heat in *demons,* you know that?"

"I do," Jask said. "But, the stronger you are, the colder you run. And buddy, I'm fucking *cold.*" Unbidden, thoughts of Vince ran through his mind. *The same is true for demons and warmth. I bet Vince is hot enough for me... in more ways than one.* He rolled his shoulder, trying to nonchalantly loosen the ache in his chest without outright rubbing it. "Demons are the only thing that ever really take the edge off."

"Right." Drazan slowly nursed his drink. "Are you going to tell me what happened yet, or are you going to keep avoiding the subject?"

Jask grinned widely, if not believably. "I'm an expert at avoiding subjects, I'm glad you noticed." He deflated at the look on Drazan's face and wrapped his hand around the glass to steady himself. "I found my mate. The one that supposedly lived clear on the other side of the planet? Yeah, that one. He's been here the entire time, just... further into the Dreads than I usually go unless I'm working a case."

All he got from Drazan was a blank stare, and Jask sighed as he realized he'd already told him that much. Jask continued, "He's gone now. I barely got a chance to see him, and the *only* time I had my hands on him, he was trying to kill me. I know that's pretty par for the course when it comes to angels and demons, *and* with the bondmates, given our histories. But fuck, D. I feel him in my bones, *and* my damn wing."

A firm hand clasped Jask's shoulder, and he leaned into the touch for a moment. Drazan sighed quietly and squeezed, then pulled back. "Listen, Jask. You're doing the right thing by staying away. I can only imagine how bad it sucks right now, but I don't think you wanna know how bad it'll get if you go to him. It's not just losing *him* you'll have to worry about. If Cidos and Edis take him out like they're supposed to, you'll never be able to look at them again, if you even survive it yourself."

"You don't think I know that? You don't think I know I'm losing all of them no matter what I do? I know where Vince is, D. I bought him a fucking house. I can't go anywhere near my family, all it'll take is them asking the right questions and Vince will be in danger all over again. I can't go to him, because I can't risk being followed. Either way, I lost them all. I don't understand it, I don't get why things still have to be this way." He scowled, looking at the liquid in his cup. "It's a shame we lost the ability to time travel a few generations ago, huh?"

Drazan nodded, sliding his barstool a little closer so they didn't have to speak as loudly. "I have my own reasons for believing that, but what difference does it make to you?"

"It makes all the difference in the world. I'd go back in time and stop myself from going to that fight. Everything was fine before then. I didn't know Vince, I had nothing to lie to my family about. I was content with sleeping around and doing pretty much whatever I wanted. Now?" Jask paused, realizing before he even uttered the words how true they really were. "I don't think I'll be able to touch anyone else. I didn't even get to have him once, D, and the fucker ruined me anyway. When my wing brushed against him in that cage..." He shuddered, his tucked wings fighting to come out.

"So, what you're telling me, is that we need to get you laid. By someone hot enough to make you forget about Vince, at least for a little while." Drazan stood, dropping some cash on the counter to pay for their drinks. "Come on, we're in the wrong bar."

Jask had serious doubts that the *right* bar existed at all, but he followed his friend outside after tipping his hat to their barkeep, and then allowed Drazan to piggyback on his teleportation powers and take them somewhere else. From what he could tell, they weren't in Ares at all anymore. "D? Where are we?"

"You don't need to stay away from demons," he said. "Just *our* demons. The ones that know you, know of the bond. These demons don't have a clue who you are, so as long as you don't run off at the mouth about your graceline, they'll probably just take you for an angel looking for a good time. And hey, at least part of that is true."

It was hard to argue with him, particularly because Jask wanted to believe him so badly. He absolutely wasn't sure if he'd be able to go through with actually sleeping with someone other than Vince, but he was more than willing to try - and either way, the whiskey would be better there.

As usual, they received a lot of less-than-welcoming looks as they sat down, but the demons realized pretty quickly that neither Jask nor Drazan appeared to be looking for a fight. Most of them stayed out of their way, and the one behind the bar turned out to be a decent guy - with *much* better alcohol.

Already slightly buzzed from that first bar, it didn't take much for

Jask to get up and change the song on the jukebox. He wasn't quite drunk enough to dance, not in the mood he was in, but the combination of good music and strong booze was at least making it easier to breathe.

He spotted a particularly broody demon over against the wall and slammed back a couple of shots, then made his move. Jask had a lot more luck this time than last, and while every damn second of it felt muted and wrong... at least he was warm.

For Jask, the next couple of weeks went by a lot like that. Get drunk, get laid, wash, rinse, repeat. After a while, he didn't have to *get* drunk anymore. He stayed that way, his body so saturated with the stuff that his grace was having a hard time burning it off. Drazan tried to help, tried to pull him back to reality with cases that needed solved, vacation plans, anything he could think of... but none of it helped. None of it made Jask want to be sober, because being blackout drunk was the only way to turn his mind — and that pain in his chest — off.

Things only got worse when he got the idea to go sleep in Vince's old bed and found the house blown to smithereens. He'd stumbled, his incoherent yells echoing through the Dreadlands as he searched the rubble for any sign of his mate, any small trinket he could take with him - but there were none. Vincenzo Riskel had disappeared from that house as thoroughly as he'd disappeared from Jask's life, and the absolute only way to fix that wasn't even an option on the table.

This was just his life now, for better... or worse.

Four

Vince

The address Johnny sent him had Vince driving a few miles past the city limit. He was grateful that it was far enough away from everything that they wouldn't be seen, and as far as he could tell, there were no neighbors or anyone close that could give away their location.

Vince pulled past the line of trees and his eyes widened. This house put the one he'd just blown up to shame. It had a wraparound porch and was a lot bigger than what he'd been expecting. He heard his mother's gasp and his sister's quiet curse as they saw it, too. They'd never have been able to afford anything like this on their own. He parked the truck and got out, grabbing his and his mom's duffle bags and walking up to where Johnny waited for them on the porch.

"Hope you don't mind, but I walked through already. Wanted to make sure there wasn't some angel assassin in the corner of a closet." Johnny took a drink of the beer in his hand. "Oh, and the fridge is fully stocked. House is furnished. Your man didn't leave anything out."

"He's not my man," Vince replied automatically, but damn, he wished Jask was. He walked in through the open front door and whistled. There was a huge couch, a couple of chairs, and a TV mounted on the wall that Lee was going to be thrilled to see.

A trip into the kitchen proved Johnny hadn't lied. The refrigerator and the pantry were both completely stocked and there were dishes in the cabinets. They had everything they needed to eat for at least a few days, and even that alone was an upgrade from their former digs.

He left his mom and sister to explore and went down the hall. At the end, he found a bedroom with a king-sized bed. The blanket was soft to the touch, and a cursory glance around the room revealed a door to an attached bathroom. He spent a minute or two imagining how two grown men would fit perfectly in that garden tub before he forced himself to go upstairs. Two smaller rooms that shared an adjoining bathroom took up the second floor. Lee and his mom wouldn't have to share a bedroom anymore.

Vince sat heavily on the top step and laid back to look at the ceiling. Jask had done all of this for *them*. Vince had run from him, had barely spoken to him, and he bought them a fucking house. His need to find Jask increased to a point that he had to grip the railing of the stairs to keep himself from running back out to the truck. He could find Jask, he was sure of that. Would that really be so bad? He was at the bottom of the stairs before he realized he'd even stood up.

"Hey, hey, whoa." Johnny held his arm out across Vince's chest to stop his progress. "Bad idea."

Vince looked down at Johnny's arm. "I just want to thank him. That's it." And if he did that thanking naked, it was no one's business but Vince's.

"I'll be sure to tell him. Look, he did this so you'd be safe - away from him. Not angel food." He sighed, taking a step back and making sure Amaranth and Lee were out of earshot. "If you want to see him that badly, you have to be smarter about it than this."

Strauss' words echo in his brain. "Johnny, if I see him, I'm not going to be able to come back."

His friend nodded, sliding his hands into his pockets. "All the more reason for you to let me handle the gratitudes, then. I'll hand it to the guy, he's a lot less horrible than I thought he'd be, but he's still a danger to you."

"What do you mean he's less horrible?"

Gesturing at the house around them, Johnny gave him a look that suggested the answer should be obvious. "There's more, but I think we should probably sit down for that."

"Then let's sit." He led Johnny back into the kitchen and grabbed a couple of beers. They sat at the kitchen table and Vince listened as Johnny told him the terrifying story about his childhood. When he got to the part about Jask looking for him, Vince was shocked. He let Johnny finish the story and stared at the wood. "He spent all that time looking for a demon child he didn't even know? Damn, Johnny, why didn't you tell me?"

His friend looked sad, but unapologetic. "I was scared. Scared of my father, scared someone would figure it out and make me go back. And after a while, Pavo just... didn't exist anymore. I was Johnny, and that part of my life didn't matter. I didn't think I'd ever hear that name again until Jask recognized me. Do you know how many times he must've looked at my picture to recognize me twenty years after it was taken?"

This wasn't making it easier for Vince to stay away. "Remember when I said I was fucked? It's so much worse now. I gotta do something. *Anything.*"

"Is there anything in the world I can say to stop you from going to him?" Johnny asked hopefully. "Like anything at all? All he wants is for you to be safe. You shouldn't test that."

"Tell me he hates me and wants me dead, because that's what I was holding onto." Vince stood and walked outside. He ran a hand through his hair and looked out over the yard. Spotting an axe and a pile of wood, he headed straight for it and pulled off his shirt. He didn't pay attention to Lee stepping out to talk to Johnny.

"He knows it's the end of summer, right? We won't need firewood for at least another month."

Johnny sighed loudly enough he could hear it over the wind as he swung the axe. "It's not about needing wood. Well, not *that* kind of wood, anyway..."

"That's disgusting."

"I can fucking hear you!" Vince yelled as he killed another log.

Johnny laughed, then put his arm around Leota. He lowered his voice, but not enough to get past Vince's enhanced senses. "He's in a predicament. He's in love with a man who loves him just as much, but they can't go anywhere near each other. If this is how he needs to work off steam, well... it's nicer than what he did to the Chevy, and at least it has its practical uses."

Vince hit the next log so hard he shattered the stump underneath. "I don't love him. I can't. I've said five words to him. He doesn't know anything about me, either."

"He knew enough to furnish you a farmhouse big enough for your family. Oh, and there's... one more thing." Johnny walked up behind him and reached into his back pocket, pulling out a thick envelope and smacking Vince's arm with it. "He told Pattie he tapped right before the buzzer sounded."

Vince stared at the envelope like it was going to bite him. Slowly, he reached for it and counted the money inside. "Son of a bitch."

"For once," Johnny grinned, "you're not wrong. But that's it, promise. If there are any more surprises, he didn't tell me about them. Just asked that I got you here and gave you the money."

"Did he give you a phone number?" Vince asked, still staring at the envelope. "That can't hurt, right? A phone call? Text message, maybe..."

The look on Johnny's face answered the question before his words did. "He did, but I *strongly* advise you don't ask me for it. Calls can be traced."

"Why don't you let me worry about that?"

Hesitantly, Johnny took Vince's phone and input a number, then handed it back. "Please be careful. At this point, I don't even know what side I'm on... part of me wants to drive you to him myself. But, the more logical part of my brain says that'll be great for you for about a week, and then the shit will hit the fan and it'll be my fault."

"But what a week it would be." Vince gazed at his phone for a while before tucking it in his pocket. "I need a drink. Can you stay here a bit? Just until I get back?"

Nodding once, Johnny eyed him warily. "Be careful. I'll keep your family safe."

Vince gave Johnny a grateful look before tugging on his shirt and heading to the truck. The town was unfamiliar, but he eventually came upon what was obviously a dive bar. Still, he sat in his truck for a moment and reflected on why the neon lights didn't feel as welcoming as he'd been expecting. He got out anyway and went inside, making a face at the musty air that greeted him. The bar itself was small, and Vince chose a seat near the corner as he flagged down the demon serving drinks. After ordering a glass of the strongest stuff they had, he put his phone on the wood in front of him and scrolled his contacts until Jask's name stood out to him. His finger hovered over the button until the clink of his glass hitting the wood stopped him from following through.

He thanked the girl and thought idly about how he would've been trying to take her home just a week ago. She flashed him a smile and winked at him before going off to take care of another customer. Vince considered it, he really did... but in the end, her chocolate brown eyes were no match for the ice blue ones burned into his brain. He drank the first round quickly and ordered another. Each time she dropped off his drink, Vince was staring at his phone. By the time he'd reached his fourth whiskey, he knew he needed a distraction. He switched his order to beer and walked over to the pool table.

"Taking bets?" he asked the burly looking demon at the other end.

"Depends. What're ya bettin'?"

"Even hundred?" Vince offered, choosing a stick.

"Rack 'em."

He learned the demon's name was Zazzo. Vince took his shot before he winked at Zazzo's girl and laughed when she giggled. He ignored the glare from across the table and kept up his shameless, silent flirtation. By the middle of the game, he was still playing flawlessly, but poor Zazzo was getting sloppy. It wasn't long before Vince had won the game — and, he suspected, the girl, if he were so inclined.

"Pay up, buddy," he said as he held out a hand.

Zazzo wasn't having it and broke his stick across his knee. "You scammed me!"

"All I did was play. Don't make this a thing." Vince watched as a few other men in the bar came to stand behind Zazzo. "Okay, we're making this a thing. Got it. I gotta warn you though, I'm not in a great mood, so this will *not* end well for any of you."

"There are eight of us. I think we'll be fine." Zazzo laughed at him, and Vince eyed the guy closest to him, shrugging. He dropped his own stick and stepped back, motioning for them to come at him. The first two to reach him went down easy; Vince hit one directly in the temple and the other he tossed over the pool table into a third. Four and Five yelled and jumped at him next, so Vince used his foot to toss the stick he'd dropped up into his hand and swung it wide. Four went down heavily when the wood connected with his skull, and Five sank to the ground when Vince shoved the blunt end into his stomach. He made quick work of Six after hopping over the pool table and tossing him against the nearest wall, and Seven hit the table as Vince swept him off his feet.

Proud of himself, if not a little winded, Vince turned back to Zazzo. "My money?" Zazzo handed it over and Vince left with a sarcastic bow. The fight had helped him immensely and he didn't feel the need to booty call Jask anymore. Probably wouldn't last long, but he'd take what he could get.

He sat in the truck for a bit after turning it on, trying to decide where to go. He didn't want to go back to that house yet, to be surrounded by things that proved Jask had thought about him. Not only *thought* about him, but had provided for his family, including Johnny. Vince dropped his head back against the rear window and thought about everything he'd learned. He gave himself a moment to grieve the loss of his house, of his life as he knew it. He was still close to Ares and he couldn't even go back to those things. All because of some sick twist of fate. The things he lost led to him thinking about the things he couldn't have. He looked at his phone again, but it seemed to have died sometime between the game of pool and now. He couldn't even drunkenly call his mate.

He rubbed his knuckles into his eyes to try and get the memory of

Jask falling to his knees outside of the farm out of his brain. Vincenzo Riskel didn't cry. He was a feared demonic force of chaos. He squeezed his eyes closed as the tears began to spill over anyway, apparently not getting that memo. Why couldn't things just be simple? All he wanted, all he'd ever wanted, was for life to be good for his family. He never tried to be more than what he was. He'd never asked for anything for himself, and now he *couldn't* ask. Because the one thing he wanted would get them all killed.

Vince put the truck in gear and drove out of the parking lot, wiping his cheek on his forearm before rolling down the windows. He turned on a classic rock station and turned down the first street he came up on. He drove all night, letting the wind keep his face dry as he sang along to the music. When the sun started to crest in the sky, he finally forced himself to turn back. He parked in front of the house and stumbled into the bedroom he'd explored earlier, hoping he was tired enough to not dream, but he wasn't so lucky. His sleep was plagued with dreams of things that could've been.

He woke up to the smell of coffee and bacon. He groaned and rolled out of bed, his nose following the smell. Lee shoved a mug at him as his mother put breakfast on the table, and he took a sip of the coffee in it. He gave a happy little sigh and settled in one of the chairs.

"That's the good shit. Your fella didn't skimp on the name brands," Lee said as she pointed her fork at his mug. Amaranth smacked her, then set a plate full of pancakes in front of her.

"She's not wrong. We're well stocked here. Good for a while." His mother smiled at him, but Vince couldn't get past the lump in his throat at Jask being called his "fella" to answer. He finished his breakfast in silence. His mother and sister didn't notice as they were busy talking about the new house. They were excited, and that helped the hollow ache in his chest ease a little. He left them to it as he went outside to check out the area. They were surrounded by trees as far as the eye could see, but the backyard was large enough that he could probably set a little garden up, which would give them fresh vegetables year-round and save them some money. He remembered seeing a gun cabinet, so it was entirely possible that he could do some hunting, too. If they stayed low and kept attention away from themselves, they might actually be able to stay. *No more bar fights, asshole*, Vince mentally kicked himself.

He cleaned up the splintered wood from yesterday and started scouting out the area. He made a couple of trips into town for supplies, and soon, he was working on the garden. When he had that mapped out and the seeds planted, he dug out a fire pit further out for when the cold air hit.

He cut down a couple of dead trees and built a deer stand a short distance away from the house. Johnny came by on the weekends and helped him start a fence for the backyard to keep animals away from his mother's garden. It was now *her* garden, because she said she didn't want his black thumb destroying their chance to have fresh vegetables.

The next couple of weeks flew by as he threw himself into the work on the house and yard. He filled his days with heavy physical labor so that his thoughts were completely occupied, but his nights were still filled with dreams of Jask. More than once, he'd picked up his phone and typed out a message or held his finger over the call button. So far, he'd been able to resist temptation. What if Jask didn't want him to call, anyway? He could've moved on by now. He hadn't made a move to contact Vince, which was completely understandable. The only communication they'd had was through Johnny, and now that they were settled, even that was almost non-existent.

Two and a half weeks after they'd moved in, Vince was sitting in his newly renovated backyard with a beer in hand. Johnny had just left, Lee and his mother were asleep, and Vince was completely and utterly alone. He listened to the sounds of night life around him and watched the stars. He needed sleep; he knew that he needed sleep. However, that would mean dreams of Jask, and another night of tossing and turning with no rest. He was tired. He was beginning to feel like he couldn't ignore the pull in his chest anymore, so... Vince decided he wouldn't. He slid his phone out of his pocket, opened his contacts, and hit dial on Jask's number.

Jaskian

Every day that passed without hearing from Vince, things in Jask's world got a little darker. So when he woke up from a dead sleep to the sound of the ringtone he'd specifically set for him, he nearly fell out of the bed trying to answer it. "Hel-hello? Vince?"

"Hey, angel," came Vince's quiet reply. "Did I wake you?"

His voice sounded so good it ached, and Jask shook his head despite being unseen. "Yeah, but... fuck, I'm glad you did. Are you okay?"

"Yes? Man, that's a loaded question, isn't it? Are *you* okay?"

Jask took a moment to take stock. That was the first time he'd slept at all in days, and he felt sick from his grace burning off all the alcohol. But even hearing Vince's voice was soothing something jagged inside of his chest, and he'd hang on to that for dear life if he had to. "Better now. Everything okay at the house?"

"It's perfect. I don't know how I'll ever repay you."

"You don't have to repay me, Vin. My family is trying to kill you, I'm pretty sure this one is a freebie." Jask rolled onto his stomach and closed his eyes. "I honestly didn't think you'd call."

"I wasn't going to. I've had your number for weeks, but... I wasn't strong enough to resist, I guess. Hearing you is helping," Vince admitted.

He could feel it too, and was glad he wasn't the only one. "Imagine how much better it would be if we could actually see each other. And before you freak out and hang up, I'm not suggesting that we actually do it. I just... fuck, I think about it so often it's embarrassing."

"Me too, Jask. I've caught myself driving your direction a couple of times."

Not going to him right that instant was a struggle. Jask dug the fingers on his left hand into the sheet and pressed the phone a little closer to his ear with his right. "Will you call me more often, then? I'd be lying if I said I hadn't tried to come see you, too. Johnny caught me once, actually. Said to wait, that you'd reach out if you wanted to talk. I've been dying for the phone to ring since."

"That fucker... He stopped me from going to you, too. As for calling more often, I don't think I could stop now." There was a short pause, and then, "But is it safe? They can't find us like this, right?"

Jask had gone to great lengths to make sure the lines were secured, but there were always variables. Always things he wouldn't consider, couldn't consider. "Nah," he said. "I don't think they can find you like this.

Vince sighed. "Good. That's good. So, what are you doing? Fuck, I sound like a teenager."

"Uh... well, I'm currently destroying my sheet, I think. Trying to stop myself from teleporting isn't easy." He licked his lip, slowly uncurling his hand. "I've been drunk since the day you left, I was sleeping it off. What are you doing?" He amended quickly, "Fuck that, what are you *wearing?*"

Vince let out a surprised laugh. "Uh, well, those jeans I wore the night we met. A red flannel. Cowboy hat. You?"

He lifted his head to glance down at his body. "Boxers, and it looks like they're sideways. Sorry, it's not nearly as sexy as yours."

"The way it sounds, you're not wearing much at all. That's incredibly sexy."

Rolling onto his back again, Jask snapped a quick picture and then squinted at his phone, trying to figure out how to send it to him. He heard the whoosh a couple of seconds later, then brought the phone back to his ear. "See for yourself, cowboy."

A strangled groan came from Vince's side of the call. "Shit, sweetheart, you're killing me."

"The whole point of me not having my wings around you right now is so I *don't* get you killed. I'm sorry, Vin. I'm a little outta my depth here."

"No, no. It's fine. I understand, it's just... well, anyway, you don't need to apologize. Feel free to keep sending pictures if you still feel bad, though."

Jask bit his lip and huffed a low laugh. "Something else you wanna see, Vin?" He reached down to palm himself, just in case. "Tell me."

"Yes, but I gotta make it fair first." Shuffling sounds could be heard, and then Jask's phone vibrated with the message. Vince had removed his flannel and unbuttoned his jeans so they hung low on his hips. He was framed by fire light and wore a cocky grin under his hat.

Jaskian's instincts temporarily got the better of him, and he teleported to Vince's front yard. He was back in his own bed before he even finished the swear word that worked its way out of his chest, but he was gripping the phone so hard he feared it would break. "Gods, Vin. You're the most gorgeous thing I've ever seen. Do you know how cruel it is that you're supposed to be mine and I can't come near you?"

"Jask, were you... I thought..." Vince let out a breath. "Come back. I felt you here. Or have I finally lost it?"

There it was. The invitation, the green light. The acceptance that whatever this was between them was more important than whatever stupid consequences would come from it. Except... the consequences weren't stupid, they were dire. Vince could die, probably *would* die, and nearly take Jask with him. But Jask wasn't stupid, either. While he had no idea how well or poorly Vince had fared over the last few weeks, he knew beyond a shadow of a doubt that he couldn't keep living like that. Something needed to give, one way or the other. "It was me. I couldn't control it, I was in your damn yard before I even realized I was leaving. And trust me, if I thought it was safe, I'd be with you in a heartbeat. Give me a couple of days, okay? Give me a couple of days to figure out how to do this without risking your life."

"Yeah, okay. I've lasted this long, what's a few more days?" Vince agreed after a moment.

"Torture, honestly." Jask closed his eyes, wrapped his wings around himself, and tried to remember how it felt to have Vince touch him. "I think the shittiest part of all of this... is that the only time we've made physical contact, we were fighting. That's not the impression I wanted to leave on you."

"It wasn't. Main thing I remember is how good it felt to have you under me."

That all-too-familiar bolt of lust raced through Jask's body, and he found out the hard way that palming himself had been unnecessary. "Yeah, I remember that part pretty clearly. I was ready to take you right there in front of the crowd until Johnny pulled you away from me."

"Well, they did pay to see us. We could've given them their money's worth. Remind me to smack Johnny for interrupting."

"He saved your life. No way we'd have gotten through that without someone putting the pieces together. You should thank him, I know I sure did." Jask traced his fingers lightly down his exposed chest and once more gripped his length over his boxers. He let go quickly though, his stomach still rolling from the days he'd spent completely neglecting his own self-care. "Seriously though, you guys are okay? Do you need anything else, are you running low on anything?"

"We're good. I kind of went a little crazy these last couple of weeks. Set up a garden, found a nice little area to hunt. We'll be set for a while," Vince assured him.

Jask had to laugh at that. "You've been setting up shop, and I've been on a bender. We sure that I'm the angel and you're the demon? I think we might need to be retested."

"Maybe the wires got crossed, but I'm happy to show you how bad I can be." Another heavy sigh. "Fuck, sorry. Can't seem to stop myself from saying that kind of shit."

He let out an involuntary, quiet moan at the words. "Don't stop. I need it, Vin. Need you. I haven't even had you yet and no one else has been able to come close."

There were more shuffling sounds on Vince's end. "Yeah? Me either. You know the night of the fight I went home and got myself off thinking about you. About how you'd feel in my mouth."

"Yeah?" Jask pressed his tongue between his teeth as he lifted his hips, sliding his boxers down to the middle of his thighs. He was already hard, the tip of his cock glistening with a bead of precome. "I'm kinda big, think you can take all of me?"

"I can take a lot, but why don't you show me? Just to be sure."

Smirking, Jask told him to hold on, then looped his thumb under his length and pushed forward until it was standing straight up. He didn't bother toying with the angle, he hadn't been bragging - the Veris line was gifted in this respect, and he was no exception. He snapped the photo, then took another with his hand wrapped around the shaft instead of the base, and sent both of them to Vince. He placed the call on speaker and bent his leg, resting the phone upright against his thigh so he could see anything Vince might send back. "Believe me now?"

"Holy shit." Vince sounded a little breathless. "I want to taste you, Jask. Need to get my mouth on that as soon as possible."

He started stroking himself slowly, trying not to dislodge the phone. "So take it, it's yours. Shoulda been yours years ago." Jask groaned, squeezing himself a little harder. "Your ass is outta this world, you know that? Swear I can still feel you on top of me."

"The *noises* you make..." Vince whispered, his voice deep. "Is that what you want, Jask? Me on top, so you can watch me slide down onto that gorgeous cock?"

"I want a lot of things, but yeah, that's definitely one of them." Jask rolled his hips without thinking, and the phone toppled off onto the mattress. He couldn't bring himself to care, he knew he'd still be able to hear - and now, he could reach down to tug gently on his balls as he moved his hand a little faster. Before Vince could even ask him to elaborate, Jask continued, "Want you riding me until you're spilling all over my skin, or taking me so deep in your throat I can feel it when I wrap my hand around your neck... want..." He grunted, forcing his fingers to splay out and release his length. "Want to bend you over every piece of furniture I own."

Vince let out a sound that could only be a growl. "I want that, too. Can't stop thinking about all the ways I want you. Pushed up against the wall as I lick every inch of you. Underneath me as I make you scream my name. Moaning around me as I slide into that mouth. Fuck, Jask, I'm gonna..." Vince's words trailed off, and what replaced them was arguably the sweetest sound he'd ever heard.

But, his imagination was failing him, and despite being so hard he thought he'd burst with a single touch, he couldn't quite get over the line. Breathlessly, he said, "Show me, show me the mess you made."

Jask's phone got the photo seconds later. Vince was laid back in the chair, chest and stomach covered with the evidence of his release. His hand was still wrapped around himself and he looked... *satisfied*.

"Fuck, all that for me?" Jask tipped his head back into the pillow and fucked into his fist until finally, the thought of licking Vince clean sent him over. He went boneless against the bed, still moving his hand until he was twitching from oversensitivity. "Shit, that was..."

"Best orgasm I've had in a while, and I haven't even touched you yet."

Yet. The promise of things to come had Jask feeling things he wasn't expecting. "Guess I better figure out a way to make this happen sooner rather than later, huh? I don't know how much longer I can stay away."

"Don't do anything dangerous. I'm not worth the trouble," Vince argued.

Not one part of Jask believed that. "Bullshit. You're my mate, every part of me craves you. It'll be worth it, as long as it doesn't lead to you dying." *Way to kill the mood,* he scolded himself. "Look, let's just... talk again tomorrow, okay? You can call me anytime, I've been avoiding my family like the plague."

"Yeah, tomorrow sounds good. I might actually sleep tonight thanks to you."

Post orgasm, Jask honestly felt even worse. But now, he no longer felt the urge to drink himself to the point of incoherence, which meant that maybe after a good night's sleep, he'd actually start to feel better. He smiled to himself, thinking that one day, he'd be able to wrap his wings around Vince and hold him through the night. "Then goodnight, Vin. I'll talk to you soon."

"Hey, Jask, you can call me too, you know? If you needed to talk or whatever. Or just to say hi." Vince sounded shy all of a sudden.

"Yeah? I didn't want you to think I was trying to pressure you or anything. You've got the most to lose here, and I know my side of history doesn't look great from where you're sitting." Jask closed his eyes and slowly released a breath. "I don't have a right to ask you to believe me, but I'm not like them."

"It's just a phone call, right? Not like I'm proposing marriage," he said with a quiet laugh. "I think you've already proved you're not like them, sweetheart."

Those pet names were going to be the death of him, and if that was the case, Jask would go happily. Again, he fought his instinct to go to Vince, to kiss him until they were both breathless, until the truth of their situation melted away and all they were left with was each other. "Please don't ever stop calling me that. Fuck... okay, I gotta go before I end up in your bed."

"It's big enough for two," Vince replied, delaying the inevitable disconnection.

"I know, I chose it for a reason. Did you look under the bed yet?"

"No? I'm going to now, though." The sounds of Vince opening doors and hurrying through the house made their way through the connection.

Laughing, Jask pictured Vince's face as he opened the box. He knew he was probably expecting sex toys or something kinky, when really it was just a box filled with the clothes he'd been wearing the day he bought the house. It seemed cheesy in hindsight, and probably stupid, but he'd found himself daydreaming more than once about Vince walking around wearing his shirt... and not much else. "Don't get too excited, I'm pretty sure you're gonna be let down."

"They smell like you." Vince's voice was muffled, and Jask smiled thinking about him with his face buried in his henley.

"That was the idea, yeah." And apparently, Jask was in the mood to thoroughly embarrass himself, so he spoke without thinking it through. "I tried to go to your old house, y'know. I was looking for anything you might've left behind. Clothes, books. Your pillow. I'm pretty damn glad I knew you were safe before I went there, or else I'd have thought my brothers got to you. You must have one hell of a fireball, babe."

"It was supposed to be a cover in case they did come looking. I'm sorry you don't have anything of mine."

Yeah, he thought. *So am I.* "Well, that brings me right back to needing to find a way to safely get to you, doesn't it? Maybe I should fake *my* death."

"Then you'd be stuck out in the sticks with us, never able to show your face again." A shower turned on in the background, making Jask even more reluctant to get off the phone.

"But we'd be together," Jask reminded him. "We'd be safe. The first mated pair to actually go the distance. And all I gotta do is convince the entirety of the Veris line that I'm dead."

"Could you? Do you honestly think it would work?" There was a hopefulness in Vince's voice, and Jask couldn't bring himself to let him down.

He sat up, running a hand through his hair and picking up the phone, taking it off speaker and holding it back to his ear. "On paper? Yeah, Vin. I do. But, I'd never be able to leave. I'd never be able to use my grace, not for anything. That kind of power leaves a trace, and could lead them right to us." He paused, letting that sink in. "So, you can see why it's kind of a last resort for me. When I go too long without letting off some steam, I get... fuck, I don't know how to explain it. It's like there's a hurricane under my skin trying to rip me apart. I'd be in agony by the end of the first month."

"Then that's not an option. I won't have you suffering for me."

"I'm suffering either way, but yeah. That... I don't know what would happen if I quit using my grace completely. It could kill me for all I know, I don't think any angel has ever tried it." He huffed, listening to the water run in the background. "I'll figure something else out, I promise."

"I hope so." Vince's voice was further away, like he'd put the phone down. "You gonna stay on the phone while I shower? Not that I mind, but it'll be harder to hear once I'm in."

As tempting as that sounded, Jask needed to sleep... and then plan. "Nah. Take your shower. I'll call you in the morning." He didn't give Vince a chance to change his mind before adding with a sad smile, "Goodnight, Vince."

Jask hung up, staring at the picture on his phone and taking a deep breath as he collapsed back on his bed and pulled the covers up to his shoulders. He had one hell of an uphill battle on his hands, but he'd fight it, and he'd fight hard. "Someday soon, Vin," he muttered to himself. "We'll be together. Dead or alive, we'll be together."

Five

Vince

Vince heard the line disconnect and ran his hands through his hair, tugging lightly to keep himself from picking the phone back up and re-dialing Jask's number. Hearing his mate's voice after denying himself for weeks had both soothed him and frustrated him. He wanted Jask to come back and lay with him, to talk to him until they fell asleep in a tangle of arms and legs and *wings*. He tugged a little harder on his hair and took a deep breath to calm himself down.

After a moment, he stepped into the shower and took his time cleaning up the evidence of the late-night call. He closed his eyes and remembered the noises Jask made. They'd driven him a little crazy, and now that the fog in his brain had cleared, he was sad he hadn't heard them in person. He could only hope they'd find a way to make that fantasy a reality, but for now, phone calls would have to do.

Vince stepped out of the shower and grabbed a towel. He realized that he'd forgotten to grab anything to change into, and his clothes were in no shape to be reused. His eyes landed on the box Jask had left. He didn't even remember bringing it in. He picked up the henley and slid it over his head. It fit well, so he grabbed the boxers and stepped into those, too. He couldn't resist taking a picture and sending it to Jask with a good night message attached. He yawned, officially tired now. When no return message came, Vince walked into his room and collapsed face first on the bed. For the first time in weeks, he slept soundly.

He woke up several hours later to the sound of his phone vibrating on his bedside table. With a groan, he picked it up and answered without even opening his eyes. "This had better be good."

"Is that any way to say 'good morning' to your mate?" Jask's voice was teasing, and entirely too cheery for such an unholy hour. "You look fucking amazing in my clothes, by the way. I nearly ended up in your room."

Vince rolled onto his back and smiled. "They're very comfortable. You're probably not getting them back."

"Who said I want them back? Maybe I want you in my clothes all the time."

"Yeah? Bring me some, then." Vince didn't know why he kept pushing to see Jask. Logically, he knew they couldn't, but his logical brain wasn't working well at the moment.

Silence met his request for entirely too long. When Jask spoke again, his voice was rough, like he was struggling just as much as Vince was. "Can I?"

"Yes." Vince sat up, his heart beating almost out of his chest in anticipation. A sound drifted down the hall, Leota was laughing at something his mother had said. They were probably cooking breakfast in the kitchen. "Wait! Fuck, Jask. You can't. I can't... they'll be in danger."

"Right," Jask breathed, his voice sounding like he'd raked it over hot coals. "Got it. I'll... I'll figure something out."

"I'm sorry. I wasn't thinking." He felt like the worst kind of ass. He knew Jask wanted to come, and he was leading him on. Vince dropped back onto the bed with a sigh. "Tell me about your day. Any plans?"

Jask cleared his throat. "Uh... yeah. Now that I've dried up a little, I've got a couple of cases that need solved, and I need to find out what - if anything - my family knows about this. I think as long as they don't see my wing, I should be able to control the situation."

"Your wing? What's wrong? Did I hurt you?" Vince was panicking slightly. Had he slammed Jask too hard into the floor? Was Jask in pain?

"No," he said quickly. "You didn't hurt me. My wings are white, they've always been white. But that... that spot you touched, during the fight? It's black now. Beautifully, deeply black. My guess is it was worked in as part of the original curse, so that angels *couldn't* just pretend they weren't sleeping with their demon mate. The more you touch them, the further the color change will spread."

"Will you show me?"

"Yeah, of course." A moment later, another picture came in, this one of a patch of black feathers in a sea of white.

"I'm sorry," he said again. Jask's wing were beautiful, and Vince had infected them with his demonic touch.

Jask laughed, and fuck, if it wasn't a gorgeous sound. "Don't be sorry, unless you're apologizing for not rolling around on them and finishing the job. I look like a damn Dalmatian."

"So you'll let me touch them? Run my fingers through until the job is finished?"

Vince could *hear* the shudder that induced, and the moan that came with it. Jask sounded wrecked when he spoke next. "Yeah, I want that."

Vince wondered if they were about to have a repeat of last night, but the rumbling of his stomach interrupted him. "Well, sweetheart, I'd be happy to do that for you when I see you next. Right now though, I need coffee and breakfast." He got up from the bed and pulled on some pants, keeping Jask's shirt on.

"Right." Jask chuckled, the sound a little breathless. "I'll let you know what I find out."

"Stay safe, though." Vince walked into the kitchen, ignoring the looks from his mother and sister. He went in search of coffee but frowned when there was none made.

"We're out," Leota whispered.

"Shit." Apparently, they weren't as stocked as he'd told Jask the night before. He realized at the last second Jask was still on the phone. "Sorry. Like I said, stay safe. Don't do anything to get yourself in trouble."

"I'll have Johnny bring you guys more supplies. Text me a list of what you need, okay?" Jask didn't even try to agree to stay safe, but from the look on his mother's face, Vince didn't have time to argue with him.

"Yeah, will do. I'll talk to you later?" He turned his back to her, trying to maintain some semblance of privacy.

"Absolutely. I'll call you though, as soon as I can. Feel free to text me, but I don't think it'll be good if you call when I'm with Cidos and Edis. Bye, Vin."

"Bye, sweetheart." Vince disconnected the call first this time. He grabbed some breakfast and continued to pretend he couldn't see the way his mother and sister were looking at him.

It took all of about twelve seconds for Leota to flip out. "You're *talking* to him?! Are you trying to get us all killed?"

"What are you talking about? That was Johnny," Vince lied through his teeth.

"Since when do you call Johnny 'sweetheart'?" Amaranth demanded with her arms crossed.

"Since I saw him bend over last week when we were posting the fence." He grinned at her, hoping to throw them both off.

Lee crossed her arms. "Fine, better give him a kiss then. He's pulling up."

Sure enough, he could hear the tires crunching the gravel as Johnny drove up to the house. Vince cursed internally. "Sure. No problem." He stood and went to open the front door. Seeing Johnny get out of the truck made him realize there was no way he could go through with that, so now he had no idea what to do. "Hey, Johnny. You made good time considering we just got off the phone." He tried to get Johnny to pick up what he was trying to say with his eyes.

Frowning, Johnny stepped around him into the house and took off his boots. "R...ight. I was... closer than I thought?"

"Yes, exactly," Vince smiled at both his mother and sister. "See? It was Johnny."

The look on Lee's face was predatory as she leaned forward to look at Johnny. "Why don't you give your *sweetheart* a kiss then, hm? Don't let us stop you."

Johnny whirled toward Vince, and Vince knew it was over before the grossed out "give my *who* a *what*?" was even out of his mouth.

"Fuck. Fine. It wasn't Johnny." Vince sat back down at the table.

"What in the hell did I walk into?" Johnny asked, bewildered.

Amaranth clenched her jaw and stood up, pacing in front of the table. "He's been in contact with that... *angel.* Calling him pet names and telling him to be safe, as if the angel gives a damn about my Vincenzo's safety."

Johnny raised his hands in defense. "Ma'am, I've spoken to Jaskian. Several times, he's not what you think. I'd be dead already if he was, and so would all of you."

Vince frowned at her. "We wouldn't have a place to live if it wasn't for him. Food to eat, either. He hasn't been here physically because he cares about our safety. Not just mine, but yours, too. Don't talk about Jask like that."

"He's right. He's trying to do right by Vince, I promise," Johnny added.

She didn't look convinced, but she did soften just a little. "If it wasn't for the Veris', we'd still have a home of our own, and we were doing just fine before him. Now we can't even leave, we're trapped here. Prisoners... that's what we are. We're prisoners."

"That isn't true. Jask is trying to find a way to fix this. *That's* why I was telling him to be safe. It's only for a little longer." Vince walked over to his mother and hugged her.

She wrapped her arms around him and let out a deep, apprehensive breath as Lee chimed back in. "Damn, I was really hoping you were gonna make out with Johnny. I'd have paid to see you both that uncomfortable."

Johnny flipped her off, then apologized profusely to Vince's mom for it, finally turning his attention back to Vince. "You're talking to him though? You finally called him?"

"Last night, yeah. We talked. Oh, I'm supposed to be sending him a list." Vince began to look through the cabinets as he said, "I was sitting outside after you left. Figured I might as well get it over with. So... we talked."

"Talked? Is that why you're wearing a shirt I've never seen on you before?" Leota interrupted.

"Oh, this? He left it before we even moved in."

"But it *is* his," she pushed.

"Yes, you annoying little ass." Vince started typing out a text to Jask detailing what they needed.

Amaranth smacked him in the back of the head. "Don't talk to your sister like that, how many times do I have to tell you? She's worried, we all are. He might be being nice to us, but his family won't be. The more connections you have to him, the more dangerous it is for all of us. Including you," she said, pointing at Johnny. "What if someone sees you!"

"No one pays any mind to a farm hand doing chores, Ms. Amaranth. I'll be just fine," Johnny answered with a smile.

"Not talking to him was killing me. I wasn't sleeping, Ma. Barely wanted to eat. I've talked to him twice and I feel like I can breath again," Vince tried to explain.

She still looked like she wanted to argue, but ended up nodding slowly. "I was warned you wouldn't be able to deny the bond once it set. That's why I tried so damned hard to keep you away from angels all your life. If you say you're being careful, then... I believe you. You're a pain in the ass, but you're a good boy." His mom had tears in her eyes as she continued, "I'm sorry it has to be like this for you. I hoped you'd find someone else, settle down before you ever laid eyes on your mate."

"That wouldn't have stopped it. If anything, it would've made things worse for the poor soul that had gotten stuck with me. We'll be careful, I promise."

Leota giggled behind her hand. "He's got twin brothers, right? Are they single? Let me at them for an hour or two, I bet I'll change their mind about demons, solve the whole mess you're in."

"That's disgusting." Vince gave her an offended look. "You're too fucking young to be thinking like that." Vince knew she wasn't, he'd started his own sexual escapades at seventeen. Leota was eighteen now, but she'd always be twelve to him.

She scoffed, sliding down in her seat to try and kick him. "It could've been me, you know. Just as easily as it could've been you. The Veris line has rules about that shit, we don't."

Johnny raised his eyebrows. "This isn't nothing to be gettin' jealous about, Ms. Leota. You should be thankful it's *not* you that got mated."

"I'm not jealous, I'm trying to show him that I'm not a child anymore," she countered, missing the point so thoroughly she basically proved she *was* still a child.

"Sure you aren't, Lee." Vince rubbed his hand in her hair like he'd done when she was a kid. "But I see you anywhere near those angels, I'll kick your ass like I used to do when you were little. Not even Mom could stop me. Capiche?"

His sister grumbled, but ultimately didn't fight him. "Capiche."

Johnny's phone rang a moment later and he stared at it, laughing. "Well, I'll be. Speak of the angel... do you want me to take this outside?"

"Why not take it here?" Vince asked.

He hesitated for a moment and then answered, putting the phone on speaker. "Jaskian, I wasn't expecting to hear from you so soon."

"I know, I'm sorry to keep bugging you, I know you've got shit to do. I'd ask someone else if I could, but... anyway, I've got some things I need you to take to the Riskel's if it wouldn't be too much trouble?"

Vince stayed quiet, wondering if Jask would say anything about him. "No trouble at all, what do you need?"

Jask laughed, the sound echoing through the kitchen. "How much time you got? Chain me to something so I don't go see him, for starters. It's getting harder by the fucking minute to keep away. But no, bring the truck by, I'll load it up for you. It's just some food, some clothes for Leota, and some better gardening tools for Amaranth. You said she likes to knit, right? I had Draz get some yarn from Sweden. I don't have a damn clue if that means anything or not, but I don't know shit about yarn and when I asked him where he thought I could get the best, he said Sweden. I'm rambling... feel free to tell me to shut up anytime."

Vince rubbed his chest for the millionth time. Knowing Jask wanted to see him that bad was making the ache worse. He gave his mother a pointed look at the knitting comment.

"Yeah, of course. Any specific time you want me to come by? And anything you want me to pass on to Vince?" Johnny asked.

"Just that I'm sorry for the millionth time." Jask got quieter. "I feel fucking horrible about all of this, and I'd give anything to make it go away. To make him safe, all of them. I'm half tempted to just let Cidos kill me, but I know he won't, and offering will only tip him off. So just... tell him I'm trying, okay? And I miss him, even though I've only seen him once. Fuck," he laughed again. "Yeah, you're gonna have to chain me to something, so the sooner you can get here, the better."

"I'm on my way," Johnny informed him before hanging up. Vince was up and moving before anyone could say anything. He couldn't stand hearing Jask like that, but he knew he couldn't go to him. Hopefully what he was about to do would be close enough. He dug through the box of items in his room, the few things he'd thought were worth saving. Vince gave a small yell of triumph when he found the blanket and turned to see everyone in the door watching him.

"Uh..." He handed the blanket his mother had knit for him to Johnny. "Take this to him, please. In case he gets cold, you know?"

"Yeah, Vinnie. You got it." Johnny took the blanket from him. The second he was out the door, Leota dropped her head to the table with a thud.

"Ugh," she whined. "That was *nauseating*. Seriously. Where did you find him, again?"

"Pattie's." He wasn't going to pretend he didn't know who she meant. Despite the early hour, Vince grabbed a beer. He was out of things to keep him distracted and he'd almost gotten in Johnny's truck with him. He needed to take the edge off.

Amaranth shook her head. "If you'd have just stayed away like I asked you to..." She sighed. "But I get it. He seems... sweet. I never thought I'd say that about an angel. Are you alright, Vincenzo?"

"Of course he's not alright, he's bonded to a *sap* he can't even go see!"

Leota stood, groaning like the teenager she was. "Those clothes he got me better not suck... not that I can wear them anywhere, anyway."

"You won't say shit even if he brings back potato sacks, Lee," Vince said sharply as he pointed at her. "He doesn't have to do any of this. He could've let us drive away, struggle to find a place. We would've run out of money week one. Fuck, I can't even do anything to pay him back. He's doing all of this to keep us safe, but he's also worried about your happiness, and all you can do is be ungrateful? No, I'm not okay." Vince downed his beer and walked outside to get some fresh air. He looked in the direction Johnny had driven off in. He could only hope Jask liked the blanket, since it was all he could offer.

Jaskian

Jask paced in the driveway of Strauss' farm, practically pulling his own hair out as he waited for Johnny. He wanted to take the supplies himself, sweep Vince off his feet and show him all the things they'd barely even begun to talk about, but he knew he couldn't. When Johnny's truck finally pulled in, his wings were flapping erratically behind him as he fought the ever-growing urge to go to Vince.

"Hey," he said the moment Johnny got out. "Is he okay? Have you seen him? Talked to him? Did he ask about me?"

Johnny laughed a little. "He's fine, I've seen him and talked to him. He wants to see you. I know that doesn't help, but I thought you might like to know."

It both helped and made things worse all at the same time. Jask wasn't an idiot, he knew Vince wanted to see him, and was likely going through the same thing he was. "Yeah, thanks." He started loading up the food and supplies into the bed of the truck and finally managed to get his wings to retract. "That should hopefully last them for a couple of weeks, and with any luck, I'll be with them myself by then."

Johnny checked the truck to make sure everything was set. "He also gave me something. For you."

"For me? Really?" Jask was way more eager for it than he probably should've been, but he didn't have anything of Vince's, and he wasn't foolish enough to think that having some sort of connection to him wouldn't help. "What is it?"

Johnny reached into the truck and pulled out a blanket. "He said he wanted you to have it in case you get cold."

His heart might've stopped for all he knew. He took the blanket gingerly, afraid that touching it the wrong way would cause it to disappear. "I hate being cold," Jask offered lamely, still in shock. He brought the fabric to his face and breathed in deeply, not caring how that must've looked to Johnny. It smelled like *home*, which he now knew was a person, not a place, and he couldn't even go there. Tears pricked the corners of his eyes as he looked back at Johnny, overwhelmed by such a simple gesture. "Thank you."

"Yeah, you're welcome." Johnny cleared his throat. "You need anything else? Want to write him a note or something?"

Jask shook his head, holding the blanket to his chest. "Just tell him I said thank you. I'll call him tonight, I'm gonna go talk to my family." He didn't wait for a response, knowing if he did, he'd be tempted to go with him. He stashed the blanket at his own house and then teleported to his mother's, making sure to keep his wings away.

"Jaskian, you finally decided to grace us with your presence," his mother stated when she saw him.

Smiling disarmingly, Jask took a seat across from her at her kitchen table and chose his words very carefully. "It's been a crazy few weeks. The PI's office had a pretty weird case, it took a while to close it."

"What kind of case?"

Years of carefully executed deception helped in situations like this. He shrugged a little, tapping his fingers on the table and opening up his body language. "Missing kid. Turns out, the dad did it. He's dead, kid's alive, happy ending for all."

"That's nice," she said, as if she hadn't been listening. "But surely that didn't take days to solve."

Jask shook his head slightly. "A few, yeah. But not all of them. I got a little drunk, lost track of time. You know how it is, I wasn't using my grace enough. But, I feel better now, so I'm sobered up and in your kitchen. Where are the twins?"

"I wish you wouldn't drink so much, Jaskian," she sighed disapprovingly. "They're at the firm. They'll be home in time for dinner."

He was beyond used to that tone, especially since his younger brothers joined the family law firm when Jask himself had refused. The system was rigged, basically used to put demons away whether they were guilty or not, and he wouldn't have any of it.

Thankfully, they kept the small talk to a minimum as they always did when Astarte took offense to something Jask did. When his brothers finally arrived, he tried not to let himself tense up too much. They were always nosier than his mother, more prone to picking out the half-truths he told as he was the one that taught both of them how to do it when they were younger and getting into trouble. "Cidos, Edis." He inclined his head to them both, then finished setting the table. "How are things?"

"Another day, another dollar," Edis answered, dropping his suit jacket on a chair.

"Another thousand he means. We closed that case against Irekal." Cidos kissed their mother on the cheek. She gave him a motherly pat and went back to working on dinner.

Forcing a smile, Jask sat back down. "Any chance this one was actually guilty, or did you two add to the portfolio of innocent imprisonments? It's already impressive enough as it is."

"How dare you," Cidos said, acting offended. "We do everything above board, thank you."

"It was illegal imports, he was guilty," Edis told Jask.

The lies bled through and made Jask's stomach churn, but there wasn't much he could do about it. They knew he knew, and the fact that they'd lied anyway just spoke to how self-righteous they were. He dropped it, not wanting to start an argument or give them any reason to suspect him moving forward. They helped Astarte dish up the food, and Jask ate quietly, picking at the meat and wondering how to go about stealthily asking the questions he needed answered. "So, how exactly does the ritual work where you guys kill my mate but keep me alive?"

Instantly, Cidos slammed the butt of his knife into the table like a savage. "Why, did you find the demon bitch?"

Jask shook his head, for once, grateful for his brother's colorful use of language. "No, I didn't find the bitch." It wasn't a lie, as his mate wasn't a bitch. "I was just curious how it works, and if we even needed to bother with it."

"It doesn't matter. Your mate isn't here, Jaskian. There's no need to speak of such distasteful things. Especially at the dinner table," Astarte said haughtily.

"Why so curious all of a sudden?" Edis watched him. "You've never wanted to talk about it before."

He felt like a sheep in a den full of wolves, but kept his posture relaxed and face neutral. "I'm getting older. Everyone here knows how this goes, it's never any different. Boy meets girl, boy's family kills girl, boy nearly dies. It's the nearly dying part I'm not looking forward to. And I'm curious now because I never bothered with the details before." He refrained from adding "that's all" since that would absolutely be a lie.

Astarte put her fork down and steepled her fingers. "The bond is nothing more than a spell. Any spell can be broken with the right ingredients and tools. The mark of this *specific* spell is branded on your souls. Once it's been activated - when you meet your mate... the brand demands completion. For two halves to come together. To correct the problem, we rip the brand from the demon's soul. It's completed without an actual joining needing to take place. It is a very painful process, and fatal for the demon as their very essence is ripped apart. Keeping the angel - you - alive is just a matter of keeping the body from shutting down from the stress of breaking the bond. The stronger the angel, the easier it is. You would be weak for a short period of time, but would bounce back like nothing had happened. Now, can we move on, please?"

Jask could feel the walls starting to close in around him. His insatiable need to find Vince made sense now; it was literally a matter of their souls attempting to come together... and his family, his *mother*... wanted to rip Vince's soul right out of his body. His hand shook lightly, the fork he was holding clinking against his dinner plate. "That's fucking barbaric, you know that, right? But yeah, we can move on." *Need to move on,* he corrected mentally.

Cidos kept his eyes on Jask. "It's just a demon, Jask. What's the big deal?"

That was an argument he'd been having with his brother for years. He hadn't won it yet, and he wouldn't win it now. "It's not just about a demon. It's about me. I'd rather just be left alone, y'know. Not weakened or having to have someone else keep my body functioning while my insides are effectively rearranged. I can just stay away from them, no one needs to die." He said the last bit without thinking, and he saw the moment all three of them realized it was a lie.

Silence filled the room as Astarte stared at him. Finally, she said, "Is there something you need to tell us?"

"Nah, probably just my half of the bond talking. Don't look too closely at it." Jask shoved another bite of food in his mouth, wincing as yet again, he knew they caught the lie. *Fuck, Jaskian,* he scolded himself. *Get your shit together or he's gonna die before you ever even get to hold him.* "I just think the whole thing is stupid, okay?"

"There shouldn't be a bond talking if you haven't met your mate, and I don't recall you going to China recently." Cidos raised an eyebrow.

"It isn't stupid to want to keep the integrity of our line secure," Astarte argued.

Those, he could handle. "I haven't gone to China recently, and Ma... I'm gay. Pretty sure you don't need to worry about me carrying on the line in *any* capacity, whether it's with a demon or another angel."

"Integrity lies in more than procreation. The Riskels, they are beneath us. They are not a fit match for someone of the Veris line."

Rage bubbled just beneath the surface of his skin, and he nearly couldn't stop himself from screaming that Vince was twice the person Edis or Cidos would ever be. He couldn't speak, couldn't find a single phrase he could utter that wouldn't be either hugely combative or an outright lie, so he simply bowed his head and continued eating.

Edis sighed. "Ma, go a little easy on him. It's not his fault fate dealt him a bad hand, and I'm sure when it comes to it, he'll help us do what's right."

"Will you, Jask?" Cidos leaned forward in his chair, "Help us do what's right?"

"That's enough!" Astarte clapped her hands, "I don't wish to have anymore of this talk at the table."

Knowing he could put it to bed with a single phrase, Jask ignored his mother and locked eyes with his brother. "Yes, when the time comes, I will do what's right." *You and I just have a very different view of what that is, Cidos,* he thought.

Edis relaxed immediately. "He's telling the truth, see? Everything's fine. Cidos, eat your food. Jaskian, apologize to mom."

What right his little brother had to boss him around, he didn't know, but he listened all the same. "I'm sorry, Ma. I didn't mean to upset you. I'm just a little scared, that's all... and that's not something I'm used to."

Her eyes softened. "It's alright, Jaskian. I just worry about you. I'm sorry you're struggling with this, but there's nothing to worry about. Just stay away from the demons."

Jask reached over to squeeze her hand with a soft smile, hoping she'd take that as an agreement since he couldn't say the words. The rest of dinner went as smoothly as he could've expected, and he carefully picked through the thoughts of theirs he had easy access to. Neither one of his brothers seemed suspicious, neither one was thinking anything that alarmed him. He might not have found a solution, but at least he had more information, and ruled out the possibility of getting his family on his side.

~

He texted Vince that night to thank him profusely for the blanket, then curled up in a ball on his bed surrounded by it. Jask couldn't get enough of how it smelled, how it felt against his skin. It wasn't quite as warm as having an actual demon body wrapped around him, but it was close, and it was better because it was from Vince.

They ended up texting for hours, talking about their families and stories from their pasts. Jask refrained from calling him, knowing that he wouldn't be able to hide the hurt he was feeling after his conversation with his mom and brothers, nor would he be able to stay away if he heard Vince's voice.

Now that he knew what was happening - that the bond had been activated, and was now demanding completion - it was even more difficult to stop himself from going to Vince. At least before, he could convince himself that he was being ridiculous, argue that it was for the greater good that he stayed away. But now, knowing what he did, it seemed so easy, so logical to just give in. This was nature taking its course, his soul longing - no, requiring - to be close to Vince's... and who was he to fight nature?

Over the next few weeks, Jask threw himself into his work, arguing with himself to stay sober even though the only thing he wanted to do was get obliterated. His self-control lagged under normal conditions, but adding in intoxication and the extenuating circumstances of his growing bond with Vince, and he knew he'd end up doing something stupid for sure.

The one positive that came from that was his solve rate. Since he was dumping all of his energy into working on cases and avoiding his family wherever possible, he was virtually working around the clock with very little sleep in between. The downtime he *did* allow himself was spent talking to Vince or curled up in a ball under the blanket Vince had given him.

Last time Johnny came to replenish supplies for Vince, he *had* needed to tie him down. Jask had been shaking, his wings trying in vain to lift him off the ground without permission, and he knew if Johnny didn't do something, he'd end up at Vince's. It was becoming increasingly clear that Leota and Amaranth weren't on board with him hiding out with Vince, and not one part of Jask wanted to cause the same rift with Vince's family that he'd already caused with his own.

At least *one* of them should be happy, or, at least as happy as someone could be in their situation. Their conversations got longer and more frequent, and Jask started realizing that even if they weren't bonded, he'd have loved Vince. He was funny, witty, smart, and arguably one of the most attractive people he'd ever seen. Vince made him laugh, he comforted him despite being so far away, and they had more in common than a demon and an angel had a right to.

All that served to do was make the hole in his chest almost unbearable when he wasn't talking to Vince, and when he *was*, the urge to go to him was nearly overwhelming. It was a catch twenty-two, the damned-if-you-do, damned-if-you-don't side of things that he wished he'd never have found out.

Jask began chasing natural disasters a couple of months in. The weather in Ares was turning, it was getting a lot colder outside, and Jask couldn't stand it. He traveled to long-forgotten islands and used his grace to set off a volcano just to feel the heat in his bones. But even then, all he could do was think about Vince, and how his body had felt against his own during that fight that seemed like a lifetime ago. He knew he'd only felt a fraction of the heat Vince was capable of putting off and sat daydreaming about it while the lava pooled around him. *Just how warm is he? Would it finally subdue the icy chill that's always been with me, just under the surface of my skin?*

He had serious doubts that any demon could be as warm as a volcano, but that wasn't the point. He couldn't touch the lava, not directly, not without some level of pain. Regular fire didn't affect him much, not in the way the demons' pyrokinesis did, but it would still burn, and Jask needed more than just radiating, secondary heat. He needed Vince, holding him close and heating up the blood in his veins and setting him on fire from the inside out, figuratively speaking.

Home held no comfort for him, either. Jask sat on the floor of his living room, back pressed against the front of the couch with a bottle in hand, his wings drooping pathetically at his sides. He'd reached a breaking point. Exhaustion tugged at him from every angle, and he was no longer strong enough to fight that invisible tether tying him to his mate. He took another swig of the decades-old liquor and set the bottle down, standing up and stumbling slightly. His thoughts whirred through his head without mercy, some urging him on and some sounding alarms that he was about to make a grievous mistake. There was little to be done about it now, because a single blink of his eyes later, he was standing outside of the Riskel residence. And this time, he had no intention of leaving before seeing Vince, consequences be damned.

"Vincenzo!"

Six

Vince

Vince had been cleaning one of the guns he used for hunting when the pull in his chest abruptly ceased. Seconds later, he heard his name being called from outside, so he immediately put his weapon down and ran out. He thought he heard his mother, or maybe his sister saying something, but it didn't register. He threw open the door and Jask was *there*. Vince couldn't breath, and the doorknob broke in his hand as he gripped it, because he knew if he went to him, if he *touched* him, he'd never let him go back. "Jask? What's wrong?"

"I'm tired, Vin. I'm tired and I'm cold." He started walking closer, moving slowly as if he was giving Vince a chance to tell him to leave. "I need you, and I don't have it in me to fight it anymore."

"Then don't." Vince knew the minute the words were out of his mouth that he wouldn't take them back this time. It'd been *months* of longing and torture, hearing Jask and learning about him. Loving him and not being able to see him, to touch him.

He stepped down off of the porch and closed the distance between them, pulling his mate into his arms. When his lips found Jask's, something inside of him clicked. He was *home*. Everything in him was vibrating with how right it felt as he kissed Jask like he was drowning, and Jask was the air he so desperately needed.

Strong, broad hands cupped the back of Vince's thighs and lifted him up with ease as Jask carried him into the house, not breaking the kiss as he kicked the door shut behind them.

"Um... what the *hell?*" Leota exclaimed.

"Fuck." Vince pulled away for half a second to try and explain, but looking at Jask's lips had him lost again. He pushed their lips together once more, moving his hands into Jask's hair to tilt his head and deepen the kiss as Jask set him down. He felt Jask's moan to the bottom of his feet and it made him shiver.

"Vincenzo!" This time it was his mother.

"*Fuck!*" he said again, turning to face them but keeping a hand on Jask. "I give up. I don't want him to stay away anymore." He began pulling Jask toward his room. "I suggest you do not follow."

The moment they were safely in Vince's room, Jask broke away from him and waved a hand over each of the four walls. "Soundproofing. I'm leaving the door unlocked so if they need help, they can get in... but trusting they won't."

"You're a genius." Vince grinned and backed Jask up against the door. He slid his hands up under Jask's shirt and groaned at the contact of his skin on Jask's. They were kissing again and Vince realized he'd never be able to go back to *not* kissing Jask. This is where he belonged. He somehow managed to separate them long enough to get both shirts off before diving in again.

Jask's tongue slid into his mouth as he was lifted off his feet once more, this time deposited on the bed. Jask rutted against him, kissing over his jaw and down to his neck. One of his hands traveled down Vince's body, trailing a line of goosebumps in its wake. The moment it hit his pants, Jask swore, then apported the rest of their clothes to a pile on the floor.

"That's handy," Vince gasped, then pulled Jask flush against him. He ran his hands down to Jask's ass and lifted his hips, searching for friction. When his cock brushed against his mate's, his eyes nearly rolled to the back of his head.

The soundproofing made sense based on the moan Jask let out. "Yeah? You should see what else I can do." He slowly started kissing down Vince's body, pausing to flick his tongue over his nipple as he slotted himself between Vince's legs.

"Please show me." Vince didn't even care how needy he sounded. All he knew was that Jask was *there*, finally in his bed, and he was done wasting time. He pushed his fingers back into Jask's hair like he'd been dreaming of doing since that first night.

Jask's mouth traveled lower until that glorious tongue was flicking over his tip, teasing him just for a moment before sliding down his shaft as Vince's cock disappeared in his throat. As if that wasn't incredible enough, two thick fingers eased their way inside of him - without lube, or prep, or discomfort.

Vince couldn't hold back the noises that came out of his mouth. He'd heard stories about the angels and their biokinetic abilities, but this was the first time he'd had the luck to experience it. His mind zeroed in on how good it all felt and he rocked his hips down to get those fingers deeper.

By the time Jask pulled his mouth off of him, he was a mess. He kissed his way quickly back up Vince's body and reached down to stroke himself, messily bringing their lips back together. *"Spread your legs, let me in."* The voice was in his head - but it was Jask's, there was no mistaking that underlying current of thunder.

Vince did exactly as he was asked, spreading his legs and wrapping his arms around his broad shoulders. Jask slid into him slowly, and Vince couldn't think for a second. Nothing in his life had ever felt this good. They fit so perfectly, and Vince found himself digging his fingers into Jask's ass.

"More, Jaskian, please," he begged, pushing up against him.

With deep, punched out breaths and straining muscles, Jask drove himself further inside of Vince but controlled his pace. He kissed over Vince's neck and back to his lips, using the motion of his body to create friction against his cock. And there it was again, that voice in his head that felt like it was all around him, filling him up almost as well as Jask himself was. *"Touch them, make me yours."* The words confused him for a moment, until Jask's wings unfurled from his back and spanned half the room.

Vince immediately reached for the wings and ran his hands through the feathers, then watched in fascination as they changed to black where his fingers trailed through. He felt Jask shake as he pushed deeper. "Does it feel good?"

Whatever Jask said wasn't in a language he'd ever heard, if it was even anything more than just nonsense. Jask's cock pulsed inside of him, and he dropped his head to Vince's shoulder as his movements became more erratic, more desperate. His hand snaked between them and wrapped around Vince's length, squeezing and stroking as he pounded into him harder, moaning words he could finally understand: "Don't... don't stop."

Vince cursed and tilted his head back against the pillow, his fingers tightening involuntarily in the feathers. "Fuck, Jask, you're gonna make me..." he screamed as he came, curling his legs around Jask's waist to keep him deep as he covered them both.

It only took another minute for Jask to come undone, his wings half black and shuddering as he let out a needy whine and bottomed out inside of him. Over and over, he ground against him, emptying fully until it seemed like it was an effort for Jask to keep holding himself up.

Vince pulled him down and kissed him hard, keeping one hand in Jask's feathers and rubbing the other up and down the muscles of his back. He wasn't letting go anytime soon.

He could feel the moment Jask started hardening again - it stretched him open and forced a gasp from his throat. He nipped at Vince's neck, sliding a hand under his body and lifting his hips, sliding out and slamming back in again. This time, biokinesis wasn't even necessary, Jask had come enough the first time to do the job without it. "You feel incredible, Vince. I've never... felt anything like it..."

Vince moaned, not capable of words. He arched his back as Jask slammed home again, squirming underneath him. After a few moments, he wrapped a leg around Jask and flipped them, sitting up and looking down at Jask in his bed. He could see everywhere his hands had touched the once-white wings and he didn't move for a moment, just took in the sight. "You're gorgeous, sweetheart. Most amazing thing I've ever seen."

Those ice blue eyes he missed so much stared back up at him as Jask dug his fingertips into Vince's sides. "I can't even believe you're real," he whispered, gently thrusting up.

Vince leaned down and put his forehead against Jask's, bracing his hands on his shoulders as he rocked back against him. He smiled a little. "Feels pretty real to me."

From this angle, Jask was moving *just* right, pressing against the most sensitive spot inside of him with every thrust even as cool hands ran down his back. Vince could feel the waves of grace coming off of Jask as he got closer to the edge again, moving faster, breathing heavier, that chaotic power knocking out all the lights in the house.

"Jaskian," Vince said his name like a prayer as his hands pushed back into his wings, holding tight as he met powerful thrusts. This time when Vince came, it was untouched, with another wordless cry on his lips.

His back arched off the bed as he pulled Vince's hips down. His eyes flashed that icy shade as he stared down at the mess Vince made and came again, and even that felt a little bit like grace. Jask slowed to a stop, panting, and laced his fingers in Vince's hair and dragged him into another kiss just as the bedroom door flew open.

"Why's it so dark in here?" Leota asked, annoyance in her tone. "What the hell did you two do, I was *trying* to watch tv!"

Vince covered them with the blanket immediately. "Get out, nuisance."

Laughing quietly, Jask squeezed him. "Sorry, Leota. Give me five minutes and I promise I'll fix it, okay? It was my fault, I got a little carried away. Electricity and angels don't mix."

Vince dropped his head to Jask's shoulder as Leota huffed and slammed the door. "Next date night is at your place." He rolled to the side and pulled Jask into his arms, burying his face in Jask's neck.

"Deal." He kissed his head, draping his wing over them both. "I know I just complicated things by coming here, but I just... I got to a point where I'd rather roll the dice on a chance to be happy than keep living like that forever. I'm sorry."

"I don't even care, Jask. Whatever comes, we'll deal with it. I'm just happy you're here. Been dreaming about this." Vince's attention turned to the numerous black spots on the wing that was covering them, and with a grin, he added another. "You actually do look like a Dalmatian now."

Jask laughed quietly even as he twitched from the touch. "I kinda like it, honestly. But I wonder how long it'll take before you touch every feather?"

"I can't seem to stop touching them, so I'm sure not long." Vince couldn't stop himself from kissing Jask again. He kept it slow and sweet, and would've continued if Leota hadn't knocked on the door. He pulled away with a sigh and sat up. "We should go appease the women."

With a groan, Jask pushed himself upright and gave Vince his first real look at his naked body. It was still too dark to make much of anything out until Jask waved his hand and the lights came back on. "Think that's good enough, or do you think I should go introduce myself?"

"Introductions are probably necessary, if I know my mother. Fuck, you're gorgeous. So much better than looking through a phone." Vince leaned in for another kiss before grabbing their clothes and tossing Jask his pants.

Jask smirked. "Yeah, I think it's safe to say I'd have had a thing for you whether or not we were bonded." He slid on the same outfit as Vince got dressed, then gripped Vince's chin and pulled him back in for one more searing kiss.

Vince wanted to ask if that was true, if Jask would've even looked his way without the bond. Their lives were so different that it was lucky they'd even crossed paths. He tightened his grip on the angel and deepened the kiss for a moment. It hurt him to think he almost never got to have this. Suddenly, he didn't want to leave the room. He didn't want to share Jask with anyone else, or give him a reason to leave. What if they wanted him gone? Worse, what if Jask respected that wish and left?

Vince's thoughts were in a downward spiral and he didn't know how to stop them.

"Hey, hey…" Jask whispered, running a hand through Vince's hair. "I can feel that. Stop, I'm not going anywhere, okay? If they want me gone, I'll leave and sneak back in once they go to bed. You're not getting rid of me that easy, okay? Didn't Johnny tell you how hard it was for him to stop me from getting to you?"

Vince took a breath. "Yeah, he told me when he locked me in the basement last week."

A smile broke across Jask's face. "He neglected to tell me that one. But good, then you understand. I can't fight this anymore than you can, so if you can't walk away… neither can I. I think we're in this now, no matter what." He kissed the tip of Vince's nose and trailed his hand down to lace their fingers.

"Yeah, okay. Let's get this over with so I can have you to myself again." He opened the door and led Jask out into the main sitting room. "I'm sure you're both aware of who this is, but just in case; Ma, Lee… this is Jaskian Veris." He motioned with their joined hands.

Lee made a weird nose from the back of her throat, and judging by the look on her face, she was jealous. "He knocked out the electricity, Vincent."

"Leota, you know that's not your brother's name," Amaranth scolded, then turned her steely gaze back to Jask. "So you're the one that's going to get my son killed. And you show up here, unannounced, potentially leading your family right to all of us?"

Jask squeezed his hand a little tighter and shifted his weight on his feet. "I know what it looks like, ma'am, but I promise you. Vince's safety is more important to me than my own, as is his happiness. By extension, that means I've got a vested interest in protecting the two of you as well. I'm sorry about the power… but I *can't* promise that won't happen again."

"It *definitely* will be happening again, preferably soon," Vince amended as he watched his little family. "Nothing will happen. We'll be careful. No one will suspect a thing."

"What about those?" Leota asked, motioning to Jask's wings.

Instantly, they disappeared. Jask turned in a slow circle, proving they weren't visible at all. "No one needs to know. I don't have any intentions on letting my family find out about this, so... I'll do what I have to do to either avoid them or hide my wings wherever possible."

Leota raised an eyebrow. "Speaking of intentions... what exactly *are* your intentions, Jaskian?"

"I'd thought it was obvious. I love him, and not just because we're bonded." Jask took a deep breath and continued on like that wasn't the first time Vince was hearing this. "I can feel the difference. It's like..." he paused, chewing on the corner of his lip and staring at the floor, then flicking his eyes up to Vince. "Like two different tethers. It started out as just one, but now? I can feel it. It's more than just a soulbond."

"You love me?" Vince could feel his heart in his throat. He couldn't stop himself from joining their lips again, but broke away when his mother cleared her throat.

"That sentiment is all well and good, but love hasn't ever saved a Riskel before. Forgive me if I'm hesitant to believe it'll be enough this time," she stated, then walked past them to go upstairs.

Jask let her go. His attention was on Leota, who was sitting with her arms crossed. "Nobody *loves* Vince. I don't even love him, and I'm his sister. So nice try, pretty boy. But I'm not buying what you're selling." She wobbled her head like a brat, her lips pursed.

"First of all, angels can sense lies," Jask said, grinning. "You do love your brother, and you're definitely buying what I'm selling. Which is good, because I'm not lying." He sat down across from her and opened his arms. "Come on. Quiz me."

Vince sat next to Jask immediately and slid a hand onto his thigh. Like hell he was going to stop touching him. He planned to be by Jask's side until he left, and Vince would keep him as long as he could. He listened to his sister and... soulmate? Boyfriend? Vince shook his head. That was something they should probably decide later, but for now he was content to listen to them bicker. Jask reached down and laced their fingers together. All those nights they'd talked, every small trinket they'd sent back and forth, none of that compared to how it felt to simply hold Jask's hand.

He wondered for a moment if he was still locked in the basement. Maybe this was all some elaborate dream. He looked back over at Jask and decided he didn't care. If it was a dream, he was in control and nothing bad could happen. They'd be happy like this. And if it wasn't a dream? Vince would kill anyone that tried to keep him from Jask. He forced himself to step back from that thought before he did something ridiculous — like growl. He didn't know if they would be understanding of his issues. The one thing he did know... was that now that the ache in his chest had been satisfied, Vince refused to go back.

Jaskian

Jask smiled at Leota, watching the wheels turn in her head as she thought about what to ask him. He'd taken this very same role himself with Edis' first girlfriend, and he'd have done the same with Cidos' if Ci wasn't too big of an asshole to ever *get* a girlfriend.

There was something seriously awesome about the fact that he was sitting in *Vince's* kitchen, holding *Vince's* hand, and getting stared down by *Vince's* younger sister. He was here, it was real... and he wasn't going to let anything ruin that for him.

"So," she finally said, chewing on her tongue. "If your family disowns you, what are you going to do for money? This house isn't cheap, you know."

He did know, because he bought it. He kept his expression light. "I have a job. I'm a private investigator, and no... you don't have to listen to Vince make a joke about me investigating his privates."

"Damn it," Vince mumbled, obviously prepared to make that very joke.

"Are you any good at it?" Leota asked, a challenge in her tone.

Jask raised an eyebrow. "I don't even need you to clarify if you're asking about private investigating or investigating privates, the answer is yes on both counts. Johnny and Vince can both back me up on that, respectively."

"Gross," she said, making a face. "I don't want to hear anything about my brother's privates. So, it pays well? Enough for you to keep my brother as your barefoot husband?"

"Hey, cool it, Lee," Vince chastised his little sister.

"It's okay, Vin, she has a right to ask any questions she wants." He brought Vince's hand to his mouth and kissed his knuckles, then focused on Leota. "Now, I don't know about barefoot, but... yes. If I take enough cases, I should be able to continue supporting all of you, particularly if your mom's garden does well next season and Vince keeps hunting. I can also help with that. While I can't fabricate things out of thin air, I can urge the plants to grow and draw the animals in."

"So you're serious about this? Joining the Life on the Farm: Demon Edition?" She looked skeptical, but he could tell from the emotions pouring off of her that she wasn't dismissing him.

Jask shook his head, deciding to stick to the whole truth. "Not immediately. Ideally, I'll be able to fool my family until I'm strong enough to take them on. But I won't reach the height of my powers for another sixty years or so. By that point, I should hit a sweet spot, where my father's powers are failing and my brothers haven't yet hit their prime. With Vince's help, we should be able to take them on if it comes to it." He noticed the shift in her body language and held up his other hand. "I'll never put him in danger, but I know him well enough to know he'd never let me do this alone, nor would I be able to pull it off without him. It'll be a long road, but I'll be around as much as I can between now and then, and hey. The longer I hold on to the family jewels, the better."

"You're right about not doing it alone. Besides, I can handle a couple of angels. Pretty much kicked your ass, and I wasn't even trying." Vince grinned at him.

Sighing, Jask chose not to point out that he'd stopped trying before Vince did. Leota still didn't seem satisfied, if anything, his speech had made her look even more suspicious. "You're telling me you'd fight your entire family for a few demons?"

"You should've been at family dinner a few weeks ago. I nearly fought my brothers over a demon I'd never even heard of. Imagine what I'd do for one I love." Jask leaned forward, reluctantly pulling his hand away from Vince's so he could show her he was paying attention and hearing her concerns. "I know you don't have a reason to believe me. Angels have been horrible to demonkind, and my family is determined to kill your brother. But I promise you, since I came of age, I've made it my life to defend demons. And honestly, Leota, if I wanted you dead... you'd be dead."

"He's not wrong. Give him a chance, Lee. Please," Vince begged.

She sighed, nodding once. "Fine. One chance."

Jask beamed at her, wondering if she'd actually come to like him if given enough time. He never had a sister, and he'd be lying to himself if he didn't admit the thought was appealing. His brothers were rough and rude. Leota was... crass, sure... but she was real, and he could already tell she was fiercely loyal. He couldn't exactly say that about his brothers. "Thank you, Leota. Do you mind if we head back to the room now?"

"If I say yes, Vince will probably stab me... so whatever, go knock yourselves out," she said, waving a dismissive hand.

Standing quickly, Jask dragged Vince back to his room and closed the door, immediately pulling him close. He didn't want to admit it or even think about it until then, but the house was freezing, and he was craving Vince's body heat. "So, how'd I do?"

"I was impressed, truly." Vince wrapped his arms around him. "You're cold. Want to get back under the blankets?"

"Yeah. I'm always cold, to be fair... but I guess you guys don't really need a furnace, huh?" Jask crawled back into the bed, clumsily dragging Vince with him and tangling their limbs together. "Fuck, you're every bit as warm as I hoped you were."

"No, we use the fireplace sometimes, though. If you want we can go sit on the couch. I'll get the fire started and hold you until you feel better." Vince rubbed his hands up and down Jask's back.

Truthfully, the warmth seeping into his skin was more than enough, and he didn't want to move again. "I'm fine now, seriously. I'm used to being cold, and I'd rather not be sitting somewhere that Amaranth or Leota could see us."

"Yeah? Plan on getting me naked again so quickly?"

Instead of answering, Jask simply guided his hand down Vince's body and let his grace undress them both, apporting their clothes for a second time to a pile on the floor. But oddly enough, he wasn't trying to have sex with him again - not that he'd complain at all if that's what happened - he just wanted to *feel* him. He lined their bodies up and crooked his leg over Vince's, pinning him there. "Does this answer your question? I've gone full octopus, and I don't think your family needs to see this."

Vince laughed, making sure to squirm as close as possible. "They don't need to see it, but I definitely needed it to happen. Still can't believe you're here."

There were a lot of things that Jask couldn't believe, like how amazing Vince's laugh sounded in person, how well they fit together. How instantaneously touching him calmed the wild things in Jask. "I still can't believe it took me this long." As if on cue, the exhaustion he'd been feeling before arriving started to creep back in. Adrenaline had done a pretty good job of keeping him upright and active during the sex and his conversation with Vince's family, but now that he was relatively safe and sort of sated, all he wanted to do was sleep. He moved a little, sliding his arms completely around Vince and covering them with one of his wings, determined to make contact over as many square inches of skin as he could. "Are you comfortable? I mean, I don't really care, I'm not moving either way, but... I figured I should ask."

"I've never been more comfortable, sweetheart. You're staying the night?" Vince sounded hopeful and fearful all at once, like he needed the answer but was afraid of what it could be.

Jask lived on his own, there was little chance that someone would notice he was missing, and even less chance that they'd be concerned if they did. One of the perks of being famously promiscuous was that no one looked too closely if he didn't make it home to his own bed. "Of course I'm staying. Nothing anyone could do right now could make me leave... not when I've finally got you."

Vince let out a relieved hum. "Good. Johnny isn't here to lock me in the basement. I would've followed you."

The thought made him smile despite the dangerous consequences something like that could've brought. "Well, I'm here." He kissed Vince's head, holding his lips to his heated skin and closing his eyes, finally feeling relaxed for the first time in months. "And even once I need to leave, I'll come back as often as I can. Like Leota said, you can be my barefoot husband."

"Was that a proposal, Jask? If so, I'm saying no. You didn't even bring me flowers."

Frowning, Jask tipped Vince's face up and planted about two dozen kisses all over it, just annoying little pecks randomly placed over his cheeks, jaw, eyelids and forehead. "You'll say yes without flowers and you'll like it, or I'll continue doing that for the rest of our lives."

Vince pushed Jask's face back with a disgusted noise. "Fine, *only* if you agree to never do that again."

"I can't promise anything, you have a very kissable face." Jask grinned, kissing him again on the tip of his nose. "But if it's flowers you want, flowers you shall receive."

"A demon has to have standards. If I accepted every subpar proposal I've ever gotten, I would've been married years ago. You gotta do something flashy."

Jealousy coursed through his veins, and Jask huffed a breath through his nose. "You're mine, I don't care if you accept the proposal or not." Despite his exhaustion, he rolled to hover over Vince, determined to make his point.

"I'm yours. Just as much as you're mine," Vince agreed, pulling Jask down for a kiss.

He tasted so sweet, Jask didn't know how he'd ever manage to pull away. Luckily for both of them, they didn't have to. He kissed down Vince's body, biting gently as he made his way toward his cock. Jask had spent far too long fantasizing about what he tasted like to let the moment pass without finding out - and the teaser earlier hadn't been enough.

Vince made a noise somewhere between a moan and a whimper as he ran a hand through Jask's hair. Jask sucked him in slowly, angling his head to make it easier and sliding his tongue, eager to feel and taste and experience *all* of him. It had been a while since Jask had something that large in his mouth, so adjusting to Vince's girth wasn't as instant as he'd hoped, but he loved the stretch - loved the way it pressed against the roof of his mouth and forced his jaw open, convinced his lips to spread. Vince was looking down at him, hand tightening as he bit his lip. "You take me so well."

Jask hummed, sending a tendril of grace out with it to vibrate around him, and loved the way it made Vince sound. He sucked harder, hollowing out his cheeks and putting his biokinetic abilities to uses that would probably offend his ancestors. He could feel Vince getting closer to the edge, but instead of letting him reach it, he pulled off, replacing his mouth with his hand. "Not yet, Princess." Jask stroked slowly, his fist tight, the saliva left behind from the messy affair causing Vince's cock to slide through his fist easily. "I want you to *want* it, and I don't think you're quite ready to beg for it yet."

"You can clearly see that I want it." Vince's voice was tinged with frustration.

He could, it was true. Vince's muscles were strained, sweat coating his gorgeous body and his cock was so hard between Jask's fingers that he was surprised it wasn't painful. But truthfully, he'd put his body through too much, and knew that once they were done here, he'd be sleeping for a very, very long time. So, he wanted to make it worth it. "Do you?" Jask asked, his voice playfully challenging as he slowed his hand even more, using the other to pin Vince's body to the mattress. "Are you sure?"

"Fuck, yes." Vince tried to lift his hips, but Jask held him easily. "Are you really going to make me beg?"

Sucking just the tip of Vince's cock into his mouth, Jask hummed an affirmative, even as his resolve gave out. One day, he'd make Vince beg... but not today. He moved his hand out of the way to take him fully, thankful for the grace that removed his gag reflex as that thick length pushed into his throat. He swallowed around him, flicking his eyes up to meet Vince's. *You want it?* he said into Vince's mind. *Take it.*

Vince's breathing picked up and he gave an experimental thrust. He closed his eyes for a second and then opened them quickly, like he couldn't bear not to watch as he began to move. Jask reached down to palm himself, but as Vince sped up, he couldn't hold back. He fucked into his own fist as Vince fucked his throat until Jask could barely breath, barely see, barely focus on anything but Vince and how close they both were to the edge.

"I can't... Jask!" Vince yelled as he came hard down Jask's throat, his fingers tightening in his hair.

The taste of him sent Jask's senses into overdrive, he twisted his hand and stroked roughly as he swallowed him down, then added to the mess on the sheets between Vince's legs. Pulling his mouth away was an effort, but his body was thrumming with pleasure and a need for sleep, and he had only enough energy to collapse on the clean side of the bed.

Jask closed his eyes immediately and opened his arms. "Come here. Sleep on top of me, get out of the mess. We'll clean it in the morning."

Vince crawled onto Jask and wrapped his arms around him. He adjusted until they were touching head to feet and dropped his head to Jask's shoulder. "I love you."

A whole different kind of warmth spread through Jask at the words. He'd noticed Vince hadn't returned the sentiment when they were talking to Leota, but he hadn't blamed him at the time. But now, hearing it like this, he was glad he hadn't said it back in the kitchen. This felt real, raw, uncoerced, and it felt all the better for it. Jask tilted Vince's chin up to kiss him softly and then folded his wings over them both, wrapping Vince up completely in his embrace. "Good," he said quietly. "Now sleep."

~

He wasn't sure how long he was asleep, but when he woke up, he was alone. Frowning, Jask rolled over and pushed himself into a sitting position, then stretched out his cramped wings behind him. The room was cold and the sheet was crusty, which made Jask grimace. It wasn't quite what he'd expected the first morning he woke up in Vince's vicinity to be like, but then again, few things ever went the way Jask imagined them.

Closing his eyes, he listened closely to the house around him, relying heavily on his enhanced hearing capabilities. Leota and Amaranth were somewhere toward the front of the house, discussing Jaskian in hushed tones. Much closer to him, he could hear the shower running and a deep voice singing quietly.

Jask smiled to himself as he realized it was Vince. He looked around quickly for a towel but didn't find one, so he snuck out of bed and headed for the sound of the water. Carefully, he opened the adjoining bathroom door and stayed as silent as he could, hoping he wouldn't startle Vince before he got to the end of the bluesy little number.

"They say that you're a sin... well haven't you heard that I'm the devil? I shouldn't want you like this, but I cannot resist, oh, now baby put your hands on me." Vince turned and spotted Jask, but he didn't stop singing. His face broke out into a smile and he held a hand out to Jask as he continued, "So put me outta my misery, baby! Just tell me that you feel it, too. Put me outta my misery, honey... cause baby, I've fallen for you. You a Jamie Combs fan, sweetheart?"

He had virtually no idea who that was, but he was a fan of Vince, so Jask nodded as he took his outstretched hand and climbed into the shower. "Don't stop on my account. How come you never told me you could sing?"

Vince laughed. "I only sing in the shower. No one's ever told me if I was any good." He pulled Jask close and leaned down to nip at his neck.

As much as Jask desperately wanted to feel Vince's mouth on other parts of his body, he had a pressing need to actually get clean. He let him carry on for a moment anyway, but then gently turned them so Jask could position himself under the water. "I need to go soon," he said sadly.

"How soon? Next week?" Vince took the responsibility of getting Jask clean, soaping him up and running his hands over his body. It was distracting enough that Jask didn't speak for several long moments, and when he did, he had an extremely hard time forcing the words out.

"Today. Soon. I... shit," he gasped, pulling Vince up by the hair to kiss him. "You're making this incredibly difficult for me. Staying full time is dangerous, you know that. I'll be back as soon as I can."

"I know. I *do*. I just..." Vince shrugged and kissed him again.

The thought of leaving this, leaving Vince, leaving the safety and comfort he found with him... was horrible. But the nagging reminder that staying could kill them both had him finally pulling back, his wet hair falling in curls around his face. "I'll be back as soon as I can," he repeated, then teleported naked and drenched back to his own house before he could change his mind.

Seven

Vince

Vince stumbled forward a bit as Jask just vanished from his embrace. He didn't know what he'd been expecting, but it definitely hadn't been that. They could've at least had breakfast together. Vince was sure that wouldn't have brought the damn apocalypse upon them. Hell, that had already happened hundreds of years ago. He was feeling a little jilted - which pissed him off, because he *knew* Jask had needed to leave. What hurt was the shitty goodbye. Vince finished his shower quickly — mostly because there was no one to share it with anymore — and got dressed. Jask's clothes were still on his floor, so he gathered them up with his and tossed them in the wash. The least he could do was clean the angel's clothes. He took the sheets off the bed and tossed those into the washer, too. After realizing he'd done everything he possibly could to avoid his family, he stepped out of his room and headed for the kitchen.

He didn't say anything to them, but he could feel them looking as he grabbed some coffee and a plate of food and took a seat. He looked at the empty seat across from him and wondered if maybe Jask hadn't *wanted* to stay. Vince's mother had dismissed him, and Leota had interrogated him. *I probably wouldn't have stayed in that case, either,* Vince thought to himself as he poked at his food. He went through a mental list of the things he needed to do today, and was just beginning to wonder if he might be able to get a deer bagged later when he felt those stares again. He sighed and gave both his mother and sister a pointed look. "What?"

"Where is he?" Leota asked, a hint of accusation in her voice, as if she wasn't the one that probably drove him away.

His mom shot her a warning look, but didn't end up proving to be any better. "Seems a little silly of him to tear in here like a hurricane and then leave without even eating breakfast. Did he get what he wanted and decide that was good enough?"

"You both know he was never going to stay." Vince leaned back in his chair. "That he *couldn't* stay."

Leota laughed bitterly. "Oh, brother. You're confusing 'couldn't' and 'wouldn't' again. But, whatever. I for one hope he stays gone... I happen to like my electricity."

Vince wasn't going to point out again that she probably wouldn't *have* electricity without Jask. He was tired of arguing with them, and now that Jask was gone, the ache in his chest was back. Only this time, it was so much worse, because he knew *exactly* how it felt to sleep in his mate's arms. He stood from the table and cleaned up his mess from breakfast.

"Vince..." his mother began.

"No. I don't want to hear anything else about it. He had to go, but he's coming back." He gripped the plate in his hands so hard it shattered. He cursed and grabbed the broom to clean up the glass.

Amaranth nodded with her lips pursed in a thin smile. "Of course he is. Maybe we should have dinner prepared for him next time?"

"Yeah. Sounds great." He finished cleaning up the spill and walked to the door. "Speaking of dinner, I'll be in the woods."

She didn't stop him, and Leota immediately launched into a hushed argument with her that Vince wanted no part of, so he pushed open the door and made his way outside.

Vince may have slammed the door a little harder than he meant to on his way out, so he took a deep calming breath of the cold air and closed his eyes. He was being dramatic; he knew Jask hadn't wanted to leave, but the bond was toying with his emotions. He headed into the woods without going back in for his gun, feeling the need to get his hands dirty. Vince didn't let his demonic side out often when he wasn't in a fight, but sometimes, he needed a release. Today was *absolutely* one of those days. He closed his eyes and opened his senses to the world around him. Tapping into that dramatic feeling from earlier, Vince fancied himself a predator in search of prey.

It wasn't too far off from the truth. He could hear the deer nearby and he moved quietly, his hands lighting with fire. As soon as they came into view, he focused that fire to bullet-sized balls and took aim at the larger of the two. With a flick of his finger, it went down. The second startled, but another precise flick had it joining the first.

Vince wasn't nearly as satisfied as he thought he'd be. He needed... destruction. He tossed the deer over his shoulders and carried them back to the house, then stared at the door for a few moments before turning and running back into the woods. He drew on his supernatural stamina and strength, enjoying the burn from his ever-present fire as it built in excitement. He made it a safe distance away before letting it go with a scream.

After the initial blast, he looked around to take stock. Twenty feet in every direction, the trees had been decimated. Everything was destroyed, and Vince felt immensely better. He could deal with this, and he'd been around forests long enough to know this one would survive whatever he threw at it in the process.

He eventually returned home covered in ash and burn marks, and after he finished dressing the kills from earlier, he stepped back into the house. His mother and sister were sitting on the couch, huddled close together as if they were scared. Amaranth stood the moment she saw Vince, concern lining her face as she hurried over to check him for injuries. "Did they find us? What happened? We heard the commotion..."

"Oh, you heard that? That was just me," he said as he rubbed the back of his neck.

She huffed, wiping some ashes off of his shoulder. "You haven't done something like that in a very long time. Are you okay?"

Despite the progress he'd thought he'd made in the woods, now that it was over, he certainly didn't feel as okay as he'd hoped. "Of course I am. Just haven't been to a fight in a while and had to blow off some steam."

"Leota, go to your room," she barked, earning a frustrated groan from his sister. "Now." Swearing under breath, Lee obliged, and once she slammed the door, Amaranth pulled Vince to the couch. "You're not fine, I'm your mother. I know these things. Talk to me."

"Why? So you can tell me again that I was used and abandoned?" Vince knew that wasn't fair. He knew his mother was just concerned about his well being. He sat on the couch and tipped his head back, relaxing into the cushions and belatedly realizing he was probably getting ashes and soot all over the fabric. Thankfully, she didn't say anything about it.

Amaranth sighed quietly. "I'm sorry that I reacted like that. I'm worried about you, and angels aren't our friends. Most of them aren't, anyway. I know Jaskian has done a lot for us, but there's still the fact that none of it would've been necessary if his family wasn't trying to kill you." She squeezed his knee gently. "And I don't like to see you hurting."

"His family wouldn't be trying to kill me if I'd never gone to that fight, but then I never would've met him. I don't know which would be worse."

She frowned, furrowing her brows. "I don't understand why *he* was at the fight. Seems to be a strange place for an angel, especially an angel that knows he's bonded to a demon. That didn't strike you as odd?" Her tone came off curious, not accusatory, like she was really trying to understand how all of this happened.

"At first, yeah. I think I even mentioned that to Johnny, but Jask isn't like the others. He needed those fights as much as I did."

"Chaos that will either save the world or bring it to its knees," she said quietly, her hand moving to Vince's face. "The two of you together could do wonderous things."

"If only we could actually be together," he said bitterly.

Amaranth pulled him into a hug, ignoring the evidence of his meltdown that covered him. "He's welcome here whenever. And if you need me to do anything, you let me know."

"Thank you. That means a lot." He hugged her back, taking a moment to enjoy the comfort only a mother could provide before pulling away. "I don't know what we're going to do. Just sneak around for the next hundred years?"

After a moment, she shook her head. "No, not that long. I think that boy is a lot stronger than he gives himself credit for, and so are you. I don't think the Veris' know what they're up against."

"You're saying we can beat *centuries* of hate and death? Have our fairytale ending? Life doesn't work like that, Ma."

She smiled, rubbing her thumb under his eye. "Vincenzo, life is whatever you decide it is. The only one that has power over you... is you." Suddenly, she pursed her lips and smacked him upside the head. "So stop moping around, you're making your sister almost unbearable."

He laughed and rubbed the spot she hit. "Yeah, will do. Thanks." He kissed her cheek and stood up to go shower again. He knew it would probably sound petty, but he took a second to text Jask to let him know he could've at least stayed for breakfast.

The response came quickly, just a run-of-the-mill apology and a frown. Vince huffed a laugh, then left the phone on the sink and lost himself to the pressure of the water. He tried to think of a response that wouldn't make him sound like a jilted lover; it wasn't fair to Jask, and he didn't want his mate to think it was his fault. In the end, he settled for sending back an equally generic, 'It's okay.' Vince got dressed again, and got a list of things the house needed from his mother, soon losing himself in his work.

He kept his phone on him, but both he and Jask were busy enough that they didn't talk much. He helped his mother with dinner that evening, prompting another 'husband' comment from his little sister. He ignored her, but his mind kept going back to the word and what it could mean for them. Jask coming home after solving a case and Vince having dinner ready. Jask bringing dinner in after Vince worked a long day in the sun and needed to relax. Shared showers in the morning that no one had to run from. Nights tangled up so close they couldn't be pulled apart by wild horses. He went to bed that night alternately wishing for Jask and wondering when his life had become so centered around the angel.

~

Three days. It had been three days since he'd physically seen Jask, and while they'd been full of texts, they'd only shared one late night phone call. Both of them had agreed that minimal contact was the best for everyone involved, since there was less of a chance to be caught — but Vince would be lying if he said it didn't suck. He texted Johnny and asked when he stopped by later if he could bring some liquor. He got an affirmative, and that was enough to get him through his chores.

Johnny showed up a few hours later and stayed for dinner. The conversation flowed easily, but in the end, Vince grabbed one of the bottles Johnny had brought and walked out alone to one of his demon-made clearings in the woods. He'd destroyed two more spots since that first day. He got comfortable, sitting down against a tree.

He was half a bottle in when he finally called Jask.

"Hey, I was just thinking about you," Jask said as he answered. "I'm glad you called."

"I guess that means you were thinking good things?"

Jask laughed quietly. "Always good things, babe. How are you?"

"Drunk, I think. Johnny brought some whiskey for dinner. How are you?"

"Not drunk, which I'm suddenly regretting. I've been trying to drink less, it just makes my family suspicious since I don't seem to know when to quit anymore." Jask sighed, then closed a door in the background. "Can I come see you?"

"Yes, please. I was hoping you'd ask."

A moment later, Jask was standing in front of him and looking around. "What the hell happened here?"

Vince waved with a cheeky, bitter smile. "Me. I happened." He held the bottle out to him as an offering, and Jask took it but set it down, then pulled Vince to him and kissed him deeply.

"I'm sorry, Vin. I'm sorry you have to live like this, and I'm sorry it upsets you. I wish there was something else I could do to help."

He wrapped an arm around Jask and kissed his neck. "Missed you." He refused to acknowledge the other things said.

"I missed *you*," Jask whispered back, then picked him up and held him against the tree. "I can't stay long, but I swear it's getting harder to stay away." He kissed him again, squeezing him tightly.

"How long do I have you for?" Vince asked, pushing his hands through Jask's hair and tilting his head back for better access.

Jask let out a breath as he exposed his throat further and gripped his sides. "If you keep doing that... I don't know if I'll ever leave."

"Deal," Vince murmured against his skin. He slid one hand under his shirt, scratching his nails lightly down his lover's back. Rough hands roamed over Vince's body as he was pressed harder against the tree, and piece by piece, Jask apported away their clothing until there was nothing between them but skin. His wings extended out behind him and he moved his body slowly, carefully, gasping as his length slid against Vince's ass. "Give it to me, Jaskian," Vince moaned.

Shuddering, Jask lowered Vince just enough that the head of his cock was threatening to split him open. He waited, his breathing picking up and head tipped so far back he was staring at the sky. "Vince..." he whispered, as Vince rocked down to push Jask in further.

He closed his eyes and wrapped his legs around the angel, and didn't stop moving until Jask was fully inside of him. Jask let out a quiet, broken moan, then planted a gentle kiss to Vince's lips and started thrusting, each movement causing the bark of the tree to scratch Vince's back. He stayed buried deep, grinding into him and trapping Vince's cock between their bodies, giving him just enough friction to feel amazing.

"Fuck," Vince gasped, dropping his head back against the tree. He held tight to Jask, shifting so that every time Jask pushed deep, he was hitting where he wanted him. Vince curled both hands deep into Jask's wings and asked breathlessly, "Do you trust me?"

Nodding, Jask sucked on Vince's neck and dug his nails into his ass, pulling them together over and over again.

"Good." He had to stop speaking for a second after a particularly deep thrust, but Vince eventually gathered his wits enough to finish his sentence. "Don't drop me." Vince's eyes changed to black as he tightened his fingers in Jask's wings. One of Vince's favorite abilities was the talent to send a shot of pleasure through his fingertips. He used that now, pushing it directly into Jask's wings.

An unholy moan built in Jask's chest and his knees buckled, his back arching and cock pulsing inside of Vince... but he didn't drop him. "F-fuck," Jask gasped, his wings twitching erratically. "Damnit, that feels fucking incredible." Jask started moving faster, slamming into Vince like any resolve he had to take things slow was long gone, and reached between them to stroke Vince's neglected length.

Vince cursed as Jask touched him. He tightened his legs to hold Jask deep as he came suddenly, pushing another pulse into Jask's wings. "Come on, sweetheart. Come for me."

He didn't think he'd ever seen Jask like that, trying so hard to retain control but losing it entirely. Jask grunted, biting hard on Vince's neck as he pressed him to the tree, snapping his hips almost violently as he came.

Vince gently loosened his hands from Jask's feathers and wrapped his arms around his shoulders as he kissed the side of his head. "You good?"

"Define good. I feel like jelly." Jask slowly sat down, pulling Vince with him until they were laying on the ground. "That was incredible."

Vince laughed. "Yeah, been wanting to show you that since last time. Thanks for not dropping me."

"I almost did. Next time you decide to surprise me with some demon sex mojo, make sure I'm laying down." Jask grinned, kissing him quickly and then going boneless against the grass. "Can we nap right here? I can't move."

"No, you'll get cold." Vince sat up and grabbed his pants. "But I'll carry you, if you want."

Jask absolutely looked like he was about to say no, then smiled softly.

"It's only fair, I guess. I carry you everywhere like a baby." He groaned as he sat up, then crawled into Vince's lap.

Vince wrapped his arms around Jask and stood easily after making sure he had their clothes. He debated throwing Jask over his shoulder for the baby comment, but just started walking toward the house. He couldn't stop himself from running his hands over Jask's body. Anytime they were physically together, Vince felt this need to touch him, to make sure he was really there. He stopped short of the actual house so that they were still covered by the trees, then set Jask down and handed him his clothes.

"I highly doubt my mother will be pleased if I carry you in stark naked," Vince teased.

Jaskian

Few things made Jask more inherently uncomfortable than family dinner, and yet, here he was. Astarte had insisted that since Jask kept running off, they'd get together once a week for dinner. After the way the last one went, Jask was dreading the hell out of it.

He putzed around the kitchen helping his mom as Cidos and Edis came in. Yet again, they had matching smug expressions that told Jask they'd either taken down another demon, or were about to. Jask smiled in an attempt to avoid another fight and waved his serving spoon toward Edis. "There any room left in those jails, or they full now?"

"Why? Do you need to be arrested?" came his brother's teasing response. Jask relaxed a little, barking a laugh.

"How long have you known me, Ed? Course I need to be arrested, but don't get your hopes up. I won't come quietly."

Cidos rolled his eyes as he stretched out his wings and sat down. "We know, it's not like no one in this house has ever had to listen to you have sex."

Astarte glared at Ci and he put his hands up in mock defense, but it didn't stop her from scolding him. "Inappropriate conversation for the dinner table." She turned to Jask, raising an eyebrow. "Nevertheless, he's right. I was *thrilled* the day you finally moved out." She smiled just a little, letting Jask know she didn't mean anything by it. He was just happy she was joking about it at all.

"So," Edis mumbled with his mouth full. "Jaskian. What's new? How's the private investigator business treating you and Drazan?"

Thankful for the food in his own mouth, Jask chewed to buy himself time to breathe. The only way to lie to an angel was to really *believe* it, and tricking yourself wasn't as easy as it sounded. "It's been good. We're not working too many cases right now, though."

"Then what are you doing with all your free time, if you're not working or here with us? We could use you at the firm," Ci said. "I never understood why you didn't join us."

Shit. Jask chose to focus on the second half of that question rather than the first. "You already know where I stand, Ci. I don't think we should be putting innocent people behind bars, whether they're demons or not. And the fact that you two refuse to prosecute angels doesn't sit right with me." He kept his tone light, which he suspected was the only reason their mother allowed the conversation to continue at all.

"All demons are guilty of something. Who cares what we put them away for? If it's not one crime it's another," Ci argued, but he, too, kept his voice calm. "I'm telling you, Jaskian. We could use your considerable skill set."

Edis cut in before Jask could say a word. "Wouldn't it be better if he stayed away? I mean, we haven't seen a Riskel around here in years, but still. He should be staying away from demons altogether."

Jask froze for no more than a half of a second, but it was enough for Ci to catch the scent of nervousness like a fucking bloodhound. Jask knew if they flat out asked him if he was staying away from demons, he'd have a hard time selling that lie. Or worse, if they asked about a Riskel... "It's a moot point. You two don't honestly need my help, and you're right. It's better if I stay away from the demons you two pull in." *Specific enough it isn't a lie, but broad enough they shouldn't get suspicious.*

"Are you upset that your demon mate lives so far away, Jaskian?" Ci asked, his hand gripping tight to his knife. Jask could clearly tell Cidos thought he was getting one over on him, but the relief that flooded Jask's bones at the way the question was phrased was almost laughable.

"No, I'm not." *Nothing to be upset about, because he doesn't live that far away,* he thought. *Nice try, you arrogant dick.* "They can stay right where they're at for all I care." Jask sat back in his seat, daring Cidos to continue, but hoping he didn't.

Cidos smiled slyly, suddenly looking very proud of himself, and Jask braced himself as his brother opened his mouth to speak again. "Good. From all the sneaking around you've been doing lately, I was worried you'd somehow met your mate and just hadn't told us about it. Silly of me to think that, isn't it?"

All the color drained from Jask's face. He was too caught off guard to think of a way to phrase his answer so he wouldn't get caught, so instead, he turned to his mom. "If all these dinners are going to involve Ci harassing me about something I have no control over, I'm not coming anymore. This is bullshit, mother. I didn't ask to be mated, and I sure as hell didn't ask for it to be to a demon."

Astarte smacked her palm on the table and stood up, looking at the three of them. "You three had better find a way to put an end to these discussions. When your father comes back, if he so much as hears a *whisper* about the Riskels or the bond, we will *all* be sorry. Now *enough,*" she commanded, causing both twins to bow their heads. But Ci was smirking, staring at Jask through his lashes like he'd just learned a secret worth all the money in the world.

He knows, Jask thought to himself. *He knows, and it's my fault. I should've found a way to answer... my silence said it all.* Dread filled his bones and he stood up, taking his half-finished plate of food to the sink. "I'm sorry, mother. As far as I'm concerned, it won't happen again."

"You're right, it won't." She nodded, huffing an irritated breath and sitting back down to finish her dinner. Both twins remained relatively silent until they were done eating, only speaking when spoken to. Jask couldn't help but think it was a good look for them, and that the entire world would be better off if they adopted that policy at all times.

They cleaned up quickly, and by the time Jask was kissing his mother on the cheek to say goodbye, he was aching so badly for Vince that he knew not even his brother's suspicions would be able to keep him away. The logical part of his brain knew that this needed to be the last time for a while, maybe even a couple of months, but if he wanted to get Vince on board with that without hurting his feelings... Jask was going to need to make their evening amazing.

Without a second thought, Jask teleported home to put on a suit and grab some flowers, then sat down to plan. His teleportation abilities had limits, but if he spaced and timed things right, he could get them over the ocean in a few jumps, or, he could just fly them over if Vince trusted him enough.

Once he was satisfied with his idea, he traveled to Vince's front door, knocking twice. He stood tall and ran a hand through his hair, hoping the stress he was still feeling from family dinner wasn't too obvious.

Leota opened the door, but before Jask could open his mouth to greet her, she was pushed out of the way by Vince. He'd obviously just gotten out of the shower since his hair was wet and water was dripping over his torso. It made the tattoos stand out in the light, and Jask watched a drop of water slide down Vince's stomach to his unbuttoned jeans. He must've dragged them on in an effort to get to the door first. Jask was still shamelessly staring when he realized Vince was talking. "Hey! You look great." Jask lifted his gaze back to Vince's face and watched his mate's smile falter as he asked, "You okay, sweetheart?"

"Yeah," Jask said quietly, watching as Leota turned and walked away. He pulled Vince to him, not caring about getting his suit wet - he just needed to feel him. "Family dinner. Missed you." Jask leaned in to kiss him, cupping Vince's face with both hands and relaxing as the knot in his chest loosened.

Vince kissed him back but pulled away after a second. "You're ruining your clothes."

As if Jask cared about that. He brought their bodies flush together, hugging him tightly and angling his face against Vince's neck to inhale his scent. "Go on a date with me. A real one."

"Isn't that dangerous? I mean, I want to but..." He brought a hand up to Jask's head to hold him close.

Jask was content to stay there, right there, until someone forced him to move, but he had other plans. "Not if we go far enough away. How do you feel about Tokyo?"

"I would love to go to Tokyo. A little far to drive though," Vince chuckled.

"Good thing we won't be driving, hm?" Jask brushed his lips gently over the side of Vince's neck, then leaned back with a smile. "Go get dressed. We're flying angel class."

Vince kissed him quickly and pulled away completely, sprinting back to his room. Leota rolled her eyes from across the room, and Jask smiled warmly at her. "Hi."

She crossed her arms, looking him up and down as he used his grace to dry his suit. "You're taking him out in public and you don't think that's dangerous at all?"

"Of course it is, but that doesn't mean we can live in a box forever. We're heading clear across the ocean, there's no way my family will find him."

"I hope you're right," she huffed.

Vince came out of his room wearing a dark green button-up and a nicer pair of jeans, holding a black Stetson in his hand. "I don't clean up quite as nice as you, but I think I look okay. Is the hat too much?"

Jask couldn't do anything but stare for several long moments, and he knew he looked like a lovesick idiot. Never in his life had he seen anything more beautiful than that, and again, it made him ache. "Vincenzo, you look... perfect." He walked over, placing his hands on either side of Vince's face and kissed him fully, deeply, not caring at all that Leota was standing right there and yelling at them to get a room.

Vince brought them closer for a moment before breaking away. "We should go before she gets to screeching levels."

After a quick goodbye, he led Vince outside and held him tight as he teleported them to the California coast, then let out his wings on the beach once he was sure there was no one around to see him. "It's my turn to ask you. Do you trust me?"

"Oh, shit. You weren't kidding," Vince took a deep breath and gave a nod. "Of course I trust you. Let's do this."

Jask picked him up with ease and took a breath, hoping the trip wouldn't exhaust him. He already knew it would take long enough they'd need to stay overnight before he could fly back, but he didn't want to wait another day to actually go on a date with Vince. He took off slowly, letting Vince get comfortable and adjust to the awkward shifting of Jask's wings, then set a course for Japan.

As he'd anticipated, the flight wore him out - but it happened a little quicker than he thought. He spotted a small island and landed carefully, setting Vince down and then sitting almost instantly. "I'll be good to go in a minute, just need to recharge."

Vince sat with him, putting an arm around him. "Jask, we could've gone somewhere closer."

"No, we couldn't have. I don't want to be looking over my shoulder the entire time wondering if my brothers are gonna come around the corner and try and kill you." Jask kissed his cheek, leaning into him and exhaling sharply as his muscles started to relax. "The further away we get, the better."

Vince slid back a little to better reach Jask's shoulders, then began to massage the muscles and Jask's wing joints. "Is this helping?"

Everything about it felt amazing, and Jask couldn't decide if he wanted to go to sleep right there or address the thickening cock in his slacks. "Mmm," was all he managed to get out, his eyes closed. "Mmm."

"We could stay here, you know," Vince kissed the back of Jask's neck as he pushed his thumb into a particularly stiff muscle.

"Shit," Jask whispered, tipping his head back and moaning softly. "Wanted to take you on a date, this... not a date."

"Isn't a date whatever we want it to be?" Vince stopped moving his hands after a moment, tugging Jask back against his chest. He idly began playing with his feathers. "But we can go, if that's what you want."

It was an unfair move and Vince knew it. Jask groaned as pleasure coursed through his body with each movement. "You deserve more than this, Vin. More than me. More than some stupid island in the middle of the Pacific."

"I'll compromise with you. Let me keep doing what I'm doing, and then you can take us to Tokyo after," Vince suggested.

Arguing wasn't an option. Jask palmed himself and nodded, snapping open the button on his pants. "Fuck, how am I supposed to say no to that? Your hands are incredible."

"Can you get your clothes off? Need to feel you." Vince pushed his fingers deeper into the wings, and Jask shuddered as he apported away his clothes. It felt a little weird being completely naked while Vince was still dressed, but honestly, he also kind of liked it. He liked anything involving Vince.

"Better, babe?" he asked quietly, craning to kiss him again as he started stroking himself.

Vince stopped the kiss just long enough to rid himself of his own shirt. "Much better," he crooned. Trailing his fingertips down Jask's arms, he commanded Jask to get on his knees, then wrapped one arm around his chest and moved the other to take over stroking his length. Vince pressed himself against Jask's broad back and rocked his hips forward, groaning with need.

Jask didn't bottom often, he normally didn't care for it and only did it when asked - but here, feeling Vince's bulge through his jeans, being so surrounded by him? He wanted it. "Fuck me, Vin."

There was a growl from behind him and then movement as Vince shoved his jeans down. He was pressed up against Jask again seconds later, positioning himself. "You sure?"

"Yeah, I'm sure." Jask spread his knees a little and leaned forward, wiggling his ass at Vince with a soft, throaty chuckle. "Need it, Vin. Need you."

"Fuck," Vince gasped and pushed into Jask, reaching forward again to stroke him slowly as he inched in. The feeling was insane, way better than anything Jask had had before, and he let out a quiet gasp as Vince bottomed out.

In no hurry, Jask rolled his hips experimentally, loving the feeling of Vince shifting inside of him. He added his hand to Vince's, keeping the pace slow and steady, letting the grace inside of him keep things comfortable for both of them.

Vince let Jask move, moving his free hand back to his wing joint. "I don't even have the words to tell you how amazing you feel." Vince slid out and back in slowly, and Jask enjoyed every inch of movement. He gasped, rocking back a little faster, a little harder, his wings twitching and curling backward around Vince of their own accord.

"Took us way too long to do this."

"Hell yes, it did," Vince groaned as he thrust deeper. He moved his hand from Jask's wing so he could pull him back against his chest. "Kiss me."

His lips met Vince's almost too eagerly as he wrapped his hand around the back of Vince's head. He squeezed, tugging on his hair as he sent a tendril of grace down his mate's spine, moaning into his mouth as he felt him throb.

Vince's rhythm faltered slightly but then he was returning the favor, sending a pleasure pulse directly into Jask from the hand on his cock.

He came instantly, gasping for air and covering the ground between his knees. Shuddering, Jask moved Vince's hand and bent over, his head a little too close to the mess he made on the ground. The change in angle felt amazing, as if he wasn't already thoroughly satisfied. "Take it, Vin. Take me."

Vince gripped Jask's hips and chased his own release, snapping his hips hard and almost brutally fast, pressing Jask's shoulder down until he was coming with a grunt.

Jask never knew it could feel so good, fill him up so well. He ground backward, trying to keep Vince buried inside of him as long as he could. When they finally broke apart, Jask pulled him down to lay together and kissed him deeply, blanketing them both in his wings.

Vince draped an arm over him. "We really fucked up that whole 'moment to recharge' thing."

"Yeah, we did," Jask agreed. But at that moment, he really couldn't bring himself to care. They were even safer on that random island than they ever were at home, and for the first time since their relationship began, Jask actually felt like he could relax and let his guard down. It was an amazing feeling, being able to hold his mate without fear, even if it was fleeting. One day, Jask would find a way to make it permanent... but in the meantime, he'd take whatever he could get. He kissed Vince softly and hoped that even part of him felt the same way Jask did. "It's okay. We'll get to Tokyo eventually."

Eight

Cidos

The heat was cranked up as high as it would go in his office, and yet, it was still cold. It was *always* cold, no matter what he did. Cidos glanced over to see his twin brother shivering too, and sighed. "I don't know whose idea it was to make it so the stronger you were, the colder you were, but this is ridiculous."

Edis nodded, pulling his jacket around him a little tighter. "If you think it's bad for us, imagine how Jaskian feels. I don't know how he lives like this."

That is an excellent question, Ed... and my guess is that he doesn't, Cidos thought. Rubbing his jaw slightly, Cidos sat forward. "It would probably be pretty easy for him to live like this if he had a demon to warm him up."

His brother scoffed, then outright laughed. "That's highly unlikely, Cidos. Jaskian with a demon? Mate or not, he wouldn't dare."

"Wouldn't he?" Ci stood, pacing around the front of his desk. "He's been obsessed with demons his entire life, since even before he found out he was supposed to be mated to one. Would explain all the time he spends in the Dreads, and why after all his talk about being promiscuous, we've only ever met one angel he's had sex with."

Edis studied him with his brows pinched and wings flapping slowly, thoughtfully. "Even if it's true, which I doubt... it's better than him finding his mate. It's disgusting, but... wouldn't we rather he get that out of his system?"

"He's hiding something, Edis. You know it as well as I do. Every answer he gave me was carefully worded, so that it didn't come across as a lie... but it sure wasn't the truth, either. I think it's time to do some reconnaissance of our own." Cidos trailed his fingers over the books on his shelf and smiled to himself before turning back to his twin. "I want you to go spy on him. Don't use your grace or he'll sense you, take a car. Stay out of sight, but follow him for a couple of days and report back to me. I'll do some digging of my own. If Jaskian *is* hiding something... we'll find it."

For a moment, Edis looked uncomfortable, but he ultimately nodded and stood. "I'll go now. I'll let you know if I find something."

"Oh, sweet, naive Edis. The question isn't *if*, it's *when*. I've never been so sure about anything in my life."

They shared a long look, and then Edis headed out the door, leaving Cidos to plot out his next move. He'd spent long enough hunting demons under the guise of prosecuting criminals that he knew where to go to get answers, but if he'd learned anything recently, it was that he needed to figure out the right questions first. He'd end up spinning his wheels and getting nowhere if he didn't.

So, he waited. He waited three full days, until Edis finally came back. "Well?" Cidos barked, impatience taking over. "What took you so long?"

"I couldn't find him until this morning. He wasn't anywhere, Cidos. Not at his home, not at mom's. I even went to dad's and to Jaskian's office. All empty. He came back a few hours ago from wherever he was."

Cidos stared at his brother, waiting for him to continue without being prompted. Edis looked nervous, like he'd be sweating if it wasn't practically sub-zero in that office. *He found something.* "Was he alone?"

"Yes," Edis said quickly, with not one trace of a lie. "He was alone, but... I saw... he..."

Raising his eyebrows, Cidos gestured to one of the more comfortable chairs in the room. "You look like you need to sit down." He couldn't help it, he could feel the venomous impulse to control and manipulate creeping up his spine. Though they were twins, he was several minutes older than Edis, and their dynamic had been clear from birth. His brother was little more than a pawn and simply needed to have the right buttons pushed. "What did you see, Edis?"

Looking almost defeated, Edis let out a breath. "He let his wings out. They're black, Cidos. Not... not completely, but... at least seventy percent. He's met his mate. The bond has been established."

Rage flooded Cidos and a burst of grace came off him unbidden, shattering the bulbs in the chandelier overhead and casting them into darkness. For a strenuous moment, he wasn't sure he'd be able to reign it in. "That filthy, *lying little whore!*"

"Ci! Don't, please, we'll fix it." Edis stood, waving a hand to repair the damage Cidos had done to the room. One of their assistants ran in to see what the commotion was about, but after taking one look at them, she dropped the folder she'd been clutching and bolted down the hall. Edis continued, "I think he might have been in China with her, and that's why I couldn't find him."

Pacing, Cidos shook his head. "No, not even Jaskian is stupid enough to have intentionally searched for her. It had to have been an accident to begin with, that's the only explanation. If the Riskels were clear across the planet like we'd thought, the bond wouldn't have bothered him enough to seek her out, not when he so thoroughly understands the consequences. And, he believes himself to be gay, which is even more of a reason for him to stay away. Add in the answers to the questions I asked... no, it had to have been an accidental meet. They're here, they have to be."

"So what do we do now?" The fear in Edis' voice was evident, and Cidos actually calmed down because of it. None of them wanted what was to come, but if Cidos had to be the one to take point, then he would. He would do what was needed to protect the graceline.

"While you were gone, I did some research. There is only one female in the Riskel line this generation, which means Jaskian's mate is Leota Riskel. She has a brother, though, and he's strong. If he catches wind that we know about his sister, he could make things very difficult for us.

So, we kill him first. Make it look like an accident if we can, so no one suspects anything or tries to hide her. With him out of the way, taking Leota should be a breeze. We can use her to lure Jaskian in, have mom complete the ritual, and hope that Jaskian survives it."

Sadness radiated off his twin. "Ci... what if he doesn't? What if this kills him? He's our brother."

"It's been the same for generations, Edis. It doesn't matter that he's our brother, we have to do this. You *know* we have to do this. And if we can't... we'll go tell dad. And you know how he is. He'll kill them both, just to be sure, and he won't think twice about it. At least if it's us, Jaskian has a chance to survive."

He'd apparently hit the right button, because Edis nodded once, his jaw set. "You're right. Tell me what to do."

~

Dressing down enough to blend in in the Dreadlands was a travesty all on its own. Cidos left his expensive, pressed suits behind and opted for plain clothes and contacts to hide his eyes. Only one demon needed to know who he truly was, and he'd prefer to get in and out as quickly as possible.

Edis stayed behind to distract Jaskian. There was little chance they'd be going to the same place, but Jaskian might show up for one of his cases, and Cidos couldn't let that happen. He needed his brother thoroughly out of the way from start to finish.

Walking into Pattie's was like walking into a den of bedbugs. The place was crawling with demons, and he recognized a few that he'd put away at least once. That alone had him on edge - at any moment, he could be recognized and would have to fight for his life to escape. No demon would dare touch an angel in the Gardens, but here? Angels were fair game.

He spotted Pattie playing a game of poker and walked up behind him, leaning down to whisper in his ear. "Up. Now."

The timbre of his voice gave him away, and Pattie stiffened before standing up. "I fold. Keep playing." He turned on his heel and gestured for Cidos to walk forward, then lead him to his small, cramped office. "What the fuck are you doing here, Cidos? Run out of puppies to kick?"

Sneering, Cidos nearly laughed at that. "Funny, I'd forgotten your sense of humor, Pathamros. I'm here to... offer you a deal."

"What could you possibly have to offer me, *boy*? I can't imagine I have anything you want, anyway." Pattie crossed his arms and leaned against the wall, unusually calm for someone who was steadily walking into a spiderweb.

Cidos studied his fingernails. "You do have something of use to me. Access to Vincenzo Riskel." The color drained from Pattie's face and Cidos smirked. "Don't deny it. I've long heard about this place and your... little fights. A strong demon like Vincenzo has to be a regular, am I right? All I'm asking is that you offer him a fight," he said, his voice cold.

Pattie growled, shaking his head a little. "And why would I do something like that? As I said, I don't guess you have a whole lot to offer me."

"You're right, in fact, I've really only got one card to play here. But it's a damned good card, are you ready for this?" Cidos smiled slyly, he enjoyed this part a little too much. "You know who I am. You know what I do. I've let you carry on in this cesspit for years now, but all of that can change in the blink of an eye. I can shut you down, Pathamros. Or, maybe I'll just take you out, instead. It's your choice, really... either way, I go home with a demon's head on a spike."

Neither of them moved or spoke for almost three full minutes, but Pattie finally grunted. "Who's the fight with? Vincenzo hasn't come around here in a while. It'll have to be good to entice him."

Got him. Cidos reached into his coat pocket. "The fight is with me, but you'll tell him his opponent wishes to remain anonymous. If I find out you tipped him off, I'll make sure to take *two* trophies. If he needs enticing, this should suffice." He pulled a wad of cash from his pocket and dropped it on the table. Money meant almost nothing to angels, but to demons, it was everything. No demon could resist that amount of cash. "If he gets suspicious, tell him his reputation precedes him, and his *very* generous opponent is simply looking for a good fight. Any questions?"

Pattie's eyes were glued to the cash. "When would you like this to happen?"

"The sooner the better," Cidos said simply. "I'll be ready when he is. You know how to reach me." He turned to leave but paused with his hand on the knob, looking back at the scared, cornered demon. "Oh, and Pattie? No tricks. I won't be coming alone, so if you think you can somehow get one over on me, you're very much mistaken. Don't try. If you succeed, and therefore *I* succeed, you have my word that you'll never see my face again."

"You'll forgive me if the word of an angel doesn't exactly make me all tingly with confidence," Pattie said, one last little hint of defiance sparking in his eyes. It was almost cute. "But go. You'll have your fight, and then you best steer clear of the Dreads. Folks like Vince, and they won't take kindly to you killin' someone during a fight. We have rules, y'see. A *code*."

Cidos chuckled. "Right. Demons with a code, that's a new one. Full offense, but I don't give a damn about your code. See you soon, Pathamros. Ta-ta," he singsonged with a deadly expression, then slammed the door behind him on his way out. A few heads turned his way, but Cidos barely registered them.

He was one step closer to his goal... and to being the hero of his generation. A few demons sure as hell weren't going to stop him.

Vince

Vince stared at the phone in his hand and replayed the conversation he'd just had with Pattie. A fight with an anonymous opponent that was apparently worth an obscene amount of money? On one hand, with that kind of money, he could finally get a head start on paying

Jask back. On the other, the last fight he'd been in like this had led to their current predicament. He stood and paced through the backyard as his thoughts flew through his head. Going back to his old stomping grounds was dangerous. Anyone could follow him back and leak their location to the Veris family. The odds of that were slim, though. No one knew he and Jask were mated. They hadn't exactly advertised it, and he was sure they'd been careful. Plus, the type of demons that hung around the fights were no friends to the angels.

He could meet Johnny somewhere neutral and they could go from there. That way, if someone did follow after the fight, they'd know at the drop off location. The more he thought about it, the more Vince was sure this would work. He didn't even need to tell anyone but Johnny. By the time his family or Jask knew, he'd have the money and be home recuperating, *if* his opponent could even touch him. Vince ignored the shiver of apprehension that traveled down his spine and texted Pattie that he'd be there. Convincing Johnny wasn't done as easily as he'd thought. His best friend seemed more concerned than anyone, and Vince had to beg him to not tell Jask. Eventually, they made arrangements to meet at a local thrift store and Vince prepared for the fight. He couldn't hide his excitement at getting to compete again, so he steered clear of his mother and sister as much as possible until the time to leave came. He made a vague excuse about going for supplies and practically ran out the door. Vince drove quickly and it felt like in no time at all, he was pulling into the parking lot and hopping out of his own vehicle and into Johnny's.

"Are you sure about this?" Johnny tried again to dissuade him.

"Yes, now drive, before we're late and I lose my chance at this money," Vince replied impatiently. He continued to ignore the growing unease he felt the closer they got to Pattie's. The crowd outside seemed bigger than usual, and Vince fed off the chaotic energy surrounding the audience. He stripped down to his jeans as soon as he was out of the truck, tossed everything into the back of the vehicle and headed into the warehouse in search of Pattie.

It wasn't hard to find him, he was pulling in bets left and right.

Vince headed toward him, trying to scope out the place to see if anyone was there he didn't recognize, but Johnny yammering in his ear was making it hard to concentrate.

"This doesn't feel right, Vince. No offense, but who'd pay that kinda money to fight *you?*"

"I'm the best, Johnny. Everyone this side of Ares knows it. Anyone wanting to prove themselves wants to take a shot at me," Vince answered as they approached Pattie. "So, Pat, who's the guy with a death wish?" Vince kept up his carefree attitude, despite the itchy feeling that was settling between his shoulder blades. He spared a glance behind him to see if anyone was staring, but no one caught his eye.

Pattie looked almost sad as he clapped Vince on the shoulder. "I'm afraid I can't tell you that. Swore to secrecy, it was part of the deal. You understand."

"No, no he doesn't," Johnny interjected. "This is sketchy, Pattie, even for you. He can't go in blind, it's not right."

"I did with Ja... with the last fight. It's fine. I win, we go home." Vince shrugged and headed down to the cage. A weird sense of déjà vu came upon him as he stood at the entrance - this was *exactly* what happened the night he met Jask. He took a deep breath and closed his eyes for a brief second before he stepped into the ring.

The crowd went silent as his opponent came down the stairs, a kimono shrouding him. The moment he was in the cage, Vince shifted on his feet as he felt the power coming off of him - and it wasn't demonic. It was fucking grace. His opponent finally raised his head, shucking off his robe and sneering at him as his giant, pure white wings extended out. From the size of them alone, Vince knew exactly who it had to be.

Johnny must've realized it at the same time; he frantically pulled on the gate to the cage, but it wouldn't budge, and his opponent did nothing but laugh. "That's cute. Only one of us will be leaving this cage alive, and it won't be you."

Vince wasn't one to show fear to his enemies. He grinned at him. "You came all this way to kill little old me? I'm flattered."

"Killing you is just step one. Wait till you see what Edis and I are gonna do to your sister." Cidos raised a hand, and a white-hot ball of light formed a split second before it was launched at Vince.

Vince was shocked enough at the mention of his sister that he almost let the attack hit him. He dove to the left at the last moment and rolled to his feet, throwing his own ball of fire at Cidos. "You'll never touch my sister, asshole."

Cidos threw up a shield and the fireball bounced off of it as he strode forward, showing Vince *exactly* how much Jask must've been holding back during their fight. "You're right, I probably won't lay a finger on her. But I didn't come here alone."

"Too bad the only pretty Riskel face here tonight is mine. Don't worry, I'm the better kisser." Vince was beginning to realize he might actually not survive this fight. Any amount of power it would take to win would level the building around them, but as he eyed Cidos stalking toward him, Vince started to wonder if that would be worth it.

The asshole actually laughed, pointing behind Vince. "That's what I thought too, but my associate found me a little surprise. A two-for-one deal. Sort of a... 'buy one, get one demon scum' thing. I take care of you, we go home with her." Cidos lunged, tackling Vince into the cage before he could even turn his head to see what the hell he was talking about. Pain lanced through his body as Cidos landed the first blow right to his cheek, followed by a second.

Vince cursed and belatedly brought his arms up to block. Cidos backed off just enough that the kick he aimed at Vince dropped the demon to one knee, but he clenched his teeth and forced himself up and into Cidos' stomach. Vince lifted with his shoulder and tossed Cidos as hard as he could into the cage wall. He spun to see what Cidos had been talking about and witnessed a grinning angel holding his struggling sister by the arms. His heart froze in dread as he realized he couldn't get to her. She got one arm free long enough to slap her kidnapper, and Vince watched to see if it made a difference. He knew it wouldn't, but he had to hope. He was too distracted and it cost him; the punch aimed at his chest sent him flying into the opposite end of the cage. Vince coughed and struggled to his feet again. *Definitely at least one broken rib,* he thought as he stood to his full height.

Cidos gave him a smug grin. "Do you see? We've already won. Give in and die like the worm you are."

"Not really my style, but thanks for the offer." His eyes went black as he hit Cidos with a bigger ball of flame. The angel tossed up a shield again, but this one at least made him stumble back. It was long enough for Vince to get his eyes on Johnny. He pointed to his sister and the angel. "Get her out of here!" He watched as Johnny realized what was happening, but then Cidos was punching him again. Vince blocked the next hit and countered with one of his own, feeling no small amount of satisfaction when his fist connected with Cidos' nose. Another blast from the feathered bastard knocked Vince backward and he could feel his skin burning. Never again would he fight shirtless. He slowly rose to his feet again and glared at Cidos.

"Stay down!" Cidos practically growled at him.

"Fuck you," Vince spat as he tackled him to the ground. Cidos bucked him off and then straddled him before he could recover, the punches coming hard and fast. Vince covered his head and tried to get free, but nothing he did was working. Eventually, he stopped blocking the hits and put both palms on Cidos' chest, sending the strongest pain wave he could through his hands. He grinned as Cidos screamed and rolled away from him but didn't waste those precious, hard-earned seconds. Vince turned over and dragged himself to the wall of the cage, then used it to pull himself up to a standing position - but Cidos was on him again, tossing him right back to the ground. From his new point of view, Vince could see Johnny and Lee. The demons in the crowd had finally noticed an angel trying to kidnap a young demon girl, and weren't reacting kindly to it. Vince didn't have time to work out why she was even there in the first place, but heaved a sigh of relief as he watched Johnny grab her and lead her toward safety.

Suddenly, Cidos kicked him in the side. Vince groaned and tried in vain to get away, but the attacks kept coming. In the background, he heard what sounded like metal being torn apart, but he didn't care; he couldn't even *think* as a particularly heavy kick made his head swim. Then, abruptly, the violence stopped and Vince was being hoisted to his feet.

When his vision cleared, he was surprised to see a very familiar face holding him up. "Well, son of a bitch. That really you, Kos?"

"Don't get used to it." Kos led him through the ripped cage as Cidos was swarmed with angry demons from the crowd. He leaned heavily on his former enemy as he carried him out, watching with no small amount of satisfaction as the other angels suffered a similar fate to their employer. "Serves those fuckers right."

"Wonder why they thought they'd get away with that shit here," Kos muttered as he led them out of the warehouse.

"They're arrogant assholes. Over there, Johnny's truck." Vince waved what he was pretty sure was a broken arm. A loud explosion came from the inside the warehouse, and Vince cursed at Kos to hurry up. "Get us out of here and they'll leave everyone in there alone."

Kos tossed Vince over his shoulder, ignoring the grunt of pain from his unwilling passenger. He ran toward Johnny's truck and Leota threw the door open as they approached, and Kos deposited him unceremoniously into the seat then waved them away.

"Go, I'll distract them," the big ruffian said as he turned and ran back to the warehouse.

"Fuck me, never thought we'd be on the same side." Vince closed the door. "Drive, Johnny!" His friend didn't need to be told twice. He floored it out of the lot and didn't slow down until they were miles away, giving Vince plenty of time to take stock of his injuries. He counted several broken bones, burns covering the top half of his body, and he was pretty sure he had a concussion. A sniffle from his left had him turning his head with a wince.

"I...I'm so sorry..." Leota said as tears spilled down her cheeks.

"What the *fuck* were you even doing there, Lee?" Vince demanded.

"I heard you and Johnny on the phone! You were talking about going out and I didn't think it was fair that you kept going out and I was stuck in the house. I hadn't been anywhere in months, Vince! I thought" —

she hiccuped — "I thought I could watch the fight. I didn't know there'd be angels there! How was I supposed to know?"

Vince didn't answer. He couldn't answer. He'd almost died tonight at the hands of his mate's brother. He took a deep breath and closed his eyes, needing a glass of whiskey and a week's worth of sleep. What he *really* needed was Jask, but that would have to wait until he healed, or he'd have to explain a lot of things he didn't have the strength to explain at the moment. He honestly wasn't sure he ever would.

Jaskian

Jask stared down at the phone in his hand with a horrified expression. Johnny had texted him to tell him that his mate and brother were seriously injured, but sent no explanation whatsoever. He had a split second where he wasn't sure who to go to, but he reminded himself that Cidos would heal from whatever was ailing him faster than Vince would, and at the moment, he cared more about his mate's well-being than he did his asshole brother.

He'd been working a case to try and make some money but excused himself from the witness' house, then teleported to Vince's place and walked right in. "Vince! Johnny?"

Johnny darted out of Vince's bedroom and held up a hand to stop him. "Look, don't freak out."

"What *happened?*" Jask asked, pushing past the demon to get to the door, ignoring all of Johnny's efforts to stop him and explain before he went in. He just needed to see Vince.

When he spotted him on the bed, Jask's heart sank in his chest. He looked mangled — his skin was charred and more than one of his limbs was bent the wrong way. "Vince?" The word came out broken, and he rushed over to the bed and gingerly climbed up, hovering his hands over Vin's body. "Where does it hurt the worst?"

"I'm fine, Jask. Already hea..." The word broke off into a scream as a bone audibly snapped back into place. Vince took a few deep breaths and smiled weakly. "As I was saying... already healing."

"Demons don't really have *healing* powers, they have a second wave of pain," Jask muttered bitterly, hating the fact that anything good for demons came at a price. He closed his hand, reopening it as a ball of his grace appeared. "Hold still, babe. This should feel a little better." He slowly started healing the burns, clenching his jaw as he watched the skin scar over instead of heal completely. Even with his powers, Vince would bear the marks of whatever happened forever. "Who did this to you?"

Vince relaxed a little, closing his eyes. "You have magic hands, sweetheart. We don't really need to talk about what happened."

"It was Cidos," Johnny said from the doorway.

"Johnny," Vince warned, but he was cut off by his friend.

"No, Vince. He deserves to know!"

Jask's stomach rolled with nausea. All of his fears were coming true, but his mind quickly caught up with the meaning. "Well, then. He's apparently decided he doesn't care if I die." He realized belatedly that it was an incredibly selfish thing to say, but his mind felt like a rock skipping over water - only catching a few, scattered thoughts. He continued working, setting Vince's bones the best he could. Jask wasn't a trained healer, he knew Vince would still likely be in some level of pain, but at least he'd be able to move again. "I'm so sorry, Vince. I'm so sorry."

"Not your fault." Vince lifted his now mostly healed arm and touched Jask's cheek, before letting it fall back to the bed. "You didn't know... and I don't think he knows about us."

Frowning, Jask shifted so he could hold Vince. "What do you mean, he doesn't know? Why would he come after you if he doesn't know?"

Vince rolled into his arms, laying his head on Jask's chest. "Leota was there. Cidos was trying to kill me, and some other asshole was trying to kidnap Lee. I think they're under the impression that she's the mate."

"That makes sense, it's always a male and a female. But..." Jask's confusion only grew. "What do you mean *there*? Why were you two away from the house at all?"

"You know, my head hurts and details are pretty fuzzy so..." He stopped talking and buried his face in Jask's neck.

"It was Pattie. Called Vince in for a fight. Lee heard the call and snuck out to watch," Johnny said darkly.

"Fucking hell, Johnny. Get out of my room."

Jask shook his head. "No, he can stay, since apparently he's the only one that wants to tell me the truth here." He kissed Vince's head and glanced over at the other demon. "Pattie was in on this? How did Ci even know about those fights? And what the hell could *possibly* possess you to go, Vin?"

"It was a lot of fucking money, Jask." Vince sat up with a wince.

"We didn't stick around to find out about Pattie, but I can go ask," Johnny said at the same time.

"Yeah, do that." Jask nodded to Johnny then focused on his mate. "Vince, if it was money you wanted, I could've given it to you." Sadness crept through his bones when he realized if he'd have just done a little more, Vince wouldn't have taken his brother's bait. "Just tell me what you need. More food? Clothes? Toys?"

"The money was for you! So I could start paying you back for all of this." He waved a hand and then frowned at Jask. "Toys?"

That almost made it worse. "You didn't have to pay me back, I never asked for that. All I wanted was for you to stay safe, and the exact opposite happened." He sighed, now agreeing that he just wanted Johnny to leave. "And yeah, toys. Four wheelers, TVs, game consoles, dildos. *Toys.*"

The sound of the door closing had them both looking over. Johnny was gone, and Vince sighed. "I know you didn't ask, but you don't have to provide for me. I can take care of myself. This is nothing, I've had worse."

The lie snaked down Jask's spine and he sat up, leaning against the headboard. "No, you haven't. And right now, you can't take care of yourself. It's not your fault, Vince. It doesn't make you weak or incompetent. My brother is little more than a duty-driven psychopath right now. Isn't that what love is supposed to be about, supporting each other when we can't support ourselves?"

"And when have I supported you? All these months, name one time I've done something for you," Vince asked, his voice quiet.

"Vince, you can't look at it like that. Right now, my family is trying to kill you. It's my job to make sure that doesn't happen, by any means necessary. We'll probably live another hundred and fifty years, you really think there won't ever come a time when I need you to support me?" Jask dropped his eyes to the bed and closed them slowly, knowing that Vince wouldn't accept that as an answer. It just wasn't how he was wired, and it was one of the things Jask loved about him under normal circumstances. He didn't need a knight in shining armor to save him, which was good, because Jask was anything *but*. All that meant at the end of the day was that the only way he was going to be able to keep Vince safe would be to leave. Reject the bond, reject him. And he didn't know if he was strong enough to do it. "Come here," he said softly, his arms outstretched. "Just lay with me."

Vince slid back down and fitted himself into Jask's arms, putting his head back on his shoulder. "I'm sorry. I should've at least told you."

"You should've, but I get why you didn't. And maybe in the end, it's good you didn't. There's no way I'd have let Cidos fight you, and he'd have known straight away that Leota wasn't my mate. Where is she now, by the way?"

"In her room. I may have said some pretty mean shit to her when I woke up," he admitted.

Nodding, Jask held him a little tighter. "I think you both need to rest, but Vince... I think you and Lee need to leave. Amaranth, too. Now that my brothers know for sure you're here, they won't stop, and Lee's in danger now, too." The thought made him sad, but maybe if the Riskel's cooperated, it would be easy to explain why Jask wasn't coming around anymore without hurting Vince directly.

"We can send Mom and Lee away, but I'm not going anywhere."

"Vince, what happens when Ci finds her? You realize they think *she's* my mate, right? They won't be looking for you, they'll be looking for *her.* If you're not around to protect her, she'll die." Jask hated even saying it out loud, but if there was one thing he knew beyond a shadow of a doubt, it was that Cidos wouldn't stop until the Riskel family was wiped out completely. If he had the chance to stop their line from continuing at all, he would.

"I can't just leave you here. They may not know I'm your mate, but they know the bond has been established. You're in danger, too!" Vince pushed away from him again, looking him in the eyes. "You can't stay here alone."

Jask let out a slow breath and stayed steady. "I have to. It'll be a lot easier for them to track me than it'll be for them to track you. I'd be surprised if Cidos wasn't already trying it."

"No." Vince shook his head. "*No,* Jask. This isn't the only way."

"Seriously? Vince, why can't you see that I'm trying to keep you alive? That I'm trying to keep your entire family alive?" Jask asked incredulously, climbing off the bed to stand up. "It *is* the only way, and you know it!"

Vince tried to stand too, but that wasn't working for him, so he sank back against the headboard. "Because in a couple of days I'll be like new, and we'll be able to take on anything your family throws at us. Together."

As much as Jaskian wanted to believe him, he couldn't. When it came down to it, truly came down to the bare bones of the matter, this was him stuck in the middle between his brothers and his mate. Why Vince couldn't see the position that put him in was beyond him, but Jask wasn't going to point it out unless he had to. "And what if we don't *have* a couple of days, Vin? Do you really think Cidos and Edis are just going to sit around waiting patiently for you to recover? No, they're gonna *know* you're weak, and they'll come after you now. You need to move, I can't take them on alone."

"You won't be alone if you don't make me do this," Vince pointed out. He clenched his jaw and put a hand to his side. "Fuck. Ribs are the worst. Where would we even go, Jask? Everything we have here is because of you. All we have is that old truck."

Jask walked over, gently placing his hand on Vince's side and tried again to heal him, hoping the extra effort would make it easier for him to walk. "There's a safe full of cash in Leota's room behind the mirror. The combination is the date we met. Take what you can, and go. It's better if you don't even tell me where." He kissed him fiercely, stopping any potential reply and trying to pour all of the hope and love and fear he felt into it, then braced himself and teleported home - or rather, to his house. His home was with Vince... and now it was gone.

Nine

Vince

Vince immediately grabbed the phone on his nightstand and called Jask, but there was no answer, so he cursed and threw the phone across the room. That disappearing thing was really starting to piss him off.

Everything still hurt, but it was a manageable pain thanks to the healing Jask had provided. He rolled out of bed and headed for the mirror to check out his scars. They were everywhere, and those energy bombs Cidos had thrown at him had pretty much ruined his tattoos, as if he needed another reason to be in a shitty mood.

The door opened just as he was bending to pick up his phone. "Vince, you should be in bed!" Johnny chastised as he walked over and looked at the destroyed phone. "What the hell happened?"

"Jask took off. Preached a bunch of nonsense about keeping me safe and fucking left. Without a goodbye. *Again*."

Johnny took the phone from him. "I'll get you a new one when I go to talk to Pattie."

Vince gave a halfhearted nod and sat on the edge of the bed. "He wants me to run. I'm tired of running."

"Vince, one fight with Cidos and you had six broken bones. He may have a point."

"Fuck him *and* his point. Cidos distracted me. In a fair fight... where I didn't have to hold back? He wouldn't have lasted."

"Right. Say it enough and you might believe it," Johnny scoffed.

"Fuck you, too," Vince snapped.

"Look, I know hiding is hard for you but did you ever think this might be an issue for Jask, too? He's literally stuck between you and his family. We might not be their biggest fans, but they're all he's had for his entire life. Cut him some slack," Johnny tried. When Vince didn't answer, Johnny sighed and left the room.

Vince laid back on the bed and closed his eyes, thinking about what Johnny and Jask had said. Keeping his family alive was the most important thing to Vince, but he included Jask in his definition. He never really thought that Jask might feel the same about his asshole brothers.

He ran a hand over his face and took a deep breath. With only so many options available, Vince decided he would do this one thing at a time: he'd count the money in the safe, figure out how far it would get them and then try to talk to Jask again. Beyond that, he was too tired to think. One thing was certain. If they thought Lee was Jask's mate, they wouldn't hesitate to kill Vince — and if they did that without breaking the bond first, *Jask* would die. He wasn't too worried about himself, but he couldn't let anything happen to his mate.

With a groan, he forced himself back up and into the bathroom. He'd shower, eat, and count the money. One foot in front of the other. Once he was completely healed, he and Jask would decide what to do together. He kept that thought at the forefront of his mind. *Together, or not all, damn it,* he decided. The alternative was too painful to think of.

~

The next day, Vince was able to move a little easier. He stretched his sore muscles as he stood up from bed and shuffled into his bathroom to brush his teeth. Lee still hadn't left her room, and Vince didn't feel stable enough to try and coax her out. He left the new phone Johnny had brought back on his table as he went to the kitchen for coffee. His mother eyed his healing body sadly, but kept her thoughts to herself, and Vince wasn't sure which was worse - the silence, or the lecture she could be giving him. After what he thought was a suitable amount of time, he walked back to his bedroom and checked his phone. No new messages, no missed calls. He opened his texts to Jask and scrolled through, tormenting himself with all the unanswered pleas and questions. He ran a hand down his face and forced himself to believe it was fine. He could wait.

~

The second day after the fight, Vince's bones finally finished mending. He stood in front of his mirror again and noted that the discoloration from the bruising was much better. He may even be able to salvage some of the tattoos if he could find the right artist. He grabbed a shirt and went to drink his coffee. Jask had finally texted him a one-word response the night before — Vince had been begging Jask to at least let him know if he was okay, and Jask had replied in the affirmative and then went radio silent again. Lee stayed in her room, Amaranth stayed quiet, and Vince stayed waiting.

~

"It's been three days, Vin," Johnny said softly, spinning his own coffee mug on the table.

"And?" Vince asked before sipping from his.

Johnny blinked, like he shouldn't have to be explaining this to him, "And you need to count that money, start making plans!"

"Not until I hear from him." Vince absently checked his phone again, but there was nothing new waiting for him.

"I told you I saw him yesterday, he's fine."

"Then why can't he talk to me?" Vince raised an eyebrow at his best friend. As Johnny stuttered and tried to come up with an acceptable reason, Vince stood and dropped his mug in the sink. The problem was that no matter what Johnny said, Vince wasn't going to find it acceptable. Even if Jask was trying to placate his family, there was no reason for the completely frozen communication. Vince went for a walk after

Johnny's failed attempts to explain. He destroyed another part of the woods on the property, and he waited.

~

The fourth day, he received a text from Jask asking if he'd counted the money, and if he'd made plans. Vince responded that he hadn't and invited Jask over to help him, but as expected... he didn't answer. Instead of breaking another phone, he punched a hole in the wall, then spent the first part of the day fixing the damage he'd caused.

His sister came to find him and they sat down, having an incredibly long discussion about what happened and could happen in the future. She was terrified, and Vince knew leaving would be the best way to battle those fears. Still, he waited.

~

The fifth day came, and he finally counted the money. There was more than enough to get them out of town. Out of the state, if they were careful. They could even sell some of the things from the house to make it further. Vince stared at the cash on the table, his hands clenched into fists. There was enough money to get all *five* of them away from all of this - if only Jask would give him something, some indication that he may agree to go with them. A life lived on the run would be unbearable without his mate. These five days had been torture enough.

He called Jask again and his heart broke a little when the call didn't even go through. He wiped away the tear that fell, and he continued to wait.

~

"Vincenzo," Amaranth said on the sixth day, "He's not coming back. We have to do what's best for us. For our family."

Vince ignored her and continued to work on dressing the deer he'd killed that morning. It hurt hearing the words out loud, even if he had been saying them to himself all morning. Vince couldn't just leave, though. Jask was probably being held against his will. His family could be torturing him to give up Vince's location, all while Vince sat there elbow deep in animal guts — doing nothing, unable to support Jask even now. So he said nothing, he acknowledged nothing. He turned up the radio station to drown out her, and his own thoughts. He hummed along, and he waited.

~

On the seventh day, Vince blinked at the ceiling in his bedroom. He wasn't sure what time it was, but he knew he'd normally be up by now, so he sat up and ran his hands over his face and into his hair. The fact that he hadn't been able to do anything to help Jask so far was weighing heavily on him, and he wished he knew what to do. Vince flopped back onto the mattress and put a pillow over his face, hoping that if he held it there long enough, he'd eventually pass out and stop thinking.

Unfortunately, that didn't happen, though he still nearly lost consciousness when Lee dove on top of him and drove her elbow into his rib. "Get up, moron. We have company coming according to Johnny. Don't you wanna look pretty for your asshole boyfriend?"

Vince sat up. "Jask is coming?" He pushed Lee onto the floor and hopped out of bed, running into the bathroom to shower. He knew Leota was being a jerk when she asked him if he wanted to get pretty for Jask, but the answer was obvious. He hadn't seen Jask in a week. Vince wanted to at least look presentable, so he at least made sure to get clean and put on something that covered his scars. He spent a little too long on his hair before coming out and holding his arms wide. "Admit it, I'm incredibly sexy."

She rolled her eyes and crossed her arms right before Vince felt Jask's presence. A second later, he knocked. "Great," she said sarcastically. "See you when you two are done blowing out our electricity again." She slammed her bedroom door as Jask went ahead and opened the front door on his own.

He was wearing a suit, his long hair tied back. There was definitely something different about him, like the spark Vince usually saw behind Jask's eyes had completely gone out. "You're still here," he muttered. "I told you to leave a week ago."

Vince frowned and walked forward. "I've been waiting to talk to you. I've been trying to reach you for days." He placed a hand on Jask's cheek. Jask leaned into it for the barest second before pulling away. "Jask, what's wrong?"

His voice was more rolling, distant thunder than anything else. "You need to leave. You shouldn't have stayed - I'd have thought my silence was proof enough of that."

"I thought..." Vince stepped back now, his fists clenched. "I thought maybe you were being cautious. That your brothers were watching you, or *had* you. Are you telling me you've been ignoring me on purpose?"

Jask nodded once, his eyes empty. "I had tried to do this without a confrontation, but it seems that you need me to actually say it. So, I'll say it. I'm leaving you, Vincenzo. I'm not coming with you because I don't *want* to come with you."

"You're lying. Jask, you *have* to be lying. What did they do to you? What are they threatening you with?"

Nothing changed on Jask's face. "That's not what this is. I've set you up with enough to get you started in your new life. Take it as a token of whatever you think we once had. It's over, Vincenzo. You need to move on."

"Move on? After... you can't just... What the *fuck*? We're mated! This wasn't some fling." Vince could feel his world dropping out from underneath him. Something was incredibly wrong. He looked around for help, from Johnny or Lee. Anyone that could tell him he was having a nightmare and what was going on wasn't really happening. That Jask wasn't really saying these things.

Slowly, Jask slid his hands into his pockets. "I'm sorry you saw it like that, because you're wrong. Goodbye, Vincenzo."

"No. No, fuck you. You don't get to do that. You can't disrupt my entire life and then come in here like it doesn't mean anything!" He looked at Jask, trying to catch a glimpse of any emotion. When Jask's blank expression gave away nothing, something snapped inside of Vince. Before he realized what he was doing, his fist had connected with Jask's face. This time, he didn't pull the punch.

Jask flew backward, crumpling in the grass several yards behind the end of the porch. He stayed there for a moment, then slowly pushed himself to his feet. He glanced at Vince like he was going to say something else, but didn't, and vanished into thin air.

Vince stared at the spot for much longer than necessary, but Jask was gone. Really and truly gone this time. He felt his back hit the wall and he slid down to the floor. That damned ache was once again settled in his chest, and he rubbed. Over and over again, he ran his hand over where it hurt the most, but it didn't ease.

"Vin?" Leota sat next to him and put her hand on his shoulder.

"He left. He *actually* left, Lee. I don't… I don't know what to do."

"Fuck him. He never deserved you." She slid her arm all the way over his shoulders and squeezed. "Let's go far away from here. Leave all this shit behind us."

Vince dropped his head in his hands. He didn't move right away. Some part of him told him Jask had been lying. He hoped, maybe, if he waited long enough, Jask would come back. That they would talk, and this would all be explained. He took a deep breath and pushed himself back up. "I'll be back." He walked into his room and grabbed his phone. He didn't call Jask, but he *did* send him a text: "I'm sorry." It wasn't enough, but maybe it was a beginning.

Another week went by without anything from Jask. Another week of his family trying to persuade him they needed to go. Another week of everyone wanting him to run. Vince was in the woods, axe swinging and wood flying around him when Johnny showed up. Vince didn't want to listen to whatever it was he had to say, so he kept swinging. When it was clear that Johnny wasn't going to go away, Vince dropped the axe and looked up to the sky. After a few calming breaths, he looked at his best friend and didn't care for what he saw on his face. "Someone steal your puppy?" Vince asked.

"No, but I feel like I'm about to steal yours. Can you just... step away from the sharp objects for a minute? We need to talk."

Vince frowned and stepped over to where he'd left his shirt, and grabbed a bottle of water. "So talk."

It looked like Johnny would rather do anything but that, but he nodded anyway. "Jask... he... he's fine. No injuries, he's moving around freely. He's working for the family law firm now, and he's... well." Johnny shifted on his feet and took a deep breath. "He has a boyfriend."

Water shot into the air as Vince crushed the water bottle in his fist. He didn't speak for a long moment, then his hand slowly unfurled from the destroyed plastic. He had to clear his throat before he could speak again. "He has a *what?*"

Johnny blinked rapidly, taking a step back. "He has a boyfriend. I saw them together. It's another angel, I don't know much else about him."

"You saw them?" Vince looked down. "You saw them doing what, exactly?" Maybe Johnny was mistaken. Maybe it was just Jask with Draz. Vince didn't look up as he waited for the answer he didn't actually want to hear.

Johnny's voice got softer. "Look, I didn't expect to see what I saw. But they were... they were kissing, and the guy had his hands in Jask's wings."

It was like a physical blow to his stomach. Someone else was touching Jask's wings. The wings that had been marked by Vince, that he knew so intimately. Everything up until now, Vince had shrugged off or had rationalized, explained away. He had started to think Jask was just trying to keep them safe and that his departure had been some sort of a sacrifice. All along, he'd just wanted something else, some*one* else. Another angel to erase the feeling of sleeping with a demon, perhaps. Vince realized he hadn't responded to Johnny, but he couldn't even bring himself to move, much less speak. He kept imagining someone else getting to hear the noises Jask made when his wings were touched. That wasn't supposed to be for anyone but him. A white-hot rage built inside him, fueled completely by hurt and jealousy. He dropped the remains of the water bottle as his hands lit with flame, but he forced himself to focus it in a straight line so it wouldn't hurt Johnny. He let it all out in one blast, and when it was done, there was a demon-made trail in the woods. Vince huffed out a breath and shook his head.

"I'm sorry, Vince. I am. I didn't want to have to be the one to tell you any of this. I thought Drazan and Jask were just friends, but what I saw... that wasn't just friendship."

"Drazan? Well, fuck." Vince laughed, and kept on laughing. It'd been Draz all along. He knew he sounded crazy, but the laughter wouldn't stop. "Shit. That's probably why he never stayed. Nights with his dirty demon secret and then brunch with his angel boyfriend. Son of a bitch." He didn't have the energy left to be upset. He grabbed his things and turned to smile at Johnny before walking back to the house.

"Vince? I know this is a stupid question, but are you okay?" Johnny asked as he followed behind him.

"Peachy, Johnny. Things have cleared up for me, that's all." He walked into the house with his friend close on his heels.

Lee looked him up and down, noticing something different. "We leaving?"

"Tomorrow morning. Get your shit packed." Vince watched as she jumped up to do exactly that. His mother gave him a sad smile and followed, so Vince grabbed a beer out of the fridge and turned to his best friend. "You coming? We got room for one more."

Johnny hesitated, but ultimately agreed. Relief and something a little like a shadow of happiness spread through Vince as he realized that he wouldn't be alone, not really. Even if Jask decided to throw him away, Johnny never would.

They packed all night.

Jaskian

Jask threw up for the third time that day while Drazan rubbed his back. "Jask, I think you need to stop taking those blockers. They're making you sick."

"It's not them." Jask rolled to sit down next to his toilet, looking up at the only friend he had in the universe. "It's the entire situation. Lying to Vince like that was fucking horrible."

"You know it's for the best. The stubborn bastard wouldn't give up, otherwise." Draz stood and filled a cup with water, handing it to Jask.

He drank it quickly, closing his eyes. "I don't know much longer the blockers will fool my brothers, anyway. You think our little show worked? The sooner Vin actually gets outta here, the better."

"That little demon kid took off pretty quick when he saw us. My guess is he went straight to Vince. So, odds are he's either on his way here to kick your ass," Draz said as he sat on the edge of Jask's tub, "or, he's on his way out of town."

Jask nodded as nausea rolled in his stomach again. He swallowed hard, tipping his head back. "No offense, but you touching my wings made me physically ill, I think. Let's not try that again."

"No offense taken. We had to sell it, though. I think that did the trick. You ready to move to the couch?"

Carefully, Jask pushed himself to his feet and tried to make a joke. "At least you're a good kisser. It could have been even worse." He walked out to the living room and plopped down on the couch, wincing from his lingering injuries. When he'd first confronted Cidos, their argument had quickly turned into a fight... and both brothers were still sporting the consequences. "How long do you think I have to keep this shit up before my brothers move on?"

"Honestly? I don't know if they will. Ci seems a little... fanatical about this. Edis you could probably convince to back off, but I'm not holding out much hope for the angry twin." Draz went into the kitchen and came back with a bottle of whiskey. "For the pain."

Jask laughed bitterly and took the bottle. "Thanks. How's my face look? Vince hits a hell of a lot harder when he actually wants to hurt someone."

"It looks fine," Draz said in that voice someone uses when they're lying to make you feel better. "I still can't believe he actually hit you, though."

Me either, Jask thought with a pang in his chest. "It's for the best. If I know Vince, he'll be back on his feet in no time. And I'd rather him be angry than sad."

Draz looked at his face again. "Yeah, you definitely pissed him off. So... what's next? What happens when he's safe and long gone?"

Not one part of Jask wanted to think about it. "I wait a decade or so, play house with my brothers... and then I'll leave. Get far away from Ci and Edis so I can stop taking the blockers, and I'll just... exist. I don't know what else to do."

"Sounds lonely," Draz sighed. "Guess that means I'm inviting myself along on your self-imposed exile."

Company sounded great, but Jask knew that Draz would never be able to keep that promise. "You'll be married by then, but I appreciate it. Who knows, maybe they'll just kill me first." Jask took a long drink, wincing as it burned his throat.

"Who says I'm ever getting married? Also, you know you aren't going to let them kill you, because that will kill Vince. The bond is still established. There's only one way to break it."

If anything, that only made him feel worse. "You'll get married cause you're a catch, Draz. You're easy on the eyes, know your way around a kiss. You're almost annoyingly selfless. You can cook. I can go on, but now I'm getting nauseous again." Jask grinned, but he knew it didn't meet his eyes.

"That solves it. You and I will get fake-married and I'll let you kiss me on Wednesdays. Only Wednesday though." Draz smiled back.

Jask's laugh was a little more genuine that time. "Sounds like a raw deal for you, if we're being honest."

"Nah. As long as you're willing to turn a blind eye to my infidelity, we'll be golden." Draz stole some whiskey.

"Ah, and now we're right back to it being a raw deal for *me*. I accept your proposal nonetheless. Congrats, Draz." Jask snatched the bottle back and grimaced as he set it down, tipping his head back against the couch. "Go to work for me tomorrow. I don't want to look those two in the eyes right now."

"I accept on the condition that I get to play an overly doting boyfriend to annoy the hell out of your stuffy asshole brothers," Draz said, leaning back in his chair.

Jask rolled his eyes with a soft smile, knowing damn well he didn't deserve a friend like Drazan. "You kind of have to, they'll never believe I ditched the bond for you if they don't buy the fact that we've always been secretly in love."

Draz blinked at him, affecting an overly dramatic, shocked expression. "Are you saying we *haven't* been? Jaskian, I'm wounded."

"Want me to kiss it and make it better?" Jask asked, trying to smirk but failing miserably. "Fuck. I'm gonna be the one that screws this up, I can feel it."

"I won't let you," Draz answered quietly. "Wouldn't be much of a friend if I did."

Jask nodded, pushing himself up. "You can take the bed tonight. I'll sleep on the couch." He disappeared to get himself a pillow and a blanket, feeling like shit that Draz couldn't even go home. They'd de facto moved in with each other to sell the lie.

He made his way back out a couple minutes later and dropped his stuff, scratching the back of his head. "You need anything else?"

"I'm not taking your bed, Jask," Draz shook his head. "I'll stay in here with the whiskey, thank you."

"Look," he said, sitting down. "You're giving up your life to help me. The least I can do is sleep on the damn couch."

"You have a king sized bed, Jask. We could share. I promise, I'm done kissing you for the day." Draz smiled, but it did little to relieve the tension in his chest. Jask knew it was wrong to sleep next to anyone but

Vince, but if he was being honest, Cidos could show up at any moment and them sleeping together could only further prove the lie they were trying to sell. He nodded once, accepting the compromise, and they took that bottle of whiskey to bed with them.

He barely slept, but Draz kept his word and stayed on his own side. In a way he'd never admit out loud, it was nice not being alone, even if he had no interest in holding Draz the way he used to hold Vince. That very same thought filled him with sadness as he realized Vince probably had no one to keep him from being alone, whether it was real or not.

Jask eventually drifted off wondering how long it would take for Vince to move on for real, and how long Draz would stick around before finding someone he didn't have to fake it with. Everyone involved deserved better, and for what? Because Cidos couldn't let go of a centuries old feud?

Sleep evaded him almost entirely, and when he woke up, Draz was still sleeping. Jask watched him for a few moments, thinking to himself that if things were different, and he'd never met Vince... he could've loved him. He doubted Drazan would've felt the same, and it was a moot point either way, but Jask could still see that simple life playing out in his mind.

They'd have gotten a huge house somewhere, probably near the Dreads so they could've continued working. Maybe a cat or two, but no kids. The sex would've been fine, but nothing to write home about. They'd have never fought, never hurt each other. It would've been perfect.

And Jask would've been bored to death.

He wanted Vince, and his warmth and wittiness and arrogance. He wanted a tiny house in the woods somewhere with absolutely no privacy from each other. He wanted fights and arguments and *passion*. A fleet of kids, a dozen dogs... he wanted it all. He wanted *Vince*, and he wanted Drazan by his side as his best friend.

Aching, Jask pushed himself out of bed and took a shower, then made breakfast for Draz before heading off to work.

Walking into the family law firm was torture. He hated that place, hated what it stood for, and hated the things he had to do now that he was a part of it. Jask waited until the last possible second to take the blockers that would stop his brothers from sensing his moods or knowing when he was lying, then pushed his way in Edis' office. "Good morning. Sorry I'm late, I had a little trouble getting out of bed this morning." He smirked, hoping Edis would take that as an innuendo.

Edis frowned. "I really don't want to talk about what you do in bed."

"And that's why I like you better than Cidos. I had to recount it for him... in detail." Jask straightened his tie and tried to keep the hatred from his eyes. *The blockers need to kick in soon, I can't do this forever,* he thought. "What demon am I condemning today?"

"We have a drug possession charge," he said, then tossed the file to Jask. The defendant was only fifteen.

Jask clenched his jaw and huffed a laugh through his nose, covering his revolt. "Perfect, nothing better than locking them up nice and early." He scanned the file, seeing the complete and utter lack of evidence. "Do you have *anything* on him at all other than his shadowline?"

"Only the area he was in when arrested. West corner of the Dreads," Edis answered as he typed something on his computer, "He was caught with three others. We can probably also prosecute with intent to distribute if we can get some witness statements."

You mean coerce and blackmail your way into some witness statements, he thought bitterly. "Great. Should be a slam dunk, right?" He tapped the file on the desk and turned to leave, but stopped. "I'll push for intent to distribute if you cover for me with mom tonight. I'm not coming to dinner."

Edis stopped typing. "That is not a fair trade. No one is allowed to miss the weekly dinner."

"Look," he lied, testing the blockers, "Draz just got some new toys in, and we're too impatient to wait til tomorrow. It's gotta be tonight."

Edis made a face. "I'll cover for you if you never tell me about Draz's toys again."

"My toys?" Draz walked in with a travel mug of coffee. "Are you telling him about the harness? Also, hi. You left your coffee," He kissed Jask on the cheek and pushed the coffee into his hand.

Jask took it with a genuinely grateful smile. "Thanks, babe. And that's not actually the one I was talking about, but I'm pretty excited for that one, too." He nudged Draz, and Edis groaned.

"Okay. Go to work, we're not paying you two to flirt with each other."

"You got it, boss. Hey, question though, say Jask and I are on a stakeout and things get heated... Are you saying you *won't* cover the dry cleaning bill?" Draz asked innocently.

Cidos walked in and leaned against the door, scoffing. "I highly doubt things will get heated between you two... so sure. We'll cover the dry cleaning bill."

It was said like a challenge, and Jask ignored him completely. "Edis, please tell Cidos his opinions on the matter weren't requested."

"I'm not doing that. We aren't teenagers anymore." Edis pointed to his twin. "He's right there, tell him yourself."

"As fun as this conversation is," Draz said as he took the file from Jask, "It seems we have a case. The sooner we get done, the sooner we can try out the harness. Shall we?"

Jask nodded, taking Draz' other hand and leading him out past Cidos, shoulder-checking him on the way out. He may have to pretend he didn't care about Vince and was in love with Draz, but Cidos absolutely deserved the hate and Jask wasn't above dishing it out.

The moment they were away from the firm, Jask turned to Draz. "Look at the file. That kid is innocent, or at the very least, it's not his fault."

Draz opened the file and started reading through it. "This absolutely sounds like a wrong place, wrong time situation at the least, a deliberate frame at the worst."

"Knowing those two, my money is on door number two. Add this to the list of things I'll kill Cidos for one day." He hated saying it out loud, but he knew he meant it. Ci wouldn't stop, he'd never stop.

"If that's what you decide to do, I'll be right there with you. I could think of at least one other person that would be there for you, too." Draz dropped the folder, continuing quickly before Jask could dwell on Vince. "We could mess this case up, you know. Find the actual dealer. Man, that would piss Ci off."

Jask grinned. "Y'know, if it was Wednesday, I'd kiss you for that. No angel knows the Dreads better than us." He let out his wings, refusing to look at them. "You ready to go? I think my old car is still parked at our office."

"Yeah, ready when you are." Draz tucked the file in his jacket.

He teleported them both to his car and piled in, and Jask started the engine using his grace. He chuckled as it sputtered pathetically to life and put the car in drive, taking off out onto the road. "You may wanna put your seatbelt on, D."

Draz looked like he was about to argue, but conceded and put it on. "Where to first, Captain?"

"Same as the old days. Let's head to the scene of the crime and see if we can pick up anything Cidos purposefully ignored."

It felt good to get back on the road with Drazan, and even better when they actually succeeded and exonerated that teenaged kid. The look on Ci's face was priceless... and Jask couldn't wait to make it happen again.

~

Jask made it through the rest of the week, but barely. By Saturday morning, he was laying in bed and couldn't bring himself to get out. He couldn't stand to take the blockers if he didn't have to, and he missed Vince so much he couldn't breathe. Jask pulled the blanket up on himself a little higher, desperate to take the edge off the cold in his bones, but nothing helped.

The door opened and Draz walked in holding a large, steaming coffee. "Look, it's me, your devoted, fake boyfriend. I come bearing gifts."

If he didn't crave the heat so much, he'd have sent him away. Jask sat up slowly and reached out for the mug, taking a slow sip and shivering as he felt it spreading through his chest. "Thanks, D. What are you doing home on a Saturday?"

"You seemed a little sad last night. Didn't think it would be a good idea to leave you alone," he said as he shrugged.

"Yeah, it hit me pretty hard last night. You don't have to stay though, seriously. I get it. I'm not a lot of fun most of the time."

"That's because I'm the fun one, Jask. You're the broody one."

Even the word 'broody' made him sad. Jask frowned at the steam rising off of the mug and ran his thumb over the rim. "Believe it or not, Vince was the broody one with us. He was adorable though, I couldn't take him seriously."

"Do you really want to talk about this? I mean, if it helps, then I'm all for it, but I don't want you spiraling. You'll go straight to him." Draz sat on the bed after kicking off his shoes.

Jask shook his head, absentmindedly rubbing the spot where Vince had decked him. "No, I won't. He's better off without me. It was hard the first couple of days, but now... I don't feel that insane pull anymore. He's far enough away, I think. And either way... no, I don't really wanna talk about it. I shouldn't have brought it up." He finished his coffee and laid back down, staring up at the ceiling. "I just wanna know when it gets easier, y'know?"

"I wish I had an answer for you, but we're kind of working without precedent. It's been ten generations since this last happened."

"And even then, we still don't have an accurate precedent. As far as the history books show, no one's ever tried to fight it like this. They all just... gave in. Let themselves have each other until the Veris' caught on and put an end to it." Jask threw an arm over his head and let out a breath. "Guess one way or the other, this'll be the end of it. We'll be the last."

"That isn't necessarily true. If Leota and either of your lovely brothers procreate this is just going to continue. The children don't have to come from you. Just your graceline," Draz said, sounding apologetic.

Jask looked him in the eyes for the first time all morning. "I'm well aware of that, D. But I never said I was planning on letting Edis live

through this, either. Leota can pop out as many babies as she wants...
the Veris line ends with us."

Ten

Vince

They had driven for twelve hours before stopping at a motel just off the main highway. They'd now been at the motel for a week, and Vince and Johnny had saved themselves some money by offering to do repairs for the elderly owner. She was a widow and gave them free room and board for the work they'd done.

Collectively, they agreed they probably weren't far enough away and needed a plan. Vince laid on the hood of the truck in the parking lot, listening to Johnny and Leota bicker. He watched the clouds float by as they debated which direction to go, until Leota's voice was reaching that octave that set his teeth on edge. "That's enough!" he yelled as he sat up. "I'm going to save Cidos the trouble and turn myself in just to get away from you two!"

"You promised me the beach, Vin!" Lee stomped her foot.

"We need to go somewhere secluded," Johnny argued.

"We *need* to agree. If I have to do this without..." He took a breath. "If we have to do this, I don't want anyone unhappy." *Anyone but myself,* he amended silently.

"You're telling me there's no such thing as a secluded beach?" Lee shrieked, her face inches from Johnny's. "It doesn't even have to be the ocean, I'm trying to compromise here!"

Johnny looked lost, like he had no idea how to successfully argue that logic. He turned to Vince, holding up his hands in mock surrender. "I'm just the driver. You tell me where to go."

Vince ran a hand down his face. "I don't know." He pulled his phone out to search the nearby area and began to laugh. "Actually, I do know. And we're only an hour away." He turned his phone around to show Johnny.

"Devil's Lake," Johnny read out loud.

"It has a beach, it's been abandoned for years. Almost immediately after the apocalypse. Plenty of game to hunt, and I'm sure between the two of us, we can find a fixable house. What do you say?"

Lee shoved Johnny out of the way to take a look and grinned. "Looks like a beach to me. It's a little lacking on the hot guys and tiki bars, but like I said... compromise."

After fixing his shirt, Johnny nodded. "Devil's Lake it is."

Vince hopped off the hood of the truck. "Let's get our things and tell Ms. Mabel we're checking out." Everyone ran to do what they needed, and an hour and half later, they pulled into Devil's Lake. The closest civilization was a forty-five minute drive away. They explored until they found what looked to be a sturdy home, and Johnny finally stopped the truck.

"We got about four hours of daylight, how much do you think we can get done?"

Vince got out and grabbed the tools they'd brought from what he'd been referring to as 'the *other* place.'

"Oh, I think we can get plenty done," he said as he walked into the house to check it out.

Johnny followed, and Leota immediately dragged Amaranth to the beach. Johnny stepped through the front door with his flashlight on and knife in his other hand. "Let me just... scope it out first."

"You're kidding, right? What would be in here that your knife would kill faster than... well, me," he said, motioning to himself.

"I'm trying to be cautious!"

"Yeah, okay." Vince took no caution as he inspected the rooms. The house was old, but the foundation was strong. A little love and work and it could be a very nice place. Vince started making a list of what they'd need and how much money it would cost as he waited for Johnny to finish his scouting mission.

He came back a few minutes later, pointedly not looking at Vince. "Clear. There are only two bedrooms, though."

"Guess you and I are sharing, roomie." Vince grinned at him. "Until we can do some renovations, anyway. I think I saw an old hardware store in that last town. We should go stock up on what we can, get some dinner, and start getting ready to camp here for the night."

With a nod, Johnny grabbed the keys and headed back out to the truck. Once Vince climbed in, they drove down to where Leota and Amaranth were and yelled out the window that they'd be back. Navigating was easy enough, but trying to figure out the necessities was a different story. Anything they could possibly find at the house or in the woods around it didn't get purchased, and even still, when they loaded up the truck to head back, they had considerably less money.

"Fuck, that generator was way more expensive than I was expecting," Vince sighed. He and Johnny unloaded the truck and got to work. Soon, the home was lit and Vince had a fire going in the fireplace. The work had kept him distracted, but now that everyone was inside and finally safe, he checked his phone again. There was nothing new from Jask, and he dropped his head back against the wall he was sitting against and stared into the fire.

"Do you think we'll be able to stay here for a while?" Amaranth asked. "Or will we need to move again soon?"

Johnny cleared his throat, taking the pressure off of Vince to answer. "We should be safe here, Miss Amaranth. I don't think the Veris' will come looking anymore, and even if they do, we covered our tracks. You should be able to settle in this time."

"Why won't they come looking?" Lee asked, looking at Vince.

"Because Jask has moved on. We're not a threat to them anymore." Vince waved his hands in a grand gesture. "So welcome home."

Lee scoffed, curling up on the couch. "I told you he was an asshole. The pretty ones always are."

His mom looked like she was going to scold his sister but decided against it, instead, she glanced at Vince with sadness in her features. "Well, you'll just have to move on, too. Show those Veris' that they messed with the wrong Riskels this time."

"Sure, plenty of options out here on the lake. I'll just go find myself a bikini clad co-ed tomorrow." He put another log on the fire, leaving the words he wanted to say unsaid. He didn't want to move on. He wanted to find Jask, and he wanted to stab Drazan. He wanted what he was never going to have again.

"We won't have to hide forever, Vin," Johnny said quietly. "Give it a couple of months just to make sure Jask and Drazan stay together and don't give Cidos a reason to come back, then we should be able to live normally again. Just... here, not there."

Leota groaned. "Should've just stayed away from the prick in the first place, I miss my friends."

"I didn't look for him on purpose, Lee. I didn't ask for any of this," Vince reminded her.

"Maybe not, but you didn't have to jump into bed with him," she accused. That time, Amaranth did interject.

"Enough. Leota, you know better than to talk about things you don't understand, and the past is the past. Vincenzo has worked very hard to undo the damage Jaskian did, you should be grateful to him."

"She's right. I didn't even last a whole month. I called *him*, not the other way around. Everything that's happened is my fault." He stood abruptly before realizing he had nowhere to go.

"Come on." Johnny got to his feet too. "Let's go for a swim."

Vince followed him out without thinking about it. "We should've hit the liquor store."

Johnny stripped down to his boxers and tossed his clothes on the sand. "First stop tomorrow, you have my word. In the meantime, this water is probably gross enough that if you drink it, you'll get some kind of a buzz."

Vince followed suit. "I'm not drinking the water. You feel free, I'll bury you somewhere nice." He walked out into the water, grimacing as he noticed how right Johnny actually was about it.

"Ouch," Johnny said sarcastically. "After all I've done for you, the most I get is a nice rock for a headstone?" He headed into the water, sighing with relief. "It's cold, it feels amazing."

"You think Jask threw away my blanket?" Vince asked. Johnny's words made him worry about Jask getting cold since Drazan wouldn't be able to keep him warm. He scoffed when he realized it was ridiculous for him to even care anymore. "Never mind. Don't answer that."

Johnny seemed to sense where his mind went. "If he did, he's probably shivering in bed next to another angel. Twice as cold." He splashed Vince in an attempt to distract him, then dove underwater.

Vince waited for Johnny to resurface before splashing him back. "That doesn't make me feel any better. Only person he should be in bed with is me."

"Do you think it's real, then?" Johnny asked carefully, wiping the water from his face and moving closer. "I thought maybe, even with everything, it was all some elaborate scheme to keep you safe. I just don't get it, he seemed so..." He trailed off, hovering his palms over the surface of the water. "I'm sorry. You probably don't want to think about it anymore."

"You're the one that saw them, and honestly it makes sense. Right? Angels belong with angels. Tell me that makes sense, Johnny."

His friend looked at him sadly, tipping back to float on the water. "It looked real. It pissed me off like it was real. And if we were talking about anyone other than Jaskian Veris, I would say yes, angels belong with angels. But even before you, Jask preferred demons. He'd slept with a hell of a lot of people, but his preference was *always* demonic men."

"Sounds like you've done your research." Vince looked up at the night sky. "Shit. He could be in bed with Kos right now. I would drive off a cliff if I found that out."

"I didn't have to do my research, Vin. He told me. We spent quite a bit of time together thanks to all of this." Johnny shook his head. "Kos would've killed him first."

"Kos couldn't kill him. He would try, but he would lose." Vince swam a little further out. "If something were to happen to Jask, I'd bet money it's because of Cidos."

"Yeah, but no way Cidos could take him, either. Jask is stronger, right?"

"Yeah," Vince agreed. "He's the strongest, but like you said. They're his brothers. He wouldn't even see it coming."

Johnny dove underwater again and stayed down for almost two minutes, then came back up and shook his head to displace some of the water. "Thought of something else while I was down there, but you're not gonna like it. Him and Drazan... it *has* to be real. His brothers would sense if it was a lie. I'm sorry, Vin."

"Fuck." Vince laughed. "You give the worst pep talks I've ever heard, but like I said. It makes sense. He was always telling me not to call at certain times. He never stayed for breakfast. At first I thought it was because of his family, but he only sees them once a week."

Heading toward the shore, Johnny called back, "Let's go egg his house or something. Fuck that guy... I can't believe I actually trusted him."

"I'm not driving the entire night just to egg his house, Johnny." Vince stayed where he was.

"Fine, then at least come to bed. We have a lot of work to do tomorrow and I've known you long enough to know how cranky you get when you didn't get enough sleep. Come on." He waved to Vince, stepping up onto the beach. "I promise I'll keep my hands to myself if you promise not to fart anywhere near me."

Vince began to swim forward. "That's such a messed up compromise. Does that mean you're going to molest me if I do? I gotta tell ya... these are some real mixed signals, roomie."

"It's meant to deter you from farting in bed with me. So yeah, but do you have to word it like that?" Johnny grimaced, picking up his clothes.

"You said it, not me." Vince grabbed his own things and they walked back into the house. Lee and his mother had already made their way to bed, so Johnny and Vince didn't waste any time, either. Soon, they were settled in the dark, quiet house. Vince stared up at the ceiling with one hand on his chest. The ache wasn't so bad now. If he'd actually left the first time, he might've avoided all of this. He never would've gotten to know Jask. He never would've fallen in love with him. He could've met a nice demon somewhere and moved on with his life. Those thoughts felt wrong; they made his stomach roll and his eyes burn. He took a deep breath and forced himself to calm down so he could sleep.

Johnny sucked in a breath like he was about to say something, but cleared his throat and rolled onto his side. He faced away from Vince, causing him to frown and turn his head to look at his friend's back. "What?"

"Nothing," Johnny said. "I just don't like seeing you like this, that's all."

"Seeing me like what? I'm fine. Totally normal." The words sounded fake to his own ears.

Johnny scoffed, then muttered, "I'm the one person on this planet you don't need to lie to, and yet, you're doing it anyway."

"What do you want from me, Jay? Want me to sing some sappy song and we can cry over some ice cream? You can tell me I'm still pretty, and I can do so much better than him, too." He couldn't keep the bitterness from leaking into what was supposed to be a sarcastic comment.

After a few moments of tense silence, Johnny quietly said, "I didn't mean any harm by it, Vincenzo. Goodnight."

Vince sighed. "I'm sorry. Honestly, I am. I know you're trying to help but talking about it sucks. Like... *really* sucks, and I can't seem to stop myself from doing it."

"I know that. And I don't know how to help, which is strange. Before, if you were upset... the fix was easy. A night at Pattie's, some booze and sex. I can't give you any of that at the moment."

"Technically," Vince began with a laugh, "You could help with one of those things."

Johnny paused for a beat. "If we're getting technical, I could help with all three. Though I wouldn't put up much of a fight, and I'd have to drive into town to get alcohol."

"I don't want to fight you and that would take two hours. Isn't worth it." Vince put his hands under his head and stared at the ceiling again.

He shifted a little, but still didn't roll back over. "So... you were talking about the other thing, then."

"I feel like that was obvious. Was it not obvious?" Vince kicked one foot out from under the blanket.

Johnny froze to the point that Vince didn't even think he was breathing. "And that... that would help you? Make you feel better?"

Vince wondered how far Johnny was willing to go with this, and decided to push that button until he found out. "You know what they say: best way to get over someone is to get under someone else."

A soft huff escaped his friend and he nodded, swearing under his breath. "Okay. Right, um... it's not gonna be weird tomorrow, right? This isn't... it's just..."

Vince stayed quiet for half a second before he started laughing. "Holy shit. You were actually going to do it."

Johnny sat bolt upright and dug his palms into his eyes, making a disgruntled noise. "You're an asshole, Vince. You know that?"

Vince couldn't answer. He was laughing so hard he couldn't breath. He laughed until Lee yelled from the other room for him to shut up. When he could breathe again, he wiped the tears from his eyes. "Fuck, Johnny, I needed that. Thank you."

In one, swift movement, Johnny stole the only blanket they had and stomped toward the door. He paused, muttering "asshole" again, and then dragged the blanket out to the living room.

Vince continued to laugh and let Johnny leave with the blanket. He *had* actually needed that humor; it had reminded him that his life didn't revolve around Jask, and that he'd been somewhat happy before all of this. He eventually let himself fall asleep with a little hope.

The next day dawned bright and early. He and Johnny spent the day repairing what they could; Johnny still grumbled about Vince being an asshole, and Vince still laughed. When they were done, they cleaned up as best they could and Vince convinced Johnny that they needed to find a bar.

They found a small place about an hour out and went inside. Two hours of hustling pool and darts later, they actually had a good amount of cash. Johnny nudged him and pointed to a black-haired beauty that had been eyeing him since they'd walked in. "Yeah, I saw her." He downed his shot and stood. If Jask could do it, so could he. He calmly walked over and sat next to her, offering to buy her a drink.

She told him her name, but he forgot it almost instantly. They exchanged obligatory small talk for a short time before her hand found its way to his knee. "You wanna get out of here?"

He didn't. The entire interaction was making him feel so much worse, but he grinned and gave her a nod. She pulled him outside and had him pushed against the wall before he could even ask where she lived, and then kissed him. It was a perfectly acceptable kiss, but it left him feeling empty. He pushed her gently away, apologized, and went to find Johnny. They drove home in silence.

Jaskian

Something was making Jask sicker. Whether it was the blockers, being away from Vince, the weight on his shoulders, or some combination thereof, he wasn't sure.

It was getting harder to make it through the day without getting drunk, and he found himself relying on Drazan a lot more than he thought he would. But Draz was the only person he could be honest with, his only friend in a vast sea of people that cared more about ancient grudges than him, and they both knew it.

Cidos had been stingy with the cases he'd given them after they'd caught the correct culprit the last time, so they made due with what they got. Day after day, it was the same thing. Some marginally guilty demon being taken down for crimes far beyond anything they were likely even capable of. *Hell, maybe that's what's making me sick,* Jask thought.

"Think anyone would care if I went back to Patties?" he asked Drazan.

"Probably not, with Vince gone. And we can make sure to keep it anonymous," Draz answered easily. "You feeling antsy?"

Jask scoffed. "That's an understatement, D. I haven't had sex *or* let off any of this bullshit since I confronted Ci. I feel like my organs are gonna come parading out of my body."

"That sounds gross and potentially really cool all at the same time." Draz stood and stretched. "Well, let's go see Pattie."

Despite having serious doubts that Pattie would let an angel anywhere near his fights after what happened with Cidos, Jask followed Drazan out there, anyway. He needed the release to even think clearly, so he'd take the chance.

He lifted his hood over his head and nodded for Drazan to do the same, then made his way inside of the building and approached Pattie, careful not to draw attention to himself otherwise. When he reached him, he leaned in close. "Hey, got anyone willing to fight tonight?"

Pattie had been counting bets when Jask spoke, and his face immediately broke into a scowl. He kept his voice quiet. "What're you doing here, Veris?"

"Don't lump me in with those assholes. I kicked Ci's ass for what he did." Jask crossed his arms. "Let me fight."

"He almost killed Vince!" Pattie points to the side of the warehouse currently being rebuilt. "The other one blew up my wall. You expect me to be happy that you gave him a slap on the wrist?"

"That isn't fair, Pat. You know if Jask said he kicked his ass, he kicked his ass. We've brought you good money in the past," Draz pointed out.

Pattie huffed. "Fine. Go, fight. Don't bring the building down."

Jask let out a relieved breath, but was also a little concerned he'd do exactly that. He clapped Pattie on the shoulder then nodded to Drazan before pulling off his shirt and flexing his shoulders. "Ready to watch your fake boyfriend kick some ass?"

Draz fanned himself. "Be still my heart. Go get 'em, tiger." He slapped Jask's ass, and Jask grinned before knocking someone out of the way while they were trying to get to the cage. Since he wasn't officially on the roster, he had to make his own way.

He stepped in, turning in a slow circle as he watched the crowd around him. "Anyone want to get a little revenge on a Veris? C'mon!"

There were loud boos and shouts from the assorted crowd, but only one stepped forward, his arms crossed. "You weren't here for that. Bring us the other two."

"Whose orders do you think they were here on?" Jask spread his arms and shifted on his feet. "Those two don't do anything without my permission. Come on." His eyes sparked with icy promise and he paced around his side of the cage. "I'll even let you choose a tag team partner, just this once."

The demon jerked his head up and another joined him. They entered the ring together and the second one sized him up. "You fought Vince last year."

The mention of Vince only egged him on. "You're right, I did. You two should be no match for me then." He decided to cheat, knowing two-on-one wasn't all that fair. Jask disappeared, teleporting behind them and knocking their heads together with a deafening crack.

They sank to the ground, both unconscious. The angry shouts grew deafening as another stepped into the cage.

"You gonna fight them all?" Draz called from outside.

Jask chuckled and stepped over one of the bodies to get to Draz, and put his face right up next to the bars. "Hell yeah. Gonna kiss me for good luck this time, or should I just bend over so you can smack my ass again?"

"Why not both?" Draz stuck his arms through the bars, one going to Jask's ass and the other to the back of his head. He kissed him thoroughly before pulling away and whispering, "We were followed." Draz stepped back and winked.

Fucking Cidos, he thought. Jask bit his lip in what he hoped was a seductive stare, then turned to face the demon that took the other two's place. He allowed himself a single moment to lament the fact that he wouldn't be able to get laid that night since he was being spied on, and started looking for the traitorous twin. To his surprise, his eyes landed on Edis - not Cidos. *Enjoy the show, little brother.*

The demon lunged, tackling Jask back into the bars he'd just walked away from. The pain felt fantastic, and Jask let out a laugh before planting his feet and launching the demon across the cage. He stalked forward, running his hand down his abs. "Get up."

The demon growled and stood, then aimed a punch at Jask's face. Jask steadied himself and let it happen, exaggerating the blowback a little bit. It hurt, and he'd likely have a mark, but realistically it was going to take a lot more than a low-level demon to do any kind of real damage. Not to mention, if he didn't let them get in at least the occasional hit, no one would fight him.

He rubbed his jaw. "You've got quite a love tap. Let's see what happens when I piss you off." He created and released a ball of energy, connecting with the demon's midsection.

The demon flew back, rolling like he was on fire as soon as he hit the ground. After a moment he stood and charged at Jask, managing to get an arm around his waist.

For a moment, the heat felt so good Jask nearly let that happen, too. He wrapped his arm around the demons back and held tight, lifting him off the ground and slamming them both to the cement. It nearly knocked the wind out of Jask, but he rolled quickly and pinned him to the ground. He decided to put on a show for his brother. "Screw saying uncle. Say Veris!"

"Fuck you!" The demon struggled to get out of his hold.

"Put him out of his misery!" Draz yelled from outside.

Anger at Edis, Cidos, Vince, himself and all of his ancestors welled up inside of him, and Jask blacked out for a moment. When he came back to reality, he was screaming, his hands white-hot with grace as the demon under him burned with it.

The demon screamed, trying harder to get away. "*Veris!* Let me go, damn it!"

Jask backed off immediately, crawling backward across the cage. He hadn't meant to lose control like that, and now that he had, he was scared to do much else. His eyes flicked to Draz, looking for some sort of direction - some sort of salvation that he knew he wouldn't find on a dingy, bloodsoaked warehouse floor.

Draz stepped into the cage immediately. He kicked the demon away nonchalantly and lifted Jask to his feet, holding his hand in the air. "To Veris goes the victory. Thank you, and good night!" He walked back out and tugged Jask with him, hurrying out of the warehouse. The demons sneered at them and whispered as they left.

He didn't stop until they were standing in front of the car. "You wanna talk about what just happened in there?"

Jask shook his head, opening the passenger door and tossing Drazan the keys. "You drive." Once he got in, Drazan stared at him until he remembered that the car wouldn't start on its own, even with the keys. He placed his hand on the dash and brought it to life, then leaned back in his seat and closed his eyes as Draz started driving away. "I got mad, that's all."

"Yeah, Jask, I could see that. Was that for your brother's benefit, or what?"

"As with everything else, why can't it be both? For my brother and... 'or what'?" Jask realized with a frown that he'd left his shirt there and poked at a couple of the bruises. "That was honestly a waste of time. I don't feel any better."

"What would help?" Draz asked, checking the rear view.

Vince, he thought bitterly. *Nothing and no one but Vince.* Jask decided to play along, if for no other reason to distract himself. "Marathon sex. Fratricide. A whiskey bottle big enough to sate me."

"I can help with possibly two of those. Dealer's choice," Draz said as he got them back out onto the highway.

Jask laughed quietly. "What, three's asking too much of you?"

"I don't think I could find a whiskey bottle that big, honestly," Draz grinned at him. "I was hoping the other two would be enough."

"All those obligatory make out sessions making you curious, D?" Jask glanced over at his friend, wondering if some no-strings relief wouldn't do them both some good. Drazan had pretty much given up his life to help Jask sell the lie and keep Vince safe, the least Jask could do is hand out a few orgasms. Especially because they both knew at the end of the day, it wouldn't mean shit. No one would ever mean anything to Jask again.

"Considering you normally throw up after we kiss, I think I'll take a rain check on anything further."

Jask rolled his eyes but couldn't blame him. "So, in other words, you're offering to help me kill my brothers and absolutely nothing else. Got it." He tipped his head against the passenger window and let out a breath. "You should know I'm still pretty damn grateful for that."

"Yeah, they're assholes. And hey, we can also buy a lot of small bottles of whiskey and just hope it's enough? And then if you're drunk enough, we can revisit the third thing."

They didn't have much time to dwell on any of that, or exactly how much whiskey it would take for Jask to be able to touch someone else, because Edis was standing on their front porch when they pulled in. Jask glanced quickly at Drazan. "Hope you're ready to visit that third thing right in front of my brother. I didn't take my blockers today."

"Why the fuck is he even here?" Draz demanded. "Yeah, fine. Whatever you need me to do, you know that."

Jask knew he could live a million years and never be able to pay Drazan back, but he'd have time to sort that out later. He got out of the car and headed for the porch, tilting his head and trying to clear his mind. "To what do we owe the pleasure, Ed? Did I miss someone's birthday?"

"We need to talk. Are you going to let me in?" he asked.

Gesturing to Drazan, Jask shrugged. "You know I like to fuck after a fight. And I know you saw that fight, so... put two and two together."

Draz was already pulling off his shirt. "He's right, so I suggest you say whatever you need to quickly."

It was a good thing that Draz really was handsome - despite not having the urge to do a damned thing about it, at least Jask didn't have to fake the impressed look on his face when he took in Drazan's body. "Yeah. Real fast would be great, Ed."

They walked into the house and Edis crossed his arms. "Something about this doesn't sit right with me. I've refrained from talking to Cidos about it, we both know what a fanatic he is, but Jask... I'm not an idiot."

"Respectfully, I disagree. Is that all you came to argue about?" Draz sat on the couch and took Jask's hand, tugging him down beside him.

Jask fit easily at Drazan's side and smiled a little, genuinely happy to have him around in a pinch. "He's right, Ed. You are kind of an idiot, especially if you're still questioning this. What proof are you looking for, exactly? Want me to ride him in front of you?"

Edis' face didn't change. "I know about the house. I know about the money you took, and all the times you snuck off to see her. I also know that Drazan wasn't your boss before this... *you* were the investigator. I saw your name on the door to your office when I came looking for you, I just never told Cidos. Which means... you've figured out how to lie to us."

It felt like the walls were closing in around him. "What?"

"You should go, Ed. I won't have you accusing Jask of things you know nothing about. Having part of the story doesn't make you an expert," Draz said, putting an arm around Jask.

The contact grounded him. Jask forced a laugh and relaxed again, tilting his head to kiss Drazan's chin. "You're right. I helped them, wouldn't you if you learned your life force was tied to someone else's? Last time I checked, it wasn't a crime for me to want to live. I'm with Drazan, and I haven't had any contact with my mate in weeks." Every line was the truth, plain and simple... even if it wasn't the *whole* truth.

Edis nodded. "I know. And I get it. I probably would've done the same thing... which is why I'm here. I owe you an apology for what we tried to do to Leota."

"Wow. I'm shocked. I didn't think you two knuckleheads knew what an apology was." Draz ran his hand up and down Jask's arm, watching Edis.

"Cidos doesn't," Edis said. "I do, which is why I'm here alone. I'm sorry, and I came to make sure you were okay, Jaskian. I know fighting the bond must be incredibly difficult."

Fuck. Here's where I have to be a wordsmith, he told himself. "That would make sense, right? That's what we were told, anyway. But Drazan, he just has an uncanny ability to make everything easier. I don't know what I'd do without him."

Edis smiled at Drazan and watched the path of his fingers. "Weird you two waited so long to get together though, isn't it?"

"Well, there was that one time in college." Draz grinned and moved his hand from Jask's arm to his waist, tracing a pattern.

It was actually making Jask kind of horny, which was horrible for him as a person, but wonderful in the situation at hand. Jask smirked. "Neither one of us were ready to settle down in college. We got so close he could piggyback off my powers, though, and that closeness hasn't wavered. Sometimes, things happen exactly as they should."

Edis nodded. "I can see that. I'm happy for you both, especially since the two of you being together is stopping a war."

Jask glanced up to Draz with humor in his eyes. "You hear that, babe? Our love affair is stopping a war."

Draz laughed a little before kissing Jask quickly. "Guess that makes us heroes."

"So, is that it then?" Jask asked as he turned his head back toward Edis. "We're good, and I'd very much like to get off in the near future."

"Your wish is my command," Draz said, slowly sliding his free hand into the waistband of Jask's pants.

"I'm still right here." Edis pinched the bridge of his nose, but Jask knew they had to really sell it.

He flipped over, straddling Drazan's lap and kissed him deeply, rolling his hips until Edis *clearly* got the message that he wasn't going to want to stick around for what happened next.

But he didn't move, he didn't say anything other than: "You can stop now."

Draz pulled away from the kiss, breathing heavily. "Edis, if you don't leave, I may have to kill you." He ran his hands down Jask's back to his ass, holding him close against him.

Not even Jask sensed a lie there. He kept his wings tucked tightly, knowing that would be a sure fire way to ruin whatever the hell was about to happen, and kissed him again as he heard Edis get up.

"Okay, you two are gross. I get it. Have fun," he called, then shut the front door behind him.

Draz dropped his head to Jask's chest. "Jaskian, you're my best friend. I would die for you. So please don't take this the wrong way." He knocked Jask off his lap onto the couch and stood abruptly.

Jask landed softly and rolled to look at him, frowning. "What the fuck was that for? I'd have moved, I was just waiting for him to actually be gone."

"Look, I know I flirt and whatever, but I'm not a saint. You can't" — he stopped and gestured broadly — "and expect me to *not*" — he swung his hand in another broad gesture — "You know what? That whiskey sounds like a great idea." He walked into the kitchen, leaving Jask on the couch.

His mind raced trying to figure out what Drazan meant, and the only explanation he could come up with was a sexual one. Jask didn't have long to ponder that before Draz was back with whiskey and two glasses, and they both slammed their first ones so fast it was a miracle either of them tasted it. The second went a little slower, and Jask started to feel more relaxed. "You gonna tell me why you threw me off your lap yet?"

"You didn't notice?" Draz raised an eyebrow and then poured them a third. "I was enjoying it, Jask."

Jask swirled the liquid around and took a cautious sip. "So was I. Didn't know that was a crime."

"I don't want you doing something you'll regret." Draz took a much *less* cautious sip.

I'll regret absolutely everything that isn't Vince for the rest of my life, anyway. Why should that mean I can't at least try to enjoy life in stupid, fleeting little bursts? The thoughts gave him courage, and the whiskey only helped it along. He finished his drink and stood up, walking slowly over to Draz. "Tell me to stop and I'll stop. If not... you're right. We're best friends. It doesn't have to mean a damned thing."

Draz watched him walk closer, finishing his own drink. He sat it down and then pulled Jask down onto his lap again. "Just friends helping friends?"

"Just friends helping friends," he agreed, running his hands over Drazan's torso. "No one's in love, no one gets hurt. Just us reliving that night from college." Jask tipped Draz' chin up and kissed him again, tasting the whiskey and pressing his tongue between his lips, chasing more.

Draz opened for him, his hands going back to Jask's ass as he rocked his hips up, and somehow Jask knew he wouldn't be throwing up when they were done.

In the end, Jask had a hard time getting Vince off his mind, but it still felt damn good. It felt even better when Drazan seemed to read his mind and wrapped his arms around him afterward. If he closed his eyes hard enough and ignored the biting cold, he could almost believe it was Vince, and so for one, stupid, fleeting little night... he didn't feel quite so alone.

Eleven

Vince

Vince was proud of the work they'd completed on the house. It had taken two weeks of repairs, cleaning, and slight renovations, but the addition that would become Johnny's room was coming along nicely, and with a little magic and a little light theft, they now had full power to the house. Running water had been harder to pull off, but even that, they managed to do thanks to a few tricks Vince's father had taught him before he died.

The last two weekends, he and Johnny had hit the bars. They hustled pool and cards, making just enough to replace most of the worn-out furniture that had been left behind and even upgrade a couple of appliances. Afterward, Vince always tried to leave with someone new. Each time, he'd given up before leaving the parking lot.

Despite that, his spirits were high. They were safe, Jask was happy... even if it wasn't with him. His sister loved the beach, his mother was at peace, and he and Johnny had worked out a good routine. Things were actually starting to look up for them for once, so when Johnny approached him looking serious, he knew he wasn't going to enjoy the conversation.

"You got that lost puppy face again," Vince said, scratching the beard he'd let grow since they'd arrived.

"I just thought you might want to talk about what happened last week."

Vince went back to sanding the board he'd been working on, looking away from Johnny. He thought back to that night. They'd been on the roof, patching the holes made known to them by a heavy rain the day before. It was beyond late by the time they'd finished, and Vince had been standing, looking at the moon. He'd been about to ask Johnny if they had any beer left when a bad feeling had overcome him. He'd put his hands on his knees, leaning forward to breathe through it. He couldn't shake the feeling of *wrongness*. After a moment, it finally seemed to pass — he'd stood up straight and smiled at Johnny right before toppling off the side of the roof when a wave of dizziness hit him. It'd taken an entire painful day to heal, and he still didn't know what happened. "Why would I want to talk about it?"

"Well... I mean, what if it's the bond? What if you're weakening or something?"

Vince laughed. "Johnny, it was one night. We'd worked outside in the sun for fourteen hours, and then kept going well into the night. I was probably dehydrated or some shit."

"I don't believe we *get* dehydrated, Vince." Johnny took his hat off and set it down before sitting on the porch. "I'm worried about you, that's all."

"You shouldn't be. I'm..." Vince was going to say great, but the lie froze on his tongue. He wasn't great. He was surviving. He missed Jask, and not just because of the bond. He forced a smile and willed himself to keep talking. "I'm okay."

Johnny nodded like he didn't quite believe him but was taking him at his word. "You'll tell me if you're not, right?"

"Of course I would, but that's not going to happen," Vince assured his friend.

He nodded once. "Okay, then. How's Miss Leota feeling?"

"She's still feeling off, but that kid is tough as nails. She'll be fine in no time."

Lee had started coughing a couple of days ago. She'd been okay for the most part, but her energy had been slowly draining. Last he'd seen, she was cozy on the couch with some tea and a book he'd gotten her from the thrift store.

Johnny smiled a little. "'Tough as nails' runs in the family, I think." He watched him work for a moment and then sighed, getting up to help. "Figure a couple more weeks, we'll finally be able to relax?"

"If Cidos wanted us, we'd have been found. Go ahead and relax." Vince handed him a saw and tried not to dwell on why Cidos didn't find them a threat anymore. He'd been doing better not picturing Jask with Drazan, but every now and then, his brain would helpfully fuck that up. He'd get a clear mental picture of Draz with his hands in Jask's wings and his lips on Jask's neck.

Vince blinked when he realized Johnny had been talking. It took him a couple of minutes, but he caught the drift of the conversation and continued it like nothing was wrong. After a while, his mother asked them to go into town to get Lee some more tea, and if they could find it, decent medicine. They cleaned up and took off in the direction of the closest city.

Johnny stared blankly at the small aisle of medicine available. "Did she have any symptoms other than a cough?"

"Uh... no? I mean, like I said she hasn't had any energy but... we don't get sick. I don't know what any of this is." Vince scratched the back of his head as he picked up a box that said "cough", but it also had a list of other symptoms below it. "She doesn't have any of that."

Slowly, Johnny licked his lips with his brows pinched. "We do get sick... but with only one illness. And if that's the case, none of this is going to help her." Johnny set the box down and eyed Vince a little nervously. "Any chance she's faking for attention?"

"It's not that, and *don't* say that around either Ma or Lee." Vince grabbed a couple of different medications and dropped them in the basket. "One of these has to work."

Johnny looked like he was fighting himself about something, but instead of shutting up like usual, he actually spit it out. "These medicines are expensive, Vincenzo. And they're most likely useless."

"I gotta try something, Johnny. You know, we didn't even have the money to *try* to save my dad. Lee was a baby, so she doesn't remember, but I was fifteen. I watched him waste away. *No one* would help. I can't let that happen to her."

Sadness washed over his friend's face. "Okay, then we'll try. If it really is the Void Sickness..." he trailed off, leaving the rest of it unsaid. It didn't *need* to be said. Only a demon could contract the Void, and only an angel could cure it.

"It isn't. It *can't* be, because there aren't even any angels out here. She'd die. So... it isn't." He said it knowing that his denial wouldn't be enough, then dropped the useless basket on the ground. "We still need to get tea."

"Tea, we can handle." Johnny grabbed a box of Amaranth's favorite and frowned at it. "Is this the one Miss Leota likes? No... that's..." He snatched another box from the shelf and held it up. "Got it. Anything else?"

"Since we're not getting the medicine, we can probably afford to get them some chocolate or something?" Vince suggested. "Maybe it'll cheer her up, help her shake it off."

They got what they could reasonably afford, and Johnny didn't say much at all on the drive back home. He kept looking at Vince from the corner of his eye, though... like he was afraid Vince was going to freak out at any moment.

"Stop looking at me like that," he said, finally acknowledging him.

Johnny looked away abruptly and nodded quickly. "Right. Sorry." But not two minutes later, he was staring at Vince again.

Vince didn't freak out, but he did give up holding it in. He watched the road as he began to speak quietly. "It's just... things were good back home. The house was small, but it was ours. I had honest work. Lee had her friends. We were all happy. Then I went to that stupid fight and it's been one hit after another. We had to leave everything behind and start over. Had to rely on our *literal* mortal enemy for everything... and even then, it wasn't so bad. The house was great, we were really making a life for ourselves. Jask was there when he could be." Vince paused at a stop sign and didn't start talking until the truck was moving again, the rumble of the old engine soothing him. "And then I went to the second fight. Because apparently, I didn't learn my lesson the first time. Now Drazan has Jask, we can never go home, and Lee... Well, you tell me, Jay. When do the hits stop coming for people like us? What do I have to do to stop them from coming?"

The answer didn't come right away, but when it did, Vince could barely make out the words. "They don't, Vince. We're demons, and this world belongs to the angels. It always has." He reached over, lightly squeezing Vince's lower thigh. "We just have to keep moving forward."

Vince laughed a little. "Then what the hell am I even running for? Should've let Cidos kill me."

"No, that's ridiculous, don't even talk like that." Johnny moved his hand. "We'll make it through this, Vince. You said yourself that Cidos doesn't care about us anymore, which means we can live a normal life again. And we'll save your sister."

"And then what? Wait for the next blow?" They pulled up to the house and Vince took a breath as he put the truck in park. "Doesn't matter. Let's go see how Lee is doing."

Neither said anything else as they got out of the truck and headed into the house, both of them too afraid of what they'd find waiting for them inside. Amaranth was sitting on the couch with her head in her hands, their bedroom door was shut, and Leota was nowhere to be found.

Vince dropped the bags and went to his mother immediately. "Where's Lee? What happened?" When they'd left, she'd been fine on the couch. Vince's heart was beating so hard he was sure the others could hear it. "Ma, what happened?"

"She's in the room, Vincenzo. You must stay away." She stood, crossing the room quickly and holding out a hand to physically stop Vince from disobeying, her eyes shining with tears. "You *know* what this is. You can't touch her."

"No. You're wrong. It isn't. It's just a cough, right? She's fine." He stepped forward, pushing against her hand. "I have to go make sure she's fine."

Johnny stepped in front of the door and joined Amaranth in an attempt to block his path. "I'll open it, but Vince, you *can't* touch her. You *can't.*"

Vince kept his eyes on the door and slowly nodded his head. When Johnny swung the heavy door wide, Vince could *feel* the heat radiating out of the room. Demons naturally generated a higher level of heat, but this was too much. Leota's body wouldn't be able to stand that temperature for long.

He swallowed hard as he saw her on the bed. Her eyes were closed, and her skin was pale. Even from where he was standing, he could see the black lines in her neck, confirming the Void sickness had taken hold. His earlier denial stuck in his throat. He couldn't pretend any longer. His sister was dying.

"How did this happen so fast?" Johnny asked quietly, still standing next to him. "Did it move this fast with your father?"

"No," he whispered, not taking his eyes off of Lee. "It took weeks for him to get this far. I don't understand. She was healthy." He turned to his mother. "There has to be something."

Amaranth crossed her arms across her chest and shook her head slightly. She tried several times to say something but began wailing, collapsing back on the couch as the grief became too much.

Johnny clenched his jaw. "He can save her, Vincenzo. Call him."

"No. He won't answer, and if he does, he'll lead Cidos right to us. We'll find someone else, a doctor. Somehow." Vince closed the door — he couldn't continue seeing Lee like that — then went into his room to find his phone. He hadn't even turned it on since they'd gotten there and when it blinked to life, he cursed. "No cell service. Because we're in the middle of fucking nowhere!"

He could hear Johnny and Amaranth talking in hushed tones, and his mother repeatedly pleading for Johnny to do something. A moment later, Johnny knocked on the door. "I'm taking the truck. I'm just going into town to get some ice packs for her, I'll be back. Stay here with her, she shouldn't be alone if..."

"Yeah, yeah. Go." Vince waved him away. He paced the bedroom

floor, trying to think of anything that could help. He was cursing himself for ever thinking coming this far out was a good idea. He eventually moved back out to the living room to sit with his mother, and they
hardly spoke at all. There simply wasn't anything to say.

When Johnny finally returned, he wouldn't look Vince in the eye.
"It's done, Miss Amaranth. He'll be here very soon."

At first, Vince thought Johnny had found a doctor. He stood in relief, opening his mouth to thank him, but then he saw that sad look on
Johnny's face again. He turned and looked at his mother and then back
to Johnny. "You didn't. Tell me you didn't. They think she's his *mate*,
Johnny! They'll let her die!"

"No, they won't," Johnny said quietly. "It's precisely *because* they
think she's his mate that they'll save her, which means you have to go
along with the lie."

Before he could even process it, he felt the change in his chest that
signified Jask was close. A split second after, he knocked on the door.

"*Fuck.*" Vince's legs gave out and he sat back down. Being this close
to Jask after so long was… difficult; it was taking everything in him to
not run to him. Johnny opened the door and Vince's stomach clenched
at the sight of Jask, because directly behind him… was Drazan. Vince
closed his eyes as they walked in, unable to stop the tear that fell down
his cheek. Lee was dying, the only one that could save her was in his living room… and he'd brought his fucking boyfriend to rub it in Vince's
face.

"Save her and get out," Vince growled.

Jask recoiled like he'd been slapped, but followed Johnny's outstretched hand into the bedroom and closed the door without a word.

"Well hello to you too, gentleman." Drazan sat down like he actually
belonged there, like he was actually welcome.

"Why are you here?" Vince asked, running his hand through his
beard in an attempt to stop himself from hurling a fireball at Drazan's
face.

He frowned. "Thought that would've been obvious. No way Jask would leave here willingly, someone has to drag him back home kicking and screaming."

"Why would Jask want to stay here? He has you and the twins back home. No need to stay in the backwoods with the hillbillies."

Drazan blinked and then laughed. "Wait, what? Are you serious? He's been crawling out of his fucking skin wanting to come back to you. It's fake, Vince. It's all fake. The relationship, him playing nice with his brothers. It was the only way he could keep them away from you."

Vince stared dumbly at him. "Johnny *saw* you. You were... you had your hands in his wings."

He grimaced, looking at Johnny. "Guess you didn't stick around long enough to see him throwing up all over my shoes after, huh?"

Johnny shook his head. "Didn't want to see what happened after."

Vince stared at Draz. "This *entire* time, it's been fake?" Vince shook his head. "As soon as Lee is cured, we're all having a long, *long* talk."

"Take that up with him. I'm only here to drag him out by his hair if he tries to stay." Drazan headed for Leota's door right as Jask came back out, wiping his brow.

"I have to call Edis. I can't do it, and Drazan won't be able to, either."

"What do you mean you can't do it?" Vince stood up and began gravitating toward Jask before forcing himself to stand still.

Jask didn't make eye contact. "I've never seen it spread that fast. If you'd have called me at the first sign, I might've been able to help. But she needs a healer, a trained healer, and Edis is the only one I've ever met that might be willing to help a demon."

Johnny scoffed. "He tried to *kidnap* her, why would you think he'd help you?"

"Because," Jask said simply. "He believes she is my mate, and therefore if she dies, I will die. Cidos may be willing to let that happen as a means to an end, but Edis isn't. And for the record... as far as I know, Ed wasn't even there that day. The kidnapping thing was all Ci, and I kicked his fucking ass for it."

"And what's to stop him from running back and telling Cidos where we are? Or kidnapping her to try and complete your stupid ritual?"

Vince asked sharply. He tugged on his own hair, mentally reminding himself he needed to focus on the bigger picture. If they let Edis help, Leota *might* die. If they didn't let Edis help, Leota *would* die. As much as he hated to admit it, they didn't have a choice. "Fine. Call him, but if Cidos shows up... I'll kill him."

Jask nodded once, then disappeared onto the front porch. Draz just looked sad, which almost made things worse. He said, "Vince, go easy on him. I've never seen anyone try so damn hard."

"My sister is dying in the next room. Apparently the only person that can save her has a vested interest in seeing her dead. He's also the brother of my mate — the mate who a month ago told me he didn't want me anymore, and last I heard was sucking face with *you*. Forgive me if I'm not feeling welcoming to either one of you right now."

Drazan just shook his head and sat down and let Johnny fill the silence. "There's obviously more to that story than we know, Vince. Maybe we should give them a chance?"

Vince huffed and walked to Lee's door. He leaned against the wall next to it and crossed his arms, standing guard. He wanted to talk to Jask and hear from *him* that it was fake. He wanted Lee to be okay without having to endanger everyone he ever cared about. He wanted all of this to be over... and he wanted to shake the feeling that the next blow was about to land. He just... *wanted.*

Jaskian

"Edis, please," Jask begged, for what felt like the eighth time. "I need you, and I need you to not tell Cidos."

From the other end of the phone line, Edis sighed. "Jask... you're putting me in a really rough spot. If word gets out..."

"It won't," Jask said quickly. "Save her life and I promise that'll be the last anyone hears of it. She's my mate, Ed. I'll die if she does; I can already feel it." It was a lie of the highest degree, but the distance helped. Jask shoved his hand in his pocket to make sure he had a blocker with him and took a breath. He never begged for anything in his life — he rarely even said "please" — but here he was. "Ed, *please*... I don't want to die."

Silence stretched for too long, then finally, "Fine, but you have no idea how much it's gonna cost you. Text me the address." Edis hung up after that and Jask held his phone tight as he sent the message, nearly buckling with relief.

Jask headed back inside and took the blocker dry, nodding to Drazan. "He's coming."

"That's good. I half expected him to say no," Draz admitted, standing and patting Jask on the shoulder. Vince watched them from his spot on the wall, and Jask's chest ached at how good he looked with a beard. His mind wandered involuntarily, conjuring up the ghost of a guess as to how it would feel against his skin.

He looked at Draz sadly, pulling himself back to the matter at hand. "He never does anything for free, D. You know that." He avoided eye contact with Johnny and Vince, but spoke to both of them. "Please don't take what happens next personally. It's an act," he said, but wondered if it even mattered what they thought anymore. He couldn't have Vince either way, and wouldn't it be easier for Vince to think Jask had really moved on?

"Is it? You two look pretty cozy," Vince accused.

"He's my best friend, asshole." Draz dropped his hand, but despite hating himself for it, Jask reached out to pull him back for two reasons. One, to stop himself from going to Vince, and two... to prepare for Ed's arrival.

"It's not —"

He felt his brother's power flood the area a mere moment before he heard the knock. Jask clenched his jaw and opened the door, stepping aside to let him in. "She's in the bedroom."

Draz took his hand, silently giving the support he had to know Jask needed. Vince pushed himself off the wall as he said, "I'm going in there with him."

Johnny intervened. "Vince, you can't." Edis ignored them both, letting them argue amongst themselves as he looked at Jask. "I just have one question. I came to apologize and you kicked me out so you could have sex, but now you're calling me to ask for favors?"

The other side of the room grew quiet and dread pooled in his gut as he realized he couldn't lie, not this time. "It was one time, Edis. And I already apologized for it."

"Was it Thursday of last week?" Vince asked abruptly, his voice quiet.

Edis frowned at him. "How'd you know that?"

Vince didn't look away from Jask. "I... *Leota* was sick that day."

Jask felt the lie, and he knew Drazan and Edis did, too. It took everything in him not to panic, not to scream and yell and throw things until the world stopped spinning wildly out of control. Instead, he held himself together and turned to Edis in an attempt to distract him. "I said I was sorry, though I didn't realize getting fucked by my boyfriend was something I needed to apologize for. You could've called first."

"I don't have time for this. Where's the girl?" Edis demanded with a sigh.

"This way." Johnny opened the door, and Edis walked through it and closed it in Vince's face.

Jask wanted to go to him right then; wanted to hold him and kiss him until everything else disappeared. He watched as Vince turned — stopped from opening the door again by Johnny — then walked over to where Jask was standing entwined with Drazan and looked at their joined hands. He said quietly, "so much for fake, right?" and then disappeared out the front door. Traitorous tears pricked his eyes and when Draz tried to pull back, Jask only held tighter. He'd let a lion into their house, and now, he had to play his part perfectly.

Johnny whispered, "Edis might save Miss Leota... but you're going to kill Vince." He followed his friend outside, and Jask sat down in a heap on the couch.

Draz joined him instantly. "It's better this way, Jask. You know that."

"I can't breathe, Draz. He's hurting, and fucking all of it is my fault, but at least half of it is bullshit." Jask dropped his forehead to Drazan's shoulder and took a deep breath. "He hates me."

Carefully, Draz put his arm around him. "Pretty sure what he's mad about is both our faults. He doesn't hate you, Jask. If he hated you, he wouldn't care."

Jask let himself curl against Drazan, knowing if Johnny or Vince looked in the window, their point would be proven. But Drazan had been right - it was better this way, and Edis was right there. "Okay. Sell it by whatever means are necessary."

Draz sighed and kissed him gently on the forehead. "Whatever you need, sweetheart."

They'd used pet names before, but Jask had *always* refrained from using that one with Draz. Vince was his sweetheart, and nothing and no one would be able to change that, no matter how bad things got. Jask nodded against his chest and then sat up straight, needing distance but not wanting to go too far.

Edis was in there for what felt like hours — so long that Vince and Johnny eventually came back in, and Johnny nodded to them in lieu of a verbal greeting. "Any update?"

"No, nothing. But this isn't an easy thing to cure, I hope you both know that. It's not just a matter of Edis snapping his fingers and making her better."

"All we needed was a yes or no," Vince said from the corner he'd sat himself in.

"I'm gonna kick his ass," Draz mumbled to Jask, prompting Vince to laugh.

"Yeah? Think you could?"

Instantly, Johnny stepped between them, looking every bit as exasperated as Jask felt. "This isn't the time or place."

Jask locked eyes with Vince and stood slowly, letting go of Drazan's hand. Edis' words about how much this favor would cost him echoed through his mind, and all the pain he'd felt and endured to keep the Riskels safe followed. And for what? Vincenzo wasn't grateful. He didn't understand and didn't *want* to understand. "If you don't want our help, then fine. I'll go in there and get Edis, and you can find your own fucking cure."

"Fuck you, Veris," Vince growled, but right as he was about to say more, the bedroom door opened and Edis finally came back out looking exhausted.

"It's done."

Jask found himself glad for the excuse to look away from Vince and focused instead on his brother. "Thanks, Ed. Since I'm sure no one else in this house knows the fucking meaning of the phrase, I'll say it for them."

"Thank you, Edis," Vince forced out with a sharp glance at Jask. "I know you didn't have to come."

Drazan stood and placed his hand on the small of Jask's back. "We should go."

"Yes, I'm sure this would be painful for Jask's mate to see," Vince agreed. "Can I see my sister now?"

Edis nodded, stepping out of his way. "Go ahead. But, this is the last time I offer my services. And if my brother finds out, I will not hesitate to throw every single one of you under the bus." His eyes focused on Jask, and Jask knew what he really meant. Edis would blame it all on him and let Ci sort it out from there.

The thought of leaving before he had a chance to explain himself was making him ache, so he attempted to buy himself time. "I understand, Edis. Can I see her before we go? Just to make sure I won't die in my sleep?"

"Are you doubting my ability, Jask?" Edis frowned.

"No, he just wants to check on the girl. Go home, Ed. I'll make sure Jask doesn't linger longer than necessary." Draz stepped up and took Jask's hand again, which he was grateful for.

His brother suddenly looked skeptical, so Jask stepped even closer to Drazan and leaned in to kiss his cheek. It was about all he could stomach at the moment."No need to worry, Ed. I have absolutely no interest in being with Leota."

When Edis relaxed, so did Jask. Ed disappeared a moment later, and Jask immediately backed away from Drazan, his eyes flicking toward the bedroom door.

"Go," Drazan said.

He didn't hesitate to head into the room. His first concern was Vince, but after what had just happened, he wasn't sure if Vince was even willing to listen to him. "Lee? Are you okay?"

She smiled weakly at him. "I think so. Pretty sleepy, though. Thank you, Jask. I know I haven't always been nice to you."

"Don't apologize, Lee. You had every right to hate me. I'm so, so fucking sorry for... everything." He understood in that moment that this wasn't about him and Vince... for Vince, this was about his sister, and his presence was more of a hindrance than anything. He headed for the door, mumbling "I hope you feel better quickly" before dropping his eyes to the ground and joining Drazan and Johnny once more. "We can go, Draz."

"You sure?" Draz asked.

No, he thought bitterly. *I'm not fucking sure, but this isn't about me.* "Yeah." The word sounded a lot less convincing than Jask had hoped, and when he tried to actually leave, his feet wouldn't budge. His hands were shaking slightly; every ounce of him was screaming to go to Vince, and the pieces of him that weren't in complete turmoil over leaving were trying to savor the peace brought on by proximity to his mate. "You gotta... I can't."

Draz took one more look into the bedroom before giving him a nod. He took Jask's hand, and together, they made it to the porch before Jask heard his name and then Johnny shouting, "Vince, no!"

"Shit." Draz tightened his grip and moved faster.

He tried to fight it. He tried to allow his friend to take him away from there, but hearing the strain in Vince's voice was too much. They needed each other, and Edis wasn't there anymore to tell them no. This was a fight they'd lose every time, and it was beyond Jask why Drazan didn't just piggyback on his powers to teleport home like they'd done in the past. "Stop," he said suddenly, jerking his hand out of Drazan's and sprinting back into the house. "Vince?"

"Jask," Vince said again, tears in his eyes. "Wait." Johnny was in front of him with his arms braced on the door frame, struggling to keep Vince in the bedroom.

If Jask didn't know any better, he'd have thought his ribs were cracking from the pain lancing through him. He was halfway to Vince with a wild look in his eyes when Draz caught up to him and threw him over his shoulder. "Vince!" Jask squirmed and thrashed, but Drazan's hold was sound, and all Jask could do was watch as he was carried away from his mate.

When Drazan finally set him down, they were almost a half a mile away. He collapsed, wheezing, and then punched Jask in the face. "That's for all the times you fucking kicked me. I was doing what you told me to do."

Jask rubbed his jaw and lifted Drazan back to his feet, knowing he absolutely deserved that. They weren't quite far enough away to quell the urge to go back, but they *were* far enough out that Jask could at least think more clearly. He clenched his jaw and let out a frustrated scream before teleporting them back to their house.

"You told me to do whatever it takes. That's why I was there," Draz said as they landed. "Are you okay?"

He wasn't sure he'd ever be okay again. "I hate this. I hate all of it. I'm sorry, Draz. I can't... fuck, I'll never be able to thank you for everything you've done for me. I don't deserve somebody like you."

"You definitely don't, but I'll stick around anyway." Draz smiled, obviously trying to make Jask feel better.

Jask grabbed a bottle of really old bourbon and poured them each a glass, then handed Drazan his. "Well... here's to you being saddled to me forever, cause it doesn't look like there's a light at the end of this tunnel. Just a gaping fucking hole... and not the good kind."

Draz drank it quickly, ignoring the bad innuendo. "For what it's worth, I'm sorry I had to make you leave. And I'm glad the girl is okay. What do you think Edis is going to ask for?"

"Well, I'd say my firstborn son, but I'm pretty sure he knows how gay sex works. So I don't know, but I can tell you it won't be nothing." Jask fidgeted with his pocket where he could feel the outline of his phone. The device never rang anymore, and when it had earlier, he'd almost jumped out of his skin hoping it was Vince. "Do you think Vince will ever know the truth?"

"He already knows the truth, he just doesn't believe it. I don't know if he ever will, but there's not much we can do about it." Draz shrugged and topped both glasses off.

"You're right." Jask said bitterly. But try as he might, he couldn't stop thinking about the tears in Vince's eyes. Maybe he just hadn't been ready to listen. He pulled out his phone and texted him, hoping he might have better luck that way.

Jask: *I'm sorry, Vin. All I can say is none of this is what it seems.*

"He was hurt. Fucking Edis had to bring up the sex..." Draz shook his head. "Let's just drink. We'll worry about it tomorrow."

He stared at his phone and realized he probably wouldn't get a response, then pocketed it, grabbed the blanket Vince had given him, and curled up on the couch next to Drazan. He held his glass to his lips and smirked, returning the favor of trying to relieve the tension. "At least it was good."

"Sex with me is always good, Jask. You didn't complain either time." Draz laughed, nudging him. They drank for another couple of hours, reminiscing and talking on the couch when Jask's phone finally buzzed.

Vin: *No apologies needed. Enjoy your night with your boyfriend. No hard feelings here.*

The smile Jask had barely managed to muster disappeared as he read the words. He knew Vince was hurt, and tried to remember how things must've looked from his side. If Drazan had seen Johnny and Vince together, Jask would've lost his mind. But still, after everything he'd done to help the Riskels, and everything he was putting himself through to keep him safe, the text pissed him off almost as much as it hurt him.

Jask: *thats not fair, and he's not really my boyfriend. We tried to tell you it wasn't real. We had sex once, it was a mistake, and hasn't happened again.*

"What's wrong? Who are you even texting?" Draz asked, trying to look at the screen.

Vin: *Congrats. You don't owe me any explanation. Thank you again for saving Lee.*

The text was followed immediately by another:

Vin: *Don't come here again, Jask. I was wrong to call you back.*

He stared at the words and couldn't hold back anymore. He stood, throwing his phone toward the wall, but it smacked into the window with enough force that it shattered. Jask's wings came out on their own as a response to the sudden stimulation, and the moment Jask saw the blackened tips, he screamed again. Wave after wave of unrelenting pain coursed through him until he was on his knees without even realizing it. He understood suddenly why no mated couple had ever managed to stay away from each other before - — rejection, real rejection — was quite literally tantamount to torture. The house started to shake around them as the chaos in Jask reached a peak, and he vaguely registered Drazan coming toward him. "Go," he yelled, not wanting anyone around him. If he didn't figure out a way to reign it back in, he was going to level the entire block and everyone in it.

"Jask, I'm not going to leave you like this." Drazan held up his hands. "You have to calm down though before you do some major damage."

In that moment, Jask didn't care about the damage he'd do. He'd already done more damage than he felt could ever be repaired, and had little regard for what happened to him because of it. It was Drazan's continued presence alone that had Jask fighting to regain control - for all of Jask's own faults, Drazan absolutely didn't deserve to die. "I... fuck, Drazan... *fuck*." Jask dropped his head to the carpet and fisted his hands in his hair.

"You have to tell me what happened, Jask." He slowly knelt next to him, like Jask was a wild animal he didn't want to frighten away.

Struggling, Jask used his grace to call the phone back to him. One glance told him the messages were still visible despite the cracked screen, so he shoved the phone into Drazan's hands. "That."

Draz read it and sat back against the couch. "Shit. Jask, I'm sorry..."

Jask didn't respond, but he knew he didn't need to. He went to every happy place he'd ever created in his mind and pushed away all thoughts of Vince, his brothers, the bond, and virtually everything else that was currently making his life as an angel a living hell. Gradually, the house around them stopped shaking enough that Drazan was able to repair the window. Jask sat up, but one look at the blanket Vince had given him had nausea rolling in his stomach. "Drazan... can you do something with that?" He nodded to the blanket, and Draz took the hint. With a flip of his wrist, the blanket was gone, and Jask could breathe a little easier. "Okay," he said finally, pushing himself up and brushing off his shirt. He knew what he was about to say would come across as a lie, but he needed to say it anyway for his own good. "It's time to move on."

Twelve

Vince

After Jask walked out of the bedroom, Vince's heart broke all over again. He could feel each step that took his mate further away from him. Unbidden, Jask's name had fallen from his lips and he stood. Johnny had jumped in front of the door, arms spread and pushed against each side of the frame. "Vince, no!" He'd made it to the door of the bedroom as Jask burst back into the house and tears welled in his eyes as he heard Jask say his name.

He could move Johnny, but not without hurting him, so he did the only thing he could — he called out his mate's name. Vince had to swallow before continuing; his throat was so tight he only managed to get one more word out: "Wait." He hoped it conveyed everything he was trying to say. *Wait. Don't leave me again, stay and tell me you still love me. That this is all a terrible mistake.* Then Drazan was there, and Jask was taken. Being forced away from him. Vince saw Jask struggling and all thoughts of not harming Johnny flew from his head. He knocked his best friend to the side and had made it to the front door when everything went black.

Vince woke an hour or so later on the couch. "What the fuck?"

"Ms. Amaranth" — Johnny said from his chair, holding up an iron skillet — "hit you with this. She may be your mother, but she's still a Riskel."

"Son of a bitch." Vince dropped his head back down with a wince.

He could feel Jask's absence, and it was as bad as the first time they'd left. It would take weeks for it to go away this time. He stood and knew he wouldn't be able to deal with this sober, so he looked at Johnny and asked quietly, "Lee?"

"Both she and your mom are asleep," he answered as he got up. "Bar?" Vince gave him a nod and they drove to the nearest one they could find. Vince was two whiskeys and a beer in when his phone vibrated in his pocket. He'd forgotten it was even there. He opened the text and his heart dropped to his feet. There it was. Jask apologizing, offering an explanation. Johnny caught him staring at his phone and Vince handed it to him. "You do it. I can't."

Johnny looked down at the phone. "What do you want me to tell him?" Vince told him what to type, his hands shaking as he fought the urge to take the phone back and call Jask... to admit the things that were being sent weren't the things he really wanted to say. At the last part, Johnny gave him a sad look. "Vince, are you sure?"

"Send it, Johnny. You have to." Vince cracked the beer bottle in his hand. The bartender brought him a new one, then cleaned the spill and gave Vince a wink as he walked away.

"Any answer?" Vince asked as he watched the man.

"No, Vince. No answer."

"Well, that settles that then." Vince stood and walked to the other end of the bar. "Evening, handsome. You working late tonight?" After a few moments of flirting and flashing his charming smile, the bartender got a coworker to cover the front. He led him to the back room and Vince pushed him against the door as soon as it closed. What they shared was quick, fun, and dirty... and it didn't help Vince one bit. The bartender — he never bothered to get a name — seemed happy enough, so Vince walked back out and caught Johnny's eye.

Johnny hurried to him. "No. There aren't that many bars out here, don't get us kicked out of this one."

"I'm hurt that you think so little of me." Vince looked around the bar, but Johnny caught on almost immediately.

"Damn it, Vince, that's your 'looking for a fight' face!"

"Johnny, buddy, it's just my normal face." Vince slapped him on the back and walked over to a big lump of muscle by the jukebox. Vince could feel Johnny's concerned gaze on him, but that didn't stop him. Vince huffed at the memory of telling Pattie if there was one thing he was good at, it was pissing people off. He did that now, and didn't stop until the big demon slugged him in the face. *Finally*, he felt something. Soon, the entire bar was in on the fight, and Vince was feeling better than he had in weeks. He was standing in the middle of a group of fallen enemies, breathing a little heavy as he looked for his next victim. Someone was running at him with a pool stick, but suddenly the man dropped it and backed away.

"Enough!" a new voice called, and Vince turned to face it. A man stood behind Johnny with a knife to his throat. His smile made Vince's blood run cold and his eyes turn from their normal bright topaz to a deep, dangerous black.

"If you know what's good for you, you'll let my friend go." Vince took one step forward, letting the raw fury radiating off of him speak for itself.

"Of course. I only want to talk." The man pulled away from Johnny, who hurried over to Vince.

"Then talk." Vince dragged an assessing gaze over his friend, and once he was assured there was no lasting damage, he focused all of his attention back on the newcomer.

"The name is Damian. This is my place. Well, this and a few others. I've been watching you for a while." He pulled a chair from one of the tables and sat like there weren't unconscious men everywhere.

"Watching me?" Vince demanded.

"I suppose you can say Devil's Lake is my territory. They call me the King. I knew the moment you stepped foot into my space, Mr. Riskel. That *is* your name, isn't it?"

"The fuck do you want?" Vince was getting annoyed, if not a little afraid that they'd been discovered.

"To employ you. You see, I knew you were strong. Like I said, I've had people watching you, but what I didn't know was that you could *fight.* I need someone like you." Damian smiled again.

"What, exactly, could you need someone like me for?"

"Oh, this and that. I pay very well. I'm sure we could come to an arrangement."

Vince froze for a moment before sitting with the man. Johnny objected, but Vince waved it off. He was feeling *just* self-destructive enough to listen to whatever bad idea this was. Damian, it turned out, actually did own a large part of Devil's Lake. He was looking for what he called an enforcer, and Vince almost had a heart attack at the amount of money he was offering. After a few vague questions and even more vague answers, Vince shrugged and agreed. How bad could it possibly be?

Driving them home, Johnny kept looking over to glare at him, and finally, Vince couldn't take it. *"What?"*

"You just joined the fucking mob!"

"You're being ridiculous. I'm drunk, but not that drunk." Vince scoffed at him. They didn't speak for the rest of the drive, and Vince passed out on the couch as soon as they got home. He'd made plans to meet with Damian the next morning, so he needed his sleep. He left in the morning before anyone had woken up and met Damian at the same bar.

"My rules are simple," Damian began. "No harm to women and children. No destruction of property. If you get information, you bring it directly to me. And the final one? Do what you're told."

"Seems simple enough. You said something yesterday about a war?" Vince asked.

"A territory war. I've been in charge of Devil's Lake for years, but recently this young hothead showed up. Thinks he can take my home away from me. I've taken out a few of his guys, but haven't gotten close to him. And if you want to kill a snake, you cut off it's head," Damian explained.

"What's his name?" Vince looked over some of the documents Damian had on the table.

"Malus." Damian pointed to his picture.

"Latin for bad? That's a little on the nose, isn't it?"

"I didn't name the kid. You in or not?"

"Yeah, why the fuck not? I got nothing else going on." Vince had the sense to realize it sounded too good to be true, but he wasn't exactly in a position to argue. They needed the money, and if he could fight for it like he did before everything went to shit, well... he'd take that deal any day of the week.

Damian drove them to the first location Malus' men had set up, and they made quick work of the idiots inside. Vince barely broke a sweat, and it was over in moments. Damian sent one of the less injured cronies to send a message to Malus and that was all she wrote. It was quick, simple, and clean... and it smoothed the dark edge in Vince that had been growing sharper by the day before Damian had found him.

The days flew by as Vince took out Damian's enemies. Thoughts of Jask were pushed into the back of his head and all he focused on was violence. After the fourth takedown, just the sight of Vince had them surrendering.

"You're magnificent!" Damian laughed, paying him for the day. Vince counted the money and thanked him as always, then left before he could be made to do anything else.

That night, Vince took the truck further out and got some things for his family — new blankets, clothes, food, a bedframe for his mother, and a small TV for Lee. Finally, Vince was able to provide for his family with no help from Jask.

"This is wrong, Vince. This is blood money," Johnny whispered as he helped him unload. He'd agreed with Vince that Lee and Amaranth didn't need to know what Vince's new career was, only that he'd found employment.

"Yeah? Better than angel money, and besides, I haven't killed anyone. Just a couple of busted heads here and there."

His friend didn't say much of anything else, and the next day, Vince went right back to Damian. "Do I actually get to fight today, or will I just be looking pretty?" Vince asked as he walked into the bar.

"You think you're pretty?" Damian laughed.

"I *know* I'm pretty, there's a difference." Vince stole a beer from behind the bar and sat down, legs splayed and posture relaxed. He was finally being put to a use he understood, and that made a world of difference to him.

"You'll get to fight today. There's a larger group that's been causing trouble. They burned down a bar that's very important to one of my employees. Ms. Eleanor has been running that bar for twenty years. She has a family that depends on the income. She got hurt in the fire." Damian sounded more emotional than Vince had ever heard him. "So, even if they don't want a fight, we're giving them one." They drove out to the area, further out than Vince had been yet. This building was a little more heavily fortified than the rest.

"You think your guy is here?" Vince looked out the window.

"Malus? No, my intel doesn't put him here. Just a couple of punks." Together, they stepped out of Damian's vehicle and went to knock, which in this case, meant that Vince blew the door in and yelled something to the effect of: "Knock, knock, motherfuckers, the party is here!"

Damian had been right, there was a fight waiting for them, and Vince allowed himself to get lost in it. The first guy went down quickly, the second even faster. They were met with less and less resistance as they fought their way deeper. When they made it to the main part of the base, Vince leaned nonchalantly against the wall and watched as Damian gathered the information he needed from their files.

After a few minutes, noise drew Vince's attention and he stepped out into the hall to find a kid with a raised gun standing at the end. He couldn't have been any older than his sister. "Nice toy you got there, kid." Vince crossed his arms and stood his ground. "Put it away before someone gets hurt."

"You're the one that's been taking out our guys," the kid said, his voice wavering. He didn't lower the gun.

"Yeah. That's me. Want an autograph?" Vince grinned.

"I want you dead! Malus killed my brother because of you!"

Vince's smile fell. "What?"

"He's killing the ones that fail to protect their areas. Everyone that fails him." The kid cocked the gun. "I won't fail him."

"Look, I didn't know. You tell me where Malus is, and I'll go kill him slowly." Vince unfolded his arms and brought his hands up in front of his chest.

"You're lying. You don't care if we die," he accused in a small voice, the gun shaking in his grip.

"That isn't true. I haven't killed any of you."

"He's telling the truth," Damian said as he stepped out of the room. "All we want is Malus. No one else has to die." The gun now swung between them. Vince watched as the nervous kid pulled the trigger, the gun pointed at Damian. Vince cursed and pushed Damian out of the way. He tackled the kid, but he used too much force, and a sharp crack echoed throughout the room as the boy's head slammed into the concrete floor.

"No. Fuck. *No!*" Vince shook the kid, trying to get him to react but it was no use. The boy's eyes were unseeing, and it was Vince's fault. He vaguely realized Damian was pulling him away, but he couldn't stop looking at the body. They were almost back when Vince spoke again. "I want Malus."

All Damian gave in response was a curt nod. Thankfully, the information Damian had collected led them right where they needed to be. Vince kept his promise to the nameless kid and killed Malus slowly and painfully.

Back at Damian's bar, he drank... and drank... and drank some more. The memory of the boy's eyes staring up at the ceiling wouldn't go away, no matter how many glasses of whiskey he had. Somehow, he managed to stumble outside and did the one thing he thought might help: he called Jask. The phone rang three times and connected, but any elation Vince felt vanished as the voice on the other end said "hello".

"Of course, you have his phone. Fucking hell." Vince leaned back and slid down the wall, wiping his beard. He could hear fabric shuffling and then the sound of a door closing.

"He's sleeping, Vince. What do you want?" Draz demanded after the noises had stopped.

"Him. I want him. I *need* him." Vince took another drink out of the whiskey bottle.

"You're drunk. You know that's not going to happen."

"No. Because he has *you* now. He doesn't need me or my fuck-ups. And man, did I fuck it up this time," Vince said with a bitter laugh.

"What's wrong? Is it Lee? Your family?" Vince was surprised that Draz sounded so concerned.

"I killed a kid. Couldn't have been a year older than Leota, if that. Barely an adult, and I killed him. I killed his brother too, indirectly. Fuck, why am I telling you this? Not like you're going to tell him. You're not even going to tell him I called..."

"No, I won't. I can't, Vince. You saw what happened, I had to drag him away. Not telling him is for the best."

"Fuck you. Fuck 'for the best'. Fuck absolutely everything." Vince hung up the call and turned off the phone. He couldn't call Johnny to pick him up, there was no cell service at the house. He couldn't drive and risk wrecking their only vehicle, and walking would take all night. He sighed and dropped the bottle on the ground, enjoying the sound it made when it shattered. He sure as hell wasn't staying at the bar. He decided to take a chance on driving, and somehow made it home relatively unscathed just to sleep on the couch again.

When he woke up the next morning, sober with a throbbing head, all he could think about was all the lives lost for nothing. The kid at the base, all the ones Malus had killed for not being able to stop Vince. That blood was on *his* hands.

Leota came to sit next to him. "You're in trouble, aren't you?"

"Me? No, of course not," he lied, rubbing his face.

"You are," she insisted gently. "You can talk to me, Vince. I know you see me as some immature pain in your ass, but I'm not a little kid anymore. I've been on the run, I nearly *died*. And I know trouble when I see it."

"I'm not in trouble. I just... did some things I regret." He almost laughed at how inadequate that was.

She didn't ask what he did, but simply, "Can you stop?"

"Yeah, already have." He barely recalled the drunken conversation he had with Damian, but he knew he told him he was done. With Malus dead, Damian didn't need him, anyway. He pulled his phone out of his pocket and handed it to Lee. "Do me a favor, though. Keep that away from me. Seems I can't be trusted not to drunk dial."

"Hope you don't have Edis' number in here, or I might just end up making it worse." She stared at the phone with a frown on her face. "I hate him, and yet..."

Vince took the phone back immediately. "No. That's... just no. *Edis*, Lee? Really?"

She blushed, looking outright ashamed of herself. "He was cold. And it felt... good. I know I was dying and pretty much everything would've felt good, but... you know how it feels to have an angel heal you. I miss that feeling already."

"Yeah, can't blame you there." Vince let his head fall back on the couch and closed his eyes. "Drazan answered Jask's phone. It was two in the morning. I'm pretty sure they were in bed together. Draz left the room to talk to me. And as for *your* angel crush... the only reason you aren't dead is because he thought he was saving Jask. Looks like falling for the wrong person is a family trait."

"I didn't say I was falling for him." She didn't sound as defensive as he expected her to. "I barely know him. A lot of my memories from that day are... hazy, y'know? But... I remember the look in his eyes. His wings... he was gentle. I didn't expect that. And... nevermind." Lee looked over at Vince and pursed her lips in a strained smile. "I'm sorry about Drazan. But Johnny said they're not really dating... are you sure they were sleeping together?"

"Drazan literally told me Jask was sleeping. I'm assuming that's why he answered and if they're not dating, then they're at least fuck buddies." Vince turned his head to look at her. "Edis wasn't a dick? You sure that wasn't a fever-induced dream?"

Lee nodded. "I'm sure. His words were... fucking mean, but his movements and his hands were *not*. I think he hates me because he thinks I'll be the reason Jask dies." She paused, tucking her knees to her chest. "Maybe Jask just wanted to feel something, and right now, Drazan's probably all he has. If they were telling the truth, then Jask is hiding a lot of things from literal walking lie detectors. It can't be easy."

"He hates you — *us* — because of what we are. Nothing more, nothing less." Vince sighed, he didn't really want to acknowledge the rest of what she said, but knew he needed to, anyway. "And does it make sense that it would hurt less if it wasn't Draz? If it had been some stranger at a bar, I wouldn't have to worry about Jask catching feelings."

"I think it's better because it *is* Drazan. They've been friends for a really long time. If he was going to catch feelings, it would've already happened. I'm sorry, Vince. I know you miss him." She paused, then asked quietly, "Should we move again?"

"No. I'm not letting them push us out of another home. Especially one I've put so much work into. This is ours, and I'll fight anyone that tries to change that." Vince deliberately ignored confirming that he missed Jask. He was sure it was obvious.

After a moment, she stood. "Me too. Now get some sleep... it looks like you need it." She disappeared quietly into her room, leaving him alone with his thoughts.

Vince couldn't go back to sleep if he tried. After a few moments of staring at the ceiling, he got up and made coffee. He might as well get ready for the day.

Jaskian

The bed shifted and Jask's eyes opened. He'd barely been asleep anyway, so even that slight disruption was enough to make him sit up. He looked over and noticed Drazan's form settling back down, and he considered not bothering him, but knew he wouldn't be able to go back to sleep. "You okay?" he asked, sleep lacing his voice.

"Yeah, had to take a call. I didn't mean to wake you." Draz put the phone on the bedside table. "Go back to sleep."

"You know that's not gonna happen, D." Jask rubbed his jaw and looked down at him. "You should get some sleep, at least you'll get the bed to yourself for a few hours." He smiled a little and pushed himself off the mattress, stretching as he stood.

"Jask, you just got to sleep a couple of hours ago. That's why I answered the phone so you wouldn't have to wake up. Come back to bed, I'll sing you a lullaby." Draz grinned.

It was hard to ignore the exhaustion tugging at his bones, but when he slept, he always dreamt of Vince. And waking up to Drazan instead was almost like losing Vince all over again, so he avoided it wherever possible. But he craved comfort — comfort that for some reason, Drazan was still willing to provide — so he climbed back into the bed without argument. "Who was it, anyway? It's the middle of the night."

"No one important." Draz pulled the blanket back over them both.

The lie was faint, but it was there. Jask assumed maybe Drazan finally found someone else and just didn't have the energy to confirm it. He had no right to ask Drazan not to do it, but knowing he'd be alone again soon wasn't something he wanted to look too closely at. "Well go on, then. Sing to me."

"Oh. I wasn't expecting you to actually want that." Draz cleared his throat and started to sing. It wasn't pleasant, and after a couple of bars Jask reached over and clamped a hand over his mouth.

"Okay. Now I'm gonna have nightmares, so thank you for that."

Draz licked his hand and grinned when Jask pulled away. "You're very welcome. Always happy to help."

Jask rolled onto his side facing away from Draz, figuring he deserved a night off from Jask being a giant baby. Sleep didn't come easy, but it did eventually come.

In the morning, he made breakfast for Drazan. The furnace was working well, so he had his shirt draped over his shoulder and moved around in just his boxers. When the food was ready, he yelled for Drazan to get his lazy ass out of bed.

Draz walked in rubbing his eyes. "It's too early for you to be shouting. And why are you naked?" he grumbled as he sat at the table.

"I'm not naked. Are you complaining?" There was no sarcasm behind it, they were still trying to navigate the boundaries of their fake relationship. He started to think maybe he was getting too comfortable, but flipped the bacon and let Drazan answer for himself.

"About the shouting? Yes. The other stuff?" Draz shrugged.

Jask chuckled but got dressed as the bacon finished up, then started on the pancakes. "Sorry, I guess sometimes I forget where the lines are."

"Are there lines anymore?" Draz asked as he stood to pour some coffee. "And speaking of, I have a... proposition."

"Well, we stopped sleeping together, for reasons I don't even think *I* understand. So yeah... there are lines somewhere". Jask frowned as he added some cinnamon to the pancakes. It wasn't as though he wanted Drazan that way, but sex and violence were the only two things he'd found that made him feel anything at all without Vince. "What's your proposition?"

"We should get married." Draz turned to look at him, sipping his coffee.

Jask kept his hands busy. "I can't ask you to do that, D. For me, marriage is pretty much only upside. I get my family off my back, and it's not like I'll ever settle down with anyone else... but for you? I can't saddle you like that. You deserve to be happy, and we both know you're not happy with me." He flipped the pancakes with a frown and stared at them, not wanting to see the look on his friend's face.

"I asked you, not the other way around and really, Jask, what else have I got going for me? No one is gonna want me. I drink too much, curse like a sailor. There's no one..." he paused, taking another drink. "There isn't any angel that would put up with me. At least you're my best friend, that's more than I thought I'd get."

A consolation prize for us both, he thought bitterly. He'd always imagined if he got married, it would be a huge event. He'd get obscenely drunk, embarrass himself and his family, and act like an idiot all in the name of love. And while he loved Drazan, he didn't love him like *that*. But he couldn't deny the benefits of getting married. Rumor was that his father was asking questions, and if that became the case, nothing short of marriage would actually fool him. "Least I can kiss you without puking now, huh? Might've put a damper on the ceremony."

"Yeah, thanks for not throwing up after the sex, by the way. Not sure my ego would've recovered from that. So, that's a yes?" Draz nudged Jask's arm.

"The sex was great, D." Jask knew he was stalling, but actually agreeing to marry someone other than Vince was harder than he thought - even knowing it was fake. "Yeah. Yeah, we can. Thanks, I..." He pulled the pancakes off the skillet and leaned forward against the counter. "You can still sleep with whoever you want. For you, nothing changes."

"What a moving acceptance to my marriage proposal." Draz grabbed some bacon and sat back at the table. "Congratulations, Jaskian. We're engaged!"

"You expect me to be happy I'm ruining your life?" Jask served Drazan and sat down, not hungry anymore. "I know it has to be done, and I'm so grateful for you I could die... but this isn't gonna be fun, D. It's just not." *Especially since you can sleep around and I can't,* he added silently.

"Jask, look at me." Draz waited until Jask looked him in the eye. "You aren't ruining anything. Tell me if I'm lying."

He wasn't, but for some reason, it didn't do much to make him feel better. He smiled a little and decided if Drazan was willing to make this sacrifice for him, the least he could do is make it easier on him. "You're stuck with me, then. No take backs. I just... need ya to tell me what I'm allowed to get away with and what I'm not, you know how handsy I am."

"I feel like that's going to be a day by day discussion," Draz answered honestly. "Also, I know how nice my ass is, so it'd be cruel of me to not let you touch it occasionally."

Jask cracked a smile. "I'd like to see you try and stop me, honestly. I'm bigger than you."

"Not where it counts," Draz smirked.

"That's true..." Jask turned the corners of his lips down briefly. "Guess I'm a lucky man, then. Or, I would be, if we were actually sleeping together in the sexy way."

"Maybe later, if you're a good boy." Draz threw a piece of bacon at him. "Now eat, you'll need all your strength when you take me to family dinner to make the announcement."

Jask knew what that would mean, so he sent a text to his mom and an email to his father. By the time he actually ate his pancakes... they were cold.

Several hours later, Jask tied his long hair back and straightened his tie, glancing in the mirror to watch Drazan as he got dressed. "You should take a blocker too this time. My father will be there."

Draz sighed. "Yeah, probably. Damn." He took one from Jask and swallowed it down with a grimace.

"I'm sorry." Jask doubled up on his, knowing he needed to be rock solid. If Athar found out this was all a sham, he'd kill Drazan, and Jask wasn't about to let that happen. He turned to him once he was dressed and held out his hand. "I owe you big for this, D."

"You don't owe me anything, Jask. If the situation was reversed, I know you wouldn't hesitate to do the same." Draz took his hand easily.

Jask didn't answer out loud, but as he looked at his friend, he knew that wasn't true. He wouldn't be faking a relationship... he'd have killed the people threatening to hurt Drazan, no matter what it took. Part of him was grateful that Draz reacted differently. "Okay, then. Let's go act like the happiest couple of assholes this side of the Dreads." He closed his eyes, and teleported them to his mother's front door.

Before he could even knock, Edis opened the door and stepped out onto the porch, using telepathy to communicate with him directly. *"I've been trying to call you. He asked me how you were still alive. He knows she had the Void."*

A stunned expression spread across Jask's face as he put the pieces together. There was no way Athar could know Leota was ill, unless... "Drazan, this is a mistake," he muttered as quietly as he could. Angelic hearing wasn't perfect, but it was far more pronounced than it had a right to be and he couldn't risk anyone overhearing. "We should go."

Edis gripped his arm, barely making any noise at all. "It's too late. If you run, he'll only be suspicious."

Jask quickly fished one of the blockers out of his pocket and shoved it into his brother's mouth, forming the silent word, "swallow," with his own. Edis looked panicked for a moment but obliged out of instinct.

Draz squeezed his hand. "It's now or never, darling. Smile and let's go tell everyone the good news."

Not seeing another option, Jask held him tight and stepped through the door with a smile he hoped didn't look as forced as it felt. "Hey! Sorry we're late. I find it's getting harder and harder to get out of bed each day." He smirked at Draz, grateful there was more than one reason to be bedridden.

Draz let go of his hand to wrap his arm around him, pulling him into his side, "Darling, it's rude to talk about how *hard* it is in front of your mother." Draz smiled at Jask's parents, then winked at Cidos, who was currently glaring at them both.

Astarte smiled and hugged them tightly. "I'll forgive it. It's good to see you both."

"Dinner's ready," Edis said. "Father is already in the dining room."

Jask nodded and pulled Drazan along, bracing himself for whatever was about to happen. "I'm glad everyone could make it on such short notice. It's been what... two years since our father has come around? Surprised he could clear his schedule."

"Some matters are more important than family," Athar said coldly as everyone entered the room. "And others aren't."

Draz looked like he was about to say something that would've gotten them both killed, but his face broke out into that same charming smile. "Welcome home, Mr. Veris. I trust your trips were pleasant?"

"Of course, Drazan. Not that they're any of your concern." He tilted his head challengingly, and Jask stepped protectively in front of Drazan.

"Good to see you haven't lost your impeccable manners since I last saw you," Jask said sarcastically. He took a seat, pulling Drazan next to him as the others filed in. Dinner was already spread out around the table, and as per Veris custom, Jask served Drazan before serving himself.

Cidos sneered at them like he was about to win some long-fought war. "Jaskian, I'm sure father would love to hear about your recent... adventures. Why don't you tell him all about it?"

"C'mon, Ci," Edis cut in, taking a bite and waving his fork. "It's rude to talk with your mouth full, we should eat first."

"I always knew Edis was the smart twin." Draz took Jask's hand and kissed it before picking up his own fork.

They ate in silence after that, though Jask could feel his father staring at him. When they were done, Drazan and Edis helped his mother clear the table, and Jask adjourned to the living room with his father and Cidos. "I'm assuming one or both of you has something to say, so... say it."

"I've heard about your little indiscretion," his father said with a sneer.

Jask sighed like the comment was nothing more than an inconvenience. "Yes, and it's over. I'm with Drazan now, as it should've been from the beginning."

"What I don't understand is why the girl hasn't been brought here? The bond should've been broken weeks ago."

Laughing quietly, Jask gave the answer he'd practiced a million times and trusted the blockers to do their job. "There's no need. Weaker Veris' of the past might not have been able to fight the bond, but I can. The girl means nothing to me."

"Then there should be no problem with completing the ritual." Cidos smiled at Jask.

He gave his father a pointed look as Drazan came back, silently sitting next to him. "Do you want the turf war? I don't, nor am I excited to be laid up for weeks in recovery from something unnecessary. Unless, of course... you two *want* to see me injured?"

"Of course we don't, you're being dramatic. Recovery wouldn't take nearly that long. You owe it to Drazan, at the very least. The bond could pull you two apart at any moment." His father looked at Draz for back up.

"I have no reason to think Jask would leave me for the girl," Draz said as he took Jask's hand again.

Jask kissed him with a fond smile and turned back to his family. "Interesting, then, that you've both tried to kill her recently. You know what happens if my mate dies before the bond is broken, and yet..." He tilted his head, ignoring the pang of sadness spreading through him and focused on Drazan. "Seems to me my father and brothers want the bond broken so badly, they don't care anymore if I die in the process."

"We were only trying to get you to come to your senses. Plus, sometimes sacrifices must be made." Cidos shrugged.

"Threaten Jask like that again, there *will* be a sacrifice made," Draz warned quietly.

"It is curious that the girl survived both attempts," Jask's father interrupted before the fight could go further.

"It's not curious at all," Jask said, holding Drazan's hand like an actual lifeline. "She found a healer for the Void, and... oh, thank you, by the way, for admitting that was *your* fault. I hadn't been positive, but since you didn't deny trying to kill her, I'll assume it was your handiwork?"

Athar merely pursed his lips. "No angel would've agreed to save her. It shouldn't have been possible."

"Ah, I guess the demons are smarter and more resourceful than you think. Either way, I'd like to put this mess behind us. Drazan, would you like to do the honors?"

"Oh, I get to tell them?" Draz smiled and waited a moment for everyone to focus on Jask and himself. He smiled brightly at the Veris clan as he announced, "I asked Jask to marry me. He said yes."

Astarte squealed with delight and immediately launched into a list of things she needed to do, barely even in the room before she was hurrying back out to grab her notebook. Edis relaxed, clapping happily and ignoring the dual glares they were receiving from Cidos and Athar. "I knew it would happen soon. You two are meant for each other."

"We are," Jask agreed, banking heavily on the blockers still being effective even after a large dinner. He smiled dopily at Drazan and pulled him into a kiss, doing his best to sell it.

Draz deepened the kiss, tilting Jask's head back. They were interrupted by Edis clearing his throat. "We don't need a repeat of the last time, thank you. You can't kick us out of here."

He hadn't had the motivation to get himself off in days, which proved to be a blessing. Jask's body responded eagerly to Drazan, so when they broke apart, the evidence of his lust was noticeable. "Sorry, Ed. Don't worry... we don't invite you on the honeymoon." He grinned, facing his father again with the last ounce of resolve he had. "Now do you see why breaking the bond isn't necessarily? Draz and I are entering into one of our own, and I'd like to be healthy for it."

"I suppose we'll see." His father shrugged.

Draz pulled Jask a little closer. "Let's talk more about the honeymoon part."

"Not here. Let's go home," Jask said, his voice surprisingly steady. "I think I've been a good boy, right?"

"Yes, absolutely," Draz stood and pulled Jask with him. "Thank you for dinner. Now we're going to go have dessert."

Edis was laughing as Cidos looked ready to kill someone. "What's the matter, Ci?" his twin asked. "Jealous no one's ever called you a good boy before?"

The two broke out in a wrestling match, which Jask took as the distraction he needed to get them out of there and safely back in their own living room. The moment they landed, Jask collapsed on the couch.

"That was fun." Draz sat next to him, closing his eyes and letting out a heavy sigh.

It had been the opposite of fun, and Jask got the distinct impression that Drazan had no intention of sleeping with him, despite his earlier promise about him being good. But at that moment, he couldn't bring himself to care. As nice as the release would be, he'd just gotten confirmation that both his father and brother were willing to kill him, and while that was devastating, at least now he knew that he wouldn't end up having to marry Drazan. It was clear they'd never stop, and if Jask had any hope at all of saving Vince and Leota, he'd have to make a move in less time than it would take to plan a wedding.

He just hoped he was ready.

Thirteen

Drazan

Draz waited until he was sure Jask was asleep to step into the bathroom. He took the knife and sliced his palm open, putting the required symbols onto the mirror and reciting the incantation from memory. He waited for the glow to fade before climbing through and exiting into a dirty bar bathroom. He texted the person he was supposed to meet and straightened his clothes. He was still in the suit from dinner, so he was going to stick out like a sore thumb, but nothing could be done about it now. Draz put his phone back in his pocket and walked out, ordering two beers.

Twenty minutes later, he heard a familiar voice behind him. "I wasn't expecting to see you again so soon. Miss me already?"

Draz smiled and turned, holding out the second beer. "I'd be lying if I said I didn't."

"You look good," Johnny said with a smile, then leaned in to kiss him. "Sorry it took me so long, had to make sure Vince was knocked out."

Draz pulled Johnny in for a much more heated kiss before letting him go. "Yeah. Jask drank almost an entire bottle of bourbon before I could get him in bed."

"Is he doing any better?" Johnny asked as he sat down.

Draz dropped his head to the bar. "Jask needs Vince, but his dad is back in town because of all of this. It's the *worst* possible time for them to even think about seeing each other."

A comforting, warm hand touched his shoulder. "How bad is it?"

"Well." Draz turned his head to look at Johnny. "His father and brother don't care if he dies, if they find out Edis helped, they'll kill him too, oh, and Jask and I are getting married." The last part was said in one breath as quick as Draz could get away with it. He half hoped Johnny hadn't heard it.

His face fell, which ruined that hope. "Oh. First of all, that's terrible, and I want to make that clear so it doesn't sound like I'm a horrible person when I immediately segway to my next question. Are you guys still... sleeping together?"

"Technically, yes, because we're sleeping in the same bed. Cidos has some kind of obsession with outing us, so if he shows up in the middle of the night..." he trailed off, sure that Johnny could put the pieces together. "But, we are no longer having sex. Just the one time."

Johnny relaxed, grabbing the front of Drazan's shirt and pulling him in for a kiss. "Good. I'm sorry, that has to be a weird line to toe with him. Does he know, or is he just accepting the fact that you two aren't kissing or touching anymore?"

"Yeah, about that. We are still kissing and occasionally touching, but only in front of his family."

The frown on Johnny's face was kind of adorable. "I'd go home and make out with Vince to get even with you, but he'd punch me in the face."

Draz laughed. "Please don't kiss Vince. For multiple reasons, but I don't want to have to fight him if he does punch you."

Johnny kissed him again, slower and deeper that time. "Just remember me when you do."

Draz dropped his head to Johnny's shoulder, wrapping his arm around him. "You could come back with me. I have an apartment you can stay in." He knew Johnny would say no, so he wasn't sure why he asked.

"You know I can't leave Vince. He got involved with something he shouldn't have, and it's affecting him worse than I thought it would. He needs me." Johnny kissed his temple. "But, I wish I could. I haven't stopped thinking about you since you showed up with Jask to save Miss Leota."

"You're talking about the kid? He called Jask and I picked up before the ring could wake him. Vince was drunk, said he'd fucked up." Draz pulled away enough to look at Johnny, who nodded.

"I don't know how to help him. He's gone through the usual list... sex, alcohol, violence. All it's doing is making him spiral."

"Sex?" Draz frowned. "Not with you, though, right? I mean, not that I even have a right to complain, but..."

Johnny shook his head quickly. "No, never. I offered once, before you and I started whatever this is. He laughed at me so hard I almost left him. I just wanted him to feel better."

"Yeah, that's what happened with me and Jask. This entire situation is so screwed up." He turned and waved the bartender down, ordering them something stronger. "We gotta find a way to fix it."

They sat in silence while they knocked back a drink, and Johnny finally said, "Let's just get them back together. Between the two of us, we can help protect them, right? It'll just get worse if we don't. There's no way Jask would be able to sneak around once you two are married, and if you're not even kissing him unless it's in front of his family, he's going to be miserable. And I think Vincenzo learned the hard way that no one but Jask can satisfy him."

"Vince told Jask to never come back. I read the texts." Draz shook his head.

Johnny grimaced. "I sent those texts. He told me to, but he wasn't strong enough to do it himself. He felt it when you two had sex. It destroyed him."

"That makes me feel extra terrible. Alright, you go home and grab Vince, I'll get Jask. Let's get the band back together. Where are we doing this?"

"It sounds like they're both extremely drunk. Should we wait until tomorrow?" Johnny asked.

"Does that mean I get you to myself tonight?"

Johnny's eyes lit up, even in the darkness of the bar. "Really? You'll stay this time? I thought you'd have to go back."

"I do, but I'll stay as long as I can," Draz admitted, running his thumb over Johnny's cheek.

"Then I'll take what I can get."

They didn't waste any more time at that bar. They went to the same motel they always did and spent the next few hours taking what they needed from each other, but eventually, Drazan knew he needed to go. Johnny didn't want to let him up, though. "Draz... he'll be fine for one night, right?"

He kissed Johnny again. "With my luck, it'll be the one night Cidos shows up. I have to go."

"Fuck. Okay." Johnny slowly got up to get dressed again. "We'll have time tomorrow, right? Once we get them in the same room, you and I can sneak off?"

"Absolutely. I don't want to be there when they decide to kiss and make up," Draz said as he reluctantly got dressed, too. When they were both done, he pulled Johnny into one last kiss.

"Okay, okay. Go." Johnny pushed him toward the bathroom and stood there with his hands in his pockets, rocking on the balls of his feet. "If all goes well, you're staying with me tomorrow night, Drazan."

"Guess we'll have to make sure it all goes well. then," He grinned and then walked into the bathroom. He repeated the ritual on the mirror and gave Johnny one last look before going home. He cleaned up the mess left from the first time and quietly crawled back into bed with Jask. Somehow, he managed not to disturb him.

In the morning, however, Jask rolled closer to him and wrapped his arm over him.

Draz woke up at the movement and looked down at Jask's arm. "Shit." A few weeks ago, this wouldn't have been a big deal. He would've even cuddled back, but doing that after a night with Johnny felt wrong on multiple levels. He lifted Jask's arm slowly and tried to roll out of bed without waking him.

"Draz." Jask sat up slowly. "Why do you keep doing that? When you said 'day to day conversation', did you just mean you had to figure out every day if you wanted to touch me or not?" He held up his hand to stop Drazan's response. "Actually... don't answer that. It's not your job to make me feel better, I get it. Shouldn't have tried. Good morning." He pushed himself out of bed and headed for the bathroom.

"Jask, that isn't what's going on," Drazan said, feeling like an asshole.

He paused with his hand on the door. "I can smell it, Draz. I know you found someone else. I'm happy for you, I guess I just gotta get used to it." He entered the bathroom and shut the door behind him, but the shattering glass made it pretty damn clear what happened.

Draz dropped back onto the bed and covered his face with a pillow. Jask had said "someone else" like they were actually a couple. He couldn't take Jask back to Vince until they had a very real conversation about where they stood with each other, which wouldn't be awkward at all. Draz threw the pillow across the room and stood up, then walked to the bathroom and knocked on the door with a sigh. "Jask?"

The toilet flushed and he opened the door, but there was no sign of a broken glass. He smiled a little and stepped out, gesturing inside. "All yours, D. I'll start the coffee."

"Before you do that, can we talk?" Draz asked, taking his hand to stop him from leaving.

"You really wanna talk before I've had coffee?" Jask raised his eyebrows, but pulled his hand back and leaned against the door. "Talk."

Draz opened his mouth and then closed it. He stepped away from Jask — out of striking distance — and began again, "Vince is in trouble."

All the light left Jask's eyes, but his face didn't change. "Your point? He rejected me. He's his own problem now, I'm doing everything I can for him. And in case you haven't noticed recently, it's taking all I've got." He headed toward the door, and asked again, "Coffee?"

"No, look, he called me. Well, technically he called *you*, but I answered. He needed you, and I told him no," Draz confessed, watching Jask.

He laughed bitterly. "What, you wanted to have your cake and eat it too? Feel bad for your boyfriend, then." He shook his head, his hand flexing into a fist at his side, but he shoved the bedroom door open and headed out to the kitchen.

Draz followed. "Damn it, Jask, this isn't about me. I was trying to protect you! I knew you'd go running to him. So I took the call, told him no, and erased it from your phone."

"Okay." His voice was lethal thunder, but quiet as a summer rain. "Consider me protected." Jask started the coffee with practiced, quick movements, and then leaned forward against the counter and refused to look at him. "You can go back wherever you were last night, and three nights ago, and last week, and the week before."

"You're making it sound like I'm cheating on you. Look, I just..." Draz stepped forward, reaching out to put his hand on Jask's arm. "I think you should go see Vince. That's all."

Jask didn't even glance at his hand. "You know I can't do that. I don't care if he called or not, he'll just end up kicking me out and I can't go through it again. I'm barely hanging on as it is." He jerked away from Drazan and grabbed a coffee mug. "You're all I have, D. I lost everything because of this. My mate, my family, my house, my job. My freedom. And I get it, you lost a lot, too, and you didn't have to. But all I had was what little you were willing to give me. And that's gone now, too."

"What little I'm willing to give? I'm giving you everything! Fuck, this is not going well. I was talking to Johnny, Vince didn't send those texts. He couldn't. He wants you back. Just go talk to him. I'll go with you, and if you really want to leave after, I'll piggyback this time and get us out."

Tears welled in Jask's eyes and he shook his head, gripping the mug hard enough it cracked. "I can't do it again. Every fucking time I get close to him, we fall apart, and it's harder for me to pick up the pieces. I'm sorry you had to give me everything, Drazan, and that your little midnight rendezvous with whoever you're fucking aren't enough for you. Call off the fucking wedding. Go live your life. At least one of us should."

Draz groaned and rubbed his face. "Jask, I need you to remember that you're my best friend and I love you. Okay? Okay." He waited until

Jask turned to him, presumably to argue, and hit him hard across the face. Jask collapsed and Draz caught him, tossing him over his shoulder. He was surprised that it only took one hit, but he carried him back to the bathroom and texted Johnny that he was ready. After one last look to make sure Jask was still out, he started the spell.

Vince

Vince was sitting on the porch when Johnny pulled up in the truck. He waited for his friend to get out and halfway to the door before he spoke. "Couldn't sleep last night. Thought I might go for a ride to clear my head. Imagine my surprise when both my best friend and my truck were missing."

His friend nodded a little, fidgeting with his fingers as he approached, then tossed Vince the keys. "We should talk, I'm glad you're awake."

"Does it have anything to do with where you were last night? Johnny, if you're fucking around with Damian..." Vince put the keys in his pocket.

Johnny wrinkled his nose. "I'm offended. No, I wasn't with Damian. I... was with Drazan."

Vince blinked and nodded slowly. First Draz took his boyfriend, and now he'd taken his best friend. Vince stood up and walked inside without another word.

"Wait!" Johnny followed him quickly, pushing through the door before it closed. "It's not what you think. None of this is what you think. Please, Vince."

"How could this not be what I think? Jask told me to fuck off so he could be with Draz. Now you're sneaking off to... what, exactly? Drink with him? Pick up girls? How come every time I turn around there's an angel causing problems?" Vince began making breakfast with aggressive, rough movements.

Johnny kept his distance. "Jaskian is *not* dating Drazan. It's been fake from the beginning, and Jask has been eating himself alive trying to get to you. But you — well, me, but you — told him never to come back."

"You heard them here, Johnny. They're sleeping together. I fell off the fucking roof because of it. And I'm pretty sure you saw them cuddling on the couch." Vince motioned to the living room as if they were still in there. "So, yeah. I told him not to come back because seeing him with Draz makes me physically ill."

"Vince. Listen to me. I'm a hundred percent positive about this. Drazan and Jask slept together *once*, because Drazan was trying anything he could to make Jask feel better. It didn't work, and they didn't do it again. Edis was here, they were putting on a show - to protect *you*, to protect Miss Leota. Listen to reason."

"Your new best friend told you all of that?" Vince didn't look over at Johnny as he scrambled the eggs a little harder than necessary. Panic rose in his chest because if what Johnny was saying was true, then he told Jask not come back for nothing. That was a mistake he didn't think he could fix.

Johnny let out an exasperated sigh and took a noticeable step back. "He's not my best friend. He's... well, we haven't exactly put a title on it, but... he's my boyfriend. I know he's not sleeping with Jask, because he's sleeping with me."

Vince set the bowl down and turned to fully face Johnny. "I'm sorry. You're what?"

Holding up his hands defensively, Johnny's eyes widened a little. "I'm sleeping with Drazan. I've been sneaking out every few days since they saved Miss Leota. Jask loves you, he's half-dead without you."

"I don't... you're... with *Drazan*? How did this even happen? You've met him twice!"

Johnny swallowed. "Well, the first time I didn't think much of it. The second time, though, he was looking at me like he wanted to eat me when he wasn't putting on a show for Edis and Jask. Again, didn't think a whole lot of it, until he left, then I couldn't really think of anything else. I reached out to make sure Jask was okay, one thing led to another, and here we are. Please don't hit me."

Vince sat at the table. "I'm not gonna hit you. Johnny, what if he's playing both of you?"

"Wow." Johnny laughed a little bitterly. "He's not playing anyone. He asked Jask to marry him to get Athar and Cidos off Jask's back, I know all about it. And judging by his... *appetite*... he's not getting any from that arrangement."

"Fuck. So you're telling me I fucked this up, too. He was right there, Johnny. He was trying to get back to me. I told him not to come back and then I fucked the bartender."

Sadness crossed his friend's face. "Well, the good news is that you're going to see him. Soon. He should be here" — he checked a watch he wasn't wearing — "any minute."

"Why would he be coming here?" Vince asked, but the answer was interrupted by a loud crash coming from their bathroom.

"A little help?" Drazan's voice echoed through the house.

Johnny smiled nervously at Vince and then bolted toward the bathroom. Once he was out of sight, Vince heard a hushed conversation, a grunt, and then Johnny came back into view, helping Drazan suspend what appeared to be an unconscious Jaskian. "He's alive," Johnny said quickly.

"Son of a bitch." Vince was in front of Jask in an instant. He lifted Jask's face by his chin and saw the mark on his cheek. "You fucking hit him?" Vince pulled Jask away from them both and moved him to the couch.

"Come on, sweetheart, wake up."

"He'll be fine. A hit from me isn't going to do shit to someone as strong as him in the long run," Drazan assured him.

"One more word from you, and I'll blast you with a fireball. I don't care who you're sleeping with." Vince didn't even look at Draz as he spoke, checking Jask over.

Slowly, Jask blinked his eyes open, then smiled and abruptly closed them again. "Fucker finally killed me, huh?"

Vince couldn't help it, he laughed. "Nope, not dead yet. Just got sucker punched. Can you sit up?"

"I *told* him Jask would be fine," Draz whispered to Johnny.

"Cut him some slack, he's had a rough morning," Johnny muttered back.

Jask opened his eyes again and grinned, reaching up to touch Vince's face. "First of all, fuck you for those texts. Second of all..." He let out a breath and lunged forward, kissing him heatedly. Vince put both hands on Jask's face and climbed onto his lap.

"This should probably be the part where we leave, right?" Draz asked.

"Wait." Vince pulled back, taking a breath. "We gotta talk. Right? I mean... Johnny said you're getting married and a bunch of other shit I'm having trouble remembering."

"Can we talk later? God, you feel good." Jask ran his hands over Vince's body and shuddered. "Need you, Vin. The rest can wait." He kissed him again, wrapping both arms tightly around him.

"Yeah, we should... go," Johnny said. "Come on."

Vince heard Johnny and Draz leave, but all he could focus on was Jask. "I missed you. I can't let you go again, Jask."

"So don't. I'm here. If you think I've got the strength to ever leave your side again, you're sadly mistaken." Jask buried his face in Vince's chest. "Fuck, I missed how warm you are."

Vince held him there for a moment longer before standing up and pulling Jask with him. "Mom and Lee are at the beach, but they could be back any second. We can't stay in here."

Jask followed willingly like a lost puppy. "Bedroom? Tokyo? Paris?"

"Bedroom, don't want to wait for the travel time on the others." Vince led him into the room and closed the door behind them, then yanked his shirt off over his head and kissed his mate again.

One by one, Jask's powers stripped away the rest of their clothes until finally, there was nothing between them but skin. Jask picked him up and spun around, gently laying him down on the bed and kissing over his jaw and down to his neck.

Vince guided his hand into Jask's hair, running his other one up his spine. "Your wings. Let me see them."

They carefully unfurled from his back and extended out, covering almost the entire length of the room. "I don't advise touching them," Jask said with a smirk. "It's been too long for... everything. I won't last with your fingers in my feathers." He dipped down, teasing Vince's nipple with his teeth.

Vince moaned. "You can't tell me that, now all I want to do is touch them." He ran his fingers very lightly over the wings, making Jask twitch.

"I lied, I don't care. Touch them. They missed you. I missed you." He kissed lower, nipping Vince's hip and ghosting his lips over his length.

There was nothing better in this world than the feeling of Jask's mouth. He rolled his hips one more time before moving his other hand to a wing joint, shivering with pleasure and trying to move Jask off of him. "Wait, stop. Trade with me. Want to taste you."

He shook his head and fought Vince's grip, trying to suck him back in. "After."

Vince laughed and pulled Jask up, kissing him before grinning up at him. "Same time?"

"You are a genius." Jask kissed him again and then flipped around, straddling Vince's face. He didn't waste any time, licking over his length and taking him deep.

"Fuck!" Vince gripped Jask's thighs and took a breath before returning the favor. He moaned around Jask as he felt the back of his throat. If Jask kept that up, *he* was going to be the one that didn't last.

Jask started moving, jerking his hips up and thrusting back down, sliding along Vince's tongue and shoving into his throat. Each time, he mocked the movement on Vince's cock, taking him deeper until they were both fully buried.

Vince slid his hands up Jask's ass back into his wings. He planted his feet so he could circle his hips while he pressed against Jask's length with his tongue, and all it took was a handful of seconds of that before Jask was coming with a growl.

Swallowing him down with a moan, Vince followed seconds later. Jask pulled away and flipped himself around again, and Vince latched onto him, wrapping his arms and legs around him. "You leave this time, I'm coming with you."

"I'm tired of fighting it, Vin," Jask whispered, holding him tight. "I wasn't kidding when I said I don't think I have the strength to leave again."

Vince buried his face in Jask's neck. "Are you really marrying Drazan?"

"Apparently not. I was going to, but if I'm staying with you, there's no point in marrying him." Jask's wings stretched out and closed around Vince's body. "I didn't want to, anyway."

Vince relaxed. "You know that means you can't go back? They'll know."

Jaskian

He'd been hoping to avoid this part of the conversation for longer than twenty minutes, but in the end, he wasn't surprised. Jask owed Vince a long, *long* explanation. "Yeah, Vin. I know I can't go back. You got room for two more here? Drazan won't be able to go back either, and after everything he's done for us, I can't leave him behind."

Vince huffed a laugh. "We don't even have room for the four of us, but we'll figure it out. I'll talk to Damian if I have to."

"Who?" Jask frowned, pulling back a little bit.

Vince sighed and sat up, running a hand down his face. "Draz really didn't tell you?"

Jask blinked, trying to remember his conversation with Drazan before he was knocked out. "He told me you were in trouble and that you needed me, but no, he didn't go into details. I didn't really give him a chance to, I... freaked out on him a little bit."

Vince frowned at him. "What's a *little bit*?" He was obviously trying to change the subject, but Jask knew if he had any hope of fixing any of this, he had to tell the whole truth.

"Maybe more than a little bit." He grew quieter, but relayed the conversation to Vince. When he was done, he looked away. "And then he knocked me out and brought me here."

"Fuck, you didn't even want to be here." Vince laid back on the bed. "I mean, you're right. It was — *is* — my problem."

Jask stayed still, giving Vince his space. "It's not that I didn't want to be here, it's that I thought I *couldn't* be here. I felt it when you rejected me. And when you moved on. And then Drazan started sneaking around and I just..." He looked down at his hands. "I wasn't in a great place. I'm still not. I know I deserve all of it and then some, but laying in the bed I made is easier said than done, I guess. Who's Damian?" he asked again.

"Moved on?" Vince looked at him like he'd lost his mind. He sat back up. "Jask, I didn't *move on*. I mean, I fucked a bartender who's name I still don't know, and then after that, I basically tried to get myself killed. I rejected you because I thought you were happy with Drazan, and seeing that destroyed me. I couldn't watch him hang all over you and not want to snap his neck. And Damian? He found me that same night." Vince stopped talking and looked down, his hands twisting in the blanket.

Slowly, he told Jask about Malus and everything he'd done. The words seemed more forced near the end. "I killed him, Jask. He was basically a child. I... I didn't mean to." He looked up then, his face full of despair.

It was hard for Jask to pin down one particular emotion, but he knew in that moment, it wasn't about him. He brought their bodies together and planted his chin on Vince's head. "You didn't kill him. You were trying to stop both of them from dying, if anything... *Damian* killed him, he started all of this."

Vince wrapped his arms around Jask, holding him close. "No,

Damian takes care of his people. That's all he was trying to do. I killed Malus."

Jask furrowed his brows, but held him. "Vince, he wanted you to murder someone. He's taking over, how do you not see that he's a problem?"

"Because he's helping people. People like me." Vince pulled back to look at Jask. "And I told him I was done. So, it's over."

"Then let it be over, sweetheart. What happened to that kid wasn't your fault." Jask still had a bad feeling about Damian; it sounded like he wasn't doing anything but using Vince, but he also knew he wasn't going to make any progress with that conversation just yet.

Vince sighed and dropped his head back to Jask's chest. "It was, but I really don't want to fight when I just got you back. Speaking of, I should probably go tell Mom and Lee you're here."

He nodded, planting his lips to Vince's head. "And I need to talk to Drazan."

Vince kissed Jask one more time, slow and gentle, before standing and pulling on his pants. He held out his hand. "Together?"

"Actually, Vin... I think the conversation I need to have with D would be better in private. And after everything that happened, I don't know if I wanna see the look on your mom's and Lee's faces when you tell them I'm back to fuck their world up again." He took Vince's hand anyway and stood, using his grace to dress himself. "I won't leave the property."

Vince didn't look pleased, but he agreed to the compromise. He opened the door to the sight of Johnny and Drazan making out on the couch.

"What the *fuck?*" Jask barreled past Vince, his eyes wide. "Are you — is this — *seriously?*"

"You didn't know?" Vince asked as he walked out behind him.

Draz stood up. "I didn't exactly get a chance to tell him. Jask, I can explain."

Every part of him knew he didn't have a right to be mad. He knew that, he *did...* and yet. "Wow. So, the demon kid I spent years searching for is sucking face with my fake fiancé." That alone was fine, and he was happy for them both... but Drazan had been sneaking around for weeks. The fact that he didn't trust Jask enough to tell him hurt, and also made him change his mind about the conversation he'd been about to have with him. "Congratulations guys, seriously. Makes it a lot easier for me to tell you you gotta stay here." He nodded to Drazan, then looked at Vince. "Guess I'll come with you after all."

"Stay here? What do you mean we're staying here?" Draz didn't sound upset, just confused.

Jask laughed a little incredulously. "You fucking knocked me out and brought me to my *mate*. What did you think was gonna happen here, Drazan? Course, now" — he gestured to Draz and Johnny — "it all makes sense. You get me outta your hair and get to be with Johnny. Clever move on your part." He knew he sounded like an ass, but Jask was starting to feel a little out of control. It didn't seem like anyone around him had their feet on solid ground, and now that he was here, he was going to have to make a move on his family. He couldn't put it off anymore.

"You know what, this is starting to sound a lot like the fight we were having before I knocked your ass out. I'm not trying to get you out of my hair, I was trying to do what's right! Why can't you see that?"

"It's fucking *Johnny*, Drazan! Why didn't you just fucking tell me? Did you think I wouldn't understand? You thought it was better to let me try to get *something* out of you night after night, just for you to push me away or disappear completely?" He realized then it actually *did* sound like he was accusing Drazan of cheating. "Fuck." He turned, heading out the front door but didn't move off the porch, he just needed air. Things were spiraling for no reason, and he needed to get himself under control before he said or did something he would regret. "What the hell is wrong with me?" he asked himself.

The door opened and then Vince pulled him into his arms. "Nothing's wrong with you."

"There's plenty wrong with me, Vin. Drazan's the last person I should be yelling at right now, I should be happy for him. I just feel like a dick and wish he would've told me." He squeezed Vince a little tighter, curling his fingers against his back.

"Yeah, don't think we aren't going to talk about that night after night comment later, but playing devil's advocate here... Maybe he didn't tell you because he felt guilty being happy when he knew you were miserable."

Jask sighed. "Look. You gotta understand. I told him he could be with someone else, it's not like I ever wanted him that way, even before I met you. But when he asked me to marry him, I knew it was over for me. He could sneak around, but I'd never be able to. I'd never trust anyone other than you and Draz not to rat me out, and I couldn't have you. Yeah, it was stupid and selfish, but I tried with Drazan. More than once, but once was all he gave me. After a while I stopped trying to sleep with him and just wanted... comfort." Jask felt like an idiot as he stared at their hands and felt the tears welling in his eyes again. "And I didn't want to be the reason Drazan was miserable too, and I thought maybe if we just..." He shook his head, sucking in a breath. "But even that, he was pushing me away. If he'd have just told me, I'd have stopped trying."

"I'm sorry, Jask. I wish I could've been there so you didn't have to try in the first place. You want to talk to him? I'll take Johnny to go talk to my family."

"He's got the same enhanced hearing that I do. Unless you somehow soundproofed the walls, he heard me." Jask sat down and fidgeted with his nails. "Go on. Warn them before it's too late."

Vince leaned down and kissed the top of his head before walking down to the beach. Johnny followed silently a few moments later and Draz sat next to him. "I'm sorry. I should've told you."

"Don't worry about it, guys. Seriously. I'm happy for both of you, I'm sure it wasn't easy to make the sacrifices that you did. I just feel like an ass about it." Jask smiled a little, watching the way they leaned into each other. "You two have nothing standing in your way. That's good."

"We don't, you're right. Which conveniently frees us up to help you and Vince." Draz put his hand on Jask's shoulder, and Jask offered him a nod.

He watched Vince's retreating form. "Johnny, you might wanna put that offer to use and go help him. Something tells me the women in this house won't be happy to see me."

"Right." Johnny got up and started walking away, but stopped and turned to kiss Drazan before hurrying after Vince.

Once he was out of earshot, Jask turned to his friend. "You know what has to be done now, right?"

"War, basically," Draz leaned back on his elbows. "Question is, do we strike first or build a defense?"

Jask let out a breath that sounded a lot more like a whine, but knew his friend would understand. "Do you really wanna sit back and wait for them to come to us?" He flicked his wrist and conjured a ball of energy in his palm, focusing on it as it grew and shrank at his will. "Someone has to save my mom. That's my only request."

"I'll make sure she stays safe," Draz promised. "You know the twins and your father... they won't stop. They'll fight to the end. Are you sure you're ready for that?"

"You're asking me if I'm ready to kill my father and my only siblings?" He laughed a little, staring at the beach where he could still faintly see Vince and the others. "I don't know, honestly. But it's not just about me and Vince anymore. It's Leota and Amaranth and you and Johnny... and everyone that'll come after us. If I end the Veris line, the curse ends, too. So yeah, Drazan. Whether I'm ready or not, it has to be done. It should've been done generations ago, but if I have to be the asshole... then I have to be the asshole. I just hope the rest of you can forgive me when it's done."

Fourteen

Vince

The elation that Vince felt at having Jask so close again was making him dizzy. He couldn't stop touching him when he was near and when he wasn't, Vince normally had his eyes on Jask's ass. That's where they were right now, watching Jask bend over to hammer in the stakes for the tent they'd be sharing later. Vince knew he should be helping his mate, but Jask was so damn distracting. There was a smack to the back of his head and he glared up at Drazan.

"Stop looking at my best friend like he's a piece of meat," Drazan said with a grin.

"Yeah, ditto, asshole." Vince nodded over to Johnny, who was currently working on the house shirtless.

Drazan's eyes were immediately glued to the demon. "Fair point. You're a worthy adversary, Vincenzo."

"I don't know if I'll survive living in a small space with you." Vince sighed and walked over to Jask, stepping behind him and fitting himself against Jask's ass.

Jask wiggled back, smirking as he looked back over his shoulder. "Can I get the tent up before you fuck me?"

"I'm already pitching a tent." Vince wrapped his arms around Jask and kissed his neck. "See what I did there?"

With a wave of Jask's hand, the tent erected itself. He turned to face

Vince and kissed him as he backed them up into it. "See what *I* did there?"

"To be honest, no. I was still looking at you," Vince kissed down the line of Jask's jaw to his neck. He couldn't seem to get enough of Jask, no matter what he did. "Jask, I gotta tell you something. I think I love you." He hoped Jask heard the teasing note in his voice as he kept up the kisses.

Laughing, Jask grabbed him and flipped them both, laying Vince down and biting his lip. "Just now figured that out, huh?" He rutted against him, lacing their fingers and pinning their hands above Vince's head.

"I knew I was feeling something. Seem to be feeling something extra now, too." He lifted his hips to match Jask's rhythm.

Jask let out a soft moan and tipped his head down, moving a little faster. "Shit. Push me off of you or I'm gonna end up coming like this... you feel so good under me."

Vince didn't have to be told twice. He flipped them and straddled Jask's waist. "You realize it's the middle of the day and our friends are fifteen feet away?"

"I do, yeah." Jask pulled him down into a kiss and slid a hand over his waist, sending their clothes to a pile on the ground next to them. "I'll fight every single one of them if they try to interrupt, I need you, Vin." He reached between them to touch Vince gently, just teasing him. "Don't you need me?"

"Always need you, Jask." Vince moved back until their lengths were lined up and took them both in hand. He squeezed lightly as he thrust forward, and Jask's eyes fluttered closed as they rubbed together. They tried to say silent, but each passing second had them moving a little faster, becoming a little needier.

"Wanna be inside of you, Vin. Ride me."

Vince gazed hungrily down at Jask's naked body. He thought back to the night they met, and the fantasies he'd had since then about having Jaskian just like this. Under him, willing, and utterly his. He lifted himself up as Jask's grace surged through him, then bit his lip with a sly smile as he sank back down and split himself open. Even with the magic, it was an overwhelmingly powerful feeling, and Vince lost himself in it more than once before he finally started moving.

With a soft whine, Jask rocked up to bury himself deeper, the muscles in his body flexing as he tried to control himself. "Not gonna sound-proof. Wanna see how quiet we can be, and if not... I want them to hear it." He reached to close his hand around Vince's cock with a dangerous gleam in his eyes.

Vince moved in slow circles and cursed quietly before stopping completely. "Gonna need you to be quiet, because the noises you make? Those are only for me, sweetheart." He leaned down and kissed Jask, tangling a hand in his long hair and tilting his head back so he could slide his tongue between those gorgeous teeth. He felt his mate's moan in his bones as he started moving again, drowning in the cold waters of Jask's touch. Moving his lips to the sweet spot on Jask's neck, he trailed his fingers over the sculpted muscles of his torso and sent small, quick bursts of power through him.

"*Vin,*" Jask gasped, his free hand fisting in the sheet above his head.

He hushed him, but couldn't manage to stay quiet himself as the feeling of Jask completely filling him made him unravel. Vince leaned back, planting his hands on those thick thighs as Jask sped up.

Everything about it was perfect, from the angle to the intensity of his mate's gaze. With a muffled grunt, he painted Jask's chest with his release.

Groaning desperately, Jask licked his thumb clean and stopped holding back — something Vince hadn't even realized he'd been doing. He fucked into him hard enough the sound echoed around them, and when he came, the very ground below them trembled.

Somewhere behind them, Leota started swearing loudly. It broke any lingering haze the two were under and Jask huffed a laugh as he pulled Vince into a kiss. "Well, I guess we know how she feels about it."

When they came out of the bathroom a little later sharing private smiles, Amaranth already had lunch waiting on the table. Vince and Jask took their places across from everyone, and would've ignored the way Lee was looking at them if it weren't for the bags under her eyes. Vince studied her a little more closely, noting the paleness in her cheeks. "You feeling okay?"

"Of course. I'm fine." She smiled but it didn't quite reach her eyes.

"You're not lying, right? Jask said last time that if we'd caught it earlier, he could've helped."

"No, Vincenzo, mind your business," Leota sighed. He glanced over at Jask in concern and Jask's hand made its way to his knee.

"She's fine. There's no trace of the Void," Jask assured him quietly.

Vince relaxed a little when the six of them managed to have a peaceful lunch, but he wasn't stupid. There was no way the peace would last with everyone stuck there, especially if he had to put up with Draz on a normal basis. The tent was a great temporary fix, but it wouldn't last long. Vince needed to talk to Damian. He ran a hand down his face and went to find Jask.

"I have a favor to ask," he said quietly as he walked up next to him.

"Anything, Vin." Jask looked over with a small, sincere smile. "There's nothing in this world I wouldn't give you. What's up?"

"I need to go into town and talk to someone. I want you to stay here and keep an eye on the girls."

He nodded a little, his eyes flicking to Vince's lips. "Who is it?"

"I should've known you'd ask. It's Damian."

Jask paused, then shrugged slightly. "Sure, I'll stay back. But you're taking Drazan with you."

"Why the hell would I do that?"

"Because I don't trust Damian. Arguably, Drazan is more powerful than Johnny, so as bodyguards go... he's the better option. Unless you'd prefer *I* go with you." Jask smiled with his mouth closed, looking smug.

Vince really didn't want to spend any extended amount of time with Drazan, but had his own reasons for not taking his mate. "I don't need a bodyguard, Jask. There's nothing to worry about, and I'd feel safer with you here, so you going with me isn't really an option."

"Then Drazan's going with you, and this is not a negotiation. I'm not even saying that Damian is an issue — though, I'm pretty fucking sure he's an issue — but you leaving here alone isn't gonna happen, anyway. If Cidos finds you..." Jask trailed off, assuming he didn't need to elaborate on that.

Vince sighed and looked up to the sky. "And no chance you'd be satisfied with it being Johnny?"

"Johnny can't heal you if something goes sideways," Draz said as he opened the door.

"Were you eavesdropping?" Vince kept his hand in Jask's, squeezing a little harder than he probably should.

Jask cut Drazan off before he could answer. "It doesn't take much for us to eavesdrop, we pretty much just have to be awake. He's right, though. All around, it makes more sense to take D with you. Do you have some kind of problem with him?"

"No. Nope. Of course not," Vince lied through his teeth.

"We can sense the lie, dumbass," Drazan said, shaking his head.

Shifting, Jask pulled his hand away from Vince's. "You have something to tell me, Vin?"

Vince frowned down at their now unclasped hands before shaking his head. "No, nothing. I'll take him if it makes you feel better."

It was clear that Jask wasn't going to let that slide for long, but he nodded nonetheless. "Alright then, I'll see you two when you get back." He leaned over to kiss Vince and then stood, grasping Drazan's shoulder. "Damian tries anything he shouldn't... kill him."

"You got it, babe." Draz grinned. Vince clenched his jaw to stop himself from saying anything. He knew Draz was doing it to get a rise out of him, and Vince wasn't going to take the bait.

"If you're coming, get moving," he barked as he walked to the truck. Draz jumped in and instantly started messing with the radio, which had Vince debating how mad Jask would be if he left Draz on the side of the road somewhere. One glance at Jask watching them from the porch told him that wouldn't be a good idea.

The drive took longer than normal thanks to Drazan's incessant babbling, and by the time they pulled up to the bar, Vince was imagining the many different ways he could kill him. He'd spent the last half hour talking about how close he and Jask were. If Vince had to hear one more story about how they'd woken up cuddling in college, he was going to drive them both off of a cliff.

Vince got out of the truck and almost ran into the bar to find his former boss. The sooner he got this over with, the sooner he could go home to Jask and forget everything Draz had said. Damian was at his normal table in the back, and Vince pulled up a seat without asking. Drazan stood behind him with his arms crossed and a menacing expression.

"Who's the muscle?" Damian asked.

Vince made a face. "Apparently, my bodyguard."

"You don't *need* a bodyguard."

"That's what I said!" Vince took the beer the waitress brought and made sure Draz took one, too. The last thing they needed was to offend Damian. They were there to ask a favor, after all.

"So, I doubt you're here just to have a drink. What can I do for you, Vince?" Damian leaned back in his chair.

"I need a place to stay. The home we took over, it was fine for the four of us. But we've recently acquired two more. There's no way we'll all be able to stay sane in such a small space. I was hoping you could help get us into something bigger?" Vince asked, hoping that would be enough of an explanation.

"Of course, Vince." Damian smiled. "I owe you everything. Will next week be soon enough?"

Vince sighed in relief. "Yes. Next week is perfect. Thank you, Damian. I appreciate this. I'll see you then?" Damian nodded and Vince stood after shaking his hand. He walked back out to the truck with Draz and as they drove home, not even Drazan's stories could mess with his good mood.

Jaskian

By the time Vince came back, Jask had questions. Johnny had outright refused to answer any of them, and Leota couldn't seem to focus enough to string more than a few words together. He'd checked her again, and it wasn't a recurrence of the Void, but there was definitely something off with her. He pulled Vince aside and sat him down. "Talk."

"Hi, honey. I missed you too," Vince replied, sitting back and crossing his arms.

"Yeah, great. You gonna explain to me what your beef with Drazan is?"

"Do I have to?" When Jask didn't answer, Vince looked away. "Don't make fun of me, but... he's had you in every way I've dreamed of. He got to live with you. Go out in public with you. *He* got to propose to you and have people be happy about it. You and Draz didn't have to sneak around. I know it was fake but..." Vince trailed off and shrugged.

"I almost cried when he proposed to me, and not in a good way. It wasn't some big, public thing... I said yes like I was agreeing to a death sentence." Jask shifted, staring at the ground. "And neither of us wanted it, Vin. Drazan didn't want me, he never wanted me. All those things you mentioned, it wasn't something he *got* to do, it was something he *had* to do. And I missed you the entire time." He reached out to take Vince's hand. "Ask him how many times I threw up when he touched me, and how long it took me to stop."

Vince laced their fingers, staring at the way they fit together. "Logically, I know you didn't want it, but he seems to get some kind of sick amusement out of reminding me. He's your friend, so I'll try to be the bigger person. Especially since I have you back."

"Ever think he's doing it to distract you from the fact that he's fucking your best friend?" Jask raised an eyebrow, but grinned. "And don't let him fool you, anyway. He was almost as miserable as I was, and he's probably just trying to find some humor in it now." Jask pulled Vince in slowly, kissing him and wrapping his arms around him.

Vince melted into the kiss, moving until he was in Jask's lap. "Yeah, those are all fair points. I suppose I can look past his terrible personality as long as I have you around to kiss me and make it better. Plus, we'll be in a bigger house soon. That'll help."

Something about that raised a red flag for Jask. "Oh? How's that? I can't exactly go steal the funds from the family at this point, and I can promise Pattie won't let either of us back."

Vince shrugged, attempting to look innocent. "Damian is handling it. It'll be a bitch to move everything again, but I think it'll be worth it."

"The hell do you mean, handling it? What are you doing for him? No one just hands out a house without a motive." Jask frowned, those flags getting a lot bigger.

"Can we go back to the kissing, please? That was nice. No arguing, no questions."

Taking a deep breath, Jask kissed his temple. "You can talk to me, Vin. I'm not going anywhere this time, but you gotta be honest with me. If you start hiding shit..." he trailed off, hoping he wouldn't have to say the rest out loud.

"I'm not hiding anything. Damian said he owed me. He didn't ask for anything in return. Ask Drazan." Vince laid his head down on Jask's shoulder and snuggled close, sending small waves of power through him as a distraction.

Jask let out a soft moan from the sensations snaking through him. He knew that the conversation was far from over; it was sounding like he'd end up having to kill Damian too — but that list was getting out of hand, and Jask didn't particularly want to think about it anymore. "Okay."

"I hear the word, but the tone sounds definitely *not* okay." Vince looked up at him. "I promise, I wouldn't do anything to jeopardize this. Trust me."

He nodded a little. "I don't trust him, Vince. And I'm not comfortable taking anything from him. But we're already facing shit from all sides, and I don't want to fight with you. So if you trust him, and you think this will be okay... then I'll trust *you*."

"That's all I'm asking, sweetheart." Vince smiled as he ran a hand through Jask's hair, and Jask leaned into the touch.

"I love you. And I'll be damned if I let anyone get between us, I don't care who they are. When are we leaving?"

Slowly, Vince licked his lips and jerked one shoulder up. "Damian said it should be done by next week. You're stuck in the tent with me for a bit."

Dread pooled in Jask's gut. "It doesn't strike you as odd that he can find a house for six people in a single week?"

"There are plenty of abandoned houses out here, Jask. This one for instance. Stop worrying so much."

He knew that wasn't going to happen for several years, but he didn't want to bring Vince down any more than he already had. "Okay. You did good, Vin. Thank you for finding us a place to stay."

"I know you're just saying that to make me feel better, but I like it when you tell me how good I am, so I'll allow it." Vince kissed him, and Jask decided it was time to shut up. He deepened the kiss, sliding his hands up under Vince's shirt with every intention of telling Vince *exactly* how good he really was, but they were interrupted by Johnny rushing in.

"Hate to break this up, but Miss Leota just stole the truck."

Vince was off Jask's lap in a heartbeat. "She *what?*" Vince ran out of the room, but Jask knew if it were possible to catch her on foot, Johnny would've just done it himself.

Jask attempted to teleport inside of the truck but miscalculated and landed in front of it. He threw out a hand, using his powers to kill the engine just in time to stop it before it hit him. He rushed around to the driver's side and yanked open the door. "Lee, what the hell are you doing?"

"I have to go back." She had tears in her eyes and her hands were white from how hard she was gripping the wheel.

A weird sense of familiarity and foreboding filled Jask and he slowly peeled her fingers away from the wheel. "Hey, hey... talk to me, Lee. Where do you need to go?"

"I don't know. Just home. Something is wrong and I need to go home," she babbled.

"Okay. Come on," he said quietly, guiding her out of the truck and wrapping an arm around her. "Let's go back to the house and see if we can figure out what's going on, huh? This isn't like you."

"Can't you take me back? Back to Ares. Please, Jask?"

"There's nothing in Ares for any of us anymore but death, Lee. You know this." He hugged her fully, resting his chin on top of her head. "Haven't you had enough of almost dying?"

"I don't care. I can't stay here anymore, there's something... I don't know what it is. What's happening to me?" The tears were falling freely now as she fisted both hands in the front of his shirt.

Although he had no proof, he was starting to think he knew exactly what was happening to her. "Lee, hey. Shh, it's okay. Can you tell me when this all started? When did you start feeling like this?"

"After the Void. You all left and I couldn't shake the feeling that something was still wrong. Is this a side effect? Am I always going to feel this way?"

"I need to know what happened in that room, Lee. It's not very often angels save demons from the Void, but no. This isn't a normal, documented side effect." He leaned back a little to look at her, but didn't move his arms from their protective barrier around her.

"I don't remember much, honestly. Except his hands. They were so cold, and he was so gentle. It was the best thing I'd ever felt." She frowned a little. "I remember him saying some mean things about demons, but his touch and his actions, they didn't match."

Nodding, Jask let out a breath. "He's a healer, he knows enough not to let his own prejudices affect his work, but... Lee, is that what you're trying to get back to? Edis?"

She blushed and looked down at her hands. "I..."

Her words were cut off as Vince came running down the road. "What the fuck is going on?"

Jask would have laughed if he wasn't so sure he was correct. "Vin, leave her be. We've both done the same shit, neither of us have room to judge her."

Lee stepped a little closer to Jask and crossed her arms over her chest. "I'm sorry, Vince. I wanna go home."

"Home? As in, back to Ares?" Vince looked between them. "That's not home anymore."

"It's more like back to *Edis,*" Jask said gently. "I think when he saved her, some kind of connection was established. I've never seen anything like it, but she's acting exactly like we did when we were separated."

"That's great." Vince's voice was laced with sarcasm. "That's exactly what we need. Let's just get her back to the house, and we'll figure this out from there."

Jask frowned but fixed the truck. "Actually, this might be exactly what we need... if Edis feels it, too."

"He doesn't. He's an angel, if he felt it... he'd have come for me." Lee wiped the tears from her face and climbed back into the truck, holding herself.

"You don't know that. He still thinks you're my mate, Leota."

Vince climbed in beside her and put an arm around her. "Jask is right. We don't know what's going on, but we'll figure it out. Can you drive?" He turned to Jask as he asked the question, and Jask complied quickly.

"Guess this means I'm going back to Ares for a bit," Jask said quietly. "I need to figure out what they know and start planning anyway, but now I can talk to Edis and see if he did this on purpose, or if he's just as confused as we are."

"I don't know if it's a good idea for any of us to go back. Can't we just stay here and forget they exist?" Vince asked him.

Jask shook his head as he drove, hoping that Vince would extend the same level of trust to him that he'd extended to Vince. None of them would ever be able to live in peace until it was over, and the only way to bring it to an end was to quit hiding. "I think we both know the answer to that."

Edis

Edis paced in Jask's house, waiting for him to come back. He ran a hand through his hair and tried to talk himself into leaving a dozen times, but for some reason, he couldn't bring himself to do it. He had to know how she was.

It took almost two days for Jaskian to finally show up. When he did, Jask immediately conjured a ball of energy and poised it to throw, but Edis held out his hands defensively. "Wait! Wait, I'm alone."

Slowly, Jask looked around and the ball disappeared. "What the hell are you doing here, Edis?"

"I've been asking myself that for days. Speaking of, where have *you* been, exactly?"

Jask went pale like he'd been caught in a lie. He muttered something about blockers and rocked his weight to his other foot. "Ed... please. Just... don't ask. Please."

Any other time, Edis may have pushed, would've kept at it until he knew what Jask was hiding. However, right now there was only one thing he wanted to know. "How is she?"

"She's... wait, who?"

"The demon girl." Edis knew her name, but this would keep Jask from looking too deep into his interest.

Jask stayed silent for a suspiciously long time, like he was trying to carefully choose his words. "Well, I'm alive. She's alive."

"Yes, thank you for telling me something I could see with my own two eyes." Edis huffed and ran a hand through his hair for the hundredth time. "This was a mistake. I should go."

"Ed, wait." Jask stepped forward, looking more conflicted than he'd ever seen him. "Just... wait. What happened that day that you healed her?"

"Nothing." He knew Jask sensed the lie from the look on his face.

"Damn it. I don't know, okay? I just can't stop thinking about her. Honestly, if I didn't think her brother would attack on sight, I probably would've gone back." He rubbed his hand over his mouth. He'd said too much and now he could never take it back.

Jask actually grinned. "Worried about *her* brother but not your own, huh? Doesn't that strike you as odd, since you're convinced she's *my* mate?"

Edis frowned at him. "What exactly are you implying? I just wanted to make sure she recovered well." The excuse sounded flimsy to his own ears.

"Y'know, she told me that having your hands on her was the best she'd ever felt." Jask took a step forward, crossing his arms. "Did you enjoy having your hands on her?"

"I..." Edis turned away from him toward the other end of the house. The sight of Jask's bedroom door reminded him and he grasped at the only straw he had. "Why are the runes for a teleportation spell on your mirror?"

"Because Drazan was sneaking out to see his boyfriend. Answer the question, Ed. Did you enjoy having your hands on Leota Riskel?"

"You're Drazan's boyfriend. Or fiancé, rather," Edis said to avoid the question. He was a lawyer, he could do this. He hoped he could do this.

Jask nodded. "Yep. Or, at least that's what we told you and Cidos. He's my best friend, Ed. We slept together once." There wasn't an ounce of a lie there, and Edis narrowed his eyes as Jask continued. "Now, you can either start being honest with me in return, or... well, I think you know how this ends otherwise. I don't wanna kill you, Ed."

"Damn it. Yes, I did. Happy?" Edis began to pace again. "Except now you may kill me for fantasizing about your mate."

"I would... if you were actually fantasizing about my mate." Jask sat down, his arms spread on the back of the couch to show Edis he wasn't braced for a fight. "Sit."

Edis leaned back into his seat as his brain played catch up. "The brother. He's yours." Edis remembered the lie from the day he healed

Leota. The pain on the demon's face as he'd stared at Jask. "How did I miss that?"

"Blockers. I'm surprised you didn't figure that part out when I shoved one down your throat, honestly. But yeah. Vince is mine. Leota... I had to physically stop her from coming to you, which means one of two things. Either you did something to her when you healed her... or there are *two* mated pairs this generation."

"That's impossible. That's never happened before." He shook his head and went step by step over the healing. "And I didn't do anything to her other than heal her. It has to be something else."

Jask shook his head. "It's never happened before, no. But there's also never been a same-sex mated pair, either. The whole point of the curse was to get the two lines to mix. Think about it, Ed. Me and Vince... we can't procreate. You and Leota can."

Edis started to panic. "They'll kill us both, Jask. Cidos and Father... if they find out..."

"Stop." Jask leaned forward. "I'm not gonna let anything happen to you, okay? The whole fucking reason Ci and D- *Athar* are still alive is cause I couldn't stand the thought of killing you, too. You helped me. I know you see this the way that I do... the Riskels, they're... hell, they're better than we are."

"That's where you've been. Damn it, I wish I didn't know that. How am I supposed to face them now?" He stood again, pacing in front of the couch. There was a mounting anxiety in his chest. His entire being was trying to convince him that the best thing to do was to see Leota. He shook his head at himself. "This entire situation is insane."

Jask stood to meet him, bracing a hand on his shoulder. "You should come with me. Spend some time with her, with them. You're gonna have to pick a side here, Ed."

"Come with you? Now?"

"Yeah, now. Don't you want to see her again? She's a fucking wreck without you." Jask smiled a little and yet again, he was speaking the truth. "And if you two really are mated, I know how crippling it is to be apart, and there's no way in hell I'll be responsible for keeping you two away from each other. You'll like it there, we're apparently building a small army. Just don't disrespect Amaranth, she'll beat your ass."

The thought of Leota being in pain made the decision for him. "Yes. Let's go."

A moment later, they were standing in front of a house that looked way too small for Jask's little clan to reside in, but he could *feel* her. His brother cleared his throat and glanced at him. "You may wanna stay out here, Ed. Just until I have a chance to explain."

Before he could even agree, Lee came exploding out through the front door and sprinted toward them, the look on her face almost wild. "Edis?!"

Edis' instincts took over and he had his arms around her before he could think about the repercussions. It felt like the final piece of a puzzle being placed and he closed his eyes as he held her against him.

"Lee!" Edis recognized that voice as the brother, Vince, but he couldn't bring himself to care. Jask could handle his mate, and Edis was staying with his.

"Vince, I need you to trust me," Jask said, followed quickly by a grunt. "Edis, let your wings out."

Edis did without a second thought, pulling back just enough to see Leota's face. "Hello."

Her eyes widened at the sight of his wings. "I've been dreaming about them since you left. Can I...?" She reached out, hovering her hand over his feathers for a moment, then slowly slid her fingers in. It felt incredible, like nothing Edis had ever experienced before — and wherever her hands went, the feathers turned black.

"Holy shit," Drazan said, walking out.

Edis was shaking and his wings moved forward, wrapping around her.

"Son of a bitch," Vince cursed from somewhere to his right. He knew he should let go of her and at least try and introduce himself. Speak to her family and apologize, but all he could do was close his eyes and put his forehead against hers.

She huffed a laugh and stood on her toes to kiss him, throwing both arms around his neck. Edis squeezed her, lifting her off her feet and vaguely heard a scuffle behind her as Jask and Drazan dragged Vince inside.

The kiss continued for what could have been hours before he pulled away. "I think that went well, don't you?"

"Vince will be fine, and if he's not, he's a hypocrite." She buried her face against his chest and let out a breath. "Don't leave like Jask did. Please. I'm not... I'm not as strong as Vince."

"I'll stay as long as I'm welcome." He put a hand on the back of her head and held her. "How long do you think we can hide out here?"

She gripped the back of his shirt and shook her head slightly. "I don't think we can, but... Jask made it seem like we wouldn't have to. Maybe you should talk to him?"

"Yes." He took her hand and entwined their fingers. "Let's go face the firing squad." Leota led the way into the house, and Edis almost laughed when he saw Jask sitting on Vince, literally holding him down.

"Hey, look at that. You two managed to quit suckin' face way before we did," Jask joked. "How's it feel?"

Leota threw a pillow at him and scoffed. "Mind your business, perv." It was clear to Edis that Jask had been there for a while; he'd built a relationship with all of them. He belonged there.

"Okay, okay," Jask said, rolling off a squirming Vince. "Seriously, though. Your wings are turning black, which confirms my theory. You two are mates."

"Congratulations! Welcome to the team, Ed!" Drazan clapped from his spot on the couch.

"Who said he could join the team?" Vince grumbled but quieted down at a look from Jask.

Edis cleared his throat. "I have a lot to apologize for and I'm grateful you're giving me the chance to do so."

"You wanna apologize? Help me deal with Cidos and dad," Jask said, all humor gone from his face. "You know they'll never stop."

Edis looked around at the faces staring at him and then back down to Leota. She squeezed his hand, and his eyes drifted back toward his brother and his mate. Ignoring the slightly murderous look on Vince's face, Edis saw the way he held Jask's close. It was clear from the way Jask leaned into it that he was just as taken with Vince. Could he have that with Leota? Could they really be happy outside of the rules and expectations from their families? Would he be able to go against his own twin? One more look at Leota's citrine eyes and he inclined his head to Jask. "I'm in."

Drazan huffed. "Huh. I definitely saw that being harder."

"Nah," Jask said, bringing Vince's hand up to kiss it. "He knows not joining means Leota dies. He won't let that happen to his mate. Neither one of us ever stood a chance."

"Yes, that's another apology I have to make. If I'd known this was what you were feeling being away from Vince, I never would've played a part in keeping you from him." Edis tugged Leota a little closer.

Vince tilted his head a little. "Yes, and now nothing will keep us apart again."

"Duly noted." Edis took the threat for what it was. "As I said, I'm with you now."

Jask looked a little overwhelmed for a moment but eventually nodded. "It's okay, Ed. It's not really something that can be put into words, y'know? And dad was so fanatical about this shit that I didn't really blame you and Ci. Do you think there's *any* chance we can get Ci on our side?"

Edis hesitated. "No. I wish with everything I am that I could give you a different answer, but you know him as well as I do. He's too much like Athar."

With a sad smile, Jask nodded once. "Then there's no point in delaying anymore. I know I keep saying that, but fuck... not one part of this is gonna be easy. It's time to stop hiding. We move tomorrow."

Edis looked at the small group made up of people he barely knew. He didn't quite understand how the shift inside of him happened so fast, but he knew one thing beyond a shadow of a doubt. For better or worse, they were his family now. "Tomorrow," he agreed, sitting and pulling Leota into his lap.

Fifteen

Vince

Damian pulled through in a big way, finding them a four bedroom home. It had two full bathrooms and a small half-bath, and between the five men, it didn't take long to get everything moved. Things were going well until it was time to talk about sleeping arrangements. Vince was putting his foot down about this. He crossed his arms and shook his head at Jask. "I don't care what he is to her. He's not sleeping in her room."

"Fine, then I guess I can't stay with you either. I'm not a hypocrite, Vin. I won't stay with you if Ed can't stay with Lee, it's cruel. Not to mention, they'll just sneak around, anyway."

"It's different for us! We're..." He struggled to think of a way they were actually different. "I mean, we've already... and they..."

"It's fascinating how hard he's trying," Drazan mumbled to Johnny as they watched from the other side of the living room.

Jask chuckled, kissing Vince quickly. "I'll keep you distracted every night so you don't have to think about it."

Scowling, Lee crossed her arms. "You're not my boss, Vince. I need him." She seemed to realize what she said and clenched her jaw. "I mean... I want him. And I don't care what you say, he's sleeping with me."

"Please don't talk about wanting him to me," Vince said as he held up a finger.

"Vince, if someone tried to tell you the same, you'd stab them. You're not sleeping without Jask, I'm not sleeping without Drazan, and she's not sleeping without Edis," Johnny tried.

Amaranth made a face and stood up. "There are three angels in this room... I expect *one* of you to thoroughly soundproof this house. I don't want to hear about any of you sleeping with anyone." She sighed, heading toward her room. "Wake me when I'm needed. It's been a long... year."

As she disappeared, Jask grinned sheepishly. "Whoops. It's probably good that she's gone though. Draz, can you handle the soundproofing? We need to come up with a plan, and I'm not talking about who is or isn't fucking who tonight."

Vince covered his ears. "Come *on*, Jask! She's my baby sister, don't use that word!"

Draz gave a salute, walking backward. "Soundproofing incoming."

"Don't be like that, Vin. He's my little brother! Okay, so it's not as weird for me... but still. She's grown, and I can *promise* you, nobody makes love like a Veris."

Even Edis gagged at that. "Did mom drop you when you were a baby?"

"I'm very aware of what it's like to sleep with a Veris, Jask." Vince ignored the yelled "me too!" from wherever Drazan was. "That isn't the point!"

"Alright, look, I'll sleep on the couch. Can we move on to actually making a plan now?" Edis asked with a pained look.

Jask was laughing so hard he could barely sit up, but Lee looked like she was just told some very bad news. Jask finally calmed down enough to say, "Yeah, yeah. We should go back to Ares. Draw them out."

Vince took Edis at his word and didn't acknowledge Jask's laughter. "I don't think we should all go. Someone has to stay behind with Lee and Ma."

"Yeah," Jask agreed. "You. It'll be a lot less suspicious if me, Ed and Drazan go alone."

"That's a terrible idea," Vince argued, mostly because he didn't like the idea of being separated from Jask again.

"He's right. I don't want to leave Lee either, but if the three of us get caught together, we won't have to explain anything," Edis offered.

Jask nodded. "And I'm sure Drazan won't be thrilled about leaving Johnny. But if everything goes as planned, we can get Athar and Cidos off their guard and in the same place. Drazan will have to teach you his little mirror trick, so when it comes time, Drazan can take my mom somewhere safe, and you can join us. We'll take Athar and Cidos out and finally be able to live our lives."

Vince took Jask's hand and pulled him into his arms. "Good. That makes me feel better."

"Soundproofing is complete," Drazan informed everyone as he returned. Johnny eagerly tugged Drazan to their bedroom, mumbling something about needing to make sure.

Abruptly, Lee took Edis' hand and led him away, too. Vince almost let go of Jask to follow, but he realized they were headed for the kitchen and not one of the bedrooms. "Everyone in this house is a deviant," he sighed dramatically as they disappeared into their own room.

Laughing, Jask shut the door behind them. "It's all your fault, you know." He kissed him to shut him up and pressed him against the wall.

"Because I couldn't resist you any longer. Ergo, your fault." Vince ran his hands under Jask's shirt.

Jask smirked, but closed his eyes and let out a breath. "Mm. Keep doing that, and you can blame me for whatever you want."

Vince pulled him in until they were touching everywhere they possibly could be before leaning in to kiss Jask's neck. "Whatever happens, it's worth it if I have you."

Tipping his head back, Jask let out a quiet moan and slid his hands down Vince's body, sending his clothes to a pile on the floor. "When it's all done, you'll have me, and no one will be able to tell us otherwise."

"I like the sound of that." Vince shoved Jask back to the bed. As much as they planned and as careful as they may be, no one knew what would happen in the coming days. He needed tonight with Jask to help get him through the battles they'd face.

When Jask's knees hit the mattress, he fell back, bringing Vince with him. Another moment later and he was naked too, groaning as their skin made contact. "Need to feel you, Vin. It's been too damn long."

"You got me, sweetheart." Vince kissed down his body, settling between his legs and licking up his length.

"No," Jask said quickly, reaching down to tug him back up. "That's not what I want." He wrapped his legs around Vince's ass and tightened until they were grinding slowly against each other. "I need to *feel* you, Vincenzo."

"Oh." Vince dropped his head to Jask's shoulder and enjoyed the friction for a moment, then lifted himself back up and reached between them. The moment he felt that familiar surge of grace, he kissed Jask and inched into him with a moan. Nothing in the universe felt as good as being surrounded by his mate.

Fingertips curled against his back as Jask gasped. "I missed you, Vin."

"Missed you. Missed this," Vince agreed, tracing his hand down Jask's side until he was gripping his thigh. He angled him so that he could thrust deeper, drawing a deep moan.

Jask stroked himself quickly. His back arched and his jaw went slack as they moved together, a constant stream of praises falling from his lips. He fell over the edge first, his free hand wrapping around the back of Vince's neck and holding him close as he spilled over his own stomach and clenched around Vince's length.

Vince stopped moving for a moment, his forehead against Jask's as he fought off his own release. When he was reasonably in control, he leaned back up and ran a finger over Jask's length. "Again, Jask. I want you to come for me again, and then I want to lick you clean." He circled his hips lazily, pushing deep.

Grinning satedly, Jask let out a quiet laugh. "Greedy. I like it." His hand once again wrapped around his length and he slowly hardened once more, rolling his hips. "Here," he said, his voice low. Two fingers swiped through the mess he already made and pressed against Vince's lips. "Just a taste."

Vince sucked Jask's fingers into his mouth and moaned as he cleaned every drop, and then began to move again, replacing Jask's hand with his own and stroking in time with his thrusts.

"Holy shit," Jask whispered, shaking slightly under him. He let out a shiver of grace and leaked precome over Vince's fingers, then slapped his hand away. "Let me ride you."

Vince cursed and rolled, pulling Jask with him. His hands went immediately to Jask's hips and he pulled him down as he guided his hips up. "Fuck, you feel good like this."

"Uh huh." Jask smirked, pinching his tongue between his teeth as he rocked down, grinding against him and sliding back up to tease him. "I know. Now hold still, let me remind you what I meant earlier." Grace flooded Vince's system as Jask dropped back down, his perfect ass pressing against Vince's hips and completely burying his cock. He stayed like that, circling and rolling until he was gasping, his hard cock neglected between them. Jask made no move to touch himself.

"Jask," Vince choked out, his grip tightening as he fought his orgasm again. He wanted this to last as long as possible, and he wanted Jask to come again first. "Let me touch you."

He shook his head quickly, leaning back just enough to change the angle. "Ahh, *fuck,* there it is," he whispered, moaning low as his movements got faster. Another wave of grace swept through them both and then Jask was coming untouched, slamming his ass down as his second release painted Vince's torso.

Watching Jask come undone like that was one of the hottest things Vince had ever seen. He planted his feet and thrust up again, unable to hold back any longer. He came with a growl and wrapped his hand around the back of Jask's neck, yanking him down to kiss him.

Jask smiled against his lips and groaned as he fought to keep Vince's softening cock inside of him. "Don't want you to go," he mumbled. "Stay."

Vince wrapped his arms around him and held him close. "Give me ten minutes and we can do it all again." He kissed the side of Jask's head before sighing. "Actually... we should probably sleep, if you're really wanting to start this tomorrow."

"I can sleep when it's over and we're together for good," Jask said, but slid off of him anyway. "If things go badly..."

"They won't. I'm not going to let anything keep us from being together. Not anymore," Vince wrapped his arms around him and pulled him as close as he could. They kissed again, because they'd never get enough, and eventually they fell asleep in each other's arms.

Vince woke slowly, the pressure on his chest telling him Jask had rolled on top of him sometime in the night. He smiled and maneuvered until he could get up. Vince wanted to surprise him with breakfast, so he grabbed some shorts and opened his bedroom door quietly. He froze immediately because two doors down, Edis was walking out of his sister's room. Lee stood behind him in nothing but a blanket and Edis' wings were decidedly more black than yesterday.

"Son of a bitch." Vince was no longer worried about being quiet. He was going to kill Jask's brother.

"Vince, wait!" Lee yelled as Vince stepped out of the room.

Edis held his hands up and took a step back. "Now, Vince, be reasonable. I'm on your side, don't forget that!" His words had gotten quicker toward the end and his pitch rose with fear, which would've been laughable if Vince wasn't already prepared to punch him.

Lee stepped in front of Vince right before he swung and Vince redirected to hit the wall.

"Ten out of ten," Draz scored the hole in the wall after opening the door to his and Johnny's room.

"You stay out of this." Vince didn't even look at Draz as he pointed at Edis. "Outside, now." As much as he wanted to hit him, his mother would kill them all if he messed up more of the house.

Jask followed as Edis led the way outside and leaned against the railing on the porch. "Don't you think there's enough fighting in our future?"

"Relax, Jaskian," Edis said. "He can hit me all he wants, it's not going to make Leota stop wanting me. And it's sure as hell not going to stop me from loving her."

"Thank you for the permission," Vince said a split second before punching Edis.

"You're not going to try and stop them?" he heard Draz ask from somewhere behind Jask. Vince ignored them both. It felt incredible to have an outlet for his anger, so he threw another punch, but Edis grabbed his arm and hauled him past him so Vince went tumbling into the grass.

Jask sighed heavily. "Seriously? This is how we're gonna fucking spend our last day together?"

Vince turned his head to look up at the porch. "It's his fault!"

"How? Cause he was doing *exactly* what you did?" Lee asked angrily, trying to get out of the grip Jask had her in. "Fuck you, Vince. You're an asshole."

Vince stood up and scowled at his mate and sister. "Never claimed to be anything else, Lee." He turned to face Edis and winced a little at the bruise forming on his cheek.

"Fuck. Fine, hit me back and then we'll all go have breakfast."

She huffed, nearly tripping over the blanket as she turned and stomped back inside. Jask shook his head at Edis almost imperceptibly, but it was enough that Edis said no to hitting Vince back. "We're done here," Edis said quietly.

Vince watched him walk in after Lee, Draz following immediately. He didn't miss the disappointment on Jask's face as he left him, too. Vince tilted his head back and closed his eyes. He had to stop fucking everything up. After a couple of minutes of quiet reflection, he went inside to breakfast.

Jaskian

Pulling himself away from Vince again was one of the hardest things he'd ever done, even though he knew they wouldn't be apart for long this time. It didn't help that he was flanked by two equally grumpy angels in Edis and Drazan, but they all understood that they had a job to do and a role to fill. It had taken entirely too long to convince Johnny and Vince that he and Draz wouldn't be kissing anymore, and even then, Jask wasn't sure it was a promise he could keep. They'd likely have to pull out all the stops in order to successfully implement their plan.

"This sucks," Edis lamented, making Jask laugh a little. "I don't care how many of these blockers you shove down my throat, I doubt it'll help. My face gives me away every time."

"You don't think I know that? That's why you're on mom duty. You should spend some time with her, anyway. If we actually do what we're setting out to do, she'll never speak to either of us again."

Drazan frowned at Jask's words. "That doesn't bother you?"

"Everything about this *bothers* me, Drazan," Jask said sharply. "Do you think I actually want to kill my brother and my father? That I want to alienate my mom for killing half her family? That I want to risk *anyone's* life in the process?"

Before Draz could answer, Edis stepped between them and held out his hands. "I just got decked, can we not fight here, too? We're supposed to be the civilized ones."

Anger radiated through Jask, and he shoved Edis' arm out of the way. "You've gotta knock that shit off, Edis. You're way more toxic than most of the demons I've met. You think I forgot about what you do for a living? What *I've* been doing to try to keep you two off my tail? Your mate is a demon, and if Vince hears you saying she's uncivilized, he'll kill you."

"Sorry, Jask," he mumbled, stepping away. "Old habits, I guess. This is new to me. I haven't been playing house with demons for years like you have."

He'd have denied it if it wasn't so damn true. Huffing, Jask straightened his shirt and looked around his house. It felt surreal being there again, especially since it was likely the last time he'd ever see it. "Enough, then. Let's do what we came here to do. Take your blockers, both of you. Ed, you go keep mom busy, Drazan and I will go invite dad and Cidos to the bachelor party." The thought was nearly laughable, but he had to hope they were still a believable enough couple to make it happen.

"Whatever," Edis said, then popped two of the giant pills into his mouth and swallowed dry. "Good luck." He disappeared a moment later, leaving Jask alone with Drazan.

"Ready to go sell this shit one more time?" Drazan asked.

Probably not, Jask thought to himself. *Guess we'll see.* He took Drazan's hand and teleported them outside of Athar's house. After taking a deep breath, Jask used his free hand to knock on the door and squeezed Drazan's a little tighter.

One of Athar's assistants opened the door, ushering them inside without much of a greeting. The house was obscenely large, especially for a man that chose to live alone without his family. Every inch was coated in marble to a point that it no longer looked real.

Genuine fear pooled in his gut, and in an effort to quell that fear, he smirked a little and leaned closer to Drazan. He whispered, "Where was all this marble when I was a kid? Bet it woulda been fun to slide around in my socks."

"You're so uncoordinated outside of the bedroom, you'd have broken your face," Drazan teased.

It worked, and Jask was almost relaxed by the time they were led into Athar's study. He flicked beady, judgmental eyes between them and sat back in his chair, his expression a lethal calm. "To what do I owe this unsolicited... well, let's not call it a pleasure."

Forcing a grin, Jask held up their joined hands. "The wedding of the century is right around the corner. Wouldn't be much of a bachelor party without the world's most fun dad." *Thank everything for these block-ers,* he said silently.

"Why on this planet would I want to attend such a debased thing?"

They'd been prepared for that, and Drazan spoke before Jask had a chance. "My father is dead, sir. You know the customs. In order to ensure purity until the moment of our union, a patriarch has to be present. In this case, that's you."

Athar was a lot of things, but someone who neglected his duties was not one of them. They'd been banking on it. He straightened up, a sense of dignity and pride radiating from him. "You are correct, and it's good to see the two of you upholding tradition. When is this bachelor party?"

"Two nights from now," Jask relayed with a smile. "Seven sharp."

His father seemed to approve the time, and jotted it down on his calendar. Jask tried not to be offended that even his own sons had to be penciled in. "Very well," he said. "You may go."

Without another word, Drazan dragged Jask out of the room and immediately teleported them to the firm they worked at, trusting Cidos would still be there. "Let's get this over with." He shuddered, likely due to the lie they were going to have to spin to get Cidos on board. Jask almost felt bad for him.

"What the hell? Where have you been, Jask?" Cidos demanded. "I've been looking for you for days."

Smiling sheepishly, Jask jerked his head toward Drazan. "Sorry. Lost track of time. Before you give me a stack of cases, though, we wanted to talk to you about something. You're not exactly easy to track down, either."

Cidos flicked his pale eyes skeptically between them. "What is it?"

"Well," Drazan started, shifting on his feet. "As you know, Jask is pretty much my whole life. Has been for years. With the wedding coming up and me not having siblings or other friends, I was - well, *we* were wondering - if you'd be my best man."

A surprised, mocking laugh left Cidos' chest. "And why would I want to do that, exactly?"

It was Jask's turn to take over. "Because. We figured you'd want to be up close and personal, to make sure we weren't somehow faking the wedding. We know you believe I'm still pining over the Riskel girl, which is fucking ridiculous, but hey. If you're his best man, that means you get to stand right next to us with your nose stuck in our business, right where you like to be."

"And why are you *offering* to let me do this?" Not one trace of his distrust was fading, but neither Jask nor Drazan was deterred.

"Because we need more people for this bachelor party, and like I said, I just don't have anyone else," Drazan said simply. "Take it or leave it, Ci. But Edis is Jask's best man, we figured it was only fair."

Cidos spent the next full minute staring at them, straining like he was trying to sense a lie in words that had already been lost to the air. "Fine. When is this party, exactly?"

"Wonderful," Jask said with mock cheer. "Two nights from now. We rented out that reception hall on Third Street."

Wrinkling his nose, Cidos shook his head and took the bait. "I'll come alone, then. Can't have anyone seeing my face in that cesspool. Did dad cut you off or something? Why can't you afford something nicer?"

"I've had an allowance for years," Jask said. "Just enough to get by. Working paid for all the fun, but since I spend most of my days climbing this one like a tree —"

"For fuck's sake, you cretin. Shut up." Cidos stormed past him and shoulder-checked him on the way. "I'll be there."

He slammed the door behind him, and Drazan waited several seconds before muttering, "I really hate him."

"Yeah," Jask agreed. "So do I."

~

Not one of them wanted to stay at Jask's house that night without their partners, and more than once, they had to stop each other from running out. Jask felt bad for Drazan since he and Edis could teleport, and there wasn't anything Draz could do about it but fight his own urges as the brothers attempted to drag each other back.

"Enough," Jask barked, slamming his fist on the table after fetching Edis for the third time. "We need to stay here."

"Speak for yourself," Edis retorted. "You've tried to get to him *how* many times?"

The truth was, he'd disappeared more than Edis had, but Jask wasn't in the mood to admit he was wrong. He did the only logical thing he could think of to avoid that, and turned the blame on Drazan. "What the hell is your excuse, huh? You keep tryin' to run outta here to the car or the bathroom, and you're not even bonded. That demonic cowboy *that* good in bed?"

"Yes," Drazan said quickly. "And just because we aren't mates doesn't mean we don't love each other."

Something about that made Jask turn his nose up. "You love him?"

"On purpose?" Edis added.

Drazan smacked him in the shoulder. "Fuck you. Yes, on purpose. Are you saying you wouldn't love Leota if it wasn't for the bond?"

Edis opened his mouth to say no, but sighed. "Actually, I probably would. She's warm, smart, witty... not afraid of me."

"Do you scare a lot of girls, Edis?" Jask teased. "Funny, I think you're the least frightening of all of us. Like a giant, frozen teddy bear."

Drazan laughed, agreeing. "He really is. That just makes him more dangerous though, he might appear innocent, but he's still lethal."

Satisfied, Edis hummed. "Don't you forget it, either. You wouldn't have invited me along if I wasn't. You're trusting me to take out Cidos, right?" His face suddenly fell, and he looked at Jask with wide, almost innocent eyes.

"No, Ed," Jask said quietly. "I just need you to keep him busy while I take out Athar, then you get Vince out of there and I'll deal with Ci. I won't ask you to kill for me."

"It's for him too, you know," Drazan reminded them softly. "It's for all of us."

How the mood shifted so quickly, Jask wasn't sure, but he'd have given anything to go back to the carefree banter they'd just been having. "It's not a negotiation, Drazan. I won't hear it."

Recognizing the dismissal for what it was, Drazan and Edis both fell silent. With his mood officially tanked, Jask pushed himself out of his chair and toward his room. "Ed, you're on the couch. Draz, you're with me. Can't take the chance of sleeping apart if we have any surprise visitors."

He knew there was nothing to stop any of them from going to their mates once the others were asleep, but he had to hope they'd all stay put, hope they'd realize that the stakes were too high to screw up now. They were halfway there... and just needed to make it to the finish line.

Preferably all in one piece.

Cidos

After storming out of his office, Cidos paced in the firm's library. Something seemed off, odd, out of place... he just couldn't put his finger on it. It had seemed that way for months, ever since Jaskian had found the Riskel bitch. But despite everything, his questions, his digging, his recon... he hadn't found anything overtly amiss. "Something's rotten," he muttered to himself. "And if I can't figure it out, I know someone who can."

He'd refrained from seeking his father's help for only one reason - Athar was the type of man to harm first, ask questions later. In the small, off chance that Cidos was wrong about Jaskian's relationship, he truly didn't want to see his brother harmed.

But the time for tiptoeing had passed. Once the two were joined in marriage, their relationship would be beyond reproach even if it *was* a total sham. He was out of time and out of options, and with that in mind, he let himself into his father's house and pushed passed his servants. "Father?" he called quietly, knocking on the frame of the open door. "Do you have a moment?"

"Cidos." Athar put down his pen. "Come in. I wasn't expecting you today."

He let himself in and closed the door behind him, taking a breath before straightening his suit and heading for the chair opposite his father. "I know you're busy, sir, so I'll get right to it. I'm assuming Jaskian and Drazan came to see you?"

"Yes, to extend an invitation to the bachelor party. Why?" He leaned back in his chair, his gaze only slightly curious.

Cidos licked his lips and tried to remain calm. He knew at the end of the day, he was firmly on his father's side, but that didn't mean he wasn't afraid of him. "I still think it's fake, sir. Their relationship. The demon is still alive."

"Do you have proof?"

No, he thought to himself. "It's just a hunch, sir. But Jaskian disappeared for days, somewhere that not even I could track him. Edis has been acting strange, and I can't sense *anything* coming from them anymore. I believe they're hiding something."

"Cidos," Athar admonished as he placed his elbows on the desk and stared hard at him. "Are you telling me you interrupted my work for a *feeling* you're having?"

Fear snaked down his spine and he clenched his jaw. "I'll find your proof, sir. I've never been more sure about anything in my life."

"Do that, don't come back without it. For now, Jaskian is here and he's going through with the wedding. He and Drazan are following proper tradition to do so. Unless you can prove otherwise, I won't waste my time on wild goose chases."

Cidos couldn't help the bitter laugh that forced its way from his chest. "*Tradition* dictates that we kill the demon bonded to him, but that doesn't seem to be concerning anyone but me anymore." He stood, stepping backward instead of turning around. "I'll take care of it, sir. I won't come back without evidence."

"If you come back with evidence, we'll do the ritual. If not, Jask will marry Drazan. He's my son. If anyone is strong enough to deny the bond, it's him."

Though he begged to differ, Cidos nodded once and exited the room before teleporting to the end of Jaskian's driveway. He stuck to the shadows, dulling his presence as much as he could as he made his way toward the front of the house. A quick perimeter search showed him that only one window was open, but he had no idea which room it was attached to - and he wasn't stupid enough to find out.

He was about to leave and regroup when a voice drifted out of the window. He immediately recognized it as Drazan. He inched closer until he could make sense of the words being said.

"No. These two assholes are the absolute worst. Wait, I can hear Vince whining in the background. He's definitely more annoying." Drazan laughed a little.

"He's terrible. I thought it might be Ms. Leota pining, but no... it's my big baby of a best friend," an unfamiliar voice replied over what had to be speakerphone.

"Is that Johnny?" Jask asked, and Cidos hunched down further.

"Go away, Jaskian. Let me talk to my boyfriend." The sounds of rustling clothing and a few grunts ensued. "Damn it, Jask, give me back my phone!"

"Johnny, how is Vince? Is he okay? Do I need to talk to him? Does he need to talk to me?" Cidos blinked as the questions flew from his older brother's mouth. *Vince?* That was the brother he'd nearly killed at Pattie's. Why would Jask need to talk to him?

"Who cares about Vince? Ask him about Lee!" Edis yelled out. Another scuffle could be heard and the sound of a phone hitting the floor.

"I swear if you broke it..." the rest of Drazan's sentence was cut off by Edis' laughter and Jask's cursing.

"Johnny, put Leota on. I want to talk to her," Edis demanded. The voice that answered wasn't Johnny, and Cidos listened once more as Vince began to speak.

"Sorry, Johnny is indisposed." He sounded incredibly calm, despite the muffled yells coming from his side of the call. "Put my mate back on the phone, please." Cidos almost choked as the realization hit him like a physical blow to the face. Vince and Jask were mated. Edis had obviously thrown his lot in with the demons, and Cidos didn't know what to do with the sense of utter betrayal he felt.

"Vin! I'm here, Drazan is sitting on me because I dropped his phone." There was a thud, and Drazan called Jask a dirty name.

"Draz, I swear to all of the Riskels before me I will dig your in-testines out with a spoon if you don't..." Vince's threat was cut off as Jask apparently took control of the phone again.

"It's fine, he's on the floor now. How is everything there?" Jask in-quired and a pillow flew out of the window, hitting Cidos in the head. He ducked into the shadows just as Drazan's head poked outside.

"Oh, hey, sweetheart. We're good, totally fine. When are you coming home?" Vince replied, much more pleasantly than he'd been speaking before.

"That was my pillow," Drazan sighed.

"If Jask gets to talk to his mate, I get to talk to mine." Edis ignored Drazan's mourning for his pillow. If this situation wasn't so completely bizarre, Cidos may have found that funny. The rest of the conversation was drowned out by a buzzing in Cidos' head as his thoughts whirled. Jask was mated to Vince, and apparently, Edis was the one actually mated to the girl. There was no precedent for this. Cidos made his way back to the end of the driveway. He wasn't focused enough to continue muting his presence, and they couldn't find out he knew. When he was far enough away that they wouldn't sense it, he teleported back to his home. Realistically, he should go back to his father and tell him what he heard. It wasn't physical proof, but Athar would know he wasn't lying when he told him the story. He opened a bottle of Scotch and grabbed a glass, but ultimately put it back in the cabinet and drank directly from the source. Some nights, he just needed the bottle.

~

The following day, Cidos finally worked up the nerve to go tell his father. He knew what it would mean when he did, and he'd be lying to himself if he said he hadn't struggled with the decision. Two mates, two rituals, two bonds broken. Two brothers that would have a hard time surviving, two brothers that might be killed anyway for deceiving their father. Was he truly ready and prepared to let that happen? He wanted to believe he wasn't, that his love for his brothers superseded anything else, but it wasn't true. He was born with such a deep sense of responsibility and duty that he knew it would only end one way.

Maybe he was born to save his brothers. Cidos just didn't know if that meant breaking the bonds... or putting them down. He decided to leave that decision up to their father.

Once again, he knocked on the frame of the door to his father's study. "Father? You requested proof. I've found it."

Athar didn't look up from what he was doing immediately. "Oh? Enlighten me."

Cidos shifted, but kept his back straight. "Sir, I need you to look at me. I need you to know that I'm not lying about what I heard, because it's... well, I wouldn't have believed it myself if I hadn't heard it firsthand. It might actually be better if you could view the memory yourself."

Athar looked up at him and raised an eyebrow. "Very well, if you insist."

Stepping forward, Cidos closed his eyes and focused intently on what he'd heard as Athar sifted through his mind. It was uncomfortable at best and horrible at worst, but when he was done, at least he could be sure Athar would believe him. No angel could fabricate memories like that. "What do you need me to do, sir?"

Athar clenched his jaw, the only outward sign of emotion as he tapped his pen on the desk. "How impressive that they managed to fool both of us. We wait. Go to the bachelor party like nothing is amiss. In the meantime, get all the information you can on the Riskels, and make the preparations for the rituals."

Nodding once, Cidos took a step back. "As you wish, sir. Thank you for your time." He backed out of the room and turned on his heel, warring with himself over what to do next. It was as he'd suspected, but he knew enough now to assume that Jaskian and Edis wouldn't come quietly, nor would they allow their bonds to be broken without a fight. The risk of something going wrong was high... and when it had just been Jaskian, Cidos hadn't been concerned. He'd been prepared to lose a brother for the sake of the graceline, but a twin? Someone he'd shared every milestone, every success and failure with from the time they'd been born? He wanted to tell himself that for Edis, he'd break the rules. That he'd go against his father, against tradition and against every single one of their ancestors.

But as he landed back in his own room, away from prying eyes and outside influences, he took a hard look at himself. With Jaskian and Edis out of the way, he'd inherit everything. The firm, the houses, the money... the brunt of his father's power once he died. With no one else standing in his way, Cidos would be the most powerful person on Earth, and maybe even beyond. He'd also finally earn the respect from his father that he'd been seeking for as long as he could remember.

Yes, Cidos knew in that moment that brotherhood mattered far less than the things he stood to gain. He would do what needed to be done to fulfill his duty.

They'd never really loved him, anyway.

Sixteen

Vince

Vince glared at the mirror and willed it to glow, change color, possibly make a noise. Anything other than show him his own damned reflection. It was past the time for Draz to have collected him.

Edis had returned almost an hour ago with a distraught Astarte, and Amaranth immediately took her in her arms and into the kitchen. They sat at the table drinking tea and awaiting news — news that should've already been delivered. Vince checked on the ladies one more time before taking his phone out of his pocket.

There were no new messages, no missed calls. Something was wrong and he *needed* to get to Jask. He began to pace again, only half listening to Edis assure Leota and their mothers that everything was fine. Johnny stood nearby with his arms crossed, his gaze glued to the mirror. He looked just as worried as Vince felt.

"Call him," Vince demanded.

"And possibly blow their cover? No." Johnny shook his head.

Vince growled low in his throat and continued his pacing. He knew Johnny was right. He had a tendency to believe the worst would happen, and he tried to push that down. Jask could handle it, Vince had to believe that. Finally, the mirror began to glow and they waited anxiously for Draz to come through.

Vince's stomach fell as soon as he saw the angel. Draz didn't step through the mirror like normal, he stumbled through and fell to his knees. Johnny was there in an instant, catching him before he could hit the ground. Johnny laid Draz over his lap and Vince took the opportunity to get a better look at him. He was covered in blood and his left arm hung at an unnatural angle. One eye was swollen shut and Drazan's good hand covered a heavily bleeding wound in his side. Johnny put his own hand over it before standing, lifting his wounded lover with him.

"Edis!" Vince shouted as he helped Johnny move him to the couch. The sound of everyone running from the kitchen was almost deafening, but Edis quickly assessed Drazan and got to work healing.

"Vince, the mirror... go. Jask..." Draz wasn't able to say much before passing out, but Vince got the drift. He turned and ran for the mirror, finishing the runes that Draz taught him days before.

He stepped through the mirror and almost lost his footing as he took in the gruesome scene before him. The room was destroyed, the walls black from energy burns and the furniture was in pieces. A fire blazed by one of the windows and Vince had to stare hard into the smoke to find Jask.

Cidos and Athar stood over his unmoving mate, and panic like he'd never felt before consumed him. Vince conjured a wave of his own fire to drive them away, then ran to Jask's side and felt for a pulse, his heart rate skyrocketing when he found it. It was weak, but it was there. Vince didn't have time to feel relief because he was tackled from the side. He rolled with the hit and tossed his attacker to the floor.

Cidos was on his feet instantly and Vince faced him, eyes going black. "He's your brother!"

"He's a traitor to our family!" Cidos swung and Vince ducked, coming back up with a punch that made Cidos stumble back.

"I don't have to hold back here, asshole. You sure you want to do this?" Vince owed it to Jask to give his brother one more chance. He watched the hesitation cross Cidos' face before a grim determination settled in. They struck at the same time, the building shaking with the force of their clash.

"Vince!" Jask called weakly and Vince spared a second to look back. Jask had managed to get to his feet but his father was fighting him again. Vince cursed and turned away from Cidos to go to him. Cidos kicked him in the back of the leg, and Vince fell to one knee. He spun and knocked Ci's legs out from under him then aimed a kick at his face, but Ci blocked just in time and landed a solid blow to Vince's stomach.

He could hear Jask fighting and knew he needed to get to him soon. He threw up his hands to grab Cidos' arm when the angel struck again, then blasted him back and jumped to his feet. The sooner he ended Cidos, the sooner he could save Jask. Vince surged forward, but got hit with an energy ball before he could make it to his foe. He ignored the agony of the burn, swallowing down the yell of pain as he hit Cidos with another wall of fire, then listened for Jask and felt some hope when he heard Athar cursing. They could do this, they would make it out of this alive. Vince would fulfill his promise to his mate and nothing would ever keep them apart again. He held onto that thought as Cidos produced a blade of pure energy and ran at him.

Vince let him get just close enough before dropping under the swipe of the blade and grabbing Cidos' arm. He twisted it back with enough force that the crack of the bone — and Cidos' following scream — echoed around the room. The blade disappeared as the angel lost concentration. Vince followed the attack with a punch to his kidney from behind. Cidos reached behind him with his good arm and tossed Vince over his shoulder. He let out a grunt as he hit the floor, but got up again in an instant.

Fighting with Cidos was taking up time that Vince couldn't afford to lose. He moved into Ci's space and gripped his throat, lifting him and slamming him hard into the ground. He brought his hand up to deliver a killing blow when a voice rang out in the room: "Enough!"

Dread filled Vince as he lifted his gaze and he knew it was over. Jask knelt in front of his father, body limp like he didn't have the energy to hold himself up anymore. They were facing Vince, and there was a very sharp knife to Jask's throat. Athar held Jask's head up by his hair and watched Vince for his reaction.

"Don't." The plea came out sounding forced, Vince having to speak around the lump of fear in his throat. There was a very real possibility that Athar would kill Jask to be rid of them both, and Vince couldn't let that happen. There was nothing more important than Jask's survival.

"Step away from my son." Athar's voice was cold and Vince stood slowly, keeping an eye on them both.

"Very wise, demon. I'm sure you see my dilemma here. I could kill Jaskian, and you along with him, but I would prefer not to do that. He is, after all, my oldest... and I'm sure once you're out of the picture, he can be *persuaded* to see the light. If you care at all for him, if you want him to live... you'll give yourself up," Athar continued in that same tiresome tone, like he was discussing the weather and didn't hold both of their lives in his hand.

"Vin, you can't." Jask grasped his father's hand in a final show of resistance, but Athar pushed the blade down.

Blood began to fall down Jask's neck and Vince stepped forward. "No!"

Athar let up on the pressure and raised an eyebrow at Vince. The question in his eyes was clear, and Vince knew what the answer had to be. He swallowed and blinked back the tears that were threatening to fall. Over the last three days, Vince had allowed himself to imagine a life with Jask. He'd been so confident that the plan would work that building a future seemed the next logical step. Either way, Vince was going to die. He had to make the decision that would be best for them both. This way, Jask still had a chance at a happy ending. This way, a part of Vince would live on in Jask's memory. He gazed into Jask's worried blue eyes and unclenched his fists.

"I'll do it. Let Jask go, and I'll participate in the ritual willingly." He spoke to Athar, but his eyes never left Jask's face. He needed it burned into his memory. Whatever they were going to do to him wouldn't be pleasant, and he would need something to hold onto in those final, terrible minutes.

"Vince!" Jask tried again to get free, but Vince held up a hand.

"Jask, you can't fight this. We can't win. This is how it was always going to end. *Fuck.*" He ran a hand down his face, wincing when he felt blood coating his beard. After everything, he was still going to lose Jask.

He'd barely gotten a chance to be happy with him. There was no time to show him how much he loved him, how much just making this decision was killing him. All the "might have beens" flashed through his mind: their wedding, their home, their children. None of that was ever going to happen now. He couldn't be selfish, because doing this meant Jask could go back. He could protect the others. He could find love again.

"I love you, Jask. More than anything. I can't let them kill you. Not for someone like me. Let me go, sweetheart. Let me do this for you," Vince's voice gave out on the last few words. Athar had lowered the blade completely, but Jask was sobbing now. He couldn't fight and they both knew it. Vince looked up as Athar nodded and Cidos stepped up behind Vince. He hadn't even seen him get up.

"Vince, *please*," Jask begged.

"It's better this way. Go find Drazan. You have to survive this, Jask. You have to live." Vince would've kept going, would have told Jask again how much he loved him. How much he wanted Jask to thrive and be happy. As he opened his mouth to continue, a white hot pain shot through his middle and he looked down. That bastard had stabbed him through the stomach. The wound wasn't fatal, but it hurt like a bitch. He heard movement and he wrenched his eyes away from the wound to watch as Jask tried to crawl to him.

Athar stepped on him, holding him down. "I suggest you do as he says, Jaskian. You wouldn't want your mate's sacrifice to be in vain, I'm sure."

Even wounded, Jask wasn't giving up. Vince felt a swell of pride when Jask rolled and pushed his father's foot away from him. He got to his hands and knees again before moving slowly toward Vince. Vince fell to his knees, one hand outstretched. If he could reach Jask, they could teleport away. Heal and try again with help from the others. Even as he thought it, the hope was ripped away from him.

"How pathetic," Cidos sneered before pulling Vince back.

"Jask, I love you. Please just... don't forget that. I'm sorry, sweetheart, I'm so sorry." Sorry that they would never get to experience a life together. That he was causing Jask this pain. Vince had to make sure Jask knew that. He tried one more time to reach Jask, but suddenly he wasn't in the same room anymore. Athar and Cidos stood above him, and Jask was nowhere to be seen.

"No! Damn it!" He slumped down and ran his hand through his hair, ignoring the blood. His wrist was grabbed and he didn't fight as Cidos cuffed him and chained him to a chair. He stared at the floor and tried to ignore the ache in his chest that happened whenever he was too far away from Jask. Would Jask still feel that when the bond was broken? He winced as his body started to heal the hole from his stab wound. The burns were already mostly done, but it would take a while for this wound to knit itself back together. He wondered if he would be dead before it finished. He could only hope Jask would honor his decision and stay away. *Please, Jask. Stay safe*, he silently begged.

Jaskian

All Jask could feel was ice and pain. Pain in his body from his father's assault, in his chest from not being able to stop Vince from being taken, and a cold so complete that he was actually surprised as he started to heat up.

Something about that didn't seem right. He blinked his eyes open slowly and rolled on the decimated, rubble-covered floor. The fires they'd started during the fight were growing, inching closer, and Jask was tempted to just let them take him under. His father might've said he didn't want him to die, but it was a lie, and Jask would rather be consumed by the flames than die from the bond being broken.

Part of Jask rebelled at the thought, pushed him, urged him, begged him to get up, to go find Vince. To stop the ritual before it happened, to save him and finish what they started. To have the life they dreamed about. But his body wouldn't obey, he barely made it halfway to his feet before the waves of burning hot air knocked him back down. He couldn't do it. "I love you too, Vin," he whispered, laying back down on the broken remains of what used to be a dining table. "See you... wherever comes next."

~

When he woke up, he heard hushed, concerned voices, but they were drowned out pretty quickly when his mind caught up to the pain in his body. He tried to do a quick inventory of his injuries, but there were too many to catalogue and he stopped trying. It seemed strange to him that he'd still be in pain in the After, and it wasn't until he heard Drazan's voice cutting through the haze that he realized he hadn't actually died at all.

"What do you mean, you can't track him?" Draz demanded. "What the fuck good are you if you can't track him?"

Edis huffed, and it sounded like he shoved Drazan. "I healed *you*, didn't I? I'm the healer. Jask is the tracker, he always has been. We have to wait for him to wake up."

Heavy footsteps sounded. "Enough, you two," Johnny said. "Arguing isn't going to help either one of them right now."

"Where is my brother!" Leota yelled, much closer to Jask's face. He startled, forcing his eyes open to look at her tear-stained cheeks. "You left him there, didn't you? Did you hand him over to your father?" Fury lined her voice and pain ricocheted through Jask as she stuck her finger in one of his wounds. "Tell... me... where... he... *is!*"

She was yanked off of him before Jask could even finish screaming. "Damnit, Ms. Leota, can't you see he's hurt?" Johnny asked, holding her back. "He did everything he could."

The words rang false in Jask's chest. Johnny was lying, he didn't actually believe that Jask did everything he could. Did Jask even believe it? Would Vince? In the end, he'd fought against his father's grip and tried.. tried to get to Vince. He coughed suddenly, as if the reminder of the blade that'd been held to his throat also reminded him of the cut it had made.

Drazan was by his side in an instant, sitting down and pulling Jask half into his lap. "Hey, hey. You're fine, don't listen to them."

Cool water ran over Jask's lips and he opened eagerly for it, drinking as much as he could before he felt the urge to cough again. "Why the fuck am I not healing?"

"I don't know, Jask," Edis said quickly, sitting by his feet. "I don't know what they did, but I think there was poison on the blade that cut you. Mom and Amaranth are looking for the antidote now. You likely won't heal until they find it."

"*If* they find it," Jask corrected gently. "No way dad would use something mom knew how to cure."

Drazan ran a hand through Jask's blood-soaked hair. "He doesn't know she's with us. No reason to pick something she can't cure if he didn't know she'd even be here. They'll find it, Jask. I promise."

"What if I'm not poisoned at all?" he asked. "What if I can't heal because they're killing him?" Suddenly, a renewed urge to fight surged through Jask and he attempted to sit up, but a gush of blood pooled out onto the couch from some unknown part of his body. Lightheaded, Jask laid back down as Edis dropped to his knees in front of the couch and ran his hands along Jask's body, searching for anything he *could* heal. "How did I get back here?"

"Edis came and got you," Johnny said. "After he healed Drazan, we got a little bit of the story. When you and Vincenzo didn't return, we got worried, and Edis finally convinced Miss Leota to let him go help. It was just... too late, I guess."

Lee burst into tears, wailing about how it was all her fault. The sound grated on Jask's ears and he groaned, raising a broken hand to his face. "It's not anyone's fault but my father's. This whole thing is his fault... if he'd have just accepted us—"

"That was never going to happen," Ed said sharply. "You know that. Especially after we lied for so long. We hurt his ego when we fooled him with those blockers, he'd kill us all just for that alone. Add in his stupid sense of duty and none of us ever stood a chance."

Jask nodded dumbly, wincing as the pain got a little worse. Drazan tried to soothe him, but Johnny didn't seem to be done yet. "What happened, anyway? Drazan didn't seem to know."

"It was an ambush," Jask said. "Somehow, they knew we were coming. They knew about all of it. Vince being my mate, Lee being Ed's. They were ready for us. Draz and I walked into a trap. Athar sat there sipping fucking bourbon as Cidos attacked Draz, and the moment I tried to help him, Athar joined, too." He let out a pained noise as Drazan shifted to help him drink some more water. "We were getting our asses kicked. I thought Draz was about to lose, so I told him to go get help. I held them off until he could get to a mirror, and hell. I didn't honestly expect to last long enough to even see help arrive."

Frowning, Johnny crossed his arms. "If you'd have died, Vince would've, too."

"No," Jask argued. "Ed was here. Drazan was here. They both know the ritual, which means they know how to keep an angel alive when the demon dies, I knew they'd be smart enough to help Vince. I wasn't trying to die, anyway. But fuck." He shivered, pressing his fingers against one of the worst wounds.

"You really couldn't take them?" Lee's voice was much softer now, like she'd really believed Jask was prepared to let Vince die before all of that. "They're that strong?"

Sorrow filled him as he realized what she *really* meant. If they were too strong for Jask, her brother didn't stand a chance. Ignoring the throbbing, pulsing pain, Jask sat up as carefully as he could and reached his unbroken hand out to take hers. "He's still alive, Lee. I wouldn't be talking to you if he wasn't. Vince is a fighter, he always has been. And as far as I know, he wasn't poisoned, so I bet he's already healed up and giving them a run for their money."

Even as he said the words, terror took hold in his chest. The thought of Vince being on his own, facing them and certain death... it was too much. He stood, bracing himself on Drazan's shoulder for support and looked down at his body. His clothes were shredded and singed, and now that he was paying attention, he noticed the smell of burnt hair. He reached a hand up to his own head and nearly collapsed when he realized that smell was coming from *him*.

"Jaskian, it's not as bad as you think," Johnny said quickly. "It's only... mostly gone."

He knew that his hair should be the last of his concerns, but it still felt like *another* part of him had been taken. Everyone was staring at him, so he straightened up a little and clenched his jaw. "Do you want to hear the rest of what happened, or can I try to get cleaned up?"

"We need to know, Jask," Drazan said carefully. "Why wasn't Vince with you?"

Nodding once, Jask recounted the story. "We were fine, we had it under control. Vince is stronger than Cidos when he's not holding back, he wouldn't have had a problem there if I'd have held out a little longer. But I was weak already from fighting them for so long, and my dad got the upper hand. Had me on my knees with that poisoned blade to my throat." Silent tears forced their way out of Jask's eyes and trailed down his cheeks. "Athar, he... he gave Vince a choice. Come quietly to save me, or we'd both die."

"He didn't hesitate, did he," Lee said, leaning against Edis for support. "The fucking idiot sacrificed himself to save you. He probably figured the same thing you did, that Ed would be here to stop you from dying when the ritual was complete." She laughed bitterly, turning to wrap her arms around him. "He's a fucking idiot."

"He's not an idiot, Leota." Jask wouldn't hear of it. After everything that had happened, the only thing he knew for sure was that Vince was braver than the rest of them combined. "He put angels to shame today," he pointed out. "Not many of us would've done the same thing. He saved my life, even risking his own. Which is why we have to go back, we have to find them, and we have to bring him home."

Drazan stood and gripped the back of Jask's arm lightly. "Let's get you cleaned up and into clothes that actually cover the family jewels again. Maybe by then, Astarte and Amaranth will have found the cure. We can't do a damned thing until you're healed."

Everyone else seemed to agree, and Jask knew he had an uphill battle in his hands, anyway. The main reason Edis hadn't gone with them from the start was because he didn't think he could bring himself to kill his brother or his father. But now, Jask knew that wouldn't be necessary. He'd do it himself, he *had* to do it himself, for revenge, for love... for everything Athar and Cidos tried to take from him. All he needed was a little help leveling the playing field.

Slowly, Drazan undressed him and helped him clean up. It was borderline excruciating, and he was shaking hard enough from the cold and shock that Drazan actually called Johnny in to help warm him up. It was so overtly *nonsexual* that Jask had to laugh. "Shame Vince couldn't see this, huh? Bet he'd level the whole building and be back here in an instant to kick both of your asses."

Johnny chuckled, his back pressed against Jask's. "I'd take that beating if it meant he got back here safely."

"I wouldn't," Drazan said. "I'd like to see him try."

Jask shook his head, wondering if his best friend and mate would ever get over their feud. He had to hope they would, but if Astarte and Amaranth failed to find a cure in time, it wouldn't matter, anyway. One by one, Athar and Cidos would pick them off until no one was left to remember Vince or tell their story. Sadness overtook him again, and he closed his eyes, focusing on the warmth Johnny provided and Drazan's gentle hands. One way or the other... healed, or not... Jask knew he had to save him.

Cidos

"Did you seriously think you could take us?" Cidos asked, amused. "As if a Riskel ever stood a chance against one Veris... let alone two."

Vince raised an eyebrow at him. "If I remember correctly — and I always do — I was about to kill you when daddy stepped in. Seems I was definitely a match for at least *one* of you."

Cidos scoffed. "Doesn't matter, you're ours now." He paced in front of the table where Vince was strapped down, his hands behind his back. "I was weakened from fighting Jaskian. Don't flatter yourself."

Vince laughed. "Yeah, sure. Keep telling yourself that. Better yet, let me up and I'll fight you one handed. I'll still win."

"Why would I do something like that? Besides, you agreed to participate willingly. Make no mistake, if you resist, my father will find Jaskian and kill him. Is that what you want?" Cidos took no small amount of pleasure in the look of pain that crossed Vince's face. While he honestly didn't want Jask to die, that wouldn't stop him from tormenting the demon with the thought.

"Fuck you. Get this over with already," Vince growled, turning his gaze to the ceiling.

"Soon enough. He's preparing the ritual now. I just wanted to see the light leave your eyes when you realize no one's coming for you." Cidos tilted his head to get a better look.

"I don't want them to. Table's comfy, room's nice and cool. Basically, it's a five star hotel in here. I'm having the time of my life, really." Vince tried to shrug but Cidos had made sure the restraints were uncomfortably tight. The asshole couldn't move, and that's just the way Ci wanted it. The spells on the cuffs, carved by him and absolutely perfect, kept Vince's powers muted as well. He tested that theory by grabbing a small hammer and hitting Vince right above the spot the stab wound sat.

Vince barely cried out before coughing, but the cough faded into a laugh. "That tickled, cupcake. Try again."

"I have no interest in feeding your sick perversions," Cidos mumbled, dropping the hammer back to the table.

"Jask does. Let me tell you, those hands? Fuck, never felt anything like it." Vince was smiling, and that just wouldn't do at all.

"Yes, and you never will again." Cidos watched the smile fall right off of Vince's face, so he continued, "Does it bother you to think of Jask with someone else? Father already has plans for his reconditioning. I'm sure it'll be painful, but necessary. The marriage will be arranged, of course. We can't have another issue like that Drazan fiasco. Drazan himself will be eliminated, if he isn't dead already. Then your entire family.

We'll end this silly bond business in one fatal swoop. How does that make you feel, exactly? To know that those lives, that blood, is on your hands because you decided your love was more important than their continued survival?" Each word seemed to make Vince deflate further. Cidos watched as Vince clenched and unclenched his fists, the only part of his body that he could move. A small flame flickered to life at his fingertips but was quickly extinguished by the magic in the cuffs. Cidos laughed. "What's the matter? Can't keep it up?"

"Very funny, but I see the way you're looking at me. Mad you didn't get a Riskel of your own? Jask got me, Edis got Leota. You're the only one left out. That must sting," Vince shot back.

Cidos picked up the hammer and swung it down on the wound again, harder this time. Vince cursed at him but Cidos didn't give him the satisfaction of a response. He walked out of the room, the hammer clattering noisily to the ground as he let it go. That line of thought was ludicrous — as if he would *ever* lower himself to that level of debauchery. Ci had plenty of options to choose from when it came to sexual partners, and a demon was nowhere on that list. He frowned as the thought kept nagging at him, swimming around in the dark recesses of his brain. Why *had* Edis been chosen? Jask was the eldest, so that made sense, but Edis was the youngest. Wasn't that spot rightfully his to have, as the oldest twin? Cidos was the one that ran the firm, he was the one that was carrying on the family's will, the one that was upholding tradition. Why did Jaskian get everything even after rejecting his heritage?

Cidos turned back toward the room and caught his reflection in a window. He blinked at himself as he realized exactly what he'd been thinking. He was jealous of his brothers for consorting with demons? The thought disgusted him enough that the emotion flowing off of him broke a nearby lamp. He shivered slightly in the aftermath and went to find the thermostat. How his father could stand to be surrounded by cold stone all day, he'd never know. Cidos ran a hand down his face as he realized that's all that was wrong with him. He didn't need a demon, he just needed heat. There were other places to find it, he didn't need to go down that road.

He found what he was looking for easily and turned the temperature up a few degrees before forcing himself to sit and calm down. Letting Vince get to him wouldn't help them in the long run. He had to find a way to keep Vince out of his head, to do what his family needed him to do. Ci closed his eyes and took a deep breath before letting it out slowly. His father would kill both Jask and Edis just for this to be over, and his mother would be devastated if he let that happen. The future of his family rested firmly on his shoulders. He knew the reconditioning Athar had planned for his brothers would be unpleasant; he could only hope they wouldn't fight it too much. Soon, the family would be restored... and all would be well.

~

A few hours later, he was back in the room with Vince. His father had given him the task of finding the location of the Riskels, and he would not fail. Vince was whistling something he didn't recognize as he laid out various tools and potions. Once he was satisfied everything was in place, he turned to face the annoying creature on his table. Vince had the audacity to wink at him. Cidos sighed heavily and said, "Tell me where they are."

"I wouldn't hold my breath, if I were you. Wait, actually, do exactly that. Hold your breath and don't stop until your breathing stops forever," Vince replied pleasantly.

"Don't make this difficult, Vincenzo. I'd prefer to not get blood on my clothes."

"Are you kidding? Everyone digs a dirty guy, cupcake."

"Stop calling me that," Cidos demanded as he grabbed a pair of scissors and cut off what was left of Vince's shirt.

"Oh, getting right to the kinky stuff, then?" Vince eyed the scissors in Cidos' hand with distrust.

"I wonder how long you'll be able to keep up the smart remarks once we really get started." Cidos raised an eyebrow at him, putting the scissors down and picking up a knife.

"Oh, I can go all day, *cupcake*. Keep it up, I—" whatever he was about to say was cut off in a choked-out curse as Cidos reopened the wound in Vince's stomach. He twisted the knife and left it there, wiping his hands on a towel. He watched Vince try to breathe through the pain as he unlocked his phone and put on some classical music.

"I hope you don't mind. I work better with something playing in the background." Cidos sat the phone back down and applied some pressure on the knife. "I think I'll leave that there for now. Where are they?"

"Fuck off. Nothing you can do to me will hurt as much as losing Jask. You've already done your worst," Vince grunted out, stopping every few words. Cidos was pleased with the amount of agony he was in, but knew he could do better.

"I'll have so much fun proving you wrong." Cidos yanked the knife out and put his hand over the wound. He healed it just enough to make it hurt before stabbing him again. He made sure the knife was embedded deep, and turned to look at his other toys. After some deliberation, he chose a hammer, this one slightly bigger than the one he'd used earlier. He took Vince's hand and flattened it out. "Where are they?"

"Nowhere you'll ever find." Vince's words were full of hate. Cidos slammed the hammer down on Vince's smallest finger, delighting in the pained groan that fell from the demon's lips.

"Save yourself the pain, Vincenzo. Where?" Cidos moved to the next finger with the hammer poised to strike. When Vince said nothing, Cidos broke that finger, too.

"Fuck! I'm not telling you anything, do the damn ritual!" Vince tried to pull his hand away but he had nowhere to go.

Cidos shook his head, feigning a sad tone as he said, "You have to know it doesn't work like that. Where are they?"

"Kiss my ass," Vince replied with a glare. Cidos broke another finger. Vince yelled out another curse, but this time, Cidos didn't stop until each finger on that hand was broken. Vince was shaking in his restraints, and Cidos was silently impressed in how well he'd fared so far.

"Where are they, demon?" Cidos pulled the knife out slowly before stabbing Vince somewhere new.

"I hope Jask kills you, and I hope he makes it slow." Vince laughed, and the sound grated on Cidos' nerves.

"Not what I wanted to hear." Cidos brought the hammer down and the crack was audible as Vince's hand broke. "That's *definitely* something I wanted to hear."

Vince struggled against the chains and straps holding him. Cidos let that continue for a moment before waving his hand over them and watching as they tightened. Vince gasped as the one at his neck began to cut off his airflow. "Never mind. *I'm* going to kill you."

"Sorry, couldn't hear you. You're sounding a little breathless." Cidos stopped the band from tightening. "Where?"

"You're pathetic. Worthless. Athar must be so disappointed that you're the son he'll be left with," Vince spat.

Cidos looked down at his shirt and sighed. "I told you I didn't want to get dirty." He struck Vince across the cheek before going back to the table. He wiped the spittle from his shirt and picked up a lighter. "Shall we find out if you're flame resistant, Vince?"

Cidos walked to the end of the table and removed Vince's boot. He lit the flame right against the bottom of his foot and smiled as Vince screamed. Cidos used his grace to make the flame hotter, watching the skin blacken. He loosened the restraints just enough to watch Vince squirm and moved to the other foot. "Where are they?"

"Start... the... ritual," Vince demanded.

"So eager to die?" Cidos turned the flame off and went back to his table. He picked up a second knife and started to slice across Vince's skin. Vince screamed again, this time it sounded angry. Cidos kept going. "You know the ritual will be ten times worse? All of this for my smug older brother. Just tell me where he is. I'll bring him right to you."

"I would suffer a thousand fates worse than this to keep Jask out of the hands of you and your father, you deranged piece of shit," Vince's voice shook as he spoke, and Cidos thought he may be getting close to breaking him. Unfortunately, he never got the chance to find out. His father came in at that moment and announced that he was tired of waiting. They would start the ritual and find the others later. Cidos couldn't hide his disappointment, but he would never disobey Athar. He put his things away and helped his father prepare.

Seventeen

Edis

The longer Vince was alone with Cidos, the more Edis started to panic. He knew his twin better than anyone else on the planet, and all that did was terrify him. Cidos was the type of person that believed the end result justified not just the means, but every single thing that happened from start to finish. There wasn't a doubt in Ed's mind that Cidos would kill every single one of them if it meant keeping the Veris line pure, and he'd absolve himself by calling them all collateral damage. He hoped his brother would at least lose a little bit of sleep over it, but something told Ed that wouldn't happen.

"Have you found anything yet?" Drazan asked Leota from somewhere behind Edis. "I think Vince is running out of time."

Leota scoffed. "Yeah, like you give a shit what happens to him," she snapped. "What is it with you two, anyway?"

"Look," Drazan said, "I might not care for him as a person, but if he dies... so does Jaskian. And *him* I care about."

Edis rubbed his temples as their argument dragged on. He didn't give a shit about the pissing match between Vince and Drazan — Ed was pretty sure they only thought they hated each other because they both wanted to believe they loved Jask more. But the truth was, Edis thought *he* loved Jask the most. He'd looked up to him from the time he was born. Jask was always there, teaching him how to walk, how to ride a bike, how to use his grace. Jask was the one that groomed his wings when they started to grow and helped him learn how to use them. Athar had always been absent. He'd left shortly after Astarte got pregnant with him and Cidos, and they had barely seen their father at all until they were old enough to join the firm. Even then, he never felt much like a dad... more like a boss.

For a while, Edis had bought into the duty of their line. 'Break the bond, save the world.' Something that not even Jask was ever aware of was the reasoning behind it all. When Cidos and Edis came of age, Athar sat them down and explained *why* they'd need to kill Jaskian's mate, no matter the cost. Legend said that the first offspring born to a Veris and a Riskel would be powerful enough to destroy the world. It would be an abomination, a monster. And once it took root inside of its mother, it would be almost impossible to kill. "It's nothing personal," Athar had said gently. "But it must be done." They'd bought it hook, line, and sinker.

Keeping that information from Jask had been hard enough. They were expressly forbidden from telling him, lest he get the idea to intentionally impregnate his mate as a means of fighting back. But now, knowing that Jaskian and Vince were biologically incapable of procreating and that Edis himself was the one at risk, things were even more complicated. He didn't have the heart to tell Leota that they couldn't ever have a child. That she'd forever need to take the strongest forms of birth control *and* he'd never be able to fill her up and mark her from the inside out like he so desperately wanted to. But there had been a night, just one night, toward the very beginning where he'd lost control. Lost himself to the heat of the moment, to *her* heat, and let himself go when he shouldn't have.

There wasn't any medical research on stopping the conception of a demon/angel hybrid. Nothing in any of his books about what to do in a situation like that, and for all of his extensive training as a healer, he didn't have a clue what to do other than pray to Veris himself that nothing happened.

"Why are you staring at me like that?" Leota asked, drawing Edis' gaze up to her eyes from where it had been intensely resting on her stomach.

"Sorry. Lost in thought, I didn't realize where I was looking." Ed stood, crossing the distance to her and kissing her gently. He could sense something different about her, but sheer hope had him denying the possibility that it was because she was carrying his child. The problem was... he wanted it. Despite knowing the consequences, he wanted to have a baby with her. A real family. He just couldn't, and he was so, so very afraid of what would happen if anyone — especially Cidos — discovered there was a chance that might be a reality. "Where are we in finding the cure? I wasn't listening."

"Astarte thinks she has it," Johnny said. "But it requires ingredients we don't have. Jask is insisting we forget about the cure and go save Vince ourselves, we won't have enough time to drive to get the ingredients *and* stop Vince from dying. As much as I hate to admit it, I think he's right."

Ed shook his head, but before he could offer a solution, Drazan spoke. "Is he strong enough to fight off whatever this is until we save Vince?"

"I don't know. It's getting worse by the hour, but truthfully, I don't know if it's because of the poison... or because of what's currently being done to Vince." Johnny crossed his arms. "Edis, you're a healer. Would you be able to tell how much time he has left?"

Nodding, he walked toward the bedroom where Jask was being kept. The stench was almost overpowering, and Ed thought for a moment that Jask might've soiled himself. But as he got closer to the bed and saw the black lines criss crossing his brother's skin, he realized what the true cause was. "He poisoned your grace," Ed said quietly, sadness and fear washing through him. "That's why you can't heal on your own. You're... you're rotting from the inside out."

Jask nodded a little, his eyes closed. "Yeah. Shit's ruining my fucking wings, Vince is gonna be pissed."

Edis wasn't sure what to make of the fact that Jask's only concern seemed to be how his mate would react to him, but he couldn't exactly say he blamed him. It was clear that their mates mattered more than just about anything else, and Jask was always the type to try and sugar-coat how he was really feeling. Sitting down next to him, Ed ignored the putrid odor and ran soothing, healing hands over Jask's body. "How fast is it progressing, do you think? They asked me to find out how much time you have left, but I don't think anyone can answer that better than you can."

"Thanks, you know I hate it when people talk for me," Jask said with a forced playfulness. "Not long, Ed. But I don't care. Get Vince out of there. Bring him home to me."

There wasn't a scenario where that was going to work. Edis might've found himself on Jask's side in the end, but he didn't have it in him to hurt his father or his twin. That was why he'd stayed behind the first time. If push came to shove, he'd be powerless against them. Nothing had changed, so there was only one thing Edis could think to do — find the cure, and then find some way to distract Athar and Cidos without outright engaging with them until Jask was strong enough to go after Vince himself.

The cough Jask let out cemented his decision. Edis didn't give a shit about Vince beyond him sort of being his brother-in-law twice over, and while he didn't wish the pain of losing a mate on Jask, he knew he'd be able to keep him alive if the bond broke. He *wouldn't* be able to keep him alive if he didn't find the cure. As Jask started slipping under again, Edis put a hand on his forehead and whispered, "I'm sorry, Jask. I hope one day you'll forgive me."

~

The cure consisted of viper garlic, storm root, and tridvar. None of those ingredients were all that rare, but they were indigenous to com-pletely different parts of the world, ensuring that only a Veris would be able to cure an angel poisoned in such a way. To his knowledge, only a demon had ever employed such a thing, and it made his stomach churn to realize that his father had done it to one of his own sons.

Bracing himself, Edis teleported as far as he could in a single leap after saying goodbye to Leota. Over and over again, he flung himself through space and time until he was in possession of both the viper garlic and the tridvar. He was exhausted from the leaps, and suddenly very afraid that even if he managed to find the root of an Eaglon tree that had been struck by lightning, he'd never make it back home in time. Teleportation was by far the most difficult of all an angel's abilities — so much so that only the Veris line had the strength to pull it off — but even then, it wiped them out almost completely if they tried to go too far, too fast.

He took an opportunity to rest and call one of the paralegals he worked with at the firm. She'd always had a crush on him, and as bad as Edis felt about using that to his advantage, he knew he didn't have a choice. He practically begged her to find out the location of every Eaglon tree in the world, and to cross reference any weather reports to see if any of them had ever been struck. He hung up, asking her to call him back when she found something, and closed his eyes. Ed knew he needed a proper amount of sleep and something to eat, but there wasn't time for any of that. He could sleep when it was all over.

When she finally called back with a location, Edis was so out of it that he didn't have a clue how much time had passed. He thanked her profusely and forced himself to his feet, calling on his ancestors to give him the strength he needed to see it through. He flung himself forward and landed in a heap at the base of the tree, pulling out his knife to hack some of the root off with a whispered apology. Now that he was in possession of the ingredients, all he had to do was somehow get himself back to Jaskian... which happened to be a task he wasn't sure he'd survive.

His muscles ached, and exhaustion was threatening to drag him under. But the chain reaction that would occur if he failed was enough to keep him going, and with a scream, he forced his tired body to leap one more time.

~

Edis woke up several hours later in the bed that Jaskian had previously occupied. Leota was crying over him, and he sat up, reaching out for her. "Lee, I'm fine, I'm fine." He kissed her quickly, then looked around the room for Jask. "Where is he? Is he okay?"

She nodded, trying to push him back down onto the bed. "Yes, he's fine. Drazan and Astarte used the ingredients to make the antidote, Jask's fine. He's pacing in the living room now, probably wearing a damn hole into the floor."

Relief flooded through him and he stood, taking her hand and leading her back out. The sight of his brother upright again settled something inside of Edis, and he grinned. "Look at you, you owe me one."

"I'm about to owe you more than one. I can't do this shit without you, Ed. *We* can't. And look, all I can promise you is that I'll do whatever I can to make sure you're not the one that has to actually kill them. I just need you to help with Vince."

Part of him knew this had been coming, and somewhere in his sleep he'd realized that *this* was his family. Not Athar, and as much as he hated to admit it, not even Cidos. Jask and Vince, Drazan and Johnny, Astarte, Amaranth and Leota... those were his people. Those were the ones he'd be spending the rest of his life with, whether Athar and Cidos survived this or not. With a nod and a heavy heart, Edis reached out for his brother. "Okay. Tell me what you need me to do."

Vince

The smell of sage permeated the room and Vince hissed as Athar branded his skin with the runes necessary for the ritual. Cidos had informed him with no small amount of glee that the branding was not necessary. They could've painted the ritualistic symbols on, but this was apparently Veris tradition. He said it as if Vince would take comfort in the fact that he was a part of the custom. All Vince could think of was the pain his ancestors must have endured. He kept his eyes on the ceiling and didn't reply to the taunts. He would do his part; he could keep Jask and the others safe. A single tear escaped down his cheek as he remembered for the hundredth time that he'd never see his family again. He closed his eyes to keep more tears from falling — no need to give Cidos any satisfaction.

He forced himself to think of something else, and Jask's smiling face was the first thing his mind supplied. He didn't know what awaited him after this ritual, but if that was the sight he'd see for the rest of eternity, then he would be content. He let his thoughts continue wandering in that direction, and soon, his mind was completely occupied with his mate. Jask's ice blue eyes lit up with amusement, the way he laughed, the way he kissed. Those were things he hoped he kept with him.

"Are you crying?" Cidos' annoying voice interrupted his daydream. "Thought you were made of sterner stuff, Vincenzo."

"Sterner than you," Vince agreed. Athar placed a brand directly over one the cuts Cidos had created earlier and Vince clenched his jaw.

"There. He's ready." Athar sliced open his hand and let his blood drip into a bowl before doing the same to Vince's broken one.

"Fuck! I have a perfectly non-broken hand over here, you know." Vince let out a sigh.

"Yes, but that wouldn't have given me nearly as much satisfaction." Athar stepped away and began adding ingredients to the bowl.

"I don't understand why this has to happen. Does the happiness of your children mean nothing to you?" Vince asked, watching Cidos as he basically vibrated with excitement.

Athar laughed coldly. "If we're pitting the fleeting happiness of my sons against the survival of the whole world, no. It means nothing to me." His voice became bored as he continued measuring and pouring. "You're dying for a good cause, Vincenzo. Take comfort in that... it's not often your *kind* are worth much of anything. This is the only scenario where a demon is ever put to good use."

"Good cause? Survival of the world? What cult are you psychos a part of, exactly?" Vince knew it was futile, but he pulled at his chains anyway.

"Don't worry about it, Vinnie," Cidos said, grinning like an asshole. "You'll be dead and gone soon enough, it doesn't concern you."

With a triumphant yell, Athar tossed the last ingredient into the bowl. "It's ready, enough talk. I suppose we'd better hope Edis is with Jaskian... or not. He had his chance."

"Is there a way to check?" Vince looked between the two angels in the room, his heart sinking as he realized they wouldn't. "You really don't care if he dies."

Cidos shook his head and walked over to check Vince's restraints. "Not anymore. And apparently, you don't either. You know what the ritual does to both parties, and yet... you volunteered for this. You're basically killing him yourself... how does that feel, I wonder? Does it hurt, or do your demonic instincts revel in that kind of thing?"

Panic threatened to choke him and he began to fight in earnest. "No! This wasn't the deal, let me go! Jask *has* to live!"

"Enough," Athar chided. "Whether he lives or dies is no longer your concern. If Edis is near him, chances are he'll pull through. And if not... I suppose you both should've thought about that before disobeying your ancestors."

Anything else Vince could've said was cut off when Cidos shoved a rag into his mouth. "That's enough, I think. Can I do it, Father? Can I say the incantation?"

Athar studied Cidos for a moment and stepped back, sheathing his knife. "Go ahead. Be the *one* son of mine to make me proud."

Nearly bursting with fevered excitement, Cidos hovered over Vince, beginning to recite words in a language Vince had never heard.

At first it seemed like nothing was happening, and Vince began to have some hope that maybe it wouldn't work. Then the *real* pain started. Like a white hot fire was flowing through his veins. Vince heard screaming as his back arched off the table, and the burn in his throat clued him in to the fact that the screams were coming from him. Cidos' recital barely registered to him as he did everything he could to just get away.

The left cuff broke off of the table, but before he could do anything, Athar was there. The angel held Vince's arm down as his body bowed away from the hard surface below him. He'd never felt anything to this degree before, and suddenly, he understood why no one survived. The pain was so intense he couldn't see, couldn't think. All he could do was scream.

Cidos' voice became faster, louder, registering even over the splintering sounds in Vince's head. All he wanted was for it to be over, to actually die and just move on, but the bastard wouldn't stop talking.

The moment the bond broke, Vince shattered from the inside out. If he'd thought he was in pain before, it was nothing compared to what he was experiencing in that moment.

But suddenly, the pain started to recede. The sharp edges became smooth corners, and the blackness in his vision began to fade. He was sure he'd died, that he'd made it to the end of the pain and would be granted some subpar, shitty afterlife as penance for the life he'd lived - but Cidos' fucking voice was still clattering around in his head. "It's too late, Ed!" Cidos yelled, which didn't make any sense. Why would Cidos and Edis be in his own little version of hell?

Vince chuckled weakly as he realized he'd answered his own question. They were here *because* it was his personal hell. All he needed now was Drazan and that would cement it. He opened his eyes slowly to see what awaited him... and came face to face with Draz himself.

"Hey there, asshole. Don't worry, I almost got you good as new." Draz grinned and then got back to work. Vince blinked a couple of times to make sure he wasn't hallucinating before turning his head slightly. The sight that met him was so strange he still wasn't sure it was real. Jask was slumped against the wall, Edis tending to him with a worried expression. Johnny was fighting Cidos and Vince looked down at himself. Drazan was healing him, tracing the runes on his skin and saving his life. He wasn't dead... they'd gotten there in time.

"Jask, he's..." Vince tried to speak, but his throat was still raw from the screaming.

"Edis has him, sit still," Draz commanded. Vince turned his head back to look at his mate. No... not his mate. He'd felt the bond break, but to him, it didn't change a thing. He still needed Jask, still loved him. Jask's eyes were still closed and Vince willed him to wake up. A noise drew his attention and he shifted his gaze. Athar was moving toward Johnny and Cidos, and Johnny was already struggling. He wouldn't be able to hold his own against them both.

"Draz," Vince coughed out.

"Almost..." Draz mumbled as he placed his hands flat on Vince's chest and finally, Vince could breathe. He felt a shiver go through his entire body and he sat up as a burst of energy flew through him. His limbs were heavy and moving so quickly had him feeling dizzy, but he slid off the table, anyway.

Draz steadied him with a hand on his arm, but Vince could feel him shaking. The healing had taken more out of him than he was letting on. They needed to finish this fight and finish it quickly.

Athar lifted a hand against Johnny and Vince reacted without thinking. He ran forward and tackled Athar back, but the angel was ready for him. He dug in his feet and grabbed Vince under the arms, flinging him sideways so he hit the wall hard.

Vince regained his footing just as Athar grabbed Drazan by the back of his shirt and threw him away from Cidos. Johnny was on his knees behind the evil twin, and Vince knew he *had* to stop Athar from getting to him.

He looked around the room and grabbed the hammer Ci had used to break his hand. He ran forward, swinging it into Athar's side. The elder angel grunted and turned to face Vince again, his face showing no hint of pain, only anger. Vince shrugged and dropped the hammer. "Oops?"

"You have literally become a pain in my side, demon," Athar growled before grabbing Vince by the neck. Vince took his wrist in both hands and somehow managed to dislodge his hold, but didn't have time to revel in his good fortune, because Athar's other hand came up in a hard punch. Vince stumbled back and shook his head to try and diminish the ringing that had taken residence in his ears. His vision returned to normal in time to see Draz take a hit from Cidos that had been meant for

Johnny. Draz flew back into the wall, and that was all Vince got before Athar was on him again.

"I should have just killed you in that room." Athar kicked Vince in the chest. Something inside Vince's ribs made a worrisome cracking noise and he leaned against the nearest object he could find.

"Yeah, but you didn't," he gasped out. "Hindsight and all that, right? I'm sure we'll all laugh about this over some margaritas later." Vince coughed and forced himself back to his feet, scanning the room. Jask was standing again with some help from Edis, and the relief that Vince felt was so profound it gave him another shot of hope. Jask was alive, and he was there with him. Nothing mattered more than that. All he had to do was keep Athar and Cidos busy long enough for everyone to get out safely. He charged forward and got a good hit on Athar, surprising both of them when the angel staggered back one step. Unfortunately for Vince, Athar was still close enough to retaliate. He grabbed a nearby chair and Vince barely had time to block before the piece of furniture hit him. He fell to one knee and watched as Draz attacked Athar from behind. Johnny had Cidos against the wall, arm against his throat.

"Fuck," Vince cursed as the cracked rib repaired itself inside his body. Since being released from the cuffs, his regenerative abilities were working again, but that was both a blessing and a curse. Draz helped him up, but Athar punched him, knocking the weaker angel to the ground. Vince stepped between them and grabbed Athar's arm before he could strike Drazan again, flipping him onto the floor. He took a deep, steadying breath and rolled his shoulders. "Let's finish this, then." Before he could attack, there was a flash of light and Vince went flying back. Athar had sent something that felt a hell of a lot like a grace bomb at them. When Vince's vision cleared, he saw Edis standing defiantly in front of his father.

"That is enough! End this now, before it's too late," Edis pleaded.

"It was too late when you chose the demon bitch." Athar's voice was low, and before anyone could stop him, Athar hit Edis with another wave of powerful, crippling grace. Edis crashed into the opposite end of the room and the wall crumbled down on top of him, burying him completely.

Jask appeared suddenly, knocking his father into the next room. Vince stepped forward to follow, but a pained shout stopped him in his tracks.

"Johnny, no!" Draz's voice rang out. Vince spun, but he was too late. Johnny crumpled to the ground, the light leaving his eyes as he looked to Drazan and Vince. Ci teleported away like a coward, and Vince watched in horror as Draz tried in vain to heal Johnny. "No!" Drazan screamed again, his wings expanding outward and shielding them both from sight.

Vince stared in shock and grief, his brain not wrapping around the fact that his best friend was dead. Johnny had done so much for them, and this was how he'd been repaid? His heart broke for Johnny, and for Drazan as the angel sobbed over the fallen demon in his lap. He didn't know how to help, what to do. That was answered for him when he heard a yell that had definitely come from Jask. He turned back in the direction they'd gone and took off running. Vince entered the room and his heart fell when he saw Athar pinning Jask to the ground, terror renewing in his gut. "Jask!" he yelled.

"Run!" Jask kicked out hard, connecting with Athar's stomach and propelling him backward. A moment later, Jask was on his feet, his broken wings spread wide and eyes brighter than he'd ever seen them. Neither angel was paying any attention to Vince at all, and he was rooted to the spot, afraid that any move he might make would cost Jask his life. "You gonna run away like Ci did, *Athar*?" Jask spat. "Or are you gonna let me finish this?"

With a flick of his wrist and a sadistic laugh, Athar lifted Jaskian from his feet. "*You*, finish *me*? In what world could that ever happen?"

A single tear streamed down Jask's face as he reached into his pocket, his feet dangling uselessly below him. "In this one," he breathed, a second before he jerked his body and flung the blade forward in a movement almost too fast to see. It landed smack between Athar's eyes with a squelch that would ingrain itself in Vince's ears for the rest of his days.

With a stunned expression, Athar lost his hold on Jask and slumped right where he was, pinned to the wall by the tip of the knife.

Jaskian

Jask felt the loss immediately and fell to his knees. He'd just killed his father, and despite knowing that very few people had ever deserved it more, he'd still committed a cardinal sin... and the fight wasn't over yet. Everything had gone so wrong so fast, and they hadn't gotten there in time to stop the bond from breaking.

With bleary eyes, Jask looked up to see a stunned Vince. He couldn't bring himself to speak, to say anything at all to justify or celebrate what he'd just done. The loss of that thin, invisible tether pulling Jask and Vince to each other was overwhelming, but he knew it was nothing compared to what he was about to face. "The others, are they...?"

Vince walked to him slowly. "Johnny, he... and Edis. It's not good, Jask." Vince held a hand out to him, and it took just about all the energy Jask had left to actually reach out to take it.

He stood on shaky legs and pulled Vince into a hug. The bond breaking was nothing more than an extremely painful formality - he'd fallen in love with Vince in his own right, and nothing would change that. "I'm so sorry, Vince." Jask knew he should go back into the other room to see for himself how badly Johnny and Edis were hurt, but he wanted one more second just being held in the arms of the love of his life.

"It's not your fault, sweetheart. None of this is your fault." Vince tightened his arms around him, burying his face in Jask's neck. Hearing the words did little to comfort Jask, because they did little to change the outcome.

Somewhere on the other side of the wall, Drazan screamed, and that alone gave Jask the strength to pull back from Vince and walk through the door. When he did, he couldn't quite make sense of what was happening. Drazan was lifting rubble from a pile and flinging it across the room, and Johnny was sprawled out on the floor behind him at a weird angle. "What... what's happening?" He didn't know where to run first, but when clearing a particularly large piece of stone revealed a crooked leg, he had his answer. "Ed?"

"He was buried, help me get this shit off of him," Drazan yelled as Jask caught up. With a wave of his hand, the rest of the rubble disappeared, revealing his brother's broken body.

Ed's eyes were closed, but his chest was still rising and falling. Drazan took a staggered step back and pivoted as Jask dropped to his knees beside Edis. "C'mon, Ed," Jask begged quietly. "Open your eyes." He was too weak to heal him, so he began checking his body for cuts that might signal the same poison was used on him that Jask had nearly died from. He seemed okay, and Jask knew there wasn't much he'd be able to do but wait and see if he woke up.

The sound of a muffled sob made Jask turn around, and it was then that he realized Johnny wasn't hurt — he was dead. Grief like he'd never known it welled in his chest and threatened to split him in two — there was a man that Jask had spent years searching for, praying to Veris that he was still alive but believing he was dead, now having given the ultimate sacrifice. "Pavo?" Jask said weakly, not daring to step any closer.

Vince knelt slowly next to Johnny's body. "We have to get them home. We have to..." Vince ran his arm over his eyes.

Drazan pulled Johnny back into his arms. "This can't be how it ends. Not him."

"This kid survived his own asshole father just to get killed by mine," Jask said dumbly. "Fuck."

"It wasn't Athar, Jask. It was Cidos," Draz corrected. "Coward killed him and ran." He planted his lips to the top of Johnny's head and his body started to shake. "When I find him..."

Jask knew exactly what was coming next, but shook his head. No one else would die for him, not if he had anything to say about it. "You've all done enough, given enough. I should've killed Cidos the moment I realized he wasn't going to stop. I should've... fuck." He dropped his head, not being able to stop thinking about the picture that hung on his office wall of the small boy just needing his help.

Vince wrapped an arm around his shoulders. "You can't blame yourself. The only one to blame here is Cidos, and we *will* find him... but right now, we have to get Edis back. Your mom may be able to help."

Horror rolled around in his gut and nearly made him sick as he realized he had to tell his mother about Athar. She'd forgiven him for a lot over the years, but he was pretty sure this would be one thing she couldn't get past. He was going to lose both his parents in one fell swoop. "Right. We should... we should take my father's body. She'll want it."

They all moved on autopilot after that, using Drazan's mirror trick to get them and the bodies back home. Jask couldn't bring himself to make eye contact with anyone as he recounted the story to Astarte, Amaranth and Leota, but he didn't have to. He could hear the pain and fear in Lee's voice as she locked herself in the bedroom with Edis' still-unconscious form, and the feelings of despair radiating off both of the mothers was nearly enough to knock Jask on his ass. "I'm sorry," he offered for the second time, knowing it fell flat.

"Sorry won't bring Johnny back," Amaranth said quietly. His own mother still hadn't spoken. Drazan was already out building his casket; he'd started on it the moment they'd gotten back with the bodies. She was right, nothing could bring him back now.

"Jask, come on. You need to rest," Vince insisted before anyone could say anything else. He took his hand when he didn't answer and tried to lead him away.

"I didn't want this to happen," Jask said helplessly, not moving. He couldn't take his eyes off of all the people that had been hurt from this. "I never wanted anyone to die. You have to know that. Mom, please," he said, his voice cracking. "Please."

Vince's hand tightened on his as Astarte blinked and nodded slowly. "Of course, Jask. I know you didn't mean for this to happen."

The words did little to comfort him, and he allowed Vince to drag him out of the room to his bedroom. When the door closed behind him,

Jask braced himself for possibly the worst news of all. "The bond broke," he started uselessly. "Do you... are we...?" He didn't have the heart to actually say the words out loud.

Vince frowned at him. "Are we what?" Vince looked down at their hands and then back up to Jask. "Are you saying you don't want me anymore? Because of the bond? Jask, I know it broke, but I still love you. I still *need* you. Is it... not the same for you?" Vince sounded so unsure of himself that Jask couldn't bear it, and pulled him into a kiss.

"Of course it's the same for me. I love you, bond or not. I'd have fallen for you no matter who we were, and I barely feel any different now than I did before it broke. It never mattered, Vin." Jask wrapped him in his arms and let out his wings, wincing a little since one of them was bent at an odd angle.

"Your wings." Vince gently touched it. "Did this happen in the fight?"

Jask nodded and refused to look at it. "Yeah, when my dad pinned me. I landed on it... it'll heal, it just takes longer than the rest of me." That reminded Jask that Vince endured hours with Cidos and Athar before they'd arrived, and Vince had been bloody and beaten when they landed. He took a step back and circled around him, looking for lingering injuries. "Are you okay?"

"I'm fine." Vince had grabbed a shirt when they'd returned, but he pulled it up now. The runes that had been burned into his skin had healed, but the scars remained. "Don't think these are going away though." He traced one of the runes with a finger, and Jask dropped to his knees to trace the same one with his lips.

"I've always found scars to be sexy," Jask said, biting his skin gently. "And nothing that happens to your body will ever change how I feel about you, Vin. Bond, no bond, scars, no scars." He continued kissing a line across his abs and slid his hands around to Vince's ass. "You're mine."

Vince ran a hand through Jask's hair as he watched him. "You're supposed to be resting."

"I almost lost you today," Jask countered. "Please, just... let me do this." He tipped his forehead against Vince's stomach and let out a shaky breath. "I can't lose you. I won't."

Eighteen

Vince

"You'll never lose me, Jask. Everything that's happened, all we've lost... we still end up together every time." Vince pulled his former mate up and led him to the bed, then sat and tugged him forward until he was between his legs. He discarded his own shirt and then ran his hands under Jask's, lifting it so he could mimic Jask's actions from earlier and kiss along his skin. They laid together, their hands exploring slowly since neither of them had the energy for anything more. Vince looked down as Jask trailed a finger over a small part of his body that wasn't covered in ink or scars. A wild idea took place in Vince's mind, and he couldn't shake it even as Jask's hand slid into the waistband of his pants. His hips rolled of their own accord.

"What's wrong?" Jask asked as Vince stopped his hand.

He kissed him gently before running a thumb over his cheek. "If I say something crazy, will you promise to ignore it if you don't agree?" Vince waited for Jask to nod before he moved their hands back to the spot right above his hip. "I want your name here. Permanently. I want you to mark me as yours."

Jask stared at him wide-eyed for a moment, then leaned down to kiss the skin there. "Are you sure?"

"Never been more sure of anything."

Slowly, Jask pressed his palm to Vince's skin and closed his eyes. Pain radiated through him followed by sweet relief, and Jask leaned down to kiss him. "You're still mine, Vincenzo. You always will be."

Vince held him there for a long, slow kiss before looking down at the spot. He smiled at the mark. "And now, anyone that sees me naked will know." He heard the growl Jask let out and laughed quietly. "It was a joke. Only one I'm getting naked for is you." Vince proceeded to do exactly that, sliding out of his pants before taking his spot back on the bed.

"You're still as beautiful as you always were, Vince. Scars and all... especially mine." He kissed the spot again and continued up his body. "I want one of my own. Will you do that for me? Make me yours again, too?"

"Yes, absolutely... if that's what you want." Vince tried not to sound as eager as he felt, but the thought of having his permanent mark on Jask made him shiver in anticipation.

Jask nodded, trailing his tongue around Vince's nipple. "Yep. That's exactly what I want." He rolled, landing softly in his back and getting rid of the rest of his clothes. "Wherever you want, just... not the goods."

Vince eyed the body of the man he loved, running his hands over Jask slowly as he tried to decide where would be best. Vince had never considered himself an artist, but seeing the canvas before him had him wishing he was. He could paint a million things about what he felt for Jask on this gorgeous body. He maneuvered between his legs and licked up his length. "So... not here?"

"Mmm. You can use your tongue there all you want, but no cuts. I think I'd rather keep it in one piece." He ran a hand through Vince's hair and thrust up, biting his lip. "Don't stop on my account."

Vince sucked Jask into his mouth and held him there for a moment before pulling off with a pop. "Not yet. I still have to find the right spot." Despite his words, his mouth was on Jask the next second as he ran his hand over Jask's right hip. Jask's name was on Vince's left and he hummed around Jask as he considered it. He traced his name with his finger, imagining what it would look like.

"Bigger," Jask whispered. "Bigger."

Vince pulled away again, ignoring Jask's whimper. "You're sure?" He trailed his finger from where it was all the way to the other hip. "Like this?"

Jask nodded, his pupils blown. "Yeah. That's good. Do it."

Vince sat up and took another long look at Jask before placing a kiss over his left hip, then began the process of marking him. He didn't have the same abilities Jask did, so this was going to take longer. His finger lit with flame as he burned the first letter into Jask's skin. "Tell me if you want me to stop."

"Don't stop," he said breathlessly. "Demon fire isn't fun, but I don't care. Kinda feels good... like a purge."

"Purged by a demon. That's a first." He moved on to the next letter, checking on Jask again to make sure he was still okay. When Jask didn't complain, he kept going until his full name was decorating Jask's body.

Jask healed quickly, barely even making a mess on the sheets. He ran his fingers over the newly formed scars and laughed quietly. "That's kind of fucked up, but I like it."

"We're kind of fucked up, so it fits." Vince shrugged. "Now, I believe I was busy with something else before that." He leaned back down and slowly inched Jask's cock back into his mouth.

Jask must've enjoyed the pain more than he let on - he was leaking into Vince's mouth immediately, groaning as his hand fisted in the sheets. "Fuck. So good, baby. Go slow."

Vince moaned at the taste, taking Jask to the back of his throat before sliding off slowly. He swirled his tongue and then moved back down until his nose was against Jask's stomach. His hips rocked against the bed as he looked for some type of friction.

With a low moan, Jask pulled Vince off of him by the hair and yanked him up until their bodies were parallel. He looked fucked out already, his eyes half closed and skin flushed as he wrapped his hand around them both. "Move, Vin. Want you to cover the scars you just made."

Vince placed a hand on the wall and the other on Jask's chest as he thrust into his fist. His eyes slid closed as he felt every inch of Jask rub against him, but he opened them again quickly — he wanted to watch Jask come undone. He moved his hand from Jask's chest to cover the one holding them and rolled his hips again, moving a little faster.

Since Jask was already halfway there, it didn't take much to tip him over. He came with a quiet moan, his cock pulsing against Vince's, but kept moving his hand. "Don't stop. Take what you need."

"Just need you," Vince gasped. Something about seeing the mess Jask made pushed him over the edge and he spilled all over Jask's stomach.

Jask went a little boneless, probably still exhausted from everything they'd gone through. He kissed Vince slowly, then smiled against his lips. "See? No difference. Fuck the bond... we never needed it. I'm crazy about you, Vin."

"You have no idea how relieved I am to hear you say that." Vince wiggled until he was laying completely on top of Jask and buried his face in Jask's neck. "Comfortable? Because I'm not moving."

He laughed, wrapping his wings around them both and holding him there. "Yeah, I'm comfortable. But we have to move soon. Ed needs help, Draz just lost his boyfriend and I still have to go kill Cidos."

Vince immediately felt a swell of guilt. He sighed and actually did move, rolling off of Jask and sitting up. "I should go help Drazan."

"Sorry, didn't quite catch that," Jask joked, but quietly enough it still sounded forced. "You helping Draz? Did the world end?"

"No, but... Johnny was my best friend, and instead of mourning him, I was having sex. I should be out there, helping..." He stopped, unable to speak the words. He should be out there, preparing his body. Helping to build the casket.

Jask kissed him quickly. "Vince, you've been through a lot. You needed me, and I needed you. I don't think anyone's gonna blame us for that. But come on, I'll go with you."

"Jask, you should be resting. You were hurt before any of this even started. I don't want you overdoing it."

"Stop," he said softly. "I won't be able to rest until Ci is either dead or in jail. He killed someone we all care about. This isn't some stupid family feud anymore, he *murdered* someone."

Vince sighed and kissed him, then stood from the bed and grabbed a fresh pair of pants. "You're right. You're always right."

Jask dressed quickly and swayed a little on his feet, then shook it off and opened the door for them. "You want Drazan or Edis duty?"

Vince frowned and grabbed the back of Jask's shirt to stop him. "I'd prefer we stay together so I can keep an eye on you. We can check on Edis, and then go help Drazan."

Nodding, Jask kissed his head and let out a breath before knocking on the door where Edis was. He opened it to reveal Leota in bed with him, curled up against him. "Did he wake up yet?"

"No," she said, sitting up a little bit. "But he's breathing."

"Have you tried poking him with a stick?" Vince cleared his throat at the glare Leota gave him. "Sorry, bad joke." He stepped a little closer to the bed and looked over Edis. He'd regained some color and looked much better than when they'd pulled him from the rubble.

Jask ran his hand over Ed's body to try and heal him, but not much happened. "I think he's okay. Just exhausted. It's not a coma or anything, at least not as far as I can tell. Our healing powers are weird… just give him a bit."

"How are you?" Vince asked Lee, wrapping an arm around Jask.

She nodded a little, running her hand through Ed's hair. "I'm alive and he's alive. I'm okay. How are you two? What happened out there, anyway?"

"Something that shouldn't have, but it's all over now," Vince didn't like lying to Lee, but she'd already been through enough. They'd deal with Cidos and then everyone could move on.

Lee laid back down and held on to Edis. "Let me guess. You'll tell me when I'm older?"

Jask nudged Vince, giving him a look that suggested she deserved to know what happened to her mate and someone she'd grown up around.

Vince sighed and dropped his gaze, unwilling to look her in the eyes. "Johnny took on Cidos while Drazan healed me. The bond… they succeeded in breaking it. Edis had to heal Jask. Drazan and I joined the fight against Cidos and Athar, but Athar was strong. He had me down and Draz came to help. Edis confronted Athar, Athar blasted him into the wall. Cidos killed Johnny."

She blinked a couple of times as she took that in. "His own father did this to him?" she asked, her voice small. "Where is he now?"

"Dead," Jask said simply. "I killed him. His body's out back, if you'd like to go spit on it or something. I know I kinda do."

Lee actually smiled a little at that. "I'm sorry about the bond. I can't even imagine."

"It's okay. Turns out we didn't need it, we made our own," Vince said.

Jask kissed him right there, and this time, Lee didn't complain about it. He pulled back, nuzzling his nose against Vince's cheek. "We did. And one way or the other, we'll be just fine without it."

Drazan

Sweat dripped down his face as he put the final nail in Johnny's coffin. It felt like such a stupid fucking cliche that he would've laughed if he didn't feel like he was being ripped in two. They might not have been bonded like the rest of them, but Drazan really did love him, and he believed Johnny had loved him, too.

It barely registered to him when the others came out. He didn't want or need their help - as much as he hated to even think it, he blamed each and every one of them for what had happened. They'd all been too concerned with themselves and their mates to give a shit what happened to him or Johnny, even after everything they'd done and sacrificed to help when they didn't have to.

He picked up the shovel and chose a particularly green patch of grass. It wasn't as fancy or beautiful as Johnny deserved, but it was the best he could do given what he had to work with. And the faster he got Johnny buried... the faster he could avenge him.

Vince walked over to him. "You don't have to do it alone. I can help."

"You've done enough," he said, a little sharper than he meant to.

"Burn Athar's body if you want to be useful. I don't want to go anywhere near him."

"Yeah... sure. I'll see if Jask is ready for that. Draz, for what it's worth... I'm sorry."

Drazan paused digging and leaned on the shovel, turning to look at Vince. "Sorry isn't gonna bring him back." He turned back to the earth, throwing everything he was into digging that grave. It was the last thing he could do for him.

Vince winced and then shook his head. "Yeah, trust me. I know, but do me a favor and don't say that to Jask. My mom already did and he doesn't deserve it."

"Doesn't he?" Drazan whirled on Vince, taking a step forward. "If he'd have fucking dealt with this the first fifteen fucking times he told me "it's time" or "no point in waiting anymore", Johnny would still be here. He'd still be alive, and instead, he's gone... and what did Jask do? What did *you* do? Crawled into fucking bed with each other. Nothing matters as long as the perfect fucking Veris prince gets what he wants!" Anger was radiating off of Drazan to a point that the grass around them withered and died. He swore, throwing the shovel and fisting his hands in his hair, dropping to his knees next to the casket.

"You know that isn't fair. Blame me all you want. I should've protected Johnny. Hell, he should've never been a part of this in the first place, but don't put the blame on Jask. He's your *friend*, Drazan. You know him better than anyone," Vince said quietly.

Drazan clenched his jaw. "Jask doesn't have friends. He has pawns. That's all any of us ever are to him. And believe me, Vincenzo," he said, his voice like thunder, "I *do* blame you." He got to his feet and called the shovel to him, then kept digging. "Leave."

Vince looked like he was about to argue, but eventually, he nodded and walked back into the house.

For a moment, Drazan regretted being so mean. But as his eyes fell on the casket holding Johnny's dead body, he stopped feeling bad about it. While it was true that Jask was his best friend, he was starting to understand that the feeling wasn't mutual. If he really *was* his best friend, he'd be out here, insisting on helping. He'd be comforting Drazan, not celebrating because he got everything he wanted.

His thoughts turned even more sour as he continued digging. They'd searched for the demon boy named Pavo for years, and all along, he'd have been better off never being found. Just *knowing* Jaskian had killed him. Knowing Jaskian would probably kill them all.

Once the hole was dug, the sun was setting, and Drazan didn't want to wait any longer. He used a combination of his own strength and grace to lower Johnny's coffin down, then sat on the edge of the grave and tossed a handful of dirt in. "I know I should invite the others for this, but fuck them. They're not gonna miss you like I will. When this whole thing started, and Jask found Vince at that fight, I had no idea what a clusterfuck everything was going to become. That I'd have to give up my life to fake date Jask, take blockers to hide the lies I had to tell to people I thought I respected, that I'd have to give up my own chance at happiness to keep Jask and Vince alive. I thought it was the end for me, but... then I met you.

"I honestly didn't think much of it that first time we saw each other, when you were checking on Jask. Just thought you were kinda hot for a demon, but in a weird... not-what-I-expected kinda way. The second time, I almost kissed you, but figured that was a bad idea for a hundred reasons, so I didn't. I kept lying, kept my mouth shut, kept doing whatever the hell Jask needed me to do. No questions asked. Then, when Lee almost died from the Void, and we saw each other again... I knew I couldn't stay away." He laughed a little bitterly at the memory, swinging his legs so his feet kicked against the Earth, head tipped back toward the sky. "I had no idea if you even thought about me or not. No one ever does, I was always the sidekick. The one that got things or did things by proxy. But you never saw me like that... as just the extra."

Tears welled in his eyes as he threw another handful of dirt onto the wood. "You saw me for me. And I'm pissed as hell that we didn't get more time together. I'm sorry I couldn't protect you... that I couldn't get there in time to stop what he did to you. All I can do now is promise that I'll get the bastard if it's the last thing I do." He dropped down carefully into the grave and laid on top of the casket. "Maybe I'll get lucky and they'll just bury me here, too."

He wasn't sure how long he stayed there, but it was fully dark by the time he pulled himself back up to surface level and got to work filling in the grave. On the other edge of the property, he could see the first sparks of the fire that would incinerate Athar, and some sick, twisted part of him was glad for it. If Athar and Cidos would've just minded their own business, none of this would've happened. But all that line of reasoning did for him was make him unsure of who to truly blame... and at the end of the day... he blamed all of them.

~

The next couple of weeks were a blur. The smell of burning flesh was still fresh in his mind, but he stayed as far away from the ashes and Johnny's grave as he could.

He'd made temporary peace with Jask and the others — as of that moment, they still had a common enemy. But he'd made up his mind at some point in the days since he buried Johnny that when it was over and Cidos was dead, he wouldn't be sticking around. Tragedy had a funny way of showing who one's true friends were, and it became glaringly obvious to him that the only true friend he had was now resting six feet underground.

When Leota and Edis called for a family meeting, he nearly didn't go. He certainly didn't feel like part of the family, but Jask practically dragged him into the room, and Drazan didn't run away just in the off chance it was news about Cidos' whereabouts.

Judging by the smiles on their faces, it didn't have anything to do with the traitor.

"Well," Leota said, one hand placed over her belly. "We know this isn't exactly the best time for an announcement like this, but we figured everyone could use some good news."

Not hardly, Drazan thought bitterly. *The only good news I want is that someone put Ci's head on a fucking spike.*

Jask was beaming, his hand laced with Vince's. It made Drazan a little sick to his stomach, but he could keep up pretenses with the best of them. He'd learned the art of deception from Jask himself, after all.

"Spit it out, Lee!" Vince said, rocking on his toes. "Is it what I think it is?"

She nodded, the smile on her face completely obscuring the pain from recent weeks. "We're having a baby!"

Drazan very nearly lost his cool. Not breaking bonds or killing mates was one thing, but procreating? Allowing the lines to truly mix? That was expressly forbidden, and Draz had heard firsthand from Athar himself *why* it was forbidden. That child would be a monster... and it would end them all. "You're happy about this?"

Edis fixed cold, dangerous eyes on Drazan. "Yes, we're thrilled. This child will not be a threat to anyone. We'll make sure of it."

"Right," he scoffed. "Like you made sure your twin wasn't a threat, either, right?" He stood, not wanting to celebrate such a thing. "While you guys pick out nursery colors, I'll go do what should've been done weeks ago." He stomped out, but this time, Jask was right on his heels. He pushed Drazan against the wall and held his forearm to his throat.

"Look," Jask spat, increasing the pressure. "I know you lost someone you love. We all did. You weren't the only one that cared about Johnny. We all did, and we all lost him. I want Ci more than you do, but we can't just go running out there half-cocked when we don't even know where he is! Someone innocent could get hurt."

Drazan shoved Jask off of him. "Like you give a shit about someone's innocence. Hasn't it always been about what someone can do for you?"

Genuine hurt crossed Jask's face. "How can you even say that to me? We ran that investigative business together. You know the kinds of people we helped. And when we started working at the firm, we made *damn* sure no one innocent was getting locked up for Ci's stupid vendetta. You know how many fucking nights I lost sleep over Pavo. How far I tracked his father to find out the truth. I killed my own *father* to keep everyone safe." He pushed Drazan, knocking him back a few paces.

"Fuck you, D. You don't get to act like I'm some kinda terrible person just because you're in pain. We're all in pain."

Somewhere deep down, he knew Jask was right. This wasn't his fault, it wasn't Vince's fault, or anyone's fault but Cidos'. He let out a slow breath, wrapping his arms around himself and trying to calm the hurricane of grief and anger and fear inside of him. "I'm sorry," he croaked out, refusing to meet Jask's eyes.

"Fuck," Jask sighed. "Come here." He pulled Drazan into a hug he couldn't reciprocate and held him tight. "Let's just go inside, be happy for Ed and Lee, and in the morning... we won't stop until we find him. Okay?"

Drazan nodded, not really believing any of it. "Yeah. I think I can do that." He watched as Jask squeezed his arm and turned to walk away, and clenched his jaw so hard he thought his teeth would snap. He had a long road ahead of him if he was ever going to find a way to move past all of this, and while not even *he* understood why he was so angry, he knew it was far from over.

But all he could do now was play along, and look forward to the day he drove a stake between Cidos' eyes. Maybe then, he'd finally find some peace.

Jaskian

He opened his eyes slowly, not wanting to face the day just yet. He could feel Vince's body heat next to him and took comfort in it, knowing that at any moment, it could be taken away. The thought filled him with fear and grief, so he rolled a little closer and wrapped himself around the man that used to be his mate. "You awake?" he asked softly, not wanting to disturb him if he wasn't.

"Hmm?" Vince wrapped his arm around Jask and pulled him closer. "Something wrong?"

Only everything, he thought, but kept to himself. "I told Drazan we'd hunt Cidos today, and not stop until we found him. I'm..." He sighed, knowing there was no use in hiding it. "I'm scared, Vince. He already killed Johnny."

Vince's arm tightened on his waist and he spoke quietly. "I'm not going to let him hurt anyone else, Jask. Not Draz, not you. We'll find him, and he'll pay for what he did."

"It's not exactly like we let him do what he did to begin with," Jask said. "I think I just have a healthy fear of what he's capable of now. I didn't before. I knew he was an ass, but not one part of me honestly believed he'd kill anyone."

"We're better prepared now," Vince tried to reassure him. "And he was outnumbered and cornered. I think he knew he probably wasn't getting out of there alive. That makes people dangerous."

Jask nodded a little and let out a soft sigh. "And I won't be making the same mistake twice. Do you think it'll really be over once he's dead?" As ridiculous as it sounded, he was afraid they'd never be free as long as Astarte lived. But he knew, no matter what, he'd never be able to kill her. He wouldn't even try.

"Yes, I do. I believe it's over now. Cidos isn't dumb enough to keep coming after us. Only reason I agree with finding him is because of Johnny."

The reminder of their dead friend made Jask close his eyes once more. "Okay. Then give me five more minutes... then we'll go."

~

More like an hour later, Jask finally dragged himself out of Vince's warm embrace and got dressed in silence. He could hear muffled explosions coming from out back and knew Drazan must be practicing, which meant if they didn't hurry, Drazan would be going without them. The last thing Jask wanted was to let that happen and lose another person he cared about. "Do you think he'll ever forgive us?" he asked Vince as they opened the door.

"I don't deserve his forgiveness, but I hope he forgives you," Vince replied, stepping out into the hall.

Knowing he was just as much to blame as Vince was, he chose not to comment. There would be time for blame and grief and guilt when it was over, and now... all he could do was try to get everyone home in one piece. "Drazan!" he yelled, keeping a safe distance. "It's time."

They watched as Drazan took a deep breath and walked over to them. His usual carefree attitude hadn't been present since the fight, and his face was grim. "Let's go."

While Jask had gotten rid of the ache he felt when Vince wasn't near him, there was a brand new one where his best friend used to be. "Right. Let's hope he hasn't moved since we did that tracking spell last night. If he has... it's gonna end up being a long day." He glanced back at the house and realized they probably should've said goodbye, but that would probably just make this harder, and they needed to go in with clear heads. Hopefully, with the three of them, it would be quick and painless... at least for them.

Closing his eyes, Jask reached out for both of them and launched them forward, landing with a heavy breath and a grunt just outside of Cidos' last known location. Tilting his head, he sent a tiny pulse of grace out to search for him. It stopped abruptly, which could only mean one thing. "He's here. And now, he probably knows we are, too. We should split up, Draz... go around back. Vince, head on in through the front door." He glanced up at the roof and clenched his jaw. "I'll come in from above. If you find him, don't hesitate. Don't try any long, drawn out hero speeches. Don't give him a chance to call for help or come up with a plan. Just strike."

Draz had already started moving before Jask was done. Vince kissed Jask quickly and then walked up to the front door, kicking it in easily.

With a deep breath and two quick movements, Jask went from the ground to the roof, then inside of the house. He looked around, twin balls of energy in his raised hands. "Ci? I know you're here, man... I just wanna talk."

"Like you talked with our father?" Ci called from somewhere in the house.

Jask tilted his head, trying to gauge where the sound was coming from. It seemed like it was coming from every direction, which wasn't helping him at all. "That bastard barely qualified as my father. And in case you don't remember, I tried the diplomatic approach. He tried to kill your twin, or don't you care about him anymore?" Aware he was breaking his own rule, Jask took a step toward one of the open doors.

"Let's not do this, Jaskian. We both know you're here to kill me. Is the tiresome back and forth necessary? Would you like me to recite a monologue for you?" Cidos asked in a bored tone.

"Wouldn't be necessary if you'd just get out here and face me," he replied, extinguishing the balls of power in his hands to go incognito. His heart rate kicked up as he started checking each room, and couldn't for the life of him figure out where *anyone* was. It felt like he was in a maze. "You killed someone I care about. It's time to answer for it."

"Did you think I wouldn't prepare for that? I know you brought the others. Curious as to why you haven't heard from them yet?" Cidos' voice continued to echo as Jask turned around to find himself back where he'd started. He went through a door to his right, but it led to a dead end. When he stepped back into the hall, the doors had moved. He turned back around to find the door he'd just emerged from gone completely. Before he could even try to catch his bearings, he heard a pained shout from Vince that had his heart in his throat.

"Vince?" Jask called out, heading in the direction he thought the noise came from.

"I'm fine, fucking asshole sucker punched me." His voice sounded further away now, and Jask turned again in a desperate attempt to locate him. "Jask! I can't... fuck, I can't *see* anything!"

"Jask!" Draz called out to him, sounding somewhere close to his right. "Cidos is using magic! I found the—" The words cut off in a shout.

"Drazan! Vince!" Jask yelled frantically, ripping open doors left and right but revealing nothing but brick walls. His knees threatened to give out as adrenaline and fear coursed through his body. "Cidos, you *coward!* You've got magic. Block them off. Face me head on!"

The next door he opened revealed a new room with four doors spread out in front of him. "Great idea, brother. They're somewhere behind those doors. Blocked off, as it were." Cidos was sitting off to the side in a chair, looking relaxed.

Being alone meant a couple of things to Jask, and surprisingly, all of them were good. "Great," he said sarcastically. "Then we can talk." Jask shifted on his feet and crossed his arms, prepared to fight at any moment - but still hoping it wouldn't come to that. "No one else has to die, Cidos. You can still do the right thing. Turn yourself over for Johnny's murder."

"For a demon? Honestly Jask, were you sleeping with that one, too? Not that it matters, they won't prosecute me." Cidos shrugged as he watched Jask.

"They will. There were too many witnesses - *angel* witnesses. Me, Drazan, Edis... we all saw it. Hell, even mom knows what you did. You'll go to jail, but at least Drazan and Vin will get some justice... and you'll get to keep your life." He took a step forward, his expression changing to something almost pleading. "C'mon, Ci. Don't make me do this."

"No!" The muffled shout came from behind one of the doors, followed by a thud. Drazan continued to yell, "I swear on my life, Jaskian, if you let him live I'll never forgive you!"

Somewhere in the darkest corners of Jask's mind, he knew Drazan would never forgive him, anyway. And he'd never be able to forgive *himself* if he killed his brother without making every attempt not to. "Ci... please," he begged, reaching out his left hand even as his right inched toward his hidden blade. "Just come with me. Do the right thing... for *once* in your life."

"This *is* the right thing. Carrying on our family's legacy, avenging our father..." Cidos stood from his chair. "I'll take care of you, and then finish off the other two. Edis won't be too difficult if you're not there to protect him."

Jask didn't understand how his brother had fallen so far. Any hope of him coming back to the light after Athar's death was extinguished fully, and Jask knew what needed to be done. "Then come on, Cidos. Give me your best shot. Just know that not one part of me will take joy in killing you."

The lie rang through both of their bodies, and Cidos' features twisted into something evil as he lunged at Jask. He barely had time to sidestep, and even still, he felt something sharp and hot slice through his side. Jask hissed, hurling a ball of energy at his brother and stalking toward him as he crashed into the far wall. "Get up, Cidos! You won't win this. You know you won't".

Cidos stood shakily and braced a hand on the wall. "I don't have to win. Just have to keep you distracted enough for the spells to kill your friend and your *mate*." Cidos said the word with disdain before barking a sadistic laugh. "Oh, that's right. He isn't yours anymore."

"Jokes on you, Ci. Turns out the bond was more of a formality." He spun, yelling for Vince to get back a moment before he shot a blast of grace at the door concealing him.

The door disintegrated, and after a moment Vince slowly stepped out, hands out before him. "Jask, I still can't fucking see!" He stopped moving forward, and more banging could be heard before Drazan yelled again.

"Let me out, Jask! Give Ci to me!"

That wasn't an option, and if Vince was blind... "No!" Jask screamed, teleporting directly behind Cidos with his blade pressing against his traitorous throat. "Undo it, Cidos. Fucking undo it, or I swear to Veris I'll kill you."

"Kill me, and he'll be blind forever." The lie bled through the words the instant they were out of Ci's mouth.

"Jask, you son of a bitch, *let me out!*" Drazan sounded like he was holding back tears.

There was only one way to fix Vince and give Drazan what he wanted, and it was a thing that might break Jask in half. But weighing his options, he knew he didn't have a choice, and he had to hope that Drazan would eventually learn to forgive him for everything that had happened. Tears pricked in his eyes as his hand started shaking, his grip on Cidos faltering. "Fuck you, Ci. Fuck you for ruining everything... and fuck you for making me do this."

With a guttural scream... Jask slit his brother's throat.

Nineteen

Vince

After Cidos died, Vince's vision returned slowly. His first sight was Jask kneeling next to the body, staring at the puddle of blood on the floor with a horrified look on his face. Vince went to him immediately and wrapped his arms around him, telling him over and over that it'd had to be done... but he honestly wasn't sure if Jask could even hear him. The gurgling, choking sounds Cidos had made as he died were burned into his *own* brain, so he could only imagine the horrors running through Jaskian's. The spell holding the doors faded and Drazan busted out, standing frozen and silent as Jask lifted his brother's body from the ground. There had been so much death... all because he'd agreed to fight an angel.

They'd returned to the house to find Astarte and Edis grief-stricken — Ed had *felt* his twin die, and after experiencing what he had with the bond, Vince didn't even want to ask what that had been like. It'd also been yet another blow to Jask, and Vince didn't know how many more he could take before he snapped.

No one said much of anything as they prepared for the funeral. Vince looked to his left to see Drazan watching the flames, wearing the expression of a man that had gotten exactly what he wanted, but found it lacking. Vince knew how he felt. Killing Cidos didn't bring Johnny back, it hadn't helped Jask, and it had devastated Astarte.

Vince could hear her sobs from where he stood with Jask, farther back from the fire than the others. He pulled Jask into his side and kissed the side of his head. It was a small gesture, but he hoped in some way, it helped.

"At least it's finally over," he said, his voice flat and devoid of emotion. "There's no one left alive that can pass these traditions down." They'd opted to burn their history books along with Cidos, Jask's one and only tribute to him. "The hatred — and the ritual — burns with him."

"Good riddance to it, and to whoever came up with it in the first place," Vince agreed. "Do you think they'll be okay?" He gestured vaguely to Edis and Astarte.

Jask fixed his eyes on them for a long moment. "They'll survive. I doubt either of them will be able to look at me anytime soon, but... I expect that Edis will forgive me before my mother does. I might've killed his twin, but he knows if I hadn't, Cidos would've killed his mate."

"I think we all knew what the outcome was going to be, I just wish I could've done more. Taken that weight off of you," Vince said with a sigh.

He shook his head slightly. "It needed to be this way. When our story is told down the line, we won't be the heroes. The truth must never be told. Someone, someday might hear it and think Athar and Cidos had the right idea, and it all will have been for nothing. Better they think I was a psycho that killed my own father and brother for power than use this as another excuse to vilify demons." Jask cracked his neck, still not used to the power he inherited when he killed his father.

Vince knew he was right. Retellings of history always twisted things, and when the real villains were made up from the most respected family around? They didn't stand a chance. He kissed Jask again, unable to stop himself. "Doesn't matter. We know the truth and we have something to fight for still. Lee and Edis, they need us."

"I know that. It seems like at least half of what we thought we knew about the rituals and mates was wrong, but if this part was correct... that baby growing inside of Lee isn't a normal child. I have a feeling our fight is just beginning." Jask watched as Drazan turned and walked back toward the house, then twitched like he was going to go after him. "He's leaving us."

Vince didn't turn to look, he couldn't exactly blame Draz. If the situation had been reversed, Vince wouldn't be handling it nearly as well. "You want me to stop him?"

"No, he said his goodbye," he explained quietly. "I heard him. There's nothing any of us can do to stop him unless we find a way to bring Johnny back, and that delves into magic far beyond anything I'm capable of... even with Athar's powers." He dropped his head down to study the grass below them, his body slumping a little. "He was the only friend I ever had."

"Not anymore, Jask," Vince said, taking his hand. "You got me. I mean, we aren't exactly friends but I'm going to be here for you." Vince looked back to the house. "And Draz will come around. He has some grieving to do, but deep down he knows this wasn't your fault."

Jask nodded. "I hope you're right. But for now, we need to get everyone somewhere safe, preferably away from here. The immediate danger may be over, but if someone finds out that Leota is pregnant, we could have bigger problems. Not all angels will be as understanding about it, and I wouldn't be surprised if a fair few demons didn't take kindly to the news, either." He glanced toward where the others were standing and heaved a quiet sigh. "We protect what's left. No matter what."

"No matter what," Vince echoed. "Where are we going to go?" He missed the farm house Jask had gotten them. He missed Ares. He even missed Pattie a bit, but he knew it wouldn't be wise for them to go back.

"On?" Jask offered vaguely, uncertain. "Maybe somewhere in the mountains? You could farm, I could hunt. At least we'd be safe until we figure out what we're dealing with. Truth be told, I don't know if we'll ever be able to stop moving."

"The mountains sound good. Easily defensible, if we find the right spot. I think between us and Edis we should be able to work out something permanent." A wave of grief hit him as he realized Johnny wouldn't be there to help him build. He glanced over to the grave site they'd designated for Johnny. He'd gotten him a nice rock, just like

Johnny had joked about at the beach. It was the least he could do for him since Draz had done most of the work.

Jask faced him fully and wrapped him in his arms, his wings slowly extending around him, too. "Hey," he said softly. "We'll handle it. I can feel... all of that. I've got you."

Vince buried his face in Jask's neck, taking the comfort he offered. "Yeah, I know. Just like I got you. I wouldn't be here if it wasn't for you."

No more words were said, because none *could* be said. They both knew it was a team effort, but they'd failed Johnny. They'd failed Drazan. They'd managed to save each other, but at a terrible cost... and celebrating their own survival felt wrong, cruel.

They stayed entwined in each other until the flames from Cidos' pyre turned to ash, and Astarte spoke from just behind them. "If we're leaving, now is the time. Where is Drazan?"

"Gone." Jask pulled back but laced his fingers with Vince's. "He said there's nothing for him here, and told me not to follow him. From now on, it's just us."

"Which, all things considered, could be worse." Vince smiled and nodded to the house. "Let's get started, then."

~

Vince rubbed the sleep from his eyes as he stepped out the back door of their new home for the third time that week. They'd been there a month already with no problems, but Astarte still swore that she heard things outside at night. They'd just gone to sleep when she'd knocked quietly on the door, and Vince had hesitated to wake Jask. Living on the run hadn't been easy on any of them, but Jask and Lee concerned him the most. That first month living out of hotels couldn't have been good for Lee's developing spawn. He chuckled a little as he remembered the fight they'd had about him using those words to describe his little niece or nephew. The laughter died out as his mind drifted back to Jask, as it always did.

Vince could tell the deaths of his father and brother were weighing heavily on him. Add to that the fact that they hadn't heard from Draz at all? It was a wonder Jask was able to function as well as he was.

Vince tried to keep everyone in some semblance of peace and happiness, but it was getting touchy. With the baby making Lee sick, Astarte's late night nightmares, and being worried about Jask... Vince was wearing thin. He'd never tell any of them that, and he'd be damned if he let them see it. He looked up at the stars and wished — not for the first time — that Johnny was there. Vince needed someone to talk to.

After looking around the outside of the house for what he thought would be a satisfactory amount of time, Vince went back in. "Coast is clear. Nothing dangerous out there." He smiled at Astarte and locked the door behind him.

She crossed her arms over her chest protectively and nodded a little. "Thank you. I'm sorry I woke you, I just..." Tears welled in her eyes, and she wiped them away quickly. "Nevermind. Have a... good night, Vincenzo." Astarte turned on her heel and went back to her room. Despite being stuck together for a couple of months, Astarte was just now getting used to being around demons and not looking down on them. He wasn't sure she'd *ever* be able to smile at them with any sincerity, but Jask had sworn to him that she had no ill intentions... and that had to be good enough.

As he made his way back to his bed, he noticed a light on in the sunroom. Curious, he made his way toward it and listened at the door.

"Just come in, Vince. I know you're there," Edis called in a tired voice.

Vince opened the door and leaned against the frame. "Can't sleep?"

"Can you?" Ed asked skeptically, then gestured to the bottle of bourbon on the table. They'd raided all of the Veris' many households before leaving, and if Athar was good for one thing in his pathetic, hateful life... it was liquor. "Care to join me?"

"Don't mind if I do." Vince poured himself a generous amount and sat across from his enemy turned... whatever the hell they were now. He observed Edis another moment before speaking again. "So, what's keeping you up? Lee's snoring?"

He shook his head slightly. "No, it's not her. It's... everything else. I suppose I'm still not over what happened... and I'm worried about what's coming next. With the baby, I mean." Ed set down his glass and shot Vince a hesitant look. "What if the stories are true?"

"Yeah. I don't think I've really gotten a chance to say I'm sorry. About all of it. Athar, Cidos... that couldn't have been easy for you." Vince cleared his throat and pushed forward. "As for the superbaby... we'll burn that bridge when we get to it, but I don't think it'll be anything we can't handle."

"It wasn't easy for any of us. But losing my twin... I wasn't prepared for how badly that would hurt. Especially since our own brother was the one that killed him. I know Jask had to do it, but... did it have to be so violent?" Ed looked at him helplessly, like he was begging Vince to give him some justification.

Vince emptied his glass in one swig before pouring more. "Cidos had gone a little crazy. He was planning on killing all three of us and then coming after you and Lee. He'd hit me with some type of blindness spell and locked both Draz and I up. Draz said the spells he used would've slowly killed us if Jask hadn't stopped him. He had to end it quickly."

Silence stretched between them, but Ed ultimately nodded, accepting what he was told. "Right. I'm... sorry too, you know. For trying to kill you. For thinking that just because we're different, I was somehow better than you. I was wrong, and I never wanted it to come to this."

"None of us wanted it to come to this," Vince agreed quietly. He'd never give up the life he had with Jask, but he absolutely wished it'd come with less bloodshed. He swirled the liquor in his glass and looked back up to Edis. "Apology accepted. The only way now is forward, right?"

Edis nodded, pursing his lips. "How are you doing with everything? I know this wasn't easy for you, either. We all lost something here, and if I know my brother, he's probably the bad kind of rock right now."

"Me? Never better." Vince shrugged and poured another glass. "And Jask is perfect. He's done nothing but be there for me."

"I wasn't trying to be mean," Ed said quietly. "I just mean that Jask hasn't always been the most open of all of us, and I... shit. I'm trying to say that I'm here if you need me. For anything. You're technically my sort-of brother now."

Vince laughed a little, surprised that the words had come from Edis. "Well, shit. I guess you're right. Welcome to the family?"

Ed grabbed his glass again and took a drink. "It hasn't exactly been the warmest welcome I've ever received, but I appreciate you for accepting me. Your mom, too. I know it couldn't have been easy, especially since you and Jaskian lost your bond and Leota and I... didn't." The last word was laced with genuine regret, like he'd wanted Jaskian and Vince to be able to have what they did.

"You know... I'm not upset about it. I mean, I miss it. I miss being able to know where he is without having to look, or know what he's feeling without having to ask. But now I can love him without someone saying it's just the bond. Now, it's just us." Vince realized what he was saying and put his glass down. "Well, that's enough of the bourbon."

He laughed quietly. "I should get you drunk more often. You're a lot more agreeable when you're like this. But speaking of Jask and knowing what he's feeling, you might want to go to him. I can hear him." His smile faded and he stared at his glass. "I'd go myself, but I don't particularly want to talk about what it was like for him to slit my twin's throat."

Vince stood and moved to put a hand on Edis' shoulder. "Jask took no pleasure in that. I held him when he cried that night. Thank you for the drink." He patted his shoulder one more time before going up to their room. He opened the door quietly and stepped inside. "Jask?"

"Please, Cidos. Don't make me do this," Jask mumbled, his body coated in sweat. Vince called out to him again, and Jask jerked, grunting and sitting bolt upright, his eyes a little wild until they landed on Vince. He cleared his throat and pushed his damp hair out of his face. It was finally starting to grow back, at least. "Hey. Did I wake you?"

"No, decided to take a moonlit stroll." Vince walked over and climbed into bed, pulling Jask into his arms. "You want to talk about it?"

Jask settled against him and shook his head, tickling Vince's beard. "Same one as always. Starts the same way, ends the same way. Nothing new. Just glad you're here now."

Vince kissed him, shifting until they were both comfortable and touching with every inch they could. "I'm sorry I had to leave at all."

"Talk to me, Vin. You good?" Jask tilted his head up to kiss his jaw and spread one of his wings over them. "What's with the midnight walk?"

"Of course I'm good. Your mom heard another noise, so I went to check it out." Vince closed his eyes and tilted his head back against the pillow. "Probably a raccoon."

Slowly, Jask trailed his lips over Vince's throat and moved until he was hovering over him. "Need a little help going back to sleep? You've taken such good care of us, Vin," he whispered, then kissed him. "I'd be happy to return that favor."

Vince hummed happily but pulled away from Jask's kisses. "You should be sleeping. Not taking care of me."

"C'mon, Vince. Don't deny me." It was said as more of a plea than a tease, and Jask slumped a little with his forehead against Vince's chest. "Sorry. I'll stop."

"Sweetheart, I'm not denying you. I just know how much you've been sleeping the last few weeks, and it's not a lot. I'm worried." He brought his hand up to fist in Jask's hair and held him in place. Vince was sharing a lot of feelings, and he'd learned it was easier when he didn't have to look anyone in the eyes. "You know I can't tell you no, anyway," he joked quietly.

Jask took that as permission and kissed down his body. They'd done this dance enough times now that Vince knew what to expect. His boxers pulled down roughly, Jask sucking him in like he was starving for it, and an occasional sudden stop if Jask felt like teasing him. This wasn't one of those nights, and Vince was sure Jask wouldn't have stopped even if the walls started caving in. He slid two fingers into Vince with a mix of grace and brute force, and when Vince came with a quiet moan, Jask swallowed all of it.

Par for the course of these after-nightmare escapades, Jask refused to let Vince return the favor. It was some sort of self-sacrificing bullshit he'd come up with to make himself feel better. Give more, take less. Vince hated it, but he wouldn't argue much if it made him feel better.

It never mattered much, anyway. Jask always gave in come morning.

Jaskian

A few months later, Jask knew it was almost time to leave their cabin hideout. He hated to do it, but they'd been there for nearly half a year, and everyone was starting to get a little too comfortable. Well, Lee wasn't, but that had little to do with their surroundings and everything to do with the child she was carrying. By anyone's estimations, she was due within the next few weeks, but they lacked the proper equipment to make sure. Astarte had *refused* to let Leota anywhere near a hospital for fear of the repercussions, and since she was technically the matriarch of their little clan, no one dared to defy her.

It wasn't as though Amaranth never tried, but when Astarte had pointed out that a pregnant Riskel would attract far too much unwanted attention, she'd backed off. No one wanted that. They all felt like they were close to true freedom - a bit longer in seclusion, and maybe they'd actually be able to join the free world again... as long as the stories weren't true.

With each passing day, Jask feared a little more for their future. If that child was truly a monster, it would either destroy them all... or they'd have to destroy *him*, which wasn't something he thought he could stomach after everything else.

Edis was convinced the child was a boy, but they had no realistic way to confirm that. What was even weirder was that none of them could sense any power coming from the baby. Usually, with angelic and demonic pregnancies, things could get... complicated. Especially for *their* families. Hiccups would blow light bulbs. Kicks would break bones that would immediately heal over. But this child seemed weak, and Jask wasn't sure if that was something he should be happy about or not.

They'd scoured the libraries at the firm and Athar's house before their stay in motels, but not one of the books they'd found mentioned anything about an angel/demon hybrid. The only references they'd found at all were simply additional warnings never to let one be conceived, which hadn't been helpful in the slightest. It was far too late for that.

Jask watched her waddle into the kitchen with a fond expression on his face. "Vince is hunting, he should be back soon if you're hungry."

"I don't know what I am," she admitted with a sour expression. She slowly lowered herself into a chair with a sigh. "That's a lie, I'm ready for this to be over."

That was a sentiment he understood all too well. "Any movement today?" he asked, nodding his head toward her bump.

"I don't think he's stopped moving in weeks. He's particularly fond of the area near my bladder, but today he seems content to be kicking me in the ribs." She put a hand over her side and winced.

Smiling a little, Jask jerked his chin up. "Want me to sing to him? Nah, he might kill you then." He chuckled, standing up to go put his hand over her belly as he kissed the top of her head. "Leave Lee alone, little guy. She gets cranky when you don't let her sleep."

"Very cranky," Lee agreed.

"How is that different from normal?" Vince asked as he walked in from the living room.

Jask pulled him in and kissed him slowly. "Done hunting?"

"Yes, but if I go back out and come back in, will you kiss me like that again?"

"You two are gross. The baby wants you to go away," Lee grumbled.

Chuckling, Jask kissed him a little quicker. "She's right, we shouldn't upset the baby. It might eat us one day if we do."

She threw something at Jask's back, which only made him laugh harder. "Screw you, Veris."

Since he valued his life, he chose to shut his mouth and not point out that screwing a Veris was exactly what got her in that condition in the first place. Instead, he laced his fingers with Vince's. "I'll kiss you like that whenever you want."

"Always, sweetheart. The answer to that is always."

Lee sighed loudly. "Where is Edis when I need him?"

Jask honestly had no idea where Edis was, but he couldn't blame the guy for needing a break. Leota was particularly needy at the moment, and while Ed doted on her, any reasonable person would need a breather now and again. "Not sure, did you ask him to change the color of the nursery again?"

"No," she said defiantly, but Jask could feel the lie. "Maybe. It wasn't the right shade! What if he doesn't like it?"

"Fucking hell," Vince sighed, dropping his forehead to Jask's shoulder. "Aren't you glad you're not the one marrying her?" He'd whispered it, but not quietly enough.

"Excuse me?" Lee almost screeched. "At least mine *wants* to marry me, Vincenzo!" Lee huffed and stood, her angry exit diminished some by her slow waddle.

Knowing damn well there'd be consequences to that, Jask hissed, "Damnit, Leota. I was nice to you!" He turned to Vince and grinned widely, hoping his dimples would make Vince forget anything had even happened.

"You know, I was going to let that drop until all of... that," he said, motioning to Jask's general demeanor. "Did you tell Lee you don't want to marry me?"

Jask frowned. "No. I told her that I didn't have any plans to propose to you, which is true, but not at all the same thing."

"It kind of is, though." Vince stepped away and to the fridge.

"How? Do you have plans to propose to *me* sometime soon?" Jask challenged, crossing his arms. "Cause if not, then that means you don't wanna marry me by your logic, which is stupid." *Good, keep talking, that hole you dug isn't big enough yet,* he thought to himself.

His former mate froze and then nodded. "You're absolutely right.

This entire conversation is stupid. No need for it to continue." Vince closed the door to the fridge and headed out the back door without answering Jask's question.

He followed, shoving the door with his shoulder as it tried to swing shut. "Can I just explain before you get all pissy and shut me out? Please?" Jask could tell from the look on Vince's face that those were probably the wrong words to use, but they were out now.

Vince crossed his arms and shrugged. "Sure. Explain."

"We're just now getting to the point where we can both sleep through the night," Jask started quietly. "My mother laughed for the first time in over six months... *two* days ago. When we get married, I want that to be a happy memory. Not crippled by all the bullshit we carry." He realized how stupid that sounded, but he meant it. Marrying Vince was near the very top of his priority list, but he didn't want anything tainting that day... or the proposal that led to it.

Vince sighed and the tension left his shoulders. He put his hand in his pocket and nodded. "Okay, I can kind of understand that but... well, yeah." He shrugged again. "We'll wait."

"Look." Jask stepped closer and reached out for him. "I want to marry you. I wanna marry you and adopt fifteen kids and watch them climb all over you and put pink clips in your hair while you're forced to read them princess stories." He kissed him. "Just not right now."

"That's a lot of kids," Vince laughed. "I like that mental picture, though. Something to plan for." He took a breath. "Good thing I found out before I asked. Would've killed me if you said no."

Jask smiled a little and shook his head. "No way I'd ever say no to you. I'd say yes right now if you asked, I was just trying to explain why *I* hadn't popped the question yet."

"This is not me asking," Vince said as he pulled something out of his pocket and put it in Jask's hand. "I hadn't finished planning yet."

He looked down, color rushing to his cheeks when he realized exactly what he was holding. "Ask me. Fuck your plans. Ask me." Jask handed the box back quickly then dropped to his knee, not remembering until he was already there that he should probably be the one standing up.

Laughing and kneeling in front of Jask, Vince retrieved the ring. He took both of Jask's hands in his own. "Jaskian Veris, will you marry me? Please don't say no after all that."

"Yes," Jask said without hesitation, then launched himself at Vince and tackled him into the grass just off the porch. "Yes," he repeated, kissing him again and again until it was getting hard to breathe.

Vince let him continue for a moment before flipping them over and smiling down at him. "You have to let me put the ring on."

Now that it was actually happening, Jask was almost too eager for it. He held out his hand, barely glancing at the ring itself - he'd rather watch the happy look on Vince's face any day. "How long have you had this?"

"Couple of months," Vince admitted, sliding the ring onto Jask's finger. The smile on his lips was almost blinding.

Jask grabbed Vince's face and kissed him hard, having no intention of stopping this time. He was prepared to let Vince take him right there in the yard. "I love you," he mumbled quickly.

"I love you," Vince said against his lips. "Get us upstairs, Jask."

In a blink, they were falling softly onto the bed. Once more, and they were naked, nothing separating them now but skin and the beard on Vince's face that was starting to get seriously out of control. The ring felt strange wrapped around Jask's finger, but for once, it was a good strange... and he didn't ever want to get used to it. "Yours," Jask whispered right before kissing his neck.

"Mine," Vince growled. He slid his hand down Jask's chest to his length, wrapping his fingers around him. "*All* mine."

Jask flipped them quickly and rutted into his hand as he began to let a steady stream of grace pulse through him. He shuddered with it, biting his own lip and then stifling his moans in a kiss a split second before leaning back. Pressing his palm to Vince's chest, he studied the way the ring looked on his finger for the first time, and after a moment, he dragged that same hand across the scars on his own body that spelled

Vince's name. "All yours," he repeated. "Now show me." He lifted himself up as Vince gripped the base of his own cock, then Jask slowly lowered himself until all he could feel was Vince. He stayed seated, his head tipped back and jaw slack. That was another feeling he'd never get used to, and never wanted to.

"Fuck, Jask. I'll never get enough of this," Vince moaned as he gripped Jask's hips and thrust up, rolling his own hips to stay deep.

Carefully, Jask let out his jet black wings and extended them wide, thankful they had a room big enough there to do it. "You won't have to. Your dumbass just signed on to marry me. We've got extremely long lives, you know that?" He smirked just as he started moving, guiding himself up and back down as his cock bounced between them.

"Yes, I do know that." Vince dropped his head back against the pillow. "And I want to spend every moment just like this." Vince's hands traced back up Jask's sides. His eyes flashed black as he sent a pulse of pleasure into Jask, and it felt so good Jask could feel his cock throbbing in the air.

"Again, Vin," he said breathlessly, moving a little faster. The second wave had him moaning loudly, bouncing and using his wings to steady himself as he speared himself on Vince's thick length. "Fuck... I'm..."

The third wave tipped him over, and Jask let go without touching himself at all. He watched as his spend covered Vince's body and kept moving, sending an answering burst of wild grace through Vince.

"Jask!" Vince yelled. He pulled Jask down for a kiss and thrust up one last time as he came, and Jask grinned against his lips.

He slowly rolled off of Vince to lay next to him, sated and tired. They had nowhere to be, and as far as they knew, they were safe, so Jask wrapped him up and kept him close. "Can we nap?"

Vince stretched his limbs around Jask like an octopus and buried his face in his neck. He kissed there lightly before answering. "Yes, and then when we wake up, it's my turn to ride you."

Nothing in the world sounded better, and Jask drifted off thinking about how lucky he was. For once, he didn't dream of killing his father or his brother, or Drazan walking out, or Johnny's body. He dreamed of the scene he'd described to Vince - a bunch of kids running around, their family safe and happy. He wasn't sure if it would ever be achievable or not, but hey. It was a pleasant dream.

Unfortunately for them, they were woken up prematurely by a knock on the door. It was Edis, telling them in no uncertain terms that they were expected at family dinner, and if they failed to show up, they'd have Astarte and Amaranth to contend with. Jask shivered as he chuckled quietly, knowing that on their own, their mothers weren't overly scary - but they'd formed a friendship over the months they'd been together and now, they were quite a formidable team. "We should go," Jask said softly, running his hand down Vince's cheek. "I think they've been playing around with spells... I'd hate it if they turned you into a frog."

"We had a date, remember? They can wait." Vince didn't move from his spot on the bed, turning his face to get more of Jask's touch.

Though the thought of ignoring everyone else was nice, the truth was that Jask was just thankful he had a family at all. A real one, not one that looked at him like he was some sort of a traitor to his graceline just for being born with what they assumed to be a curse. "Come on. I'll tease you through dinner, and we'll sneak away the first chance we get."

Vince sighed and rolled away. "Fine, I suppose I should tell everyone you said yes anyway. I expect some really top-level teasing, though."

An easy smile spread across Jask's face as he climbed out of bed and got dressed. Teasing Vince was as simple as breathing, and while it made pretty much everyone else uncomfortable... it always led to good enough things that Jask didn't care.

They made their way out to the kitchen hand in hand, and Amaranth frowned at the pair of them. "Were you going to sleep all day?"

"Sleep? Nah. Stay in bed? Probably," Jask said with a smirk. "We were celebrating."

"Celebrating what?" Leota still looked like she was angry from earlier.

"He agreed to marry me." Vince held up their joined hands so everyone could see the ring.

The moment she realized she was to blame was almost comical. She opened her mouth to argue, then snapped it shut again and raised her eyebrows. "You're welcome."

Jask clamped a hand over Vince's mouth to stop his response and bowed his head to Leota. "Yes, thank you. You making fun of him ended up working out very well for us, and I'll be sure to let you off the hook for a wedding present. The rest of you, though..." He clicked his tongue, finally dropping his hand. "You will not be extended the same courtesy."

"This is wonderful," Astarte said, but her tone suggested it was forced. Jask couldn't blame her — they'd never really gotten past what had happened, and he wasn't sure she'd ever forgive him — but he'd take what he could get.

Vince agreed. "Best thing to ever happen to me."

Amaranth came around the table to hug them. "I'm proud of you both. Now, sit and eat before the food gets cold."

"Yes, ma'am," Jask obliged. He sat down, but brought Vince into his lap and looked around the table to see if anyone was going to complain. When no one did, he kissed Vince's back and reached around him to pull a second plate closer.

Vince shifted and looked at their little makeshift family. "So, what did everyone else do today?"

"I found the new shade of paint for the nursery," Edis said, sounding tired.

That sparked an argument between Vince and Leota about giving Ed a break, and Jask ate quietly as he decided to start teasing Vince. Slowly, he ran his hand over Vince's thigh under the table, gradually moving north and sending a tiny, grace-fueled vibration through him.

"I'm just saying, cut the guy some" — Vince jumped slightly when the vibration hit, his leg hitting the underside of the table — "some slack. I'll go get your stupid paint next time."

Hiding his smile behind Vince's body, Jask traveled up a little more until he was palming over Vince's crotch. Grateful for the thickness of the table, he sent another vibration right through his hand and snorted quietly when Vince dropped his fork. Jask pulled back, leaning around him to take a bite like nothing had happened and ignored the looks he received from everyone else.

Vince was *his,* and he was Vince's. The only thing he knew for sure was that they had each other, and that bond never really mattered in the first place. And they had the rest of their lives to prove it to each other.

He could think of worse things than that.

Twenty

Vince

Vince's subconscious mind had submerged him into one of his favorite dreams. Standing back at Pattie's, he could hear the roar of the crowd as Jask crashed down in front of him. Vince grinned and shamelessly checked the angel out. They started the fight, and this time, when he pinned him... no one pulled them apart. Jask tugged him down for a hard kiss and Vince opened for him. Things were just getting good when there was a wet slap to his face.

Vince opened one eye and sighed. "What do *you* want?" He was answered with a gummy grin and another spit-covered hand to the face. His three month old nephew laid happily on his chest, and a quick glance to his left found Jask's side of the bed empty. That meant he'd been the one to bring Arrozel in. As if his thoughts summoned Jask, his fiancé walked into the room. He appeared to be carrying breakfast, so Vince chose to forgive him, but not before giving him a hard time.

"Jask, look. Arro must've learned to teleport. Only explanation I can think of as to why he's here to wake me up at this unholy hour." Vince raised an eyebrow at Jask.

"He was crying. I thought Ed and Lee could use the break," Jask said as he sat the tray down.

"Aw, you just wanted to see your Uncle Vinnie. Is that it?" Vince sat up and held Arro close. They both knew teleportation wasn't likely, since Arro was confusingly and inexplicably human. That had been a shock to everyone. Arro snuggled into his chest and Vince looked at Jask again with a smug expression. "Look how good I am with babies."

Nothing but love filled Jask's eyes as he climbed up next to them. "We already knew that, you've been handling me for like two years now. Hi buddy," he teased in a sing-song voice. "Uncle Vin scaring you yet?"

"How rude." Vince frowned at him as Arro squealed and reached out for Jask. "The *betrayal*," he said, but despite his words, he smiled as Jask took Arro from him.

Karma instantly reared her head as Arro drooled all over Jask's body, but other than a slight grimace, Jask didn't react. "When we adopt, we're going for one with teeth."

"Want to get right to the biting stage? Sounds dangerous, I like it. You bring me coffee?" Vince stood from the bed to inspect the tray.

Jask shifted so Arro could lay on the spot that Vince vacated and propped his head on his hand. "Yep. *And* I baked muffins. Somehow, you've domesticated me."

"That's adorable." Vince grabbed a muffin and tossed it in the air, catching it and taking a big bite. "This is delicious."

"I know," Jask said smugly. "It's amazing what I can accomplish with actual ingredients. Moving to a city was the best thing we've ever done."

"Kinda miss farming, but this does make things easier." Vince finished his muffin and stole the baby back. "Eat your breakfast."

Arro raised his tiny hand up to Vince and Jask smiled softly as he reached for a muffin of his own. "You think they figured out what to do with their discovery yet?"

Vince kissed the little fist in his face. "Put that down, you're not big enough to fight yet." He sat back down next to Jask and shook his head. "I don't think any of us know what to do. On the one hand, I'm relieved we don't have a dangerous superbaby on our hands. On the other" — he looked down at Arro — "he's so fragile, Jask."

"I know. This is a pretty big secret my ancestors kept, and we have to assume they had protection in mind and *not* that they were selfish bastards that didn't want the grace in our lines to diminish. If angels and demons started breeding, we'd eventually all end up as humans again."

Jask made a silly face at Arro and laughed at his squeaky giggle. "But I guess that explains where the humans that are still around *did* come from, and why we don't have any documented sightings of superbabies. No way Ed and Lee are the first two to cross that line, not when demons feel so damn good."

Vince frowned at him. "Demon. Singular. Stay away from all the other ones."

"You know I didn't mean me. You have no idea how bad the cold really gets for us. And for me, you're the only demon that could ever come close to making it go away completely. You're the only one strong enough," Jask said with a shrug. "The only one hot enough... literally."

He grinned. "Damn straight. Did you already feed the pipsqueak, or should I go get his bottle?" Vince expected Jask to talk about their plans for the day at any moment, and he wasn't exactly ready to discuss it. He'd use the baby as a distraction as long as possible.

"Yeah, I fed him... but if he's anything like your side of the family, he's probably hungry again already." Jask stood and headed for the door. "I got it, I'll be back in a sec."

Vince watched him go before looking down at Arro. "Uncle Jask thinks he's funny. He isn't, but it's cute, so we let it slide. Lesson number three hundred from Uncle Vinnie." Vince bounced the baby while he waited for Jask to return. He didn't know if it was normal to talk to Arrozel the way he did, but they'd never really been normal, anyway.

Jask came back with a bottle and a towel, handing both to Vince. "My mom said she'll watch him later so the rest of us can go."

"That's great." Vince took his time arranging the towel and the baby before settling back against the headboard. He kept his eyes on his nephew as he spoke. "Should we take something? I mean, flowers or some shit? That's what people do when they visit graves, isn't it? Do you think that's what Johnny would want?" Vince knew he was rambling, but he feared if he stopped talking, he might cry.

The air between them suddenly got a lot heavier. "I don't know. I feel like I barely knew him. I can't believe it's been a year already."

"Yeah, me either. Have you heard from Draz?" Vince smiled down at Arro as he ate. The kid really could eat a lot. He was definitely a Riskel.

"You know I haven't," Jask said quietly. "I tried calling again today, the line is still disconnected. I really thought by now he'd have come home."

Vince chose not to comment on Drazan's extremely selfish disappearance. He didn't want to think about it, and knew Jask didn't want to talk about it more than necessary. "I don't even know if I want to go today. That's pretty fucked up, isn't it?"

Mindful of the baby, Jask crawled back onto the bed and settled in close to Vince. "No. It's not fucked up. We haven't set foot there since the day after we burned my brother, and it's not like this is a happy occasion for us to return. Feels fucking terrible that our lives are all moving on and he's..."

"He's dead," Vince whispered, not looking at Jask. It had taken a year. An entire year before Vince could say those two words. He still couldn't look at Jask as he took a breath.

The soft edges of Jask's wing wrapped around him. "You don't have to go, Vin. No one's going to make you, and no one would judge you for staying back. We'd all understand... including Johnny."

"I can't *not* go. I couldn't save him, I owe it to him to at least visit," Vince said as he leaned into Jask's touch.

"I'll be with you the whole time, Vin. And you've got a few hours to prepare, Ed wants to go around sunset. I think he wants to have some kind of a bonfire, which honestly seems a little morbid, but who am I to tell him no?"

Time to prepare just meant Vince had more time to dread going. He nodded anyway, taking the bottle away to burp the kid. They'd all gotten pretty good at taking care of the baby these past few months. He and Jask had even seriously started talking about adopting after the wedding.

He realized he hadn't replied and looked up to smile at Jask. "Yeah, that sounds good."

"It doesn't sound good. It sounds fucking horrible, but we're gonna do it anyway. You're right. We owe it to him," Jask said sadly.

A knock on the open door drew their attention, and Ed was standing there leaning against the frame. "Do you want me to take him back? Leota finally fell asleep."

As much as Vince loved his nephew, he felt a need to be alone with Jask. He stood and handed Arro over to his dad with a quiet thank you.

Arro only whined for a moment as Edis tucked him to his chest and headed out of the room. "Lay with me, Vin," Jask requested, his voice soft.

Vince closed the door and crawled back into bed, then pulled Jask close and settled into the mattress as both of Jask's wings folded over him.

"I love you." Jask kissed him briefly, fitting against him perfectly. "And if it'll help, I'll actually talk about the mooshy details of our upcoming nuptials today."

"Really? Even the tuxedos? *And* the dancing?"

With a dramatic sigh, Jask nodded. "Especially the tuxedos and the dancing. The flowers, too. All of it. I'm all yours today, whatever you need."

"That's incredibly kind of you." Vince still had an ache in his chest at the thought of visiting Johnny's grave, but having Jask made everything a little more bearable.

Jask's lips found his as he hovered over him, taking his time as if they'd never run out. With practiced hands, Jask laced their fingers and pinned him down to the mattress, his hips rolling just enough for Vince to feel him. "I know. I'm a nice guy."

"Definitely feel nice," Vince agreed.

"Tell me what you want, Vin. Like I said, I'm all yours." He ducked down to kiss his neck, letting his lips trail down to the hollow of this throat.

Vince tilted his head back to give Jask more space as he considered the question. "I don't want to think. I don't want to do anything but feel you." He hoped that was clear, because he couldn't collect his thoughts enough for much else.

"I got you, Vin," Jask said steadily. There wasn't a shred of doubt in his voice, and from the way he nipped at Vince's skin and roved his hands down to his ass, Vince knew why. Jask really did have him.

It was slow, sweet, and utterly consuming the way Jask took him. Every one of his senses was on overload as Jask kissed and touched and worshipped every inch of Vince's body, paving the way across his skin with hot breath and delicious intent. Vince couldn't do anything but lay there and be swallowed whole by it as Jask spread his legs and slotted between them, unhurried in his efforts to sink inside of him. When he finally did, the warring sensations of ice and grace filled him to the brim, and only then did Jask give him what he *really* needed. He pulled Vince up until they were seated together and rocked into him, tugging him down by the shoulders to drive himself deeper, faster, *harder* until Vince didn't remember his own name, let alone the things they had yet to do.

It was hard to tell who tipped first, but it didn't matter. They came together, powerfully enough to kill the lights and shake the foundations of the house around them... despite all the work they'd done to sturdy it up. Jask kissed him slowly afterward, lazily, seemingly having no intention of ever pulling out.

Vince didn't make any effort to move. He wanted Jask right where he was forever, and he tugged Jask's hair to break the kiss just long enough to tell him he loved him.

"I love you," Jask repeated easily, running his hands down Vince's heated back. "Thank you for putting up with me."

"You sure it's not the other way around?" Vince huffed a quiet laugh.

Jask tilted his head with his lips pursed out like he was actually considering it, then grinned widely. "Pretty sure it's both. We put up with each other, and I wouldn't have it any other way."

"Me either, sweetheart. Thank you," Vince wrapped his arms tighter around Jask and dropped his head to his shoulder. "I think our tuxes should be purple." He absolutely did not mean it, but he needed to get a reaction out of Jask — something to shake off the depressive funk he'd found himself in.

"Purple?" Jask asked, his expression pained and voice nearly a squeal. "As in... purple, purple? Yeah, that would be... great."

"Yes." Vince decided to see how far this would go. "Like deep, royal purple. In velvet."

He blinked several times. "Velvet? Like the material velvet?" Jask's face turned a little pale, and Vince could feel him slipping out of his ass. "Royal purple velvet? I uh... yeah. Okay. Guess we pretty much are kings, huh?"

"And I don't think we should have cake. Also, I'm requiring you to dance with me at least six times." He kept his head down so Jask wouldn't see his smile.

Jask didn't answer right away, then asked quietly, "Are we having pie instead of cake?"

"No. Fruit salad." Vince bit his lip to keep from laughing, but he knew he wouldn't last much longer.

Jask bodily threw him back against the pillows and pinned him down. "No. I draw the line there. I'll wear your stupid purple tux and dance with you however many times you want me to, but we're having an *actual* fucking dessert or it's not happening. You can go marry someone healthy."

"I don't want to marry anyone else. I want to marry *you*." Vince forced himself to pout.

"We're already going to *look* like idiots, we don't need to *eat* like idiots, too." Jask frowned deeply, and looked a little bit like he'd been given very bad news. "Cake, Vin. Cake."

Vince laughed. He couldn't hold it in anymore, and his next words came out in gasps. "Jask. Sweetheart. Love of my life. I was kidding... about all of it. Wait, except the dancing. You agreed and you can't take that back."

He looked so damn relieved that Vince *nearly* felt bad. "Fuck. Yeah, I'll dance with you as many times as you want, just don't make me wear velvet or eat fruit."

"Deal. We can have pie *and* cake, if you want," Vince offered.

"Now you're speaking my language, babe," Jask said with a satisfied smile. He kissed him, slow and sweet, then started planting annoying little kisses all over his face.

"Ew." Vince tried to get away, but Jask was stronger, no matter how much Vince hated admitting that fact. "I take it back, I'll marry someone else. Maybe Lee will switch Veris brothers with me."

Jask stopped abruptly and narrowed his eyes. "You think my brother could ever make you shake the way I do?" he challenged, that almost forgotten undercurrent of thunder back in his voice.

Vince couldn't stop the very shake Jask was talking about from rolling through his body as he blinked. "No?"

Growling, Jask bit Vince's bottom lip a little harder than necessary. "Wanna try that again? Maybe sound more convincing this time?"

Vince shivered but shrugged. "I can't say it with confidence, I've never slept with him." He lifted his head to kiss Jask. "But I don't *want* to sleep with him, so that has to count for something, right?"

"Yeah," Jask said, even less convincingly. He flipped over and sat up, fixing the mess of hair on top of his head. "We should get cleaned up. He'll probably want to leave soon."

Vince rolled and wrapped his arms around Jask's waist, laying his cheek against his back. "Don't be like that. You know no one can make me feel the things that you do. You're it for me."

"How would you feel if I made jokes about Lee like that?" Jask paused, deflating a bit. "Don't answer that. We're getting married for fuck's sake, I don't know why I still get like that when you joke around. Guess maybe it's just because I got so close to losing you."

The thought of Jask with Lee made Vince ill. "I'll stop. I don't like the idea of you with someone else, either." He stopped himself from bringing up Draz again, but judging by the look on Jask's face, his mind had gone there anyway.

"None of that matters now. There's no one but us anymore, and in a few months, we'll be married. A year after that and we'll have a couple kids of our own to chase around, and we'll have almost everything we ever wanted." Jask turned his face to kiss Vince and gave him a bittersweet smile. "You're it for me, too."

"All I want is to be yours. Promise." Vince returned the kiss before stretching. "Are you still feeling domestic? Want to pick out my clothes for me?"

Chuckling quietly, Jask waved his hand and dressed Vince in a royal purple, velvet tux. "There. Seems pretty damn fitting to me."

"This is terrible." Vince stood and looked in the mirror, then turned to see the back of the suit before looking at Jask. "My ass looks good, though."

With a bright smile that erased all the uneasiness from moments before, Jask left the bed to pull Vince into his arms. "Yeah... but your ass always looks good."

Jaskian

Putting Vince in that suit proved to be a mistake. Despite how ridiculous it looked, Vince refused to take it off, and Jask didn't know if that was making him want to laugh or cry. Probably a little of both, if he was being honest with himself. He'd known when Vince made those crazy requests that they were false. Not lies, exactly, but not something Vince truly believed he'd wanted — and though Jask had been severely tempted to call him out on that fact, he knew that Vince craved laughter. Over the last year, it had been hard enough to keep his own head above water, but he'd done what he could to make things easier on Vince. For example, he tried to hide all the times he relentlessly called Drazan. That loss was one he didn't think he'd ever get over, because unlike Johnny... Drazan actually left them on purpose. He'd made the decision that they weren't worth much to him anymore, and after everything they'd been through, that hurt Jaskian worse than he ever thought he'd be able to admit to anyone... especially Vincenzo.

Those jealousy issues they joked about were a little too real, and Jask knew if Vince understood the depth of the love he felt for Drazan, he wouldn't be able to get past it. Sure, the love was completely and totally platonic, but it wouldn't matter to Vince and Jask knew it. It would be the same for him if he knew just how much Vince had loved Johnny. Some selfish part of them that had always been muted by the bond was a little more awake now that they were no longer secured by biology and fate. To know that — platonically or not — someone else was that close to them? And adding in everything that had happened on top of it? It just wasn't something they needed, so Jask did his best to try to work around it.

But it wasn't just Drazan's departure that still weighed on him. Killing his father and brother had done more damage than he cared to let on, but at every step of the way, Vince had been there for him. He'd supported him, held him, refrained from judgement when Jask couldn't hold back the tears. But most of all, he'd forgiven him. Somehow, Vince found a way to get past the fact that Jaskian was a murderer several times over. Saros, Taz, others... including half of his own family. Something like that shouldn't be easy to ignore, but Vince knew who he truly was. He knew his heart, and knew that Jask didn't kill without a reason. And hopefully, that particular bad habit ended with Cidos.

"What the *hell* are you wearing?" Leota asked her brother, her tone incredulous. "Take it off, you're making me want to throw up, and I did quite enough of that while I was pregnant."

Jask chuckled at the offended look on Vince's face and held up a hand. "It's my fault, I should've known better. He told me to dress him, and this was supposed to be a joke. As usual... the joke is on me."

Vince tugged on the lapels of the suit jacket and grinned at his sister. "I happen to think I look dashing." His grin faltered a little as he added, "Plus, Johnny would've found it hilarious, so..."

No one dared to defy him. He was right, and even if he *hadn't* been correct, telling him that would've just been cruel. "You're right, Vin. He would've laughed his ass off at you. All you need now is your Stetson and you've got yourself quite an ensemble," Jask said.

"Don't encourage him," came Amaranth's voice from the kitchen. "He'll be the first velvet cowboy this side of... wherever we are now."

Vince was already running back to the bedroom before his mother finished speaking. He came back with his black Stetson and had traded his dress shoes for black boots. He held out his arms and twirled. "Better?"

If it wasn't so ridiculously endearing to see the smile on Vince's face, Jask would've laughed himself into oblivion. Objectively, he looked ridiculous, and yet... "How do you manage to make even *that* look good?" Jask asked, moving himself forward and pulling Vince in for a slow, sensual kiss. "I'm the luckiest guy in the world."

"Or the dumbest," Lee teased. "The jury's still out on that one."

Vince lifted his finger to Lee in a rude gesture before turning to face everyone. He opened his mouth to speak, but Arro screeched at that exact moment. Vince picked him up before anyone else could. "What's wrong, buddy? Want to come with Uncle Vinnie?"

"He probably woke up and saw your suit," Edis mumbled.

Arro snuggled against Vince and Jask sighed like a love struck moron. While Arrozel was still kind of gross thanks to all the drool and... everything else that came along with only being a few months old, Vince taking care of him had to be the cutest thing he'd ever seen. He was already starting to regret his words about adopting an older child. "How come you never hold me like that, Vin?" Jask asked with a small smirk.

"Because you're a giant. I'll try though, if you really want," Vince replied as he rocked the baby.

Jask would honestly take any excuse he could get to be close to Vince, and hell, he wasn't above admitting that he wanted to be babied now and again, it just never happened. But as he watched the two of them, Jask shook his head. "Nah, I wouldn't want to take a second of this away from that little guy. He needs it more than I do."

"Sometimes, I swear you two think he's *your* kid." Lee crossed her arms, but the look on her face was full of nothing but love. "He's not, by the way... just in case you need a reminder."

She was both right and wrong. While Arrozel technically didn't belong to them, he was still their responsibility. They'd collectively chosen to hide him in plain sight when they moved back to a city, but every single one of them was aware that at any time, someone could figure out what he was. That in and of itself wasn't necessarily a problem - humans weren't hunted by any means, but they were incredibly rare and usually lived sequestered from the rest of the population, and so throwing one into the middle of school for angels and demons was bound to draw attention. And if anyone figured out who his real parents were, *that* would be where the issue came in.

They had time to worry about what would come as Arro started to grow. For now, they were content to just enjoy him as he was and to continue picking up the pieces. Jask snapped back to reality as Arro sharply tugged on his hair. "Ow! What was that for, little man?"

"Maybe he's saying you should cut your hair," Vince suggested. "Oh, or braid it. You'd look hot as a Viking." In reality, Arro was trying to eat the hair wrapped around his fist.

Jask frowned deeply as he extricated his hair from that tiny hand. "It just started growing back. Do you really want me to cut it off again?"

"Me? Absolutely not. I love your hair. Especially love the sounds you make when I..." Vince's explanation was cut off as Amaranth yelled his name.

"Vincenzo! Not in front of the baby!"

He grimaced as he realized they hadn't been censoring themselves at all in front of the little guy. "Sorry, Amaranth. But if you think he's not gonna be swearing up a storm by the time he's three, I'm afraid you're gonna be disappointed. Even Ed has a potty mouth these days," Jask said.

"Only because I have to live with the two of you," he countered. "Tell me again why we couldn't get separate houses?"

"Because you couldn't bear to be parted from us, Eddie. Also, we're the strongest defense you got. Against pretty much anything," Vince reminded them.

"Against anything but us," a stranger said from just behind them.

Jask whirled around quickly with a ball of energy in his hand, ready and willing to do whatever it took to protect Arro. But what he saw made him stop dead, and the light in his fist extinguished immediately. Before him stood two men, both gorgeous in their own rights... and incredibly familiar. He'd seen their photos a thousand times, heard their stories even more. "No," Jask said, stunned. "How...?" He took a step forward, staring at the one with storms in his eyes.

Vince stepped back to hand Arrozel to Edis before standing beside Jask. "Friends of yours?" He eyed the strangers suspiciously with no hint of recognition in his gaze.

"Better hope they're our friends," Jask muttered. "If not... we're in trouble. Vin, unless my eyes very much deceive me... these are our namesakes. Veris and Riskel."

Veris inclined his head with a smirk playing around the corner of his lips. "You're not mistaken, Jaskian. It's been... oh, hundreds of years at least, wouldn't you say, Ris?"

The other man nodded as he leaned against the counter like he owned the place already. "At least. Could've done with a few hundred more, myself."

"Great. Feel free to leave, then." Vince frowned at him, subconsciously stepping closer to Jask.

"Vince!" Lee hissed in a panicked voice.

Jask shook his head and put his arm out protectively in front of Vince, but some ingrained instinct told him he didn't have to. Something wasn't right here. Veris and Riskel hated each other. Bonds were meant to be broken, and mixing the lines would lead to the end of the world. Now, watching the way Veris and Riskel were looking at each other, he understood innately that everything he'd ever been told about his heritage had been a lie. "You aren't here to hurt us." It wasn't asked as a question, it was stated as fact.

"Nope," Riskel said, popping the 'p' at the end. "We're here to thank you, actually."

Vince was in the process of pushing Jask's arm down when he looked at the two with wide eyes. "Come again?"

"Sit," Veris commanded. "I think it's time you get a *true* history lesson."

Edis continued to shield Arro and shook his head, sidestepping closer to Leota. "No offense, but we don't need to be here for this. Jask and Vince can relay the message to us. Arro has a... check up."

"Lies," Veris said in a bored tone. "But as a token of goodwill, you may leave, if you so desire. I'd advise you stay, though... as the biggest thank you is owed to you and your mate."

"Can we skip the riddles and get right to the juicy bits? I'd personally like to know where the fuck you've been the entire time we've been dying!" Vince directed this to Riskel, who screwed up his face like he'd been insulted.

"Fine," Riskel said. "You want to know where we were? An island, somewhere *very* far away, enjoying each other's... company," he finished with a shrug. "After hundreds of years of watching our descendants make the wrong choices, we got tired."

Jask frowned. "You two are..."

"The original mated pair, yes," Veris clarified. "Only we did it on purpose, and I suppose that's where our story begins. Now again... I'll ask you each to *sit.*"

Without further hesitation, Jask sat down on the edge of the couch without taking his eyes off the two of them.

Vince hesitated but eventually sat close to Jask, placing himself between his family and the two dangerous beings in their space.

Ed and Lee reluctantly followed, but Astarte dropped her eyes to the floor. Jask wanted to reach out to her but knew better than to make any sudden movements. "Okay, we're sitting. What happened?"

"The world ended," Veris said simply. "Or, it tried to, anyway. The humans that were left decided to mate with angels and demons. That part of your history books is true. The rest... not so much. We were never enemies, at least not until the humans got involved. I loved Riskel as much back then as I do now. We only agreed to breed with the humans because their survival depended on it, and it should've never lasted more than a handful of generations. As you've seen with Arrozel, the offspring of an angel and a demon is nothing more than a human. We don't know why, so take your pick as to the reasoning. They inherit the light from angels and the darkness from demons, but other than that, they're completely powerless. So, eventually, the lines of grace and shadow should've faded out, returning humanity to normal."

That was already a lot to take in, but it didn't even begin to explain the questions Jask hadn't even realized he had. "So why didn't that happen?"

"Greed," Riskel said. "After getting a taste of the power we gave them, they didn't want to give it up. So they started lying. Making up stories about children with the power to destroy everything, and expressly forbidding relationships between demons and angels. We fled, knowing we'd be killed if we were discovered."

"You could've helped! Your cowardice led to the death of my ancestors. Almost led to my own, to my mate's!" Vince shifted to the edge of the couch, but stayed seated. His body was shaking with anger.

Riskel's eyes flashed blacker than night, but he didn't move a muscle. "We fought for *years*. And I don't think you have much room to talk, when all you've done is *hide*."

"That's not fair," Jask cut in as he extended his wing to hold Vince in place. "We didn't hide, and we're also not *you*." For all the original trust he'd placed in them, it was fading quickly. "Where's that thank you? I seem to have missed it."

"We were already bonded to each other. We simply made it so that every ten generations born to our lines, there would be one mated pair. We kept hoping eventually, the hatred and greed would bleed themselves out and you would figure out for yourselves that the stories weren't true. We were beginning to think it wasn't going to happen, so... we threw in a wildcard pair this generation. You two." Veris nodded to Jask and Vince. "We chose correctly."

"Thanks, that makes me feel so much better." Vince's voice dripped with sarcasm. "You decided to fuck with our lives. People have *died*. Jask's brother. My brother." Vince stopped talking and swallowed, looking down at the floor. He blindly reached for Jask's hand and held tight.

"I told you they'd hate us for it," Veris said to Riskel, pulling him in and kissing his temple. "We shouldn't have come."

Riskel shook his head. "They deserved to know the truth, even if they do hate us for it."

Jask wasn't sure if he hated them or not. On one hand, Vince was right, they'd basically been used as pawns. But on the other, he understood that this was a lot bigger than they had thought it was, and he couldn't imagine being in their shoes and having to hide for centuries. "But it's over now, right? Ed and Lee will be the last mated pair? You're done?"

"Yes," Veris said quickly. "There will be no need in the future to bond people against their will. We came back now so you'd all know the truth, and to do what we should've done a long time ago. We're offering our help to keep Arrozel safe while the truth spreads."

Vince scoffed but then gave a quick nod. "We accept. It's the least you could do."

"Hey," Ed said sharply. "Don't you think Leota and I should have a say in this at all? The last time we checked, he's *our* son. And we haven't even decided yet if we're going to tell people he's human."

Leota, in all her fiery, motherly glory, stood up and stomped over until she was standing tall in front of their ancestors. "I never said you could come anywhere near him. We don't need your help, we've done just fine."

Veris let out a sigh at the way Riskel was beaming from ear to ear. "She earns your name, that's for sure. Leota," he said, turning his attention back to her. "We won't overstep. You won't even see us. Just... know that as things progress, your son has our total protection. We would die for him. We've been waiting a long time for this."

"What do you mean, as things *progress?*" Edis asked.

For once, Veris looked truly uneasy. "I think that will become apparent soon enough. I suggest you do what you intended to do today, and we'll talk more about Arrozel's introduction to the world shortly. For now... I believe you lot have more pressing issues. Come, Ris."

"Here? Now?!" Ris squeaked, and Jask laughed like a hyena when he realized he'd taken it in a way that Veris likely hadn't intended.

He nudged Vince. "Guess that dynamic runs in our veins, hm?"

Vince rubbed his face, trying to hide his blush. "Can we go? This was exhausting, and I just want to see Johnny and then come back to sleep for a week."

Veris and Riskel disappeared without another word, but Jask felt... off. There was an underlying meaning in what Veris had said, he just didn't have a clue what it was. "You're right. Let's go, we've put it off long enough." Standing, Jask kissed Vince with all the love he could muster, then turned to the others. "Ready to go?"

"Yes," Ed said softly, handing Arro off to Astarte. "I'll take Lee, you take Vince. Meet you there."

They vanished too, and Jask took a deep breath before teleporting himself and Vince to the house they hadn't seen in a year. The outside looked the same other than the overgrown weeds and the spreading evidence of neglect. His chest tightened - part of him had hoped Drazan had at least returned *here,* and he'd see his smiling face one more time or feel the familiar imprint of his power. But there was no sign at all that the house had been occupied since they left.

After a long look, Jask tightened his grip on Vince's hand and led him out back to Johnny's grave. Leota was already crying, and as Vince and Jask stepped up next to them, he understood why. Instead of the grave marker they'd left to immortalize the spot where Johnny would rest forever, all they found was a gaping hole in the ground and displaced dirt surrounding it.

Johnny's body was gone.

The Rough Side of Paradise

Book Two of the Grace and Shadow Series
COMING APRIL 20, 2021

Please enjoy this preview:

ONE

Vince

"It's only one night." Vince let the words float around in his head as he gazed at his reflection in the mirror. His hair hung almost below his eyes and he ran a hand through it, pushing it back before placing his Stetson on his head. He brought his hand back up to his face and ran it over his chin. He'd made the mistake of letting his mother convince him to trim his beard before the wedding. With his long hair hidden and the beard much shorter, it struck him that he looked like a different person. That he looked so much closer to the Vince from "before." Before the pain, before the death, before the running. Movement in the mirror caught his eye and his line of sight focused on Jaskian as it tended to do more often than not. He smiled a little to himself as he realized he also looked like the Vince before Jask, and that person wasn't someone he wanted to be ever again. He'd take on all the pain in the world and beyond if it meant getting to keep Jask with him. Which was why the words "only one night" were so hard for him to wrap his head around. They'd had enough of being apart and yet here Jaskian stood, packing a bag to spend the night with Astarte instead of in their bed.

Vince knew he was being unreasonable but he and Jask had already spent so much time apart, just the thought of one night without him was making him uneasy. The past two months of moving and searching for Johnny's body had been hard on them both. Making the decision to move forward with the wedding had been something they'd done together. A day to look forward to, something to celebrate their love and its endurance. Vince felt excitement anytime he thought about finally being able to marry Jask. Jaskian Veris was the best thing to ever happen to him because Jask meant home to him. This stupid night before the wedding tradition could be ignored.

"Jask, neither one of us is even a bride. This is ridiculous. Stay home. Stay naked." He turned to face him, flashing what he hoped was a charming grin.

Ice blue eyes stared back at him. "Believe me, I wish I could, but our story has enough tragedy in it... why risk it? I don't want to screw this up."

"Nothing could screw this up. We're meant to be, remember?" Vince stepped closer and put his hand over Jask's, effectively stopping him from packing.

"I remember. But Vin, it's just one night. As much as I wanna stay, this tradition is important to my mom. It's more for her than anything, it's the last night I'm *just* her son and not someone else's husband."

The word husband caused a happy flip in his stomach. After tonight, he'd have the honor of calling Jask his husband. He could deal with a night of discomfort if that reward waited for him. "Alright, but let's not make this a habit."

"Wouldn't dream of it," Jask said with a smile. His hands cupped Vince's face and he leaned in, kissing him gently. "It won't be easy for me, either. I might freeze to death."

"You can take my blanket." Vince stepped away to grab it and packed it in the bag.

Jask kissed him a lot deeper after that, like he was trying to take all the heat from Vince's body. They'd have kept going and Vince might've been able to convince him to change his mind, but Edis knocked on the door to kill the fun. "Times up, gotta take him."

"If we stay very quiet, maybe he'll go away," Vince whispered, dropping his head to Jask's shoulder and wrapping his arms around his waist.

With a soft chuckle, Jask planted his lips to Vince's head. "He won't, but you're adorable. Ed, give me a minute."

"You've got two, but that's it," Ed said. The door closed a moment later.

"Vin, here." Jask carefully tried to extricate himself, but Vince wouldn't budge. "I want to give you something, but I can't until you let me go."

Vince hesitated for a second before loosening his grip. "Fine, but I'm not going far." He stepped back half an inch to give Jask some breathing room.

With a shudder, Jask let out his jet-black wings. Every trace of the white they used to have was long gone. "You gave me a ring, but I realized I never really gave you anything. So... before it was too late, I wanted to..." Jask trailed off, then made an adorably constipated face as he plucked one of his own feathers and let out an exaggerated whine. "Give me your wrist."

Vince frowned and made sure Jask's wing was okay before doing as requested. "Is this some weird angel ceremony I should know about?"

"No," Jask said as he tied the feather around his wrist. "This is just me saying I love you. And now you can have a literal piece of me with you wherever you go... unless you don't want it."

"I do! I absolutely do. Thank you," Vince pulled him close again, kissing him gently. "I love you, too."

Jask smiled against his lips and broke away only when Edis knocked again. "Times up," Jask said sadly. "I'll see you tomorrow."

"I won't sleep without you," he sighed, "but if I can handle growing up with Leota, I can handle this." He kissed Jask one more time before reluctantly letting him go with his brother. Vince stood in the same spot for a few moments as he processed the silence of his now empty house. Jask was going to Astarte's and Amaranth's home for the evening and Edis would go back to Lee and Arro. Only Vince would be without company.

He felt a sudden pang of grief, overwhelmed with a need to talk to Johnny. Johnny would've been able to distract him, help him forget about his worry that he could fuck something up. Because Vince was an expert at fuckups. He ran a hand over his face and walked into their kitchen. A flash of light from the window caught his attention and he checked to see if it was Jask and Edis. It was unlikely, as they had most certainly teleported. Vince didn't see the point since they all lived in the same cul-de-sac, but to each their own.

He directed his gaze to the buildings lighting up the night sky to his left. Settling on the outskirts of the city had been a unanimous decision, but Vince would be lying if he said he didn't miss seeing the stars.

He shook himself out of that thought and pulled open a cabinet, frowning when he saw their liquor seemed to be missing. He was sure his mother had something to do with that. She'd given him multiple lectures about being late to his own wedding, her main concern being a drunken stupor. He couldn't seem to convince her that nothing would make him late to marrying Jask. Seemed like she'd taken matters into her own hands. He slammed it closed and grabbed his keys. If he couldn't drink here, he'd go to the bar. No way was he getting any sleep without some type of alcohol in his system.

It'd taken some trial and error to find a bar when they'd first moved but eventually, they'd found a place that accepted demons, angels, and even the occasional human. No one batted an eye when Jask and Vince walked in together that first time. He started up his old truck and drove into town, whistling along with the radio as he sped down the road.

Already, being apart from Jask was making him antsy. They'd spent so long fighting the bond, so long separated. Now that it was safe for them to be together, they were hardly ever divided. They weren't joined at the hip every moment of every day, their new jobs wouldn't allow it — however, every other spare moment Jask was by his side. Until tonight. He knew it was temporary, a fleeting moment in the years they'd have, but his chest was still tight with anxiety.

They still didn't know who'd taken Johnny and that meant there was an unknown potential enemy out there. If he wasn't with Jask, he couldn't protect him. Vince huffed out a small laugh as he pulled into the bar. If anyone in their odd little family didn't need protection, it was Jaskian. Yet, the worry stayed in Vince's mind, sitting like an unwanted guest.

He wasted no time in entering the bar and waved to a few regulars. Herchel was behind the bar, glaring at a group of loud demons in one corner. Vince took his favorite stool and looked over at the crowd before turning back, hanging his hat on his knee. "Trouble?"

Herchel shook his head and dropped a glass in front of Vince, pouring him his usual. "Nothing old Bess can't handle." Herchel tapped the bar above the spot he kept the shotgun Vince knew was there. He'd seen it enough times, luckily never pointed at him. It suddenly struck him as odd that he hadn't been in a bar fight in so long. It had almost been a weekly occurrence before Jask. He shook his head as he picked up his glass. He was proud of himself for kicking that habit and he wasn't about to pick it back up now... no matter how much the men in the corner were asking for it. No matter how much he missed it. He was getting married tomorrow. Jask would murder him if he showed up with healing bruises. The idiots were getting louder, and Vince tossed back the whiskey, motioning for Herchel to keep them coming.

He could ignore them. He was not getting into a fight tonight. He took a sip of the second drink, savoring it. A few blissful moments passed as he envisioned what Jask would look like tomorrow, how he would smile when they stepped into the venue at the same time. The daydream got even better as he began to mentally plan out the honeymoon. They weren't going very far, but they'd both taken a week off work. Vince was determined to keep Jask in bed for *at least* five of those days.

He was rudely knocked out of his reverie when a small voice called out in pain. Vince couldn't stop himself from looking, turning his head to glance over his shoulder. A young angel kid, probably barely old enough to drink, had caught the attention of the ruffians in the bar. They'd shoved him to the floor and were circling him. He saw the look of terror on the boy's face and his brain flashed him back to that day with Damian. To the glassy eyes that had stared up into nothing as the blood seeped into the cold cement floor. One kid was dead because of him, he'd be damned if something happened to this one while he could stop it. Vince slowly sat the glass back on the bar before pushing his hair back and settling the cowboy hat back on his head. He watched Herchel reach for the gun and shook his head as he stood. "I got it, Herch. Leave Bess sleeping for now." Looked like he was getting into a fight tonight, after all.

He pushed a couple of the instigators out of the way and held a hand out to the victim. After a brief hesitation, the kid took it and allowed Vince to pull him up. Vince confirmed with him that he wasn't hurt badly before dusting him off and sending him away. He felt a shove from behind him. He turned, clenching his teeth and facing what he assumed was the ringleader.

"Hey," the drunk slurred. "We was just having fun."

"Oh, were you? *He* didn't seem to be." Vince took a second to roll up his sleeves.

"Angel bastards. Better to teach them early how rough the world is."

Vince shook his head. "It's only rough because of assholes like you. Herchel's is a safe space. If you can't abide by his rules, you need to go."

"Make u—"

When Vince told this story later, he would tell anyone that would listen that he hesitated. That he thought out the pros and cons of a fight the night before his wedding to the love of his life. That is *not* what happened. Vince's fist connected with the jaw of the speaker before the words had finished leaving his mouth. Almost in slow motion, Vince watched him hit the ground, out cold. A pool stick broke across his back and he turned his head with a raised eyebrow. The man looked at the broken stick and then back to Vince, who hadn't budged even an inch. With no other options, he tried to punch Vince in the stomach. Vince easily sidestepped the hit.

"Really?" he demanded before grabbing the guy by his shirt and tossing him hard into the wall. The rest of the mob jumped him at that point and Vince almost regretted getting involved. Not because he was worried he wouldn't win, but because he'd done so well in staying out of fights. He brought his elbow up and into the chin of an assailant, the vibrations traveling up his arm as he felt the man's teeth break. He ducked the next swing and gripped the man by his throat, lifting him into the air before body-slamming him into the floor.

He stood and looked back to the bartender. "Herch! Jask does *not* need to know about this!" Herch's hands went up, palms facing Vince in agreement as he shrugged. Vince could only hope he wouldn't rat him out. He was tackled from behind, stumbling forward a few steps. He reached back and grabbed the guy, swinging him forward over his shoulder and onto the pool table. After a few more moments, he had them all running out the door. He kicked the last one in the ass as he watched them flee.

"Hot *damn* that felt good!" He came back to the bar and took the bottle of water Herchel handed him. He downed the entire thing before catching his reflection in the bar. He'd managed to get a nice cut on his cheek, he lifted his fingers to it and winced. It should be healed by morning, or at the very least hidden well if he cleaned it up. He sat back down on his stool and laid his hat on the bar, picking up the glass Herch had waiting on him. A throat clearing to his left had him looking over to find the boy he'd just saved sitting next to him.

"Thought you'd left." He took a drink of the whiskey, loving the burn as it traveled down his throat.

"No, I... Well, I-I'd like to buy you a drink. For what you did." The blush on his cheeks and the stutter were adorable. Two years ago, Vince would've taken him home. Now all he wanted was to get past tonight and get back to Jask.

"That isn't necessary, but thank you for the gesture." Vince thought that would've been the end of the conversation, but the kid didn't move.

"I should be the one thanking you. Please, there has to be something I can do."

Vince finished his drink and turned to face him. "There is. Take care of yourself. Don't let assholes like that get you down." He patted the kid on the shoulder, paid his tab, and waved to Herch as he left the bar. He was just buzzed enough that his nerves were mostly settled, but not bad enough that he couldn't make it home. Once he pulled into the drive, he had a moment of weakness and started walking towards Astarte's. He just wanted to check on Jask... but something made him stop in the middle of the cul-de-sac. Jask wanted this and Vince needed to respect that. He took a breath of the cool night air and spun around, letting himself into his silent, empty home. He stripped off the clothes he'd worn, tossing them in the washer to try and stop the blood stains from setting in. After a quick shower and a cold beer, he finally sank into the bed. He rolled until his face was buried in Jask's pillow and drifted off into an uneasy sleep. It felt like seconds after he closed his eyes that he was opening them again. He stretched a little and wrapped his arms around the pillow, fully intending to go back to sleep.

~

"You did well tonight. That kid definitely has a crush," an achingly familiar voice said, hitting him like a train.

Vince was up and on his feet before he'd even made the decision to move. "Johnny?"

"Heya, Vinnie. Miss me?" Johnny smiled at him and Vince took three long strides, pulling Johnny into his arms. He knew he was probably crushing him, but he didn't care. Johnny was here and Vince was just so relieved to see his best friend again.

"I'll take that as a yes." He felt a hand pat his back and he stepped back. It was then that he actually noticed his surroundings. There were no walls, no doors, no windows. Nothing but an ongoing white around them and his bed

behind him. He turned in a slow circle before looking back at Johnny. Poor, innocent, loyal Johnny who was smiling at him still, even if it was tinged with a bit of sadness now.

"This is a dream. It's not... you're not real. Fuck..." The grief hit again, fresh and raw. Vince stumbled back until he hit the bed. He sank down into the mattress and rubbed his eyes.

Johnny nodded and took a seat next to him. "You're right, this is just a dream. But does it matter? I'm still here... in one way or another." He flashed that boyish grin Vince missed so much and nudged him with his elbow. "Miss me yet?"

"You have no idea, Johnny." Vince looked his friend over. "I'm sorry. You didn't deserve it."

He shrugged, seemingly unbothered. "I know. None of us deserved what happened that day... or the days after. You figure out who took my body yet?"

"Well, no, not exactly." Vince pushed down the guilt that was threatening to overwhelm him. "We're going to! I promise. It's just... Jask and I... we're getting married tomorrow."

Johnny beamed and wrapped an arm around him. "It's about time. I'm happy for you. But... don't think so hard about who took my body."

"No, Johnny. I can't let this slide. Like I said, you didn't deserve it, so we'll find the bastard." Vince paused, weighing his next words in his head before asking, "Johnny, are you happy? Wherever you are."

His friend shrugged, shifting his glossy eyes to his own hands. "Just confused, mostly. And tired... I can't rest until my body is at rest." Johnny shifted suddenly, turning to face Vince fully. "Why didn't you burn my body? Why'd you bury me, when you burned everyone else?"

"Draz started digging the grave..." Vince started but stopped with a sigh. He looked over at Johnny. "Truth? I should've stopped him. Should've put you on a pyre like everyone else. But doing that made it so much more real. It meant you were actually gone and I wasn't coping well with that."

For the first time, Johnny looked truly uncomfortable. "Actually, about Drazan..."

Vince frowned and waited for Johnny to continue. What could he possibly *have to tell Vince about Draz? Johnny's mouth opened, but instead of words, a loud blaring alarm replaced Johnny's voice.*

~

Vince shot up in bed as his alarm clock rang on the bedside table. His breathing was coming quick as he searched the room for the threat, tossing the blankets off of his legs. His eyes landed on his alarm clock and he sank back onto the bed. Vince reached over and turned it off, running his other hand over his face. A dream, that's all Johnny was now. He allowed himself a moment to grieve again for his fallen friend.

The phone buzzing on his bedside table had him rolling out of bed and answering his mother. A brief conversation and one hot shower later, Vince smiled at himself in the mirror. Today was the day Vincenzo Riskel got married.

Jaskian

Leaving Vince even for a single night was painful. He knew it was necessary, but still... after everything they'd lost, everything they'd suffered... it just seemed wrong to purposefully separate. He went through the motions with Astarte before she finally turned in for the night, and that alone was enough to make him wish he'd thrown tradition out the window. For two solid hours, all he heard from her was how grown up he was and how much she wished his father could've been there to see it.

Part of him was really starting to believe she'd gone mad. It had taken a great deal of effort not to remind her that Athar wasn't around for a very simple, extremely terrible reason. *I killed him,* he reminded himself silently. *Because he thought this very union was unholy enough that he tried to kill us.*

But that path was dangerous. All it ever did was cause him to think about the other things they'd lost in recent years. Athar, Cidos, Johnny... Drazan. Knowing his best friend was out there somewhere and hurting was almost too much for Jask. Drazan had given him *everything*... and how did Jask repay him? He'd gotten his boyfriend killed, and nearly got *him* killed, too.

Nothing was the same anymore. Happiness felt like something cheap, something stolen — not something to be grateful for. He wasn't sure if he'd ever be able to move past that, ever be able to look at Vince or his brother Edis and not think of all the things they'd suffered together. Sure, on some level, that brought them all closer. They'd die for each other. Kill for each other. But it didn't stop the memories from trying to swallow Jask whole.

A knock on his window caught his attention, and Jask sat up slowly from the bed. Grinning, he made his way over to peek through the glass and expected to see Vince — maybe he'd had enough of tradition, too. But when familiar, bright, hazel eyes stared back at him through the dark, he knew exactly who it was... and it wasn't his soon-to-be husband.

He opened the window so quickly that the glass actually vanished. "Drazan?!" he whispered, waving him in. "What the *fuck*, Draz! Where have you been?"

Draz climbed in through the window, straightening his clothes as he turned to face Jask. "You almost sound unhappy to see me, Jask."

Too many emotions flooded Jask's system at the sight of his best friend. He didn't answer right away. He couldn't. Instead, he surged forward and pulled Drazan into a tight hug. "Of course I'm happy to see you, you idiot."

After a moment's hesitation, Draz hugged him back, hand awkwardly patting between Jask's shoulder blades. They stayed in the silent embrace until Draz stepped back, clearing his throat. "So. Tomorrow's the big day?"

"Yeah," Jask said quietly. He ran a hand through his hair and sat on the edge of the bed, realizing pretty quickly that whatever warmth they used to share was gone. "Vince figures we've put it off long enough."

"Well, what are you doing here? Shouldn't you be out at a strip club? A bar?" Draz gave him a small smile and Jask could see a hint of the old Draz behind it. He almost missed what Draz was saying as he continued. "It's barely eleven o'clock. You're getting old, Jaskian."

It was true, but he still felt a little defensive. "Edis has a kid now, and it's not exactly like my best friend was around to plan a bachelor party for me. I don't... I don't have anyone else. Not really."

"Well," Draz said as he shrugged, pulling Jask up off the bed. "I'm here now. Let's go celebrate."

"Yeah?" Jask stepped in close, trying to take in the familiar lines of his friend's face. "Might get my ass kicked by the future missus, but I can't say no if you're offering."

"You know I'll take any chance I get to annoy Vince. Let's see if this shit still works." Draz put a hand on Jask's shoulder and Jask could feel him pull on his power. A blink later and they were outside a bar. Draz put his hands on his knees and took a few deep breaths. "Fucking hell, that's always so exhausting. I think I'll stick to mirrors."

Jask chuckled. "Aww, poor baby. Come on." He clapped Drazan on the back and lifted him upright by his shoulder. "What are the rules for these kinds of things, anyway? Am I supposed to still be a good little angel?"

"Why are you asking? Looking to get into some trouble?" Draz opened the door, revealing scantily clad dancers on poles. "Because this is where we'll find it."

The last thing Jask needed was trouble. But old habits died hard — and some died much harder than others. He stepped through and smirked over at Drazan. "Trouble seems to find us, D. Let's see what happens."

"That's what I like to hear. Go find us a table and I'll get the drinks." Draz winked and headed to the bar, eyeing one of the dancers as he passed.

Jask wasn't quite sure what to look at. Sure, the view was nice as he took a seat a little too close to one of the poles, but he still couldn't get over the sight of his best friend. When Drazan came back, he hadn't skimped on the drinks. Jask snorted as he took two of the shots off the tray and tossed one back. "In a hurry tonight, D?"

"Making up for lost time!" Draz took one of the shots and held it up for a toast, which Jask met a little too eagerly.

They killed the entire tray before the end of the second song, and Jask felt more relaxed than he had in a long time. Jask nodded his head to one of the dancers and jerked it toward Drazan. "How about one for the grumpiest man in the room?"

"I'm not grumpy," Draz mumbled as the girl straddled his lap with a smile.

"You sure look grumpy." She leaned and motioned for another dancer to join. "But we'll fix it for you, handsome."

As the music died down, Draz pointed at Jask. "*He's* the one getting married tomorrow."

"Which means I'm the one that needs to behave," Jask reminded him. "I'm... probably *too* content with just watching this." He took another drink and shook the empty glass, then stood with a wink to the girl. "Time for refills, anyway."

"You said probably!" Draz called after him. "That means one lap dance for the groom when he gets back." The laughter of the dancers followed Jask to the bar, and he couldn't shake the feeling that Vince would forgive him for whatever happened. He had to, right? Draz was back.

He refilled the tray and carried it to the table, then sat back down with his legs splayed. "Well?"

"That's my boy." Draz grinned as he watched the two move from him to Jask.

The man straddled Jask first, rolling his hips to the rhythm as he smiled. "Congratulations on the wedding. This one's on the house," he said with a wink.

On instinct, Jask's hands found the man's waist right as the girl's hands snaked down his chest from behind him. She was warm, they both were, but his eyes found Drazan in the space between them. "Thanks, D."

"What are friends for?" Draz asked quietly before downing his last drink, an indecipherable look on his face. It cleared quickly and he waved at Jask before heading back to the bar for a third time.

The moment Drazan was out of sight, Jask felt out of place. The girl was whispering in his ear about some kind of private room, but all he could think about was Vince. This was fun, but he had a fiancé to think about. "No, no thanks," he said carefully. He dislodged the demon man from his lap and stood, glancing around to see where his friend went.

Draz was waiting at the bar for the next round, having a quiet conversation with the bartender. He frowned when Jask approached. "Aren't you supposed to be getting a bachelor party lap dance?"

"Sorry, was I interrupting? I came here to hang out with you, D. You know I can't touch them, I'm getting married. Vince would kill them both."

"You don't have to touch them. You just have to enjoy the dance. Even your hot-headed demon should understand that. Besides, I was coming right back. Just getting more shots." He took the tray from the bartender and held it up to prove his point.

Jask nodded, but didn't make a move to grab one. "Yeah, would've been great if the chick was cool with keeping it like that. She offered." He slides his hands into his pockets and makes his way to a different table, a little further back. "Better to walk away."

"Alright, no more lap dances. You can't really say you blame her, though." Draz handed him a shot as they sat down, and the slight stroke to his ego had Jask shooting it back without a second thought.

"Missed you, D."

"I know. Me too." He takes another one. "But let's not focus on the past. We're here now."

The drinks flowed a little too easily after that, and toward the end of the night, Jask was undeniably drunk. He grinned at Drazan like he was the best thing he'd ever seen, but sighed heavily as it faded. "I want Vince. We should go."

Draz shook his head. "We're just getting started. We can't leave yet. Besides, you can't even go back to Vince."

"How are you still so *sober?*" Jask asked. He swayed on his feet and gripped the other side of the short bar to steady himself. "And fuck the rules, since when have I ever listened to rules? Vince was right."

"You'll disappoint your mother, speaking like that. Not to mention, when has Vince ever been right?" He waved the bartender down. "One more for the road?"

He hesitated. He shouldn't, he knew he shouldn't... but it smells delicious to him now, and it's for Drazan. *Drazan.* The best friend he thought he'd never see again. "Only if you promise to come to my wedding."

"Wouldn't miss it for the world, babe." Draz turned his back to him to grab the drinks. Facing him once more, he smiled and held up his own glass. "To love."

Something jagged soothed — or drowned in booze — inside of Jask, and he drained his glass quickly. As he set it down, he could feel his heart rate speeding up and slowing back down, over and over again. He shook it off, taking a step closer to Drazan. "I'm... glad you fff—finally came home," he slurs out.

Draz put a hand on Jask's shoulder, pulling him in for a hug. This time he didn't hesitate, just held Jask tightly for a few moments before stepping back and smiling sadly. "For what it's worth, Jask... I'm sorry about this."

"Sorry?" The word sounded funny in his head, like maybe it wasn't a real word anymore. His vision blacked around the edges as he struggled to say focused, but with each second, he felt... heavier. "D?" he asked, his voice sounding far away. "Sorry about... about wh—"

Thud.

Nikola Harvey was born in Atlanta, GA and resides there with her husband and dog.

Kiran Charles lives in rural Ohio with her daughter and three rescue dogs.